NEVADA

MCPHERSON

BALLER

BOOK 3

Outcast Press

Fiction From the Fringes

Copyright © 2024 Nevada McPherson

Cover by Cody Sexton of AThinSliceOfAnxiety.com

Formatted and edited by Paige Johnson, author of *Percocet Summer* and *Citrus Springs*

www.Outcast-Press.com

(e-book) ASIN: B0D6RB3QMW

(print) ISBN-13: 978-1-960882-15-8

For Matthew

 ONE

Everything after Jessica and Ambrose got back from France was a blur. She'd asked him to come meet her in Paris once she found out she was pregnant, and his acceptance of her marriage proposal conferred a title more "prince consort" than simply "baby daddy," since she's like a queen with all her family money and clout, though Ambrose knows he'll never be king, nor a big-time mogul like her ex-husband, Mike. At the backyard wedding thrown together so soon after returning home, he could tell her mother clearly felt she married the lowest form of commoner. Then there came the soft opening of his S&M dungeon in Noe Valley, now re-christened as Arcadia. Continuing under the name Dover, Inc. was out of the question since Miss Dover was mercilessly stalked until she went MIA in France, pronounced dead through a mysterious phone call, and even thrown a funeral the whole organization grieved over.

Yet, ever since Ambrose spotted Miss Dover, alive and glammed up more than ever, riding away from the macaron shop on Rue Napoleon in a Bentley, his sense of reality has warped. He's barely had time to get used to carrying a pistol everywhere out of paranoia—or the trauma of having blasted the right-hand man of Miss Dover's worst enemy into oblivion.

On the mundane front, Ambrose finds himself a newlywed with a baby on the way, and that's not even all. Not by a longshot.

Sitting on the patio this Saturday evening, watching his stepson Beau build a precarious structure with brightly colored blocks as water sprinklers whisper in the edges of the yard, Ambrose feels as though he's spinning in place. Calm on the outside, chaotic on the inside.

Jessica walks out from the kitchen. She's glowing, as they say, still relaxed from this morning's natal yoga class. Her long, blonde hair is swept back in a careless up-do. She's started to show and the floaty dresses, tunics, and easy-going outfits she's been wearing lately aren't that different from the at-home clothes she wears for painting upstairs in the studio, but he's detected a change.

A deep contentment infuses everything she does these days. It's like she's finished living out every repressed fantasy she's ever had and become Earth Mother, creator of life and art.

She's perfect. This is perfect, he thinks and can see her captioning this snapshot in time **#BestLife**.

"Dinner'll be ready soon," she says, pouring him another splash of sauvignon blanc from her uncle's Napa winery and setting the bottle on the table. "Let's eat out here. I'll go get the plates."

She goes back inside. His thoughts return to the first day he ever sat on this patio, pretending to be someone else. He went from scroungy drug dealer to legit entrepreneur, a husband and father-to-be.

Still an imposter.

Jessica emerges from the kitchen again, her Zen aura disturbed like ripples on a pond. She's not carrying any plates or silverware, just his mobile phone.

He pats his pockets, panicked. If she were to answer a call, there was no telling who it might be or what she might hear to make her look this way.

"You left your phone in the downstairs bathroom," she says, handing it to him. "It quit ringing as soon as I got there, but I think they left a message. It's a Texas number."

Texas. Could be a spam call. Or maybe one of his parents kicked the bucket. Or something to do with his incarcerated brother, Butch.

"Aren't you going to check the message?" she asks.

"In a minute."

"Aren't you curious?"

"Just preparing myself." He pours himself more wine. "You know. For the worst."

✳✳✳

Butch awakens to the sound of Barry jerking off in the bunk above him. The beginning of yet another day in a sea of lost time. Wasted time that he must try and make sense of just to keep putting one foot in front of the other. Let the days, hours, minutes flow over, past, and around him—or focus on minute details until they become abstractions, reduced to pure essence. He thinks of a book he read last year, *In Search of Lost Time*. That Proust was one smart motherfucker. Madeleine cookie shit and all. How the taste of cookie crumbs soaked in tea brought up so many memories it opened up a whole world from the past to get lost in. If Butch could do that, he would. Only the good parts, though, after he left home and before he got busted. Back when things were looking good, back when he was having fun and there was hope.

Above him, Barry comes and it's over. Then momentarily: "Hey, Butch?"

"Yeah, Barry?"

"Want me to suck your dick before breakfast?"

"Nah. Thanks anyway."

"Maybe tonight?"

"Maybe."

That seems to satisfy Barry for now. A few minutes later, the bunk frame creaks as he makes a move to climb down. Butch sighs, ready to get up but—*so tired*. His spirit is willing to go eat swill then make it outside for a sunlight quota and blast of heat to remind him how fast the earth is burning, but his body doesn't feel like getting up off this stale-ass bed.

Barry splashes his face at the sink, wipes his hands on his baggy pants and moves toward the cell door as it automatically opens.

Murmuring, vague profanities, coughing, and rousting by Eddie the screw all waft from down the corridor. Inmates start filing past.

Barry turns to Butch. "Ain't you coming?"

"In a minute."

Barry steps closer, sensing something's wrong.

Eddie passes, brushing his baton along the bars. "C'mon, y'all, get your asses in gear."

"Hey, Eddie," Barry calls, still looking at Butch. "Could you come here?"

The guard strolls back. "What is it?"

"I think Butch might be sick."

Eddie looks skeptical, bangs the bars with his club. "Hey, Ballard. Get on up."

Butch rolls over. He stands and takes one step before crashing to the cement floor.

Barry gasps in horror at the sight of blood spilling from Butch's nose and Eddie steps into the cell, nudging Butch's shoulder with the tip of his shiny black shoe. "Ballard? You hear me?"

Barry kneels, already in tears. "Butch? Please be all right!"

As Butch manages to roll over, a jagged, blinding pain ignites in his jaw, the whole left side of his face, spreading fast. He raises his hand to wipe away some blood as Eddie calls for help on his radio. Hearing Barry weep, tears start in Butch's own eyes. He closes them against the fluorescent glare.

✳✳✳

Phoebe Grace, fashion designer and former dominatrix known as Miss Dover, slowly paces her office as the sun sets on Paris and the lights come on. Her assistant, Gille, left a while ago and the place is quiet. The driver her friend Sergei hired is patiently waiting outside by the Bentley. Her debut collection is ready, plans for the fashion show are all set, and the atelier has been a hive of activity. Though it's taken several sharp twists, her most cherished dream is becoming real. She walks over to the window and looks out at the city. Eiffel Tower. Crescent moon. This should be a triumphant moment. Cause for all-out celebration.

So why does she feel sick to her stomach?

Because her life back in the States, that she'd severed so carelessly from the woman she is now, keeps clawing its way back. She had her own establishment there, and friends. Her deceased lover Ivan, her fairy-godfather of Russian descent with a murky past, who had ties to the criminal underworld, but loved her unconditionally, paid for her gender reassignment surgery and left her set financially.

She's been under his best friend Sergei's protection since she arrived in Paris. Even while she visited her favorite perfumerie in Montmartre, there were men following her, sent by her nemesis who's only ever meant her harm. Alexei Rusovich always thought of her as an interloper who threw everything off balance. Alexei's, Ivan's and Sergei's resentment within their circle snowballed over the years, but Ivan and Sergei had looked out for each other and now Sergei's looking out for her. True friends are there for each other, always. They don't lie to you or let you down.

She sighs but it turns into a sob as she sinks into the chair behind her mahogany desk, recalling Ambrose's face when he saw her that day. Hard to believe that really happened, but it did. *What the hell was he doing in Paris?* To everyone she knew back in the States, she was already dead—cremated, her ashes scattered over the Bay—so Ambrose wouldn't have thought to come looking for her. Unless he had some reason not to believe she was dead. Some loose end that had given her away.

Ambrose spoke at the memorial service they'd held for her at Golden Gate Park. According to Maxim Rusovich, who had been her most loyal client and the brother to her worst enemy, it was a lovely affair. The urn they'd chosen for her ashes was an original work of art. The weather was perfect. It was a send-off for the ages, everything she could have wanted for a beautiful farewell to a life well-lived. So, what the fuck was Ambrose doing in Paris?

Maybe he was just here on vacation with his rich girlfriend—now wife. Phoebe Grace keeps up with the Bay Area news, often against her better judgement. As much as Sergei thought she should make a clean break with everything and everyone there, it's easier said than done. She still has maternal feelings for Ambrose, the little runaway who needed guidance when she hired him as an assistant at her dungeon, Dover, Inc. Those feelings don't die easily. The shock of betrayal on his face still her haunts her. He'll never forgive her.

And sometimes, when she considers the enormity of her lie, she wonders if she can ever forgive herself.

✳✳✳

Even though Alexei now owns the late Miss Dover's building in the Sunset District and has an office there, he makes a point of being at his tearoom in the Richmond district for the dinner rush, arriving early for his meal in the back booth near the kitchen. Two girls work the Sunset location in the two completed suites, with more delectable Russian imports to be transported soon. Lev supervises from the Dover woman's former office, the one Ambrose toyed with for a while in her stead.

The girls pull in money, but more complicated work lies ahead: transforming the Afghan opium that's been under the parking garage for so long into a small fortune. After acquiring the Dover building, which Alexei believes should've been his all along, and which Sergei had promised him ahead of a precipitant coup, Alexei purchased the glass waterfront home he'd always dreamt about. It would be most helpful to recover the money pilfered from his account by some unknown malcontent or garden variety hacker.

It's not that he's anywhere near broke, he reminds himself, lifting his soup spoon to his lips. It's that having that money would offer a greater level of comfort. A buffer against any unexpected occurrence that could jeopardize his plans. Dimitri's disappearance still bothers him—not because Alexei cared about his short-lived right-hand man and bodyguard, but because Dimitri threatened to have "information" that could shoehorn himself into a partnership with Alexei.

I have no partners, Alexei thinks, finding comfort in the piquant flavors of Fyodor's solyanka and pleased that Fyodor didn't skimp on the capers.

He hears the door to the kitchen swing open, but doesn't turn around, figuring it's the new waitress, a Slavic languages major who works shifts around her classes at San Francisco State. She's as content with the arrangement as him: This's a quaint little place (though it's seen better days) with a concise but complete lunch and dinner menu that evolves with the seasons, a pleasing ambience with a certain outré elegance, enough flex in the schedule that allows for her studies and prime shifts for good tips. Plus, it's obvious she has a crush on the bartender.

Alexei might find other jobs for her in the future. She's saving for a new car. Might take on more hours at some point. Perhaps some *extra duties*.

Only, it isn't the waitress who comes sweeping past him. It's Lev who walks into the dining room—heavy-set, bearded, man-of-all-work who'd once run the valley operations, rustling honeybees and hustling fake caviar. He's also good at electronics and all things video. Alexei had asked him to stay in the city to handle those things and provide any muscle, if needed, in Dimitri's absence.

"May I?" Lev asks, pausing for permission before sliding into the seat opposite.

"By all means." Alexei looks around and waves over the waitress.

Short hair, this one has, and she's not the devious little sex pot that was Margarite, the prodigal whore, but she has potential. She looks at Lev. "What can I get for you, sir?'

"Stoli, please." As she goes to fetch it from the bar, Lev folds his hands, leaning slightly forward. "I have news."

"Please. Share."

"Before we moved into the new property, I had begun mapping out surveillance plans. I placed cameras in a couple of places and checked them once to see their range of view and whether the app I was using to control them worked properly. I left them in place until we officially moved in, and today, I installed some more sophisticated equipment. Discrete little machines. Small but quite powerful."

Alexei sips his tea as Lev takes out his phone. "And?"

"Before I completely disconnected the other cameras, I took a quick look at the footage they'd captured and saw something that is most interesting."

"What did you see?"

"Dimitri entering the building on the day he disappeared. As far as I can tell, he never left."

Alexei sets down his teacup. It clanks against the saucer, causing he and Lev to jump in light of this development. "Never left?"

"Maxim made a visit that day, and the only other person was that young man, the manager who usually rides a motorcycle. That day he arrived in a car, a silver Mercedes. It seems he spent the night there. Maxim left late in the afternoon, but that young man did not depart until the next morning. Dimitri never came back out."

"Perhaps he took another way back to his car."

"He very well could have. But it is a one-way street, and there's no footage of his car leaving from where he likely would have parked. Fast forward, I saw a tow truck going past two days later and caught a glimpse of the car it had collected as it drove off. It was a black BMW, exactly like Dimitri's."

Alexei sits back, absorbing this new information. Maxim left the place but not Dimitri? One might think it would be the other way around. Dimitri was out to get Maxim and bring him back here to draw up some kind of contract between Alexei and himself. Alexei would have killed Dimitri before he would've acquiesced to becoming equal partners, but someone beat him to it. Maxim fancies himself some kind of lover rather than fighter, and that young man, Ambrose, doesn't seem like the type who would face down a dark presence like Dimitri.

The waitress brings Lev's drink. Lev puts in an order for today's lunch special, beef Stroganoff, while Alexei stares at the late afternoon sunlight dancing across the tables by the tall windows. Glimpses of blue sky. The vacuum cleaner whirrs, punctuated by occasional light clatter of silverware and plates. Things have suddenly shifted. A change in perspective due to this information. Greater clarity. Like during Alexei's visit to the optometrist last week. A different lens. *"Better?"* the optometrist had asked with each click. *"Worse?"*

"You've not heard from Maxim, yes?" Lev asks.

"Nothing."

"And this young man? Where is he now, I wonder?"

Alexei looks squarely at Lev. "Find out."

✱✱✱

Randy's tossing and turning in bed again. Bennie doesn't know if it's because he can't get comfortable or if it's because he's having a nightmare. She whispers: "Randy? You okay?"

"Yeah, why?"

"Just wondering."

He turns toward her. "Am I keeping you awake?"

"Kind of. What's the matter?"

He sits up, rubbing his eyes. "Lot on my mind, I guess."

She rises, wrapping her arms around his shoulders from behind. He smells nice. No aftershave either, just his scent. Hard to say exactly what it reminds her of, but it's warm and masculine and puts her in mind of sitting on the beach at night next to a campfire. She melts closer. "What are you so worried about?"

"I've got all these things I want to do, but. . ."

"You'll get 'em all done." She sinks lower, easing her arms around his waist. He tenses, as she knew he might, because he's self-conscious about putting on a few pounds. She thinks he looks sexy just the way he is. He's so unlike most of her old boyfriends who used to traipse around the apartment naked or in their underwear—especially Rob, the guy she was living with when she met Ambrose, and the main reason she rebuffed Ambrose's tentative advances, until she found out Rob was cheating on her with one of his fellow Coasties.

By the time Bennie realized she was with the totally wrong guy (whom her mother liked, which should've a been a red flag in itself), the younger, sweet, rag-tag Texan Ambrose had already fallen for her sister Jessica, the sun-goddess herself. Then there was the comedy-of-errors flirtation with Rajit, the out-of-work techie neighbor she helped join their team at Dover, Inc., but all that drama only cleared the way for Randy: reformed bad boy, fellow black sheep. Her true love.

"Please, tell me what I can do to help."

"I've got to do this by myself."

"You mean your P.I. licensing exam? You can take it later."

"I've put it off long enough." He walks over to the window.

She curls up in the warm space he'd been lying.

"Just want to pass it the first time, that's all."

"You will. And even if you don't, you can take it again. Shouldn't put so much pressure on yourself."

He sinks into a plaid swivel chair and slowly spins it once.

"Hey, would you do me a favor?"

"What's that?" he asks.

"Get naked for me."

He smiles and there's the Randy she adores. That smile. "You first."

She gets off the bed, slips out of her nightgown then her panties.

"Wow. You look great."

"Your turn."

"I'd rather just look at you."

She takes both his hands in hers. "C'mon."

He slowly stands.

She helps him off with his shirt, then starts to strip his boxers.

"Can we get back in bed first? I'm cold."

"Sure." She turns off the lamp, climbs into bed and holds the covers up for him to slide under with her.

He tosses the boxers aside and takes her in his arms, holding her close.

She'd had thoughts of sex, that maybe it would help him get to sleep, but it's 3:30 in the morning and feels so good just lying here with him, no clothing of any kind between them. Things are so still and quiet and the mood is cozy rather than straight-up erotic.

And there's always tomorrow.

First thing in the morning.

"I love you," she says.

"I love you, too," he whispers. "So much."

#

Since they'd been to visit Butch before, seeing him in the prison hospital wasn't quite the shock to Jessica's system it might've been otherwise. Still, all the bars, automatic doors, and armed guards, along with medical personnel in scrubs. . .

Butch lies in a narrow bed, breathing heavily. One whole side of his face is black and blue, swollen.

Ambrose approaches first, and she hangs back even though her impulse is to go to him.

Butch looks so vulnerable lying there, sweating, clearly in pain. Thinking about how he was before, compared to now, she tears up as the doctor, a young serious-looking man wearing wire-framed glasses, enters the room.

"What the hell, Butch?" Ambrose says gently, grasping his hand. "How'd this happen?"

Butch murmurs.

Ambrose leans closer, trying to hear him.

"He broke his jaw when he fell, so it's wired shut," the doctor declares. "He'll be on a liquid diet for a while. Lucky we're not looking at a concussion."

"How'd he fall?"

"We're—not sure. It was an accident, but. . ."

"But what?"

The doctor glances at Butch. "Could I speak with you for a moment outside, Mr. Ballard?"

Ambrose reluctantly releases Butch's hand, looks at Jessica as he follows the doctor out, leaving Jessica and Butch alone.

Butch's eyes are bloodshot and red-rimmed, especially the left one. She takes his hand, remembering how he'd gripped both of hers that day in the visiting area, then kissed them. Even in that harsh environment, he'd radiated warmth and been so sweet to her, but now he has the look of a frightened animal caught in a trap. She thinks of an injured lion. Her heart goes out to him. She smiles. "It's going to be all right, Butch."

Tears force their way from his eyes. "Sorry," he murmurs from between his teeth.

"For what?"

He rolls his eyes, indicating the surroundings. Murmurs what sounds like: "Draggin' y'all here. Shouldn'ta bothered you."

"We needed to know, Butch. You're family." Now that he's wearing a T-shirt instead of bulky prison attire, she can see all that ink etched into his body, most prominently the cracked and bleeding heart wrapped in barbed wire. There's also a painstakingly rendered portrait of a wolf, along with other abstract designs and shapes. Anywhere else it might be an odd visual pastiche, but on his him it all works beautifully together. "Have they given you any medicine for the pain?"

He shrugs.

"I'll go to make sure," she tells him. "Be right back."

He squeezes her hand like he doesn't want her to go, even if he is in pain.

She feels helpless. Chaotic as her life gets behind the façade of her family name, she's used to getting what she wants. Mostly. Never really been the type to say, *Do you know who I am?* to get quicker service, a better room, moved to the front of the line. Beyond Palo Alto, hardly anyone knows what she looks like or who she is—outside of her growing presence in the art community. People recognize the name Intellect, the groundbreaking tech company her grandfather founded, and her dad took to greater heights before blissfully retiring. Jessica and Bennie have lived very normal lives, and she's grateful for that. Both resilient and self-sufficient—as much as daughters with a doting billionaire father can be.

Ambrose and Butch, on the other hand, are from a whole different universe, where "resilient" and "self-sufficient" mean vastly different things. For Ambrose's part, she found out he was willing to prostitute himself, then fake his identity, aided and abetted by her sister Bennie, who pretended they were working for some charity, not an S&M dungeon. But Jessica forgave them, even before realizing her own capacity for lying. . .

A nurse comes in, pushing a small cart, to take Butch's vital signs. Jessica requests the pain medication, and the nurse says she'll get him something. While the nurse goes to get meds, Jessica looks out the door and sees Ambrose talking to the doctor at the end of the hallway. She wants to go to him but doesn't want to leave Butch. Whatever it is they're talking about doesn't look good, and she's starting to understand Ambrose's hesitation to open a registered letter or listen to a phone message from this area code. It's like bracing for a punch.

She'll find out soon enough. She turns back to Butch.

He's staring at the ceiling as the nurse gives him a shot.

When the nurse goes out, Jessica returns to Butch's bedside, taking hold of his hand again. "Don't worry, Butch, you'll be able to get some sleep. Is there anything I can get for you that would make you feel better?"

He looks at her, total resignation in his eyes. He can barely talk and doesn't need her to know how he's feeling.

She flashes back to a couple months ago, in the bedroom while Bennie was helping her get ready for that impromptu backyard wedding. Jessica's mother, Pamela, had lamented in a tipsy moment that Jessica's and Bennie's choices for husbands would come back to haunt them: that Ambrose's and Randy's common-as-dirt backgrounds would spell trouble and lower the prestige of the whole Jenkins clan as well as hers, the Benningtons, and everything they ever stood for. She said to please not have children with those mongrels, for God's sake. That's before she knew Jessica was pregnant.

When she found that out, she had to go to her favorite spa at Carmel-by-the-Sea to try and process the horror of it. And she still doesn't know Ambrose has a brother in prison. She would die if she knew all the gritty details of how Ambrose met Jessica's ex-husband Mike, and how Jessica came to be with Ambrose instead.

She would just die.

Jessica looks down at Butch. He appears sleepier, his grip on her hand loosening. She barely knew anything about him for so long, and now that she does, finds herself caring for him as her own family. He's her brother-in-law, just like Randy. Regardless of what Pamela or anyone else says, *this* is Jessica's family. If the news about Butch is bad, Ambrose and Butch can't depend on either of their parents, but she can depend on her dad. She'll call him tonight. Parker Jenkins has friends in high places—everywhere. *He'll know what to do.*

Butch releases her hand, finally drifting off. She reaches up to touch his forehead, gently brushing back his hair, which is damp with sweat. Maybe it's hormones making her feel this way, or prana, that feeling of oneness with the universe that, for her at least, intensifies with pregnancy. Her intuition is heightened. She feels more connected with the things going on around her, good and bad, than she has in years. She can look at Butch and tell that, if he remains in prison, he won't live long.

They have to find a way to get him out. Soon.

✳✳✳

The new dungeon is already becoming the underground sensation Ambrose hoped for, with returning clients from the Dover, Inc. days, and new ones finding Arcadia, thanks to Rajit's efforts in optimizing their web site for better search results. He and Terrence have done wonders for Arcadia's online presence: branding, graphic design, social media accounts. They know how to ride the ever-changing algorithms of all the platforms (which is perfect, because Ambrose never touches the stuff), and with Mistress Momo back badder than ever, things are getting better.

The small bar downstairs is open Wednesday through Saturday evenings, becoming a weekly hang-out for a small but growing eclectic crowd, and the adjoining cigar club with a walk-in humidor is filled each Thursday. The cigar lounge was the brainchild of Mr. Bob, retired tech exec husband of Jessica's acquaintance, Mary-Ann. Mr. Bob frequently ventures up from Palo Alto, breaking out of his routine for nights in the city with some of his wealthy, middle-aged pals.

When this building was a residential space, the lobby might've been someone's parlor, the bar area a large dining room, the lounge a sitting room or library of some sort. Alexei's purchase of Miss Dover's building had forced them to find new digs, and this location wasn't much to look at, at first, staid and gently dilapidated, but now it's finally becoming the urban oasis Ambrose pictured—especially with the refurbishment of the back deck into its own small green space. They've added plants everywhere, potted trees, and a waterfall cascading over a brightly colored tile wall to drown out the rest of the world.

The place is starting to make money, too, though Ambrose will need more to support Butch, to be prepared for any eventuality when Butch's illness gets worse. Neither of their parents back in Texas will be any help, with their dad lying embittered in a nursing home, and their mother unable to focus on anything other than a game show for more than five minutes. Both hard alcoholics, barely able to remember that they have two sons, and barely capable of caring.

There's no other family left. No one they're close to. None who'd be willing to help take care of Butch when the going gets rough. When that happens, Ambrose is determined to step up, and doesn't want to be dependent on Jessica's money, though it is her considerable family resources working overtime to try to get Butch out of prison for health reasons. It's a long shot, but somehow Ambrose and Jessica are flying back for the parole board hearing in less than a month, so. . .

On Wednesday, just as he's closing his laptop to go downstairs and check out the new cigar shipment, Rajit walks in with a lime green Post-It and sticks it on Ambrose's desk.

"What's that?" Ambrose asks.

"A number you're supposed to call as soon as you have a moment."

"Whose number?"

"An exceedingly polite man with a Russian-sounding accent."

Always someone or something ready to grab him by the ankle. Just when Ambrose thinks he's home free. "And what if I don't?"

"That is between you and your god," Rajit says, turning to go.

"Could it've been Maxim?"

"Most assuredly not."

There's only one other Russian on Ambrose's radar. "Alexei?"

Rajit pauses. "I've never spoken to him before, but that would be my best guess. Terrence and I plan on keeping a bag packed, with our passports handy."

Ambrose walks around to the front of the desk. "You're not scared of this guy, are you? He doesn't even know what you two look like. The message was for me, right?"

"Are you saying you're not scared? Not even a little?""

Ambrose gets a bottled water out of the mini-refrigerator in the corner. "Not scared."

"Apprehensive, then? We robbed the man of a quarter-million dollars!"

"*Shhh!*" Ambrose closes the door. "Don't say that out loud."

"While it was exciting in the moment, I have misgivings. Before that, I turned down an offer for an entry-level position at a new robotics firm and now I think I should have my head examined. I'm not getting any younger."

"But you said yourself, you love working here. You're doing a great job, make your own schedule. We have fun, right?""

"But the hacking, to avenge your old boss? Again, fun in the moment, but I should've taken the time to think all this through."

Ambrose feels that familiar skitter in his gut. The shadow side of himself, the scheming and plotting that exhausts him but he must do from time to time. He's still getting over the exertion of talking Randy into going up to Tahoe for a weekend fishing trip, a ruse to get help dumping Dimitri's body, using Bennie's boat to do it.

He places his hands on Rajit's shoulders, looks him in the eyes. No matter how Ambrose feels, he's learning to alter his perspective through sheer willpower and his new mantra: *This never happened.* "You said yourself, they can't prove a thing. 'We got this.' Remember?"

Rajit stares at him. "I did say that once, didn't I?"

"You still believe it, right?"

Rajit's gaze wanders and Ambrose makes him look him in the face. "It's the truth, Rajit." Then: "Want to go get lunch? My treat."

". . .Okay. What time?"

"Meet me downstairs in like—ten minutes?"

Rajit goes out, leaving Ambrose far more rattled than he'd let on. That night, disposing of Dimitri, he'd had to shove fear away to do what he had to, and no one saw a thing. Problem solved, or so he thought, though fear of repercussions made him start packing a pistol, a .32 he scored at the pawn shop that fits in his jacket pocket. The polished nickel .38 pistol that belonged to Miss Dover is locked in his desk: the one he used that fateful afternoon to dispatch Alexei's right-hand man. What if that's *really* what this call from Alexei's about? Rajit, Terrence, nor Bennie know about that night from Hell. Only Randy.

Of all people.

Downstairs, Momo approaches Ambrose in the lobby, on a break between sessions, wearing her purple catsuit and mask with matching ears. With a half-eaten apple in one hand, flogger in the other, she does not look happy. "Hey," she says, "there's some woman waiting to see you in the bar."

"What woman?"

"She has a French accent and says she used to work for you. Is she the one that vandalized the dressing room at the old place?"

Ambrose freezes at the prospect it's Margarite, formerly known around Dover, Inc. as Mignon. Another source of anxiety arrives. He peers into the bar, and there she is, skinny jeans and a black sweater, scrolling on her phone. Momo comes to stand behind him, munching the apple, casually slapping the flogger against her thigh. Maybe she means to be supportive, but he doesn't want an audience. "I'll handle this," he tells her. "Go take your break."

"You're sure?"

"If you see Rajit, tell him I'll be right out." Ambrose closes the double doors behind her and turns to Margarite. "What the hell are you doing here?" he asks.

She looks up, smiles, leaves the bar stool to hug him. "Ambrose! How've you been, *chéri?*"

He resists the hug. "Don't '*chéri*' me. You told me to fuck off, remember?"

"I only left that message because you'd essentially told me the same thing by firing me. And I was so hurt."

"Whatever it is you came here for, forget it." He remembers how she'd put globs of lubricant on every door and handle, destroyed a bunch of outfits—the ones she didn't steal—poured tacky perfume into the furniture, and punched the message *fuck you* into the wall with her stiletto heel. It took weeks to get that stench out of the dressing room, the hallway, his nostrils. The mess she left reflected the tangle of deception surrounding her, worst of all her seduction of Jessica, which wasn't totally one-sided, but. . .

"So cruel, you are. You haven't even given me a chance to apologize. For everything." Margarite slides onto a nearby barstool, leaning in. "I made a clean break with Alexei, and with Jessica. The only reason I'm here now is because I need a job, and you need me."

"Like a hole in the head," he says, walking behind the bar, recalling the neat hole he'd made in Dimitri's head with Miss Dover's .38. On top of everything else, Dimitri was Margarite's lover, and while Ambrose would like to know the details out of morbid curiosity, he doesn't dare mention it. If she knew what happened that last time Dimitri showed up at the old dungeon, she'd find a way to turn it back on him like a flamethrower.

"Whatever happened before is the past. I can do good for you now. Let's make a new start."

"I'm not interested in starting anything new with you, and I have things to do. Would you please go now?"

She reaches into her purse, takes out a slip of paper, and hands it to him. "My new number. Call me if—*when* you change your mind." She stands down from the bar stool. "I had many loyal clients, you know, and can bring much to the table." She lingers close. Her perfume smells much more expensive than what she disposed of in the furniture.

No denying she's attractive, but dangerous, too. He wishes he could forget those nude photos she texted to Jessica, the ones he shouldn't have been snooping. He wants to trust Jessica but her fling with Mignon—real name Margarite—a brief, torrid affair, had bruised him in hidden ways.

"*Really*, Ambrose," Margarite goes on, aware she could be getting to him. "I can do so much good for you." She smiles, blows him a kiss, leaves.

He starts to tear the slip with the number on it but doesn't. Yet. If there ever *is* any good she could do, maybe it would make up for a fraction of the bad she's done. But, no, he won't ever call that number, he tells himself.

It's just another reminder not to trust anyone ever again.

✱✱✱

The following week, Ambrose parks his motorcycle and walks back up the block to the former entrance of Dover, Inc.. Still looking like another neo-post-modern-ish office. He knew there was a soul somewhere in all that corrugated metal, wood and glass, but now—nothing. Having been summoned by its new soulless proprietor, he questions his sanity as he pushes open the glass door to the old reception area. The floor is still bare concrete from when he pulled up the bloody carpet before vacating the place for good.

He stops before pushing open the next door, the one that leads to the hallway and a series of rooms: suites, offices, a cavernous space they'd called "the ballroom" that hinted at the warehouse origins of the building more than any other part, and the parking garage. Ambrose considers walking through this door and never walking out. Last time he walked into this reception area from the other direction, he killed a guy. He takes a deep breath, trying to remember just what lured him here today. The voice on the phone had been that same Dracula-diplomat voice, the man he met the day Alexei came unannounced into Miss Dover's, then Ambrose's old office, but—a bit lighter.

Alexei has a proposal and asks that Ambrose hear him out before refusing. "If the answer is no, no hard feelings." Alexei had nothing but hard feelings for Miss Dover, but Ambrose's feelings for her have turned harder than he would've ever thought possible. The hacking of Alexei's account was supposed to be retaliation for something that hadn't even happened—but nevertheless was something Alexei had coming, and the killing of his top goon?

Self-defense.

Still, in unguarded moments, Ambrose experiences an attack of conscience, wondering if he'd been badly mistaken. Maxim was sure Dimitri was there to kill him, if not he and Ambrose both, and had spurred Ambrose to action—but Ambrose had actually pulled the trigger, then was left to deal with the clean-up and consequences: physical, mental, emotional, and spiritual.

What if Dimitri wasn't really there to kill him nor Maxim, and Ambrose committed straight-up murder? Does that mean Ambrose is going to Hell? Or, if there's no actual place called Hell, maybe a lifetime of wondering, worrying, speculating. No real peace of mind.

There's a certain kind of Hell in that. But God knows what he was thinking and why he did what he did. That counts for something. Intent. And there is such a thing as forgiveness.

Being in this room again, where it all happened. Maybe that day changed his life more than he'd realized. Something froze inside him the 24 hours after he made that "blink" decision. He'd already discovered with his boss Lang, the guy he used to sling for, that once you start running, it never ends. It blew Lang's fucking mind when Ambrose finally stood his ground the last time they met.

No more running.

Ambrose is about to push the door open when he sees the hulking shadow of a man through the frosted glass.

The door opens from the other side. The man has bushy hair and a thick beard. He's wearing a Def Leopard T-shirt and jeans and has a thick accent. "Hello, Mr. Ballard. Mr. Rusovich is expecting you. Follow me, please." He holds the door open.

"Thanks," Ambrose says as he walks through it. He's hyper-conscious of Alexei's flunky following as he walks down the hallway. All the doors are closed, and for the first time, he has no idea what, if anything, is going on behind them. He thinks he hears high-pitched laughter from somewhere, but that could be some ghost-memory sound from deep in his imagination. A female voice barking insistent commands. A dull *thud*. . .

He hesitates for a split second before continuing down the hall. Miss Dover's and his former office has the only door open, and it looks a mess. There's a desk and chair, but also wastebaskets overflowing with junk food wrappers, and random electronic equipment on the desk and floor, some with the guts hanging out. *Must be the flunky's office now.*

He turns to ask his hairy guide, "Where exactly are we going?"

The guy smiles, gestures. "Just ahead, please."

Ambrose keeps walking, something Maxin had once said coming back to him. That Alexei might want to use the ballroom as his office. Ambrose hadn't believed anyone would actually do that, yet here they are at the door to the ballroom.

"Face me for a moment?" the flunky says.

Ambrose turns toward him.

"Arms up, please?"

"Why?"

The guy looks at him as if he should know. "It's only a formality."

"What is?"

"The boss wishes for me to check all weapons."

"What makes you think I have a weapon?"

The guy shrugs, still smiling. "Prove me wrong."

Ambrose raises his arms. If he makes it back outside, he won't let himself get in this position again.

The guy finds the pistol in the coat pocket, removes the bullets and stuffs them into the pocket of his jeans, handing Ambrose back the empty gun. "I'll return these when you leave." He opens the door to the ballroom.

Ambrose replaces the empty gun in his pocket and steps inside.

Morning sunlight that used to glint off the disco ball from the high windows now glints off a huge chandelier in the center of the room. Sofas, over-the-top formal, line the walls at intervals. The floor gleams with a fresh coat of wax, and, at the end of a long runner of red carpet, Alexei sits at his wide desk.

"Ah, Mr. Ballard," he graciously intones, walking around to the front of the desk, pausing between brown wingback chairs. "How kind of you to meet with me." Looks like he's wearing another custom suit. That's maybe the one thing Alexei and Maxim have in common: They dress impeccably.

Ambrose glances back toward the big Russian standing just inside the door, arms folded like a bouncer.

Alexei gives the guy a look and the hairy assistant goes out. "Please, have a seat."

Ambrose sits down.

"Would you care for a cup of tea?" Alexei asks, gesturing toward an ornate metal samovar accompanied by delicate-looking cups and saucers on a tray atop a brass cart.

"No, thanks. What is it you want to see me about?"

Alexei takes a seat in the other chair. Ambrose expected him to resume his seat at the desk to maintain his power feng-shui, but even in this setting, Alexei wants to put him at ease, even appears to be attempting a smile, though it could just as easily be a grimace. "Of course. You like to get right down to business. I appreciate that a great deal." He sits back. "I can't help but notice your work ethic, Mr. Ballard. You lost no time resurrecting your business after being forced to move from here. It's my understanding you're doing quite well."

"We're hanging in there."

"You're more than hanging, Mr. Ballard. You show a remarkable ability to land on your feet in adverse circumstances. A trait that I find most admirable. Something tells me we have more in common than you may think. I suspect we both know what it means to be betrayed by people we trusted. We both seek success on our own terms." Alexei settles back. "Not many are willing to put in the effort that takes. In fact, very few young men like yourself are willing to do the dirty work required."

"What exactly do you mean by 'dirty'?"

"Unpleasant. Difficult. Sometimes dangerous. Occasionally outside the confines of what is narrowly considered legal."

"You're suggesting I've done things that are illegal?"

Alexei shrugs. "Only you know that, Mr. Ballard."

The formality is grating, and whatever he's getting at, he wants it over with. "Call me Ambrose."

"Ambrose. You wish for me to cut to the chase."

"I do."

Any attempt at conviviality drains away and the grimness returns. "We have video footage that a close associate of mine walked into this building a couple of months ago and never left."

"What's that got to do with me?"

"You and Maxim were the only ones here at the time. Maxim was seen leaving, and later, you as well, but not my associate."

"Where'd you get this footage? Maybe he left through another door." Ambrose shifts in his chair. Yet another video Ambrose wishes he could erase. Seems impossible, but so did deleting the sex video Randy took of him and Jessica through the bedroom window when Randy was a down-on-his-luck ex-cop, before he became Mr. Bennie Jenkins. "And why were you spying on us before we moved out anyway? Around here, it was just business as usual until we had to pack up and leave."

"'Business as usual,'" Alexei muses. "You must admit, yours is not a usual business."

"But quite legit."

"Perhaps on paper."

"And in practice."

"And attracts degenerates like my dear, dissolute brother."

"Some might call it therapeutic. And it's a far cry from trafficking young girls."

"I don't like what you're implying."

Ambrose meets Alexei's cold gaze. "What are you implying? You think Maxim and I had something to do with your associate's disappearance?"

"I do."

"Well, you're wrong. He probably just went out the back way."

"In the trunk of your car, perhaps."

"Of course not."

"I would like to know whether he's still out there somewhere, or if he's gone for good."

"No idea."

Alexei stands, walks over to his desk, picking up an antique letter opener with a carved wooden handle and gold inlay, idly examining its blade. "Very well. I suppose Dimitri's fate will remain a mystery, for the time being."

"Suppose so."

Alexei balances the letter opener at its pointed end on the green desk blotter, slowly twirling it with his fingertips. "He claimed to have knowledge about who hacked into one of my accounts and drained it of funds."

"Your bank account got hacked?"

"One of them. This is a surprise to you?"

Ambrose maintains a blank expression as a familiar panic spreads deep inside his ribcage. "Sure, why would I know anything about that?"

"Indeed." Alexei puts down the letter opener, walks back to the front of the desk. "In any case, Dimitri's absence has left an opening on my staff. Lev, whom you've just met, can fill that position, for the most part. He's a very competent technician but lacks the finesse and specialized skills required for other work I need done."

"I see. Well, I hope you find the right person for that job. I have things of my own to do, so I'd better get going." Ambrose stands. "If you'll ask your boy out there to return my bullets, I'll be on my way."

"Why, Ambrose. I was just getting around to my proposal."

"Told you, I'm not interested in coming to work for you."

"I wasn't going to repeat my earlier offer of employment. I was however thinking you might be interested in an opportunity to make some extra money as an—independent contractor." Alexei draws so close, Ambrose can smell his aftershave.

Or is it cologne? Not bad, actually. Old school, classic. Royall Lyme?
"How much money are we talking?"

"For the first job, $5,000. Double that for the second. There will be more, possibly much more."

"I'd have to know what it is first to even consider it."

"Accompanying shipments of my very best product to a few well-heeled clients."

"On an airplane?"

"A delivery truck."

"Delivery truck? You don't send it, like, Next Day Air?"

"Shipping my finest caviar through standard commercial channels is out of the question. It must be kept under optimum conditions at all times. I like having control of the product from point A to point B. Fish farm to table, as it were." He fixes Ambrose with a stare. "I'm sure you understand."

"Yes, and no," Ambrose says, ready to tell Alexei to forget it, no way this is happening. For each thing Alexei's saying, there's something he's not saying. Too much to unpack. However. . . Butch'll need things when he gets out, whether that's sooner or later, and who knows if he'll be able to work. Maybe not for long, anyway. Bennie would say, *You don't need to do this,* if she knew Ambrose was sitting with the man Miss Dover warned about, said never to let in the door of this place. And here he is, coiled like a cobra, offering some crooked deal promising lots of money when all signs point to his knowing Ambrose killed Dimitri and instigated the hacking of Alexei's account. It'd be crazy to throw in with him, another stupid mistake on top of all the other stupid mistakes.

The man is a snake, Miss Dover had told Ambrose in this very room, sitting in her queen's chair on the riser, decked out in all her leather and latex glory, towering in sky-high heels. That was the day she tested Ambrose to see what he'd do if he lost it all and slapped him when he indicated he'd go back to his old ways, slinging for Lang. Whatever sense she slapped into him, he lost that morning in Paris, watching the Bentley pull away from the macron shop. Maxim had called the night before and told him to go to that address in Rue Bonaparte the next morning at 9 AM, that what he'd see there would reveal all, and did it ever.

Seeing Miss Dover's ghost, or Phoebe Grace as she now calls herself, graciously receiving her daily order of office macrons, had broken something within him and was living proof that you can't trust anybody.

She saw Ambrose, too, looked at him as if he were a ghost, before urgently telling the driver to go. She never looked back, either. And if she's somehow in cahoots with Alexei, Ambrose will get revenge on them both.

For now, he just wants to build his bank account, have a buffer against a break-up, downturn, slow weeks or months, and be able to take care of Butch on his own, should the need ever arise.

"I'll think about it," he tells Alexei. "That's all I can promise."

Alexei looks pleased. "Excellent." He turns, opens the cedar humidor on his desk. "Care for a Cuban?"

Ambrose peers into the box. Mr. Bob would be impressed.

Alexei takes one out and hands it to Ambrose. "You can enjoy this with brandy while you consider my proposal."

Ambrose slides the cigar into the interior breast pocket of his coat, fully aware this cigar isn't free.

But he's getting out of this alive. So why does he feel slightly less sure of himself than when he walked in? Maybe because then Alexei had nothing he wanted. And now, he's dangling chunks of money like juicy worms on shiny hooks. "Thanks."

"You're most welcome. I'll be in touch soon."

✳✳✳

Sergei joins Phoebe Grace for dinner Friday evening. Takeout from her favorite bistro. Mussels cooked in butter, white wine, and garlic, *pommes frites*, salad. He gifts her a bottle of Dom Perignon but doesn't drink alcohol—his ulcer—and she isn't in the mood, so it sits in the refrigerator. "My dear," Sergei begins. "I thought you'd be excited for your upcoming debut. That you'd want to celebrate. What's wrong?" He gazes at her through black-framed glasses. Those, along with his tan, thick white hair, and sport coat over open-collared shirt and linen slacks raise his aura to that of a glamorous yachtsman/tycoon. "Is it that young man back in the States?"

She dips a small crust of baguette into the butter-wine sauce, then drops it back in the bowl, her appetite evaporating. "Ambrose."

"Yes. Maxim told me he shares your concern."

"He saw me, Sergei."

"Who saw you?"

"Ambrose! He was here, in Paris, outside the Ladurée shop. I don't know why he was there, but he recognized me."

Sergie takes a deep breath. "Most unfortunate. Why didn't you tell me sooner?"

Phoebe pushes back from the table and goes to stand in front of the fireplace, gazing at the small flames slowly consuming the evening's supply of fuel. "I've just been sick about it."

"Perhaps he only thought you looked like a woman he knew."

"It was more than that."

"You're certain?"

Silence, except for the clock ticking, fire crackling quietly.

"Truly most unfortunate."

Phoebe turns to Sergei, who's staring at his half-eaten dinner, his glam aura shifting into that of a brooding ex-gangster. "It's not just 'unfortunate.' That boy was heartbroken because now he knows what a goddamn liar I am."

"Don't blame yourself. Who would he tell? And who would believe him?"

"I do blame myself. I should've never gone through with this. There were too many ways for it to go wrong and now it has."

"You must not be so catastrophic in your thinking, my dear."

"Why not? It is a catastrophe."

"Are you afraid he'll tell Alexei, just to spite you?"

"I'm afraid he hates me."

"All the more reason he might 'rat you out,' as they say."

Phoebe stares at the fire, tears burning her cheeks. "This boy is no rat. Even if he did tell Alexei, I don't give a damn anymore. I deserve whatever I get."

The room grows darker as the sun sets. Through the tall windows, the pink glow over Paris rooftops intensifies before it succumbs to night. Sergei walks over to her, flames from the fireplace reflecting in his glasses. She could blame him for talking her into faking her death, but he only gave her the idea; she went through with it.

That's the mark of a true conman, she realizes. They don't force things. They don't make you give them your money or whatever valuables in question. They make you beg them to take it. In this case, he suggested a way for her to shed her past and her problems, make lots of money, achieve real fame. And he made it so easy, at first. She shed her identity and, in the process, lost all that was good about her life and a sizable piece of her soul.

And what did he gain from it?

Control. Power over her and her new enterprise. A chance to grow his bank account as she grows her own.

She swipes away the tears, stepping back from the fireplace, the heat too intense.

"Alexei has been a thorn in my side for many years. I could have simply eliminated the threat."

"You mean you should've just had him killed? I thought you'd lost your taste for murder. Besides, I don't need another death on my conscience. My own is enough, thank you very much." She walks over to the table, tosses back a demitasse of lukewarm espresso. A raspberry tart sits on a gold-edged floral-print plate, its dollop of whipping cream beginning to melt, the cherry having already tumbled onto the doily surrounded by red stain. Nothing sweet tonight. She decides she doesn't deserve it. Feels like she should never allow herself another macaron as long as Phoebe Grace lives.

"Do you want to go back?" he asks.

"Honey, I done crossed that Rubicon. Or should I say, River Styx?" Unable to resist, she picks up the cherry, pops it into her mouth. It's soaked in Kirsch, an edible ruby. "Not even you can bring the dead back to life."

∗∗∗

When Alexei said he needed someone with finesse and specialized skills to do the jobs he had in mind, Ambrose never anticipated that meant accompanying Alexei's head stooge Lev to Missoula, Montana, to deliver a shipment of his farmed caviar to some rich cowboy who co-owns a restaurant in town. The shipment is to be delivered to his ranch, however. When Alexei offered this gig, Ambrose's first thought was to decline until Alexei could come up with some other task, but the money was harder to turn down. After all, he told himself, how hard can it really be, riding shotgun and spelling Lev with the driving when he needs to sleep?

They're supposed to go there and back, no hanging around. What isn't simple is coming up with a viable reason for going away for a couple days without inviting Jessica. They're waiting to see what happens regarding Butch's release, so she'll insist on going to Texas with him for the parole board hearing. He finally told her that Rajit and Terrence invited him to a cybersecurity summit in Sacramento.

She was in France when they'd been at such a conference a few months ago, so he just recycled the story and moved the location. Sure enough, she wasn't interested, wanted to stay home, do some painting, and continue getting things ready for when Butch arrives. He felt compelled to remind her that, while they're all hoping for an early release, they still don't know whether he'll get out or not. *That he'll get to come home*, she'd corrected. To stay in the guesthouse. And she has absolute faith that he will.

If Butch does get early release, the money from this job could pay for things he might need. As for Ambrose, these excursions could pay for things he wants, like a new motorcycle and a couple of custom-made suits. Put the rest away for later. Now that he's making money, he doesn't ever want to be street-level broke again. He's resolved that neither he nor Butch'll ever be totally dependent on Jessica. And that's not planning for failure, he reminds himself. Their marriage won't fail, but it's just common sense to be cautious. Like she was being when, pressured by her mother, she asked him to sign a prenup. He wasn't all that surprised Jessica went along with it.

Resisting the urge to turn down the blaring radio set on a '70s/'80's pop station, Ambrose watches Lev mindlessly bob his head to the music. Reminds Ambrose of his homie, Juan, who used to sling for Lang. A flash of déjà vu from the bad old days. Instead of constantly smoking like Juan, Lev constantly eats. He smokes too, but mainly eats. As the miles string behind them, Ambrose chain-smokes and drinks coffee, eating just enough to keep going.

16 hours to Missoula, and 16 back, plus bathroom stops (of which there are many because of all the coffee and, in Lev's case, soft drinks), and whatever time it takes to deal with this yahoo who's rich but still buys questionable caviar—though Ambrose knows deep down it isn't about that.

Alexei said to tell this guy, a Mr. Shane McCall, that the shipment's all there, all premium product. The cream of the crop's in the packages with gold labels and there's more where that came from, if he's pleased with this initial lot.

They arrive at the ranch around 10 the next morning. The place more closely resembles a compound with metal gates and security made up of two muscle-bound guards clothed in all-black. *We're hauling contraband, all right.*

As the guards sweep the truck for weaponry and whatever else they've been told to look for, Ambrose walks over by Lev, who's eating from a king-size bag of bright red tortilla chips. "What's in the packages with the gold labels?" Ambrose asks.

"Boss said just get it here," Lev answers, not making eye contact. "I'll assist with the unloading after you've met with Mr. McCall. Then we'll start back."

"What am I supposed to say to this guy?"

Lev smiles calmly. "Satisfaction guaranteed."

Within minutes, Ambrose is escorted into the house: a two-story that looks like an oversize cabin. Not as big as the one Bennie's family has at Lake Tahoe, but damn big. Once inside, led into the cavernous living room, Ambrose notices that the wide-screen TV over the stone fireplace looks out of place with the rustic décor, as do framed posters behind the bar of sportscars and girls in bikinis, along with a yellow **Don't tread on me** flag. There's a University of Montana Grizzlies football game from last week on mute. Rap music blares from somewhere else in the house.

"Have a seat," the guard says. "Mr. McCall will be out in a minute."

Sinking into one of the cushy leather chairs facing the window, Ambrose looks out at the mountains, once again feeling pushed onstage without a script. Like he felt when Bennie informed him his role was to play a grad student majoring in economics, and that first fancy fundraiser when he'd nearly lost it talking to that retired professor about game theory. Like he felt when interviewing Rajit, pretending to be the boss before he really became one and, again, like he'd felt opening the door to the Dover, Inc. reception area to a guy Maxim claimed was a killer, so Ambrose shot him, believing it when the guy had reached into his coat.

And now here he is once more, his pistol emptied by gatekeepers before entering a strange place "just as a precaution." Needing a shower, underdressed in jeans, T-shirt, a flannel and old boots, his stomach ominously rumbling, he feels any progress he's made is eroding, being pulled backwards in time.

But, there is the money.

When Mr. McCall appears, Ambrose wonders if this is just the teenage son, maybe, wearing a red tracksuit at least one size too big, shower slides, and a toboggan cap with a Lakers logo on it. "Hey, you made it! Drove straight though, huh?"

"That's right." Ambrose stands.

The guy gives him a fist bump and a grin. "Want a drink?" he asks, heading for the bar.

"No thanks." Then just to be clear: "Are you Mr. McCall?"

"Mr. McCall is my dad's name. Call me Shane." He pours a tumbler of orange juice and infuses it with a splash of seltzer from a crystal spritzer. "Mr. R said you guys would be here by this afternoon. You made good time." He takes a swig, walks over and flops into the leather chair facing Ambrose. "So, what's the word from San Fran? How long you been working for Mr. R?"

"I don't really—" Don't muddy the water, something tells Ambrose. "Not that long."

The guy's looking at him like anticipating some kind of status, or rundown, and Ambrose has no script. *Goddamn you, Alexei.* "The word from San Francisco is 'satisfaction guaranteed.' Mr. Rusovich is certain you'll be pleased with the product."

The guy leans forward, rubs his hands like trying to get warm. His long bangs dip below the front of his snug cap. He swipes it to the side. His eyes are large and inquisitive, and something about him puts Ambrose in mind of a shady anime character. Shapeshifter, maybe. "I got a surplus of goodfella, but this old-school shit's big with a certain crowd." And the blocks fall into place. *Square here, triangle there,* like the puzzle toy in the corner of the kitchen back in Palo Alto that Beau's nearly outgrown, but not quite. "Customers are lining up. Mostly rich boomers and X-ers. Lotta Deadheads." Shane laughs, swipes his bangs aside, setting his drink on the wagon wheel coffee table.

"Business is good, huh?" Ambrose asks.

Shane makes a noise like, *Phfft, 'good' isn't the word.*

"I didn't realize Missoula was such a party town."

"Oh, man—'Zootown'? I used to be right out there in the thick of it, partyin' all the time. My dad threatened to cut me off if I didn't go to rehab. Clean two years. But it's all good. I really gotta keep my shit together nowadays, you know?"

A sleepy-looking girl who appears barely 16 comes walking in, barefoot, wearing a halter top and track pants. She's skinny and hollow-eyed. Shane doesn't bother to introduce her.

Ambrose catches sight of a drum set over in the corner. "Are you in a band?" he asks, nodding toward it.

"Nah, that's just a relic from my younger days. I wanted to major in music and my dad made me go the business route so I could go work for him, which was fuckin' never gonna happen." Looking at the high ceiling with its exposed beams, he shoots a bird with both hands. "Fuck you, old man! I got my own fucking corporation!" He laughs as the girl pads toward them, sipping bottled water from the bar. She sits down on the arm of the leather chair and leans way over on Shane's shoulder. "I'm tired," she says. "Can I have another taste?"

Shane doesn't look at her except to shrug her off his shoulder before swiping his bangs to the side again. "Go get Bruce, babe. Can't you see I'm talkin' to this man?"

One of the guards walks in, sets a small bowl on the wagon wheel coffee table with what looks like a square piece of chocolate on it. "Sample," he says.

Shane pulls a red shaving kit from under the chair he's sitting in, unzips and sets it on the table next to the bowl. The girl gazes into space. Ambrose notices track marks down her pasty arm. "Hey,

Bruce," Shane says to the guard. "Take her back to the bedroom? Get her something."

The guy gently leads the girl back out.

"Girlfriend?" Ambrose asks.

"Just a chick who kinda took up here." Ambrose watches as Shane expertly preps the testing kit. "I don't really have time for what you'd call a girlfriend."

Ambrose tenses as Shane drips some clear liquid onto the dark brown substance. He seems pleased with the results. "Oh, hell, yeah." He swipes his bangs to the side again and Ambrose wonders why he doesn't just tuck that strand of hair into his cap. "Hey, want a taste, just to take the edge off? I got a real old opium pipe, all the way from China. Bought it in an online auction. It's, like, from the Ming dynasty days, or something."

"Tempting, but we'd better be going." Still gazing at the brown material in the bowl, one end of it turning a deep shade of turquoise, Ambrose gets up from the chair, ready to go back outside and stir around before that interminable ride back to California. "Enjoy your caviar shipment. And. . . that."

"I'll contact Mr. R. if we need to schedule future deliveries."

"Sure. Nice doing business."

"Same, man." He takes out his phone. "Hey," he says, to whoever's on the other end. "It's a go. Get 'em unloaded." He hangs up. "Red Bull for the road?"

"I'm good, thanks."

The guard comes to the door leading to the hallway, more exasperated than before. "I tried to quiet her down but she's still calling for you. Wants to see you before she goes to sleep."

"Be there in a minute." Then to Ambrose: "Tell Mr. R funds are on the way."

"Will do," Ambrose says. "I'll see myself out."

"*Vaya con dios*," Shane says with a wave, grabs his juice cocktail and heads for the hallway.

On the porch, Ambrose breathes in fresh mountain air. Its crispness reminds him of that night up at Tahoe with Randy. If Ambrose hadn't shot the guy whose body they dumped in the lake, would that guy be doing what Ambrose is doing for Alexei now? Most likely. Something unsettling about that. Ambrose paces, trying not to look impatient as a forklift removes the palette stacked with cheap caviar and fine opium from the plain panel truck in which he'll spend the next several hours with that hairy bastard Lev and his loud music.

But the money. . .

Money's on the way, the guy said. Even though Alexei had told Ambrose that this job involved finesse, specialized skills, and interacting with "well-heeled" clients. He'd also mentioned that not many young men were willing to do the "dirty work" to achieve success on their terms. If Ambrose didn't know how dirty the work would be, then. . .

He thinks of that languid young girl who's staying here, no doubt riding high on the white horse by now. And Shane had mentioned a surplus of 'goodfella,' just another name for fentanyl.

This is dirty work, all right.

Dirty enough to make Ambrose wonder if this side hustle's worth it after all.

THREE

Chopping kale on the bamboo cutting board and thinking back on the last several months, Jessica feels a growing sense of excitement. She hadn't anticipated an addition to the family this soon, but now that it's happened, she wants everything to go perfectly. Yes, there's the baby on the way, but also—Butch. After the parole board hearing went their way, Ambrose stayed in Texas for a few days while the details of Butch's release were being worked out, and Jessica came home to get the guesthouse freshened up, make an appointment with the doctor she wants Butch to see, and meet Butch's parole officer, Ethan, a soft-spoken guy in his mid-thirties with a sociology degree from UC-San Luis-Obispo. He had pictures that his kids had drawn pinned to the bulletin board in his office, which she took as a positive.

Beau is excited about Uncle Butch coming to live here. Mike doesn't know yet, but he shouldn't have a problem with it. *Should he?*

As she whisks together lemon juice, honey, butter, garlic, paprika, salt and pepper in a small bowl, she glances out the window, where Beau is riding his tricycle in lazy circles while Ambrose and Butch sit at the patio table, Ambrose sipping wine and Butch drinking a non-alcoholic beer. He's been getting settled in all afternoon. When he and Ambrose arrived from the airport, he seemed a bit overwhelmed, emotional, kept thanking them for everything they're doing. *This must be a tremendous sea change, after all those years. . .*

Butch and Ambrose are so different in many ways. Before traveling with Ambrose to Texas that first time, it was hard to think of him having any family, but Butch was the only one he cared about—with good reason. After meeting their dad, a sick old man full of resentment, and seeing how shell-shocked Ambrose was after the visit with his mother, Jessica was nervous about meeting Butch, but then found him, well. . . charming.

Now that he's here, with the prospect of their family further expanding, Ambrose's business and her own career thriving, she's feeling quite blissful as she glazes four salmon filets on a parchment-lined baking sheet with the sauce she just made and a scattering of finely chopped parsley.

She glances up as Butch walks in. Ambrose is out in the yard, talking on the phone.

"Can I help you with anything in here?" Butch asks. "Last thing I want to do's create more work."

"No trouble at all. It's great having another family member to cook for." She places the baking sheet in the oven. Then the baby kicks. "Oh—"

"Something wrong?"

"The baby's been moving this afternoon. Must know today's special." She allows Butch to gently guide her over to the kitchen table. She sits down and he gets her a glass of water.

"Does it hurt when he or she kicks?" Then: "Do you know if it's a he or she?"

"Not yet. No, it doesn't hurt. It's just different. Come sit."

He sits next to her. "Give me your hand."

She takes his hand, places it on her stomach where she felt the last kick. "It may happen again in a second."

He looks into her eyes, smiles. "This is pretty amazing."

"I know." She smiles back, her hand on his, hoping he'll get to experience that movement, hoping he'll be as excited as her. She likes to share these moments with Ambrose, too, but he he's been distant lately. Nothing to be worried about, he's just busy, she tells herself. And so is she, using this euphoric feeling of expansion and creativity to complete four more paintings for an upcoming show in Santa Fe.

The baby kicks again.

"Oh, man—I felt that!" Butch says, delighted. "I just can't believe you and Ambrose got together and made this baby. This'll be one beautiful child. If anybody would've told me this time last year that I'd be here now, I would've said, 'You're crazy as hell!'"

"We're both glad you're here, Butch."

For a moment, he seems lost in thought, still rubbing her stomach with his fingertips. It feels nice. Relaxing.

Ambrose walks in from the patio and stops short to see Butch leaning forward, rubbing Jessica's stomach.

Butch looks up. "Hey, have you felt the baby kick? That's something, ain't it?"

"It's something, all right," Ambrose replies, going to the refrigerator. "Want a drink?"

Butch straightens up. "Just one more of those alcohol-free beers. Been so long, feels like even that's going right to my head."

Ambrose gets one out and pops the top. "Here you go." He hands it to Butch, then uses one of Butch's favorite phrases: "Knock yourself out."

***

The fashion show is a resounding success: just the glamorous affair Phoebe Grace had worked for. Leggy, drop-dead gorgeous models line the stage, following the reveal of edgy-but-wearable designs: the vegan leather dresses, sexy minis, maxis with graceful flow and an exquisite silhouette, the series of shiny latex pants, tops, corsets, and stiletto boots in basic black, followed by a parade of pastels and radical brights in primary colors and neon. High fashion, but attainable. Niche, yes, but accessible to any adventurous soul looking to stir things up in the bedroom as well as the boardroom, with compatible accessories: a pop of bright, shiny latex here, glint of metal there. The show-stopper is an ultramodern wedding dress—sleek and slimming, but available in all sizes—white vegan leather with an elaborate headdress constructed out of delicate leather strips and accented with faux-feathers. The bouquet: yellow calla lilies gathered in a white ribbon.

Cameras flash and pop and beautiful people flank each side of the catwalk as Phoebe Grace makes her way to take her bow amid the din of applause and shouted praise. The stage lights are blinding, but she walks with confidence, escorted on each side by two beautiful models, holding hands, raising them, then bending forward for a deep bow, and, as she rises from the bow, there's a young man standing below the catwalk, staring up at her. Quiet, immobile, scowling: the only downbeat note in all this jubilant madness.

It's Ambrose, hands in the pockets of his trench coat, hatred in his eyes.

Phoebe feels a trapdoor opening underneath her. The noise ceases, crowd disappears, and she awakens, sweating, gasping for breath like a swimmer who stayed underwater too long. It's a relief that it was a dream, but only for a moment. The actual fashion show was all that and more, sans Ambrose at the end. That never happened, but he really does hate her. She can feel it. The scene in front of that macron shop never should've happened, but, since it did, she has to tap back into her old life to settle it once and for all.

***

Maxim likes it best when Lilly ties him to a chair, stripped to his underwear in the blue room upstairs, puts on one of her outfits and pleasures herself while eating some tempting confection from the bakery around the corner. It doesn't even have to be an overtly sexy outfit, just something that shows off her voluptuous curves. Even better if it's one size too small and she could burst out of it any moment, like cream out of a profiterole. Nice when she eats one of those, taking a bite and licking out the cream. Sometimes, she does it slowly and daintily with the tip of her tongue, and, others, she just takes a greedy bite. Sometimes she teases him, staying just out of reach, and, others, she lies the chair back to straddle his face and let him lick her, allowing him to bring her almost to climax, then rises just so he can watch as she finishes herself.

It's in the midst of such a session when Maxim hears his phone ringing over on the nightstand. He's only too happy he's tied up for the moment, literally, but Lilly hears it, too.

She pauses licking cream filling from her fingers. "Want me to hand that to you?" she asks, reaching to untie him.

"Ignore it, dear."

"But what if it's important?"

"They'll call back later."

"No worries." She goes to get the phone, straddles him again, swipes the answer button and holds it to his ear, smiling down at him.

"Eh. . . hello?" he says.

"Maxim, is that you?" A familiar voice strikes a chord in his heart. It can't be, but it is, because he knows the truth of the matter.

Lilly would recognize this voice, too. Only she would know it as Phoebe Grace.

"Dutchess!"

"I know you know, Maxim. I don't know how you found out, and I don't care, but I need your help. Are you still at Sergei's London place?"

"Yes."

"Have you seen him?"

"Not since I arrived."

"So, you're there alone?"

"Eh. . ." He looks up at Lilly, still licking sweet-sticky from an index finger. "Not at the moment."

"Who's there with you?"

"A beautiful young lady," he answers to Lilly's apparent delight. "I believe you know her. Sergei's current and your former personal assistant."

"Lilly's there now?"

"Is that Phoebe Grace?" Lilly asks.

"Eh . . . yes."

Lilly speaks into the phone. "Oh, Ms. Grace, I don't mean to interrupt your conversation, but I just wanted to thank you again for that lovely dress you sent to me." Still, when Lilly says "lovely," it comes out "loovely." Then, looking slyly at Maxim: "It changed my life from the very first day it arrived."

That's the day Maxim asked her to try it on for him, the day he knew the attraction he felt for her was mutual. The day he saw that photograph of Phoebe Grace that came with the dress, and knew the Dutchess lives! Only, along with that happy revelation came the grim consequences of having believed her dead, including poor Ambrose's efforts to avenge her as best he knew how, spurred on by Maxim's rash speculation and panic.

Dogged by guilt for leaving Ambrose all alone to clean up the Dimitri mess, and knowing there could be repercussions from Alexei, Maxim felt an obligation to convey to the boy that things weren't as they seemed, and not to commit any other crimes for the Dutchess's sake. He'd told Ambrose when to go to the Ladurée macron shop on Rue Bonaparte in Paris, that what Ambrose would see there would reveal all. Maxim hasn't spoken with anyone about the matter since.

'Til now.

"Yes, Ms. Grace. . ." Tuning back into the conversation, he hears Lilly say, "I'd be happy to help any way I can." She looks down at Maxim as she raises her eyebrows and bites her lower lip in excitement, like she can't wait to spill. "Mr. Dobrev was due back this week, but his plans have changed. Looks as though he'll be away for the entire month." A big smile. "My, that's most generous of you. . . Yes, of course. . . Let me know anything you need, and I'll get on it straight away. Shall I hand you back to Maxim? . . . Right. . . Cheers! Hold one moment, please?" She sets down the phone, hurriedly unties Maxim. "She wants to speak with you." Lilly places the phone in his hand, whispers, "I'll grab a shower and meet you in the kitchen!"

As she goes out the door, Maxim struggles to sit up, still intoxicated by Lilly's scent and disoriented by this clash of realities, past and present.

"Really, Maxim?" the Dutchess inquires. "You and Lilly?"

Maxim is surprised the impulse to fall at the feet of this voice has vastly diminished. If Ambrose felt duped by her willingness to mind-fuck the people who adored her most, so now does Maxim, her most loyal fan and longtime client. Like Ambrose must've felt seeing her that day in Paris, the thrill of discovering she's alive is tempered with bewilderment, and a feeling of betrayal. At last, Maxim can sit up, leaning against the antique canopy bed. "Lily and I have become quite good friends. With what task did you charge her just now?"

"Asked her to join my publicity team. Sounds like she's got time for a side gig, and I've worked with her before; she's a sweet girl." Her voice takes on a more hushed quality. "But I called because I really need a huge favor from you. Just *please* keep your mouth shut about the me you knew before."

"I'm sure the great Phoebe Grace has an army of assistants to carry out her bidding. Why would she need Lilly or me?"

"Maxim, there's no way to explain everything right now."

"Frankly, my dear, I don't see how there could ever be. But—Alexei thinks you're dead. Was that your primary goal when you stabbed us all through the heart?"

A few seconds' silence. "I don't have time for your guilt trip, motherfucker. If you ever gave a shit about the old me, or about Ambrose, you'll go find out what's happened to him. He saw me here in Paris. Did he tell you that?"

"He did not. Perhaps he was in shock." Maxim spies Lilly's panties on the floor. Hot-pink silk front, ruffled lace back. He picks them up, rubbing the lace between his fingertips. "Tell me, was this whole thing—the death—your idea, or Sergei's?"

Another pause.

He can hear his own breath.

"What difference does it make?" she says finally. "He's my friend and been protecting me this whole time."

Maxim can imagine her pacing back and forth, seeking justification. He should know, he's done his share of pacing, eventually making a weekly meditation of walking the labyrinth at St. Olave's Church. He's given up seeking justification and moved on to seeking absolution.

"And isn't Sergei protecting you, too?" she asks. "Not to mention you're staying in his house, fucking around with his assistant."

But Maxim isn't sure how much longer he'll be staying there. Now that he's met Lilly—whether it lasts or not—he's more mindful of all the possibilities the world has to offer, ever sicker of being caught between Alexei-Scylla and Sergei-Charybdis. When Sergei does return, crashing Maxim's and Lilly's party, it'll be time to move on, and take Lilly with him. "For now."

"Bottom line, I want you to go back to the City and see about Ambrose," the dead Duchess announces. "Stay a couple nights at a place called Arcadia. My treat."

"Lilly and I will be delighted."

"Lilly? *Hell no*, you won't be able to keep your mouth shut around her."

"I will be most discrete. If I go, she goes with me."

A pause, then: "Fine. You and Lilly can get your goddamn freak on. On my dime." Another pause, then the voice hardens. "That's Phoebe Grace's dime, and don't you forget it." Then: "You're fuckin' welcome!" The call ends.

Maxim sits still for a moment, breathing the scent of Lilly's panties, contemplating a trip back to San Francisco with his new paramour. Somehow, nothing seems as scary with Lilly at his side. Not the Dutchess, nor Sergei, nor even Alexei. And he could find a way to make his peace with Ambrose.

For leaving him hanging.

✳✳✳

"Tell me again, why do we have to go to Palo Alto tonight?" Randy asks.

It's a rhetorical question but Bennie answers anyway, preoccupied with traffic. "Because Jessica really wants us at this family-dinner-slash-welcome thing." She glances at him from the driver's seat, all sexy in her little red dress and Ray-Bans. She looked like that at Tahoe on their honeymoon, when she was showing him how to operate the boat so he could get his permit, only that day she'd been wearing her red bathing suit.

Tahoe.

That familiar chill again. Her family's palatial cabin there is the first place he and Bennie ever went away together for the weekend. Where they spent their honeymoon. It's not fair that Ambrose should get to ruin Randy's good memories there by making him his stooge and using the pristine waters for his dead-body dumping ground.

Somehow, he and Ambrose have made it this far without speaking of that since the night it happened. Ambrose got that Rajit guy to play the role of best man at his and Jessica's wedding, so Randy dodged Ambrose's presence then. When they've had to be around each other because of Jessica and Bennie, they've avoided any and all Tahoe references, like pretending not to smell a bad fart. Besides, like Ambrose said that night, "This never happened."

The fuck it didn't.

"Anyway," Bennie goes on, switching lanes, "aren't you dying to see what Ambrose's brother Butch is like? I just can't imagine."

Randy can. Probably some dead-eyed skinny bastard who looks like a chewed-up piece of gum. Covered in tattoos. Lots of weird scars. Just how they got this bastard sprung is still a bit of a mystery to Randy. Yeah, they subtracted his time off for good behavior, and he'd already served most of his hitch, but the rest. . . They said he had ALS but, once Jessica's Stanford doctors gave him a good going-over, they found out it's MS instead.

Randy gets the feeling that Jessica worked on her old man pretty hard before the awesome power of the Jenkins' fortune kicked in to grease the skids for this guy's early release. Payoff here, maybe a kick-back there. Mr. Jenkins knows important people everywhere. And high-powered lawyers can work every angle, night and day. Anyway, whatever disease this Butch character has is no walk in the park and Jessica and Ambrose are the only family he's got for when things get bad. Still, having another Ballard brother at these family gatherings is not a happy prospect.

When Bennie and Randy arrive, things seem just like always— at first. Jessica welcomes them into the kitchen, offering drinks and appetizers. The overall mood is light enough, but Randy finds himself getting that constricted feeling in his throat, which is usually a stress alert. When he and Bennie walk outside, followed by Jessica, Ambrose is over by the brick grill, stirring around the charcoal with a poker. He looks awkward, like he doesn't know what he's doing.

A guy in his late-twenties or early-thirties sits in one of the patio chairs, watching Ambrose with an amused expression, like he would get up to help, but it's more fun to just watch. He's wearing jeans, white button-down, sleeves rolled up to reveal lots of tattoos, but this guy's no dead-eyed, chewed-up piece of gum. Looks like once upon a time he might've been a bodybuilder, now a mere mortal who eats whatever the hell, no supplements. Dark brown wavy hair, graying at the temples. Maybe that's what makes it hard to peg his age. He's got mileage.

"Hey, look who's here!" Jessica calls. The new guy sees them coming and stands up. "Butch, I want you to meet my sister Bennie and her husband, Randy."

Bennie approaches first, reaching out. "Wow, it's so nice to meet you!"

"Pleasure to meet you," he says, grasping her hand, then shaking hands with Randy. He has a firm grip, looks Randy in the eye. "Randy."

"Butch."

"How do you like California so far?" Bennie asks.

"I like it fine," Butch answers. "Nice getting all this sunshine without the Texas heat."

"We do have the sunshine." Bennie smiles, inadvertently glancing at Jessica as Ambrose walks over.

"And fog," Randy offers, just to have something to say.

"You'll have to come visit us in the City when you get settled in. We'll take you out to dinner, or I'll cook whatever you like."

"'Preciate that," he says, rubbing the back of his neck. "I'll be getting out and about quick as I can. I gotta find a job."

"Don't worry about that now," Ambrose tells him.

"Is the charcoal ready?" Jessica asks.

"Uh," Ambrose glances back at the grill. "I think so."

"Could y'all excuse me just a second?" Butch asks.

"Sure." As Butch goes in the house, Jessica pulls out a chair from the patio table. "Have a seat, Randy. Bennie, want to help me bring out the kabobs?"

"Okay." Bennie follows Jessica back into the kitchen.

Randy takes a swig of beer, walking over to the grill where Ambrose stands, looking uncertainly at the briquettes. "How's married life?" Randy asks, glancing back at the door.

Ambrose worries the charcoal again with the poker. "Pretty great. You should know that by now."

"Family life, I should say. Baby on the way, brother in the guesthouse. New place of business." Another swig of beer, looking down into the smoldering embers. "You're busy as a one-legged man in an ass-kicking contest."

Ambrose looks up, unamused. "What about you? When's your private dick exam? Seems like you've been studying forever."

Touché, motherfucker. "Soon."

"Know your stuff?"

Swig of beer. "I know my stuff." Closer. "Anything else going on I should know about?"

"Like what?"

"You know '*like what*.'"

Ambrose's mouth hardens. Fine if he's pissed. Randy's been carrying around so much tension from that grim trip to Tahoe, affecting his waking hours, his sleep and even Bennie's sleep, it feels good to take a wrench to Ambrose's little "This never happened" suburban fantasy. Let his asshole pucker up; he deserves it for being such a cock-sucking manipulator.

"Nope," Ambrose says finally. "Nothing."

✳✳✳

In the guest bathroom, Butch splashes water on his face, still seeing that silver basin in his prison cell. He dries off with a hand towel before closing the toilet lid and sitting down to catch his breath. Not that he's really hyperventilating, just a lot to take in. People, places, *everything*. Doesn't seem real, landing here instead of some halfway house or that old bedroom at his mama's where such awful memories reside, finding out he has MS another shock. He can still see that prison cell when he closes his eyes, still hear Barry's whispers, feel him sliding into his bunk. . .

He rubs his eyes, takes a couple of deep breaths, trying to hold it together. *They're out there on the patio, probably wondering what's up.* Hard to really understand how all this happened, but he owes Jessica and Ambrose big. Somebody somewhere sure pulled some strings. And then all those swank doctors, that hospital, those tests. There's got to be a stack of medical bills already and soon could be mountains of them and the government ain't paying for it. All that legal help they got him—that shit wasn't free. He thought Danny was a decent enough mouthpiece, but those lawyers Jessica and Ambrose brought in were pure fire. So, he owes them, and who else? Jessica's father who he's never met? Barely got here and already in hock past his ass. Dizzy, he grasps the edge of the sink. *Make it through this evening.*

When Butch comes back outside, Jessica and Bennie chat in the kitchen while Ambrose texts by the grill. Something about him has been prickly lately, and Butch feels like the cause, landing in the middle of Ambrose's astroturf-perfect life like a belly-flop whale. They've already got one kid, and another on the way. It was never in their plans to foster or adopt a chronically ill ex-con.

Randy sits on a garden bench, sipping a beer, watching Beau, who's awakened from his nap, tooling around on his tricycle on the lawn, following the undulating borders by the rose bushes.

Butch grabs his half-full non-alcoholic beer off the patio table and gravitates toward Randy. Seems like a nice enough guy. Ambrose appears busy, with his face in his phone. *What's he got going that's so important on a Saturday night?*

Butch waves back at Beau, who's smiling and waving from the other end of the yard, before jumping off the tricycle to get a last session in on the swings before sunset. "Looks like he ain't got a care in the world," Butch says, approaching the garden bench.

Randy looks up, slides over for him to sit. "Lucky kid."

"You and Ambrose sure lucked out, finding those two gals in there." Butch nods back toward the kitchen.

"Got that right," Randy agrees.

"Where'd you meet Bennie?" Butch asks.

"At Jessica's first gallery opening. I was working security."

"Security? Thought I heard someone say you were a cop."

"I was once. Got fired."

"A cop getting fired?"

"What can I say? I pulled some shit."

"What'd you do? If you don't mind my asking?"

Randy shifts uncomfortably and Butch wishes he'd kept his mouth shut. Maybe Randy doesn't want to talk about it, but everyone here knows Butch is fresh out of stir, so it all is what it is. And Randy's staring at the ground, like he's searching there for words.

Butch lightly nudges him with his elbow. "Hey, man, never mind. It ain't none of my goddamn business."

Randy looks up, attempting a smile. "No, I don't mind. I did a lot of things I shouldn't have. Mostly involving drugs and guns that didn't quite make it to the evidence room." He takes a swig of beer. "I didn't play things smart. My police lieutenant said I stuck my fingers in all the wrong pies. But I was different then, you know?"

"I know how that is. You always wanted to be a cop?"

"I never knew what I wanted to be when I grew up. Joined the Army and got deployed to Afghanistan. When I got out, law enforcement looked like a good career track." He pauses, looking Butch in the eye. "Did anybody tell you I had a nervous breakdown my last day at work?"

"No, hadn't heard 'bout that."

"That's right, maybe just Bennie knows. I think of it as a meltdown. Right in the middle of the goddamned street. It's a wonder my colleagues didn't just slap me in jail."

"How'd you end up in the middle of the street?"

Randy glances toward the patio, speaking quieter. "Started when I had to turn in my gun and badge. I barely remember it, but, evidently, I put on quite a show. Cussed everybody out, told 'em all to fuck off. The lieutenant put a tail on me when I left the station. Two cops following to make sure I didn't go out and commit suicide or go on a shooting spree, I guess. I didn't even have a gun on me after I turned mine in. Tried to shake 'em but I just couldn't breathe, and couldn't drive anymore, and. . . I had, like, a flashback, I think." He looks sheepishly at Butch, like he's unaccustomed to talking about these things, much less to a total stranger. "Damn, didn't mean to tell you my whole life story there."

"It's a'ight. I asked. So, you got treatment? For the PTSD?"

"Meds. Saw a therapist a couple times. Could've gone back, but it hasn't happened since then." He pauses. "I mean, not really. Nothing like that time." Randy runs his fingers through his hair. Sighs. Looks like recounting took a lot out of him.

"What're you up to now?" Butch asks.

"Prepping to take the Private Investigator license exam. And I got a business plan I'm working on for a—I just want to find a way to work for myself, you know? That's on-the-level." Randy turns to him, smiles, eyes slightly bloodshot around the edges. "What about yourself? Federal prison, huh?"

"Left holding the bag in a big deal gone sour. Flew all the way from Bogota just to get busted by a couple undercover cops in Texas."

"Sucks. Who fucked you over? Somebody you knew a while?"

"Yeah, I'd known her a while."

"Her?" Randy mercifully doesn't ask her name. "That's rough."

"Is what it is." Butch glances at the patio. Ambrose must've gone inside for something. "Ever been to that place Ambrose works? I asked him about it, but he just says it's an 'urban oasis.'"

"That sounds like something he'd say," Randy murmurs into his beer bottle.

"Whatever it is, he sure stays busy."

"Oh, he's always busy," Randy says with a bit of an eye roll, then, catching himself: "I mean, your brother's a real go-getter."

"He is that."

"Guys!" Jessica calls, carrying a salad in a large wooden bowl. "Dinner's ready!"

Ambrose is back outside now, along with Bennie, placing the kabobs on a serving platter. Ambrose smiles to see Butch walking toward the patio, less so when he catches sight of Randy. Ambrose turns away, wiping his hands on a dishtowel while Bennie places the tray on the table where they're about to eat dinner.

Butch takes a seat at the table, no longer feeling quite so alien.

✳✳✳

Bennie notices that Randy's in a way better mood going home than he was driving down to Palo Alto earlier. For one thing, he's half-drunk and, for another, ended up having a good time. He even likes

Ambrose's brother, which he never saw coming. She likes Butch, too, only she's still a little nervous about his walking into the kitchen after Ambrose recklessly brought up the molly trip they took together, just as Bennie was preparing the dessert she'd brought. She'd just taken the blueberry crumble out of the microwave, about to get vanilla ice cream out of the freezer, when Ambrose walked up to her with a silky, "Hey, sis. . ." Then whispering: "Do you ever think about that night we hung out together?" Then he ran his fingers up her back, gently squeezing her neck in an affectionate way that shattered her concentration and caused her to look toward the door to see if Jessica or Randy were within eyeshot. Ambrose hadn't said it loud enough for anyone besides her to hear, but the forbidden nature of it made her jump.

Then Butch came walking in from the patio, said, "What the *hell's* going on in here?" and then laughed like he knew he'd caught them off-guard. Then he gave a kind of "*Just* kidding—*why so jumpy?*" look as he grabbed two bottles out of the refrigerator.

"You're a double-fisted drinker now?" Ambrose asked as Butch paused to pop the bottles with an opener lying on the counter.

"Just getting a beer for Randy and a near-beer for me." Then, to Bennie: "You're the designated driver, right? Mind if ya boy out there has one more for the road?"

"I don't mind."

Butch went back out and Ambrose smiled at her.

"How many beers have *you* had?" she asked, finally placing the ice cream on the counter and getting a scoop from the drawer.

"I switched to bourbon. I've eaten, though. It's not like I'm—"

"What is going on with you?"

"What do you mean?"

About then, Jessica walked in, lighted up to see the dessert preparations. "Oh, how pretty! Thank you, Bennie!" Past her, out the window, Bennie could see Randy and Butch, drinking, laughing, and talking. All evening, she felt slightly disoriented, like there was a joke or secret she wasn't in on, that, ever since Ambrose and Jessica had returned from Paris, the dynamics had shifted between herself and Randy on some level. And now—here's Butch. So different from Ambrose in every way, and Ambrose himself is different, too.

Everything is even different at the new dungeon and, though she has her own little office, she doesn't feel like she's at the controls the way she was at Miss Dover's. Rajit and Terrence are in their attic space, always working away at something. It's like there's a hidden side, a backstage she knew so intimately, but now the backstage goes deeper.

She unwillingly remembers the last scene in *The Godfather* where Kay leaves Michael Corleone in his office while she goes to make drinks, and his men approach to hug him and kiss his hand, addressing him as Don Corleone. Then one of them walks over and closes the door, darkness falling across Kay as she's standing there watching. *But that's not me*, Bennie thinks, disturbed. *I'm not Diane Keaton!*

"Hey," Randy begins, "we oughta have Butch over for dinner."

"I told him, we would. Remember?"

"He says he hasn't been into the city yet."

"Oh?"

"Yeah, what the fuck? Ambrose hasn't even taken him to see his new place."

"Jessica said before that Butch has had lots of doctor's appointments. Maybe Ambrose is waiting 'til he really has time to—"

"Bullshit."

"You yourself haven't come to see it."

"Well, what am I supposed to do there? Pretty soon you and me might be working together anyway." He looks at her. "Swear to God. I won't always be such a bum."

"You're not a bum." He looks sexy: slightly rumpled, smiling that semi-drunken smile.

"Want to pull over and fuck?" he asks.

"Sure, let me find a place to stop and we'll get in the back."

"You really called my bluff."

"Damn right." She passes a slowpoke in the middle lane and speeds up, ready to get home and take him up on his offer before he passes out. "What did you and Butch mostly talk about?"

"Different things. Prison. My former life as a cop."

"Did you tell him about your time in the Army?"

"Some." He reclines. "He and Ambrose are like night and day."

"You have an older brother. I know you said you don't get along, but is it really so bad? Maybe someday—"

"I'm night, he's day. And he hates my guts."

"What about your older sister?"

"She hates me, too. So does my mom."

Bennie glances over again. "I really don't think your mom hates you, Randy."

"She's better off if I stay out of her life."

"I don't believe that. And I still hope I get to meet your brother and sister someday."

"That'll be a cold day in Hell."

#

Jessica missed the penultimate meeting of the planning committee while they were in Texas that last time. She didn't mind missing it. In fact, the only reason she's remained involved after stepping back from philanthropic activities to focus on her painting is because it's a fundraiser for a children's art therapy program she believes has real merit.

Butch hasn't really been out of the house since arriving. He stays mostly at the guesthouse alone, except for dinner with her and Ambrose and Beau, but sometimes it's just with her and Beau if Ambrose has to work late in the city. Butch is applying for jobs. He has to work as long as he's able to as a condition of his parole so, in the meantime, he's been helping around the house, trying to make himself useful, he says. She's content having him around, but he needs something to do for his own sake.

It's like he's desperate to get a grasp on some purpose post-prison. He'd found some meaning there trying to better himself through getting his degree but, here on the outside, he says that two-year degree doesn't mean anything to anyone but him. He still has to check **yes** for the question on most applications: **Have you ever been convicted of a felony?** Seems the obvious thing would be for Ambrose to give him a job at the new place. Butch is willing to do anything, but Ambrose says he isn't sure what to have him do. Not yet anyway. She can't help feeling like Ambrose is being disingenuous, but she tries not to think about it.

She finishes eating a bowl of yogurt and granola with pomegranate avrils, watching through the wide kitchen window as Butch spreads mulch in the flowerbeds. She told him they have someone who does most of their yardwork, but he's on vacation. Likewise, Butch should be taking it easy until they hear results from the tests he's been having at the medical center. He doesn't want to sit around, though. He's in loose-fitting blue jeans and a sweat-stained T-shirt out by the back hedges, in the bright sun. She hopes his getting all hot and sweaty doesn't aggravate his condition somehow.

All the pushing, pulling, and cajoling she'd done to get her father to wield his considerable influence to get Butch out early was just the beginning. It's like Butch has become her cause. She wants him to be happy. Ambrose wants that for him, too, but Ambrose has been different lately. She's been occupying herself with getting Butch settled, his medical care, and her own health, preparations for the new baby, Beau getting ready to enter preschool. She hopes Ambrose doesn't feel neglected, but that doesn't really seem like what's making him distant. After their meet-up in Paris and subsequent wedding, she'd anticipated a beautiful new chapter. That's not unfolding quite as expected, so far. Of course, she hadn't anticipated what's happened with Butch, and neither had Ambrose. But here they are.

As she goes to put her bowl in the sink, she can see Butch wipe sweat from his face with the sleeve of his shirt. His jeans sit low on his hips. He makes his way over to sit on the garden bench. She takes a cold glass of water out to him.

He smiles when he sees her coming. "Hey, I thought you had a meeting to go to."

"It's just a briefing really, of what I missed at the last meeting. I'm going over to a friend's house. Come with me."

He looks like she just made a joke. "I better stay here."

"But you need to get out a little. Besides, you shouldn't be doing all this hot outside work. At least not until we get your tests—"

"This ain't hard work. Most folks would call it gardening."

She sits next to him. "It's too hot for gardening, so come with me. You can watch Beau. The babysitter has classes all afternoon."

"I could watch Beau here, if you want."

"This won't take long, then we'll all go get ice cream or something. Come on." He's clearly looking for a nice way to say no, and she's determined not to take no for an answer.

He sighs. "A'ight. Got time for me to go take a shower?"

When they get to Mary-Ann's and Bob's house in Woodside, Mary-Ann is sitting at a table by the pool, still in tennis clothes, gazing at her tablet, her two youngest grandkids playing badminton out on the grass. The girl, Kylie, seven, and the boy, Tyler, nine, are wearing bathing suits, and the oldest girl, Emma, thirteen, in shorts and a tank top, sits in a lounge chair, texting.

As Jessica, Butch, and Beau approach the patio, Mary-Ann slides off her sunglasses as she rises to greet them. "Hi, Jess, Beau. Who's your friend?" Then, "Oh, you must be the brother-in-law. Hello!"

"This is Ambrose's brother, Butch. Butch, Mary-Ann—Ms. Bauer, that is."

To Butch, she says, "Call me Mary-Ann."

"Pleasure to meet you, ma'am."

"Can I get you guys anything? Tea? Lemonade?"

"Some iced tea would be lovely, thank you," Jessica says, sitting down at the table.

"I'm all right, ma'am," Butch says. "Thank you just the same."

"So, Butch, how are you liking Cali so far?"

"Quite a change from where I've been, that's for sure." Butch smiles.

"I wanna go swimming," Beau declares.

"Not now, honey. Why don't you let Butch take you over to the swings while Mommy talks to Ms. Bauer."

"*Aww,*" Beau protests. "Swimming."

Mary-Ann intervenes. "It's just been chlorinated, honey. You'd come out looking like a ghost." She nods toward the kids playing badminton. "That's why they have to amuse themselves on land for a while. The pool man was late again. Says they're short-handed, but I think he and his partner just stop off and get high between here and the Montgomery's."

"See, honey," Jessica tells Beau, "you can swim next time. And we're going for ice cream when we leave here."

"Something to look forward to," Butch reassures him, winking at Jessica and Mary-Ann before he and Beau start for the swing set.

"So that's Butch," Mary-Ann says, sliding her sunglasses back on. "He's a big one, isn't he?"

Jessica looks over as he places Beau on the slide, guiding him down as the two youngest grandkids abandon their badminton racquets to head for the swing set. "He is a big guy."

Lenore, a Mexican woman in her late-forties who's worked for Mary-Ann and Bob for the last ten years, walks out of the house. Mary-Ann picks up her tea glass and holds up two fingers. Lenore nods, goes back inside.

Jessica sits back, just realizing how good it feels to be off her feet. "He's really sweet, too. He's great with Beau."

"Wonderful." Mary-Ann sits down at the table, taking some papers out of a file envelope. "What did he do back in Texas?"

Jessica had held back on explaining to Mary-Ann why she's been unavailable recently. It was easier to be nebulous about going to visit Ambrose's brother, who has health problems and is coming to stay with them for a while. But now. . . She looks over at Butch sitting in a swing, holding Beau on his lap, as Kylie hops on the other swing and Tyler shows off on his pogo stick. Watching Tyler makes Jessica nervous. *He's going to fall off that thing.* She glances at the pool, smooth as glass until a whisper of a breeze causes rippling. An idea forms.

"Jess? Did you hear me?" Mary-Ann asks.

Lenore brings their iced tea out on a tray. There's also a plate of homemade oatmeal cookies. Lenore notes Jessica's condition with a warm smile. "Figured you could use some fresh-baked cookies. Ms. Eason—Ballard, I mean, is eating for two. There's more in the kitchen if the kids want some later."

"Thank you, Lenore. That's all for today; you'd better go now if you're to make Andre's soccer game."

"Just gotta get my purse. Good afternoon, ladies." She heads back toward the house.

"Her grandson," Mary-Ann explains. "If he doesn't get a full scholarship playing for some big school, I'll be shocked." She takes a sip of tea. "Now, what were we just talking about?"

Jessica reaches for a cookie. "Actually, Mary-Ann, Butch was in prison back in Texas."

"Prison?"

"Federal prison."

Mary-Ann's mouth drops open, and she takes off the sunglasses. "What on earth for?"

"Drug smuggling. He did his time for that though. He's really turned his life around."

Mary-Ann looks over at Butch holding Beau on the swing, two of her grandkids hovering around. Butch looks at ease talking to kids. "Drug smuggling?" The way she says it, Jessica gets the idea Mary-Ann heard nothing after that phrase. "And he's living in your home?"

"Guesthouse."

"But still, Jessica. Aren't you worried?"

"About what?"

"Well, the kind of people he must've associated with. That some hoodlums or gangsters might—"

"That was a long time ago. I think most of them might even be dead by now." Jessica puts down the cookie and leans forward. "Actually, I have a favor to ask. The people who clean your pool, think they'd be willing to hire Butch if you put in a good word for him?"

"Hire him?"

"He's on parole and really needs a job and this would be perfect! He likes being outside and it's not too strenuous."

"Jessica, I—"

"He got time off for good behavior, has a college degree, and he's gone totally straight."

Mary-Ann looks over at Butch helping Beau down the slide again while Kylie waits at the top and Tyler climbs the ladder.

"Nothing bad'll happen," Jessica continues. "And even if anything did, which it won't, I'll take full responsibility. And I'll go in and talk to the boss or manager or whatever."

Mary-Ann glances at Butch again.

"I'd consider it a personal favor and I'll owe you big-time."

"You wouldn't owe me."

"I'll move Heaven and Earth to make sure this is the most successful fundraiser ever. Who knows, you might be voted philanthropist of the year! I'll nominate you myself."

"You really don't have to do that, Jessica."

Jessica leans in. "Please, Mary-Ann. All you have to do is put in a good word."

"Well. . . you understand, I can't make them hire him."

"I understand. All I ask is that you try." Quieter: "He and Ambrose had a harsh upbringing, and he's been warehoused in that prison for so long. He's such a sweet guy, just made some bad choices when he was younger. If you'd ever met their dad, you'd. . ." Tears sting her eyes just thinking about it. "Please."

Mary-Ann's uncertainty seems to dissipate, somewhat. "Okay," she says, finally. "I'll do it for you."

✳✳✳

Butch lies in bed, patio doors open, moonlight spilling over the tile and across the plush blanket Jessica brought out the other day. She was right, the nights do get chilly. Odd being more connected to the outside world. The breezes, the rain, the bright blue skies, the stars, the scent of eucalyptus leaves all around that little patio four times the size of his prison cell and that he frequently paces around in deep contemplation.

How did he get here? How did Ambrose get here? What did either of them do to deserve this cushy existence that would've been unthinkable when they lived back in Riviera, slinging for nickels and dimes and dipping into shadows at the sight of a prowl car trolling the dusty streets. As their grandmother would've said, it's only by the grace of God they've both survived to come together again like this. Purely by the grace of God.

He rolls over, hoping that thought will be enough to settle his nerves and calm his mind, but it doesn't. He glimpses his work clothes over by a chair in the corner, all washed and ready to go. The shoes don't really have to be polished, but he wiped all the smudges off. Without this job, he'd just be another hanger-on relative taking up very valuable real estate. Though no one's making him feel that way. Jessica couldn't be kinder. Ambrose, too. . .

He rolls over again, flat on his back, staring at the ceiling. Sometimes his thoughts run to Callie and the nights spent together, the things they did. He wonders who she ended up with and what she's doing now. Whether she ever thinks about him. Most likely, he'll never see her again. More likely, most definitely he'll never see her again. And why would he want to?

He sits up, sighs, pours himself a ginger ale and goes outside to smoke a cigarette, allowing his mind to wander to places it shouldn't. Mrs. Bauer, for example. She's not his type, so no problem there. He's indebted to her. Rich society lady going out of her way to recommend him for a job like that. Course she really did it for Jessica. And who wouldn't want to do for Jessica? Ambrose doesn't, that's who. Doesn't really seem to appreciate her like he should. A drag from the cigarette, watching the smoke slowly rise. But Ambrose is busy making good. Feels like he's got something to prove. Fair enough.

Butch stands, walks around the edge of the patio, drink in one hand, cigarette in the other. But the Bauer lady. Ms. Mary-Ann. Brittle, a bit uptight. Late-forties, maybe? Early fifties? Preoccupied, hurrying out to her car in one of those fitted dresses. Not ashamed of those curves. *Tap-tap-tap* of high-end high-heeled shoes. Most mornings, she says hello, sometimes just a quick wave when she sees him out cleaning the pool. She tosses her purse and a business-like tote bag into the car and gets in. Doesn't work a regular job, but she's always in a rush.

Not his type at all. Mr. Bob's got his hands full with her, in more ways than one. Except. . . He pauses, gazing into the bamboo grove rising behind the eucalyptus trees next to the back privacy fence, leaves rustling in the slight breeze. There's something about that Bauer woman that reminds him of Callie, the ex from Columbia. If Mrs. Bauer wore her hair down. If she wore something even sexier with those high heels. Showed some more skin, a little more cleavage.

Another sip. Another drag. A night in Rio. Another in Buenos Aires. And then those times at the hacienda outside Medellín. Those times her husband was watching them on camera, or from his wheelchair in the shadows. . . *Wonder if the Bauers ever go skinny-dipping?*

When Butch came outside, the clock on the nightstand said **1:39AM**. Butch crushes out the cigarette, kills the last swallow of ginger ale, and goes in to brush his teeth. The clock reads **2:05AM** as he climbs back into bed. He hears the crackling whine of a motorcycle blocks away, coming closer, getting quieter, then out front before the engine becomes muted, then goes silent. Ambrose finally parked that new crotch-rocket of his in the garage. Just another late night in the city. Doing God-knows-what.

✳✳✳

Lunch with Momo's always an adventure and today she and Ambrose are at a sleek place in Japan Town, sitting at the sushi bar of a restaurant under new management. Normally, he doesn't order the salmon skin sushi, nor the mirugai, but her uncle's working today: a chubby, bored-looking guy in his fifties who clearly knows his way around knives, cutting fish into delicate slices, turning out rolls so enticing that Ambrose is willing to give them a try. He'd balked at the *hotaru ika,* but Momo insists, and all he has to do is picture her in her new red vinyl catsuit and he complies, opening his mouth, letting her feed it to him.

It's not bad. When there's a lull, she introduces him to her father's younger brother, Uncle Ito, who only nods hello, says something to Momo in Japanese, and she answers in Japanese. Ambrose notices the guy's missing his left pinkie finger. Must've had an off day handling that cleaver at some point. Maybe he'd come to work one morning hungover. The conversation ends with Uncle Ito grabbing a pack of cigarettes from under the counter, Marlboro Reds, and heading for the kitchen as Momo resumes lunch without a word.

"What'd he say?" Ambrose asks.

"He wanted to know who you are, and I said you're my boss."

"I don't really think of myself as your boss."

"Then what are you?"

"A friend and colleague."

"Do you ever miss cracking the whip and doling out punishments like we used to together?" she asks with a smile.

"I like staying behind the scenes. You're the star attraction."

"Star?"

"Would you rather 'baddest-ass bitch this side of the Continental Divide'?"

She holds up a paper-thin slice of sashimi with her chopsticks, looking through it at the light above the sushi bar before she dips it in soy sauce and eats it. "I should put that on all my profiles."

"You absolutely should."

"Things are so different than when you and I were a team."

"Different how?"

"More tourists. More couples. More Russians."

"We've always had Russians. Miss Dover's fairy godfather's connections."

"I know, but these make me miss that crazy Maxim Rusovich. Remember him?"

"Sure."

"Wonder whatever happened to him."

Ambrose shrugs. "Maybe his work took him elsewhere." He eats another bite of crunchy shrimp roll. The wasabi makes his eyes water. "So, these new Russian clients, they haven't been causing you trouble, have they?"

"Nothing I can't handle. Some of them are weird, though. I mean, weirder than normal. And carry guns."

Ambrose puts down his chopsticks. "Why didn't you tell me?"

"It's only now becoming an issue. I'm not afraid of firearms. I carry a pistol in my purse and my husband has guns. Just seems like these guys are a *type*, you know. Nothing like Mr. Rusovich. More *gangsta*. At least that's the impression they give off, real or not."

"We'll definitely step-up security."

She sips her saki. "Isn't Bennie's husband an ex-cop?"

The last person he wants snooping around is Randy. It's hard enough keeping Bennie from asking too many questions, but, since that night on Lake Tahoe, Randy's an even worse pain-in-the-ass than he used to be. "I think he's busy with other stuff."

Momo adds another dollop of wasabi to her soy sauce dish. "Well, if you ever need a night watchman or anything, Uncle Ito's always looking for side gigs." She stirs the wasabi. "You wouldn't know it to look at him now, but he's the real bad-ass of the family." She leans closer, whispers in Ambrose's ear: "Retired Yakuza."

"Really?" Ambrose swirls his earth-tone ceramic teacup, then takes a sip of warm matcha, savoring the umami flavor of the sediment at the bottom. That's what really gets him wired. He sets down the cup, reaches into his coat pocket for his monogrammed silver cigarette case, and takes out a business card. He hands it to Momo. "Give this to your uncle. Tell him to call me."

***

Mary-Ann recalls that Julie Rudder, the wispy wife of Bob's golfing buddy, Whitt, said something about going out for drinks after today's meeting to celebrate Julie's 51st birthday. Someone suggested meeting up at Las Dalias, a beloved Mexican restaurant great for celebrations, but now Julie says her sister's taking her to dinner in the city and the ladies on the committee should go anyway.

Jessica bowed out. Something about that husband of hers (it just doesn't seem possible Ambrose's *actually* her husband). Apparently, he had to stay in the city late, her brother-in-law is home with Beau, and she wants to get home and get dinner started for them. Jessica's so very pregnant, it's a wonder she ventures into this heat, yet she rarely looks tired and, even when she does, she's beautiful. Sun-kissed California-rich-girl. One could love to hate her, only she scrambles that impulse with graciousness. She just lives on a different plane than those who never had it so easy, Mary-Ann thinks, every time she realizes she's both captivated by and jealous of her.

However, that split from Mike for a much younger man was a reminder that Jessica has weaknesses, too. So did Mike, as it turns out. He'd been running around with men behind her back before finally coming out. Whatever it is that Ambrose has that makes her crazy enough to risk her parents' ire and the whiff of scandal, must be something extraordinary. It's like a soap opera. She wanted that boy and now she's pregnant by him. She'll never escape him if things don't work out, but she's let him infiltrate her life so fully, she must love him.

Somehow the very thought of disaster looming is more sinfully delicious than the caramel gelato at La Divina, her favorite indulgence. And now Butch, that ex-convict brother of his, is living on the property, and Mary-Ann herself put in a word for him with the manager at Pinnacle Pools. So, if something goes wrong with that, will she be in for a kiss of scandal as well? Scary to think about, but—also exciting in a strange way.

After the meeting in the Cardinal Room at the country club where the ladies sip diet sodas and snack on pretzels and edamame, none of the ladies plan on going out, so Mary-Ann compiles some last-minute notes and a list of things to confirm for the gala. When she's done, around a half hour later, she puts away her tablet, swaps her readers for sunglasses and walks out to the car. That ding on the bumper that must've happened in the Trader Joe's parking lot: small but annoying. As she starts driving home, she remembers telling Bob she'd bring something home for dinner. She decides to go to Las Dalias for take-out. She can make margaritas at home. Concocting drinks in the blender appeals more than cooking, and Lenore is away for a few days—no fallback in the fridge. She calls to place the order.

The atmosphere at the restaurant is always festive. Mary-Ann enjoys walking through the ornately carved door into the gentle, sky-lighted glow of the high-ceilinged entrance, past a small fountain, down a short path lined by tropical plants and indoor palms. The azure stucco walls are decorated with colorful artwork: brightly painted iguanas, life-sized ceramic parrots, a Warhol-inspired portrait of Emiliano Zapata, and an Aztec-inspired design surrounding the wide door leading to the host's station. The place is bustling with the happy hour crowd: jovial, loud. She approaches the front desk.

The young man looks up from the seating chart as he hangs up the phone. She's seen him before. He's cute. Olive complexion, beautiful brown eyes. "Good evening. Can I help you?"

"I'm picking up a to-go order for Bauer."

He checks his screen. "Yes, ma'am, I'll have that for you in a moment." He walks toward the kitchen while she gets out her credit card. The place has small sections and nooks separated by philodendrons, cacti, and succulents in planters under the skylights. Over the din, Mary-Ann hears an exuberant laugh that sounds familiar. *Sounded like—but it can't be Julie; she went home.* Mary-Ann strolls closer to the bank of prolific aloe plants.

It's Julie Rudder and several other committee women with whom she'd just parted ways at the club, the ones who said they were going home, sitting over plates of appetizers, sipping frozen margaritas. Jessica's not with them, though. Mary-Ann has an impulse to walk over with a *"Hey, ladies, I see you changed your minds,"* but then Julie pipes up with a comment that stops Mary-Ann cold.

"I didn't think we could pull it off, but I've had enough of that bitch for one day."

"Make that a whole *season*," Sue agrees.

Alice tries to soften the tone: "She means well, but sometimes she comes off so bossy—"

"Sometimes? Come on. I don't use the C-word often but—"

"Oh, Julie!"

"I don't see how Bob stands it. He must be a saint."

"And the booze helps," Sue quips, holding up her margarita.

They all laugh.

Mary-Ann glimpses the host bringing her to-go order. She starts in that direction, disoriented. The host tells her the amount, but she doesn't hear, just hands him her credit card and soon takes the to-go bag out into the sunlight. She gets in the car and places the bag on the passenger seat, stunned. They had gone to some lengths to keep her away from their friendly little gathering. She starts the car, torn as to whether hurt outweighs anger. *Too much of a taskmaster. Too abrupt. Bossy. . . The C-word? Did she mean 'cunt'?*

Bitch.

Then again, she tells herself, this is just the price one pays to lead. She'd angled, ingratiated, and, yes, schmoozed to get to where she is. Which is where, exactly? Hated by everyone who knows her? Tolerated by her husband only because he's too complacent to leave her? Anyway, she's in this to raise money for a worthy cause, not to make friends.

But she thought those were her friends.

She glances at the clock in the dashboard. Can't figure all this out now. The food will get cold. She slides on her sunglasses, backs the car out of the parking space. Nice to know where you stand with people. Turns out they're not her friends and never were.

Anyway. Screw them.

✳✳✳

When Mary-Ann gets home, Bob is sitting at the table out by the pool in a Hawaiian shirt, cargo shorts, and Wayfarer sunglasses, smoking a cigar, sipping a beer. Really letting his hair down this evening. He waves as she takes the to-go bag into the house. Normally she'd pour herself a glass of wine, change clothes, and join Bob out by the pool, but this evening she starts for the bedroom.

"Hey," she hears, turning as Bob walks in, and goes over to the take-out on the island under the rack holding her prized collection of copper cookware. "You up for margaritas?" he asks, unpacking the food. "I'll get out the blender if you'll make 'em."

"Not tonight," she says, walking over and turning her back for him to unzip her dress. "I'm exhausted," she says. I'm going to take a shower and get into bed."

"This early?"

"Told you, I'm tired."

He takes out a sack of fresh tortilla chips and fishes around the bag for the salsa. "So how was the meeting?" he asks in a bored voice.

"Okay."

"When's the next big party-thing?"

"Doesn't matter; you don't have to go."

He looks up. "What? I always have to go."

"Not this time." She decides to get a glass of wine after all. She feels a frightening realization taking shape. "You don't have to go to another gala, benefit, or ribbon-cutting for the rest of your life."

"Oh, come on." He seems to think it's a joke. "What the hell happened?"

"Nothing."

"Something must have."

"I don't want to talk about it."

He eats a chip dipped in salsa and gets another beer from the refrigerator since no margaritas are forthcoming. "Somebody get pissed off over a lack of vegan options?"

"They all told me they were going home and then went out for drinks and appetizers without me."

He pops the top off the beer bottle and opens a foil container of cebollitas. "How'd you know they went for drinks?"

"I saw them at Las Dalias when I went to pick up the food."

"Probably just a misunderstanding. What time and where. Maybe they changed their minds at the last minute."

"It was not a misunderstanding. They were sitting at the same table we had for Payton's birthday dinner, crowing about lying to me."

"What'd they say?"

She's too tired to tell him. He'd probably just laugh, make fun. Tell her not to worry about it because Whitt told him stories about Julie, how she can be a real harpy. That should make Mary-Ann feel better, but it doesn't. "Oh, I don't know." She takes her glass of wine and starts walking toward the bedroom, dress unzipped, pride wounded, feelings hurt, over what amounted to nothing, really. Still, it's a sign other people don't see her as she sees herself, opening a realm of self-doubt.

"What brings you here today?" the doctor asks.

"I'm having these dreams," Randy answers.

"What kind of dreams?"

"Hard to explain."

"Try."

Randy shifts in the chair.

"Any images come to mind?"

"There's a woman in some of my dreams lately."

"What can you remember about her?"

"It's in a village near where I was stationed in Afghanistan. She's walking down the road, always just ahead. She's wearing this tailored suit with a fitted skirt and jacket, like an outfit from the 1940s or '50s. Desert-colored. And light brown leather gloves. And beige high heels. Pumps, I guess. And she's wearing a pink veil over her head and face. She usually stops to look at me, then turns and starts walking away. When she does, I can see that her shoes have red soles."

The doctor smiles. "Louboutins."

"Huh?"

"It's a brand of expensive shoes that have trademark red soles. My wife wants a pair." Then, "Do you think that could be what it is or—"

"Maybe. I don't really think it's blood. . ."

The doctor clicks his pen and makes a note. "What else do you remember? What's happening around you?"

"I'm in combat gear, out on patrol. Sometimes I hear gunfire, sometimes heavy. And when I see her, I want to help her get someplace safer. She watches me get closer, then walks away, and I can never get to her. And I call to her but it's like she doesn't hear me."

"Do you have any thoughts about what she might represent? Is there a new woman in your life?"

"I just got married, about four months ago."

"Oh, congratulations. Do you think that could have something to do with the woman in your dreams?"

"I don't know. My wife's the woman *of* my dreams, but I don't know if she's the woman *in* my dreams. I don't want to think it's her, because I wouldn't want her to be out in the open, in danger, and I wouldn't want her to walk away from me like that. It bothers me that she keeps walking away."

The doctor clicks his pen. "Been taking your medication?"

"Yes, sir."

"Aside from the dreams, have you been having any unwanted side effects? Nausea, dizziness. Feelings of hostility, depression?"

"Not really. I guess I get cranky when I'm not sleeping much."

"Last time I saw you, you'd been fired from your job on the police force. Still stressed about your finances?"

"I was beyond stressed before, but I have better prospects now. I'm studying to get my private detective license. . ."

"Sounds like you have a lot going on in your life."

"I guess."

The doctor removes his glasses, takes a small, blue cloth out of his jacket pocket and wipes the lenses. "You know, there are other avenues we could try in your medicinal therapy."

A weak current of anxiety. "What've I said that makes you want to change my medication?"

"Not change it, just try something different on a supplemental basis."

"More pills?"

"I don't think more pills would help." He puts his glasses back on. "You know, many veterans are undergoing psychedelic therapy now with excellent results."

"What kind are we talking about?"

"I'll give you some information and you can see if you're interested."

"I wouldn't want to like—lose control of myself or anything. Would I know what I'm saying?"

"It would be small doses under controlled circumstances. Like I said, I'll give you some information. You can see what others who've tried it say about it as well. I think you'll find it's overwhelmingly positive." He clicks his pen. "Okay?"

"Okay, I guess."

✳✳✳

Sometimes Ambrose sticks around on Thursday nights to see if Mr. Bob or any of the Palo Alto crowd shows up at the cigar bar, or whether anything's going on that he needs to handle upstairs in his office when it's quiet and he's alone and focused and no one, not Rajit, Terrence, Bennie, nor Momo, might just come walking in. Focus is harder to come by as all the daily tasks, lies, and guilt pile up, but things will settle down. This evening, he called Jessica to say he'd be late. He's been invited to Alexei's house for drinks and what else he isn't sure, but he has a feeling it's another unpleasant job. Ambrose doesn't really want to go, but he's going. There could be good money involved, and maybe one or two more "consulting" jobs like this will lead to enough of a buffer to give him peace of mind for a while.

Just as he's about take off, he hears the door buzzer and remembers there's a late check-in this evening. Some couple who was due earlier but only just arriving. Vance, the guy who mans the night desk and tends bar on cigar night stepped out to the patio for a smoke, so Ambrose slips out of his coat, straightens his tie, and goes to greet them, glimpsing their black-and-white image on the front door cam. A man and a woman, both wearing sunglasses. Ambrose starts toward the door, but something pulls him back for a second look.

The man is short, with a receding hairline, fifty-something, maybe. Looks familiar. The woman: blonde, cute, glam enough to be a curvy model. Whoever they are, they've got a suite reserved.

Ambrose opens the door. "Hello, welcome to—" He stops when the man removes his sunglasses and Maxim Rusovich is staring him in the face.

"Hello, my boy! I expected to see you but not to receive such prompt, personal service at the point of arrival." Maxim hugs him tightly. "Tell no one I'm here," he breathes into Ambrose's ear before turning to his female companion. "Allow me to present my assistant and constant companion, Miss Lilly Blackshear of Mayfair, London. Lilly, this is my dear friend, Ambrose Ballard, the proprietor himself!"

"Charmed, I'm sure," Lilly says, removing her sunglasses and looking around at the lobby. "Oh, Maxim, this place is just lovely!"

Ambrose turns to Maxim, speaking quietly: "What the hell are you doing here? I didn't think you'd be back after—what happened."

Lilly opens the double doors to the cigar bar and walks in, still exploring, *ooh*-ing and *ah*-ing.

"I'm so sorry I abandoned you," Maxim says in a hushed voice. "Can you ever forgive me?"

"I forgive you. After all, you're the one who clued me in about. . ." He glances back to make sure Lilly's not heading their way. It strikes him that that's the Lilly who Maxim mentioned in the fateful phone call back in Paris, the night before all was revealed. "You know. The undead."

"It was the very least I could do. I've been racked with guilt." He leans closer. "In fact, she called me out of the blue and sent me here." He sees Lilly approaching from the cigar bar. Vance has returned from the patio and is busy mixing something in the blender.

"Maxim," she calls, "I'm having a pina colada. What's your pleasure?"

"One moment, dear." Maxim smiles, then, to Ambrose. "I'll explain later. What there is to explain."

"I have a dinner engagement tonight, but make yourselves at home," Ambrose tells him. "Drinks are on the house."

Maxim smiles. "Thank you, my boy. Most generous." Lilly guides him back into the bar.

Ambrose grabs his coat and walks outside, stunned. Maxim and his girlfriend Lilly. Miss Dover's vicarious meddling. And now off to Alexei's for drinks. Clash of civilizations. None of this is happening, yet here he is mounting his new Ducati to ride out to a glass house on the edge of a cliff.

Cruising along the Coast Highway, the sunset is spectacular. He imagines what it would be like having Jessica's arms tight around him, if he were going out to dinner somewhere with her, the way it really should be. Pregnant as she is, she might not want to ride the motorcycle, but the Mercedes has a sunroof and this weekend he'll prioritize her because, the more he reaches for, the more he can feel slipping away, and that's not why he's doing all this. These extra activities are just a means to an end, security for himself and Butch. But he's got that, he'd like to think, if he'd just have a little faith. Why is having "just a little faith" so much harder than it sounds? He rolls to a stop at the turn that leads down the driveway of the glass house, glowing like a lightbox as night falls.

Alexei's car is the only one here. Maybe there'll be no Lev guarding the door or grazing in the kitchen. Ambrose rings the doorbell and Alexei answers.

He wears white linen pants and a black shirt. Ambrose has never seen him dressed so casually. "Ah, Ambrose. Come in." In the foyer, Alexei helps Ambrose off with his coat and lays it across the back of a white chair. "This way." Ambrose follows Alexei into a grand living room with a floor-to-ceiling fireplace, all white, with sofas and chairs in shades of black, white, and gray. The only splashes of color are the red chess pieces in a large painting over the mantel. A bar with chic glassware. Nothing overstated, outdated or outré here, not like the tearoom or his ballroom office at Miss Dover's old building.

This is all modern and minimalist, with a priceless view of the Pacific Ocean beyond. There's a well-curated spread on a glass table by the open patio doors. Caviar in an iced bowl, accompanied by a small bowl of sour cream, a plate of what looks like thin silver-dollar pancakes, champagne chilling in a silver bucket, crystal flutes. The ocean breeze slightly ruffles the calla lilies in a delicate vase. Pop music pulses from unseen speakers, the woman singing in Russian makes him think of someone beautiful. He can't wait to get home to Jessica.

"I take it you had no trouble finding the place?"

"No trouble at all."

"Please, help yourself to the food." Alexei pours two glasses of champagne, hands one to Ambrose.

"Thanks. Expecting more company?"

"My lady friend is coming over tonight, but not until later. I wanted us to have time to talk."

"I see. This is a beautiful place."

"Maxim arranged the purchase before he—disappeared."

Mention of Maxim reminds Ambrose to stay on guard. *Tell no one I'm here. Game face.*

"I miss having him around to see to my affairs." Alexei shrugs. "But the show must go on."

"True." Ambrose sips champagne, easing toward the open patio doors. The moon is rising and its reflection on the water makes him want to sit in one of the nearby chaise lounges and just stare. "The show must go on."

"Please, have a seat," Alexei offers.

"I really can't stay long."

"But you've come all this way. Do sit down." Alexei steps outside, sits in one of the chaises, puts his feet up and sits back, champagne in hand.

Still wary of getting too cozy, Ambrose finally follows suit, gazing out at the most stereotypical romantic scene imaginable, only he's here with Alexei.

"I have some shorter delivery runs coming up, and then another more lucrative job for you, if you're interested."

"What kind of job?"

"Another long-distance delivery. Miami, Florida."

"That's a hell of a road trip."

"Indeed. Most likely the last one."

"Honestly, I don't know if I can get away for that long."

"I will make it worth your while."

"I'll think about it." Ambrose sips champagne. "What would I be delivering, and to whom?" Never used 'to whom' before. It felt correct.

"A large shipment of our best to a most well-heeled customer."

"Our best—what?"

"Caviar, of course. Top domestic grade."

Ambrose sets his glass on the cube-shaped table between them, rolls over to look at Alexei. Something about this feels too cozy by half, like rolling over in bed. He straightens up, too tired to keep playing nice. "Cut the bullshit. It's a long drug run. What kind of drugs?"

"Best opium the world has to offer."

"And they turn it into heroin, right?"

"What my customers choose to do is their own business. If they wish to adulterate the product with—"

"How'd you hook up with that Shane guy in Montana?"

"Networking, my boy. I have contacts all over the world." My boy. Maxim's the only one who usually says that. Could that be Alexei's left-handed way of letting Ambrose know he's aware Maxim's back in town? "As they say, I know a guy who knows a guy, who knew Shane was in the market for such goods and had the capital to purchase without tiresome negotiations."

"Guess it could be tiresome to a guy like yourself, negotiating with a spoiled Zoomer who has his own mini militia."

Alexei laughs. "I was only aware of the essentials. He wanted to buy, had the money, and has as much to lose as me by running his mouth. However, your take on things is most enlightening." Alexei gazes up at the stars. "You're quite mature, you know, considering your tender years. Fearless, in many respects. I find you to be a most impressive young man."

"Again, please cut the bullshit."

"No bullshit." Alexei takes a big sip of champagne. "Perhaps my dealings with you will help keep me young."

Ambrose thinks of that night at the country club when Mr. Bob had talked about retiring as head of his company but staying on the board to keep young. Alexei is no Mr. Bob, but he's probably around Mr. Bob's age. . .

"In spite of your past allegiance to that Dover person, I'm glad she's gone. Her ties to my old enemies kept me shackled to the past as well. Now I'm looking forward, and so should you."

"What makes you think I'm not?"

"When my cache is converted into liquid assets, I'll no longer seek to be the Western distributor for Afghan aunti."

"So back to being part-time restaurateur, part-time pimp?"

"I don't really care for that word 'pimp.' However, I must say, my plans are evolving on that front. There's been some unpleasantness at an apartment building I own near Bakersfield that could invite unwelcome scrutiny from the authorities. That's the last thing I want." He turns to Ambrose. "So, after careful thought, I've decided to divest from that side of things, for the time being. Greater focus leads to greater clarity, yes?"

". . .Sure"

"You understand. You're driven. Action-oriented. Very adaptable to changing circumstances. You are an inspiration."

Ambrose drinks champagne, mixed feelings rising to the surface like the starry bubbles in this slender glass still half-full of Bollinger. "Thank you, I guess."

Alexei stands, goes over to the handrail. "Speaking of past associations and cutting through bullshit. . . I've given Dimitri up for dead. I prefer that, actually. I believe he sought to create trouble for me even as he claimed to have information about restoring my hacked account. I believe, had I made him a partner, he would have ended up killing me to take over my business. So, to whomever killed him first, I salute you." He raises his glass to Ambrose then turns toward the ocean, drinks the rest of the champagne down. *Whomever.*

Ambrose gets up off the chaise and joins Alexei at the rail. Even though no one's around, he feels compelled to speak quietly. "Just to be clear, you don't still think I had anything to do with either one of those things, do you?"

Alexei stares calmly straight ahead. "I said I'm looking forward these days, not back."

Silence for a few moments, only the sound of the waves below. Ambrose remembers that swishing, hissing swirling seawater that faded into white noise the night he was hanging by his fingertips on the end of a pier. He was hiding from the police following the bust of a drug deal where the drugs turned out to be fake. The night he met Randy, who was all lean and mean back then. That was right before they both hit rock-bottom and had to start climbing back.

Finally, Alexei turns to him, smiles. "Let's have some caviar, shall we?"

They start inside. Ambrose catches a whiff of Alexei's aftershave. Definitely Royall Lyme.

"This is not my domestic brand, but Russian beluga sturgeon. The very best." He serves Ambrose a small plate. Caviar on a cloud of whipped sour cream, balanced beautifully on a golden blini like a picture in one of Jessica's cooking magazines.

"I've never had this before," Ambrose admits, picking up the blini that contains the primo fish eggs.

"This is the caviar against which you'll measure all others."

Ambrose takes a bite. It's nothing like he thought it'd be, and nothing like he'd hoped. But not the worst, either. Reminds him vaguely of the next-level sushi Momo was feeding him recently. But creamier. Fishy in a different way. Alexei's watching him. He shrugs, nods. "It's good."

"It is an acquired taste."

"My taste buds aren't very sophisticated."

"Not for long." Alexei prepares his own plate, dipping caviar with a mother-of-pearl spoon. "You'll learn to love it."

✳✳✳

The following Wednesday, Mary-Ann stays in bed until nearly noon, when she forces herself to get up and go take a shower. The last meeting before the gala is tomorrow and, feeling like she does, she doesn't see how she can go to the meeting or the gala. She knows she shouldn't let those women keep her from fulfilling her duties as committee chair, but something's shut down inside her and she finds herself barely able to function. She's never really been prone to depression, not like this, but, somehow, her entire sense of reality's been shattered. She's fallen headlong into a black hole and the walls are too high and smooth to climb out.

Not believing what she said about never making him go to another charity function, Bob asked which tux he should wear, and she told him not to worry about it. They're not going. He was at a loss, like a tame animal set free in the wild, not knowing what to do. He's getting worried, never having seen her like this, withdrawing from her beloved social scene. It's a shock to him.

After her shower, she contemplates getting dressed, but doesn't have the energy, so goes back to bed and doesn't get up until late afternoon. She tells Bob to order himself something for dinner; she's not hungry. He says he ate a late lunch and what did she end up having for lunch, by the way? He never asks things like that, so this is Bob getting frantic. She tells him she ate a salad, just to calm him down, and then he puts on a swordfish-print Hawaiian shirt and topsiders before going out by the pool for a beer and cigar.

Their son, Payton, drops by with Kylie and Tyler. His oldest daughter's prom is in a couple of weeks and Mary-Ann had ordered her a dress from an L.A. boutique. It arrived a few days ago, before Mary-Ann's reality check and, grasping at any chance for this day not to be a total waste, Mary-Ann gets the dress to show Payton. "Think Emma will like it?" Mary-Ann asks. "She saw the picture, but it's even prettier in person. So chic and modern."

"She'll be crazy about it," Payton says. "I could use a soda. Want another beer, Dad?"

"Not yet." Bob puffs the cigar as the kids head for the swing set. Payton's not a fan of cigars, giving Bob one of his "*those things are gonna kill you*" looks as he walks past. Mary-Ann stands there, holding the dress. She wanted to see Emma try it on, but maybe better just to let Payton go ahead and take it to her. Emma's growing up and certainly doesn't need her grandmother's approval. Mary-Ann goes and puts the dress in Payton's car, then walks into the living room and collapses into Bob's recliner, again exhausted. The television's off and she can hear Payton taking a phone call in the kitchen.

"Well, can you find somebody else? . . .I don't get it, she knew we were counting on her. . . She knew it was all but definite. . . I'll ask, but I can't promise. . . I know, but they sometimes get busy, too. . . Okay, okay. . . I said I'd try."

"Try what?" Mary-Ann hears Kylie ask, having come in from the swings. The refrigerator door is closing.

"Jennifer can't come over to watch you kids tonight, so your mom wants me to ask if you can spend the night here while we go to Britt's baby shower."

"Aw," the little girl whines. "Let Tyler stay here. Why can't I just go spend the night at Dakota's?"

"Because it's a school night and we can't do that to Dakota's parents without okaying it in advance."

"I don't want to stay here. Emma can be our babysitter."

"Emma has a study date with Matt."

The kids opening/closing the refrigerator door again. The sound often gets on Mary-Ann's nerves, but now, combined with the whining resistance to spending the night, it's giving her a sick headache. She stands, thinking it might be a good time for an aspirin and a sleeping pill, then back to bed, when Kylie inquires of Payton, "If I stay, how much will you pay me?"

"Cut that out, I'm not paying you this time. Don't you like staying here?"

Mary-Ann peers into the kitchen where the girl is sullenly rearranging fruit in a wooden bowl on the counter.

"It's boring and Grandma's too bossy."

"She takes you anywhere you want, buys you anything you want."

"Not stuff I really want."

Mary-Ann avoids the kitchen as she heads for the bedroom, headache intensifying. Through the window, she sees Bob walking to his car. Looks like he's getting something from the glove compartment, his phone charger. As he starts back toward the patio table, she goes out to him through the side door. "Bob!" she hisses.

"What?" He turns to her in the waning light.

She nears. "Payton and Edie are going out tonight and the babysitter can't make it. He wants us to keep the kids."

"So? Might cheer you up."

"It will not cheer me up," she says, tears closer to the surface than she'd realized. "I have a splitting headache and—" She almost tells him what Kylie said but doesn't have the energy. "If he asks, tell him no. Not tonight." The tears spill over. "I just can't." She barely glimpses Bob's concern as she turns and makes her way back into the house, into the bedroom where she turns out the light, falls onto the king-size bed, and burrows under the covers.

✱✱✱

Bob heads back out by the pool, sensing this could be something other than one of Mary-Ann's typical moods. He plugs his phone into the charger with plans of listening to tonight's Giants game, another reason why, if those kids stay here, he'd want Mary-Ann to cater to their spoiled-rotten whims. The boy's not so bad—not yet, but the little girl's fast becoming a tween terror and the oldest has morphed into a straight-up teen bitch. Getting Mary-Ann's go-ahead to say no for once is a tremendous relief.

Payton walks out, sliding his phone into his pocket. He pastes on a smile when he sees Bob rolling a Cubano. Payton and Edie hate the cigars. If he doesn't quit smoking for himself, Edie likes to say, he should do it for the grandkids. Payton approaches, Kylie following behind, dancing some steps she maybe saw on TikTok or some Disney movie. "Hey, Dad, Edie and I have an event to attend, and the babysitter flaked on us. Think you and Mom could babysit tonight?"

"Your mother's not feeling well."

Payton shrugs. "Maybe having the kids here would—"

"I said, your mother's *not feeling well*," Bob repeats. "Not a good night for it."

Payton looks down at Kylie, who's oblivious, still dancing that goofy dance. "If you're sure. Mom usually loves spending time with the kids."

Bob settles back in the chair, puts his feet up on the adjacent one, preparing to re-light the cigar. "Not tonight. Some other time."

Payton seems taken aback. "Oh. . . well. If you say so."

Bob flicks the cigar lighter, puffs, producing smoke that drifts toward Payton. "I say so."

"All right, then." Payton, unaccustomed to his dad calling the shots in a situation like this, looks down, pats Kylie on the head. "Come on, kids. We'd better go." Tyler tosses the soccer ball into the air and catches it, starting toward the car, Kylie trotting along behind. "See you guys later," Payton says over his shoulder as he follows.

"Later." When they're gone, Bob draws deeply on the cigar, releasing a cloud towards the sky, where the first star has just appeared. A breeze ripples the swimming pool. He finds the game on his phone. Just started. Sinking further into the chair, he relishes having just dodged a bullet that would've spoiled the whole evening. He'll check on Mary-Ann when he goes in for another beer.

For now: Peace.

As Butch cleans the Bauers' pool on Monday, he realizes Mary-Ann hasn't been around much. She used to constantly come and go, dressed up, in a hurry, but lately she's been absent, even though her car is here. He sees Mr. Bob every so often, getting in from a round of golf or heading off to one. Sometimes he's dressed casually as if for an afternoon meeting: slacks and a polo, maybe a sportscoat. His schedule hasn't changed but Ms. Mary-Ann seems to have dropped off the face of the earth. And Mr. Bob looks pensive. He's normally one of those poker-faced guys, but, the last couple weeks, that neutral expression has shifted into one of unease.

Today, When Butch goes around the corner to clean the hot tub and sow it with chlorine, the back drapes are open and Ms. Mary-Ann's inside, lying on the bed, wearing an emerald-colored nightgown with black lace. She has her back to him. Seeing her through the window like that in her gown, only partly covered by the crisp, white sheets. . . He turns away, aware he was maybe looking too closely. Maybe they have some camera out here. But anybody would look, even if just wondering if she's all right. Is she? He turns to look again. She's sleeping. Usually never asleep this time of day.

Mr. Bob's been so distracted, Butch hasn't had the nerve to ask, but curiosity finally gets the best of him. The next time he's over, he sees Mr. Bob coming out of the house, summons all his courage, and walks closer to the car as Bob beeps it unlocked with the key fob. "Hey, Mr. Bob."

"Hey, Butch."

"I haven't seen Ms. Mary-Ann in a while. How's she doing?"

Mr. Bob pauses. "She's, uh. . . Hasn't been feeling too well."

"Oh?"

Mr. Bob opens the car door, about to get in, like he wants to pause and talk about it, but then again, he doesn't. "She'll be fine in a couple of days. Just—needs some rest."

"Tell her I hope she feels better."

For a split second, Mr. Bob looks him in the eye, a rare occurrence. He's worried. "I'll tell her."

Butch mentions it at dinner. Tonight, it's just him and Jessica and Beau. Ambrose is working late in the city.

"That's all Bob said?" Jessica asks. "Mary-Ann didn't return my last call, so I just thought she'd been recuperating. I knew something must be wrong when she backed out of going to the gala. She said she'd come down with the flu and turned everything over to Julie Rudder. Julie was thrilled to do it, but still. Mary-Ann's never missed anything like that before."

"Social butterfly, is she?"

Jessica laughs, like that's a huge understatement. "Yeah. At least she used to be. Now that I think about it, I saw one of our acquaintances at the grocery store the other day and she said Mary-Ann's quitting the Woman's Club, too." A pause as Jessica seems to connect some dots. "Tell you what, I'll cut some roses for her in the morning and make a bouquet. It'll be a get-well present from all of us."

"I'm going there tomorrow. I'll drop it off."

Beau asks to get down to watch TV and when she gets him set up watching one of his kid channels, returns to the table.

"What time's Ambrose getting home tonight?" Butch asks.

"Soon, I hope. Wouldn't want to think he stays out so late because. . ."

"Because what?"

"Because he doesn't want to come home."

"Surely you know better than that."

She sighs. "I feel like I've had this same conversation before."

"Same conversation?"

"When Ambrose first came here, we were talking after dinner about why my husband Mike never really wanted to come home. Ambrose made me feel so—" She stops, then, "Let's just say he helped me through a rough time." She looks down, toys with the silver filagree at the end of the unused spoon by her plate. "It's another reason I fell in love with him."

Butch leans forward, props his elbows on the table. "Why do I feel like there's something you're not telling me?"

"This staying out a lot. He says it's for work and I want to believe he's being honest with me." A pause. "How much do you know about how Ambrose and my ex, and I, met?"

Butch sits back. "Well, I know he came to stay in your guesthouse, 'cause that asshole I knew back in Texas threatened him." He realizes now how little he does know. Just that Ambrose had hit the jackpot in every way possible: Jessica's rich, looks like a movie star and Miss America rolled into one, she's kind, a perfect mom already, and about to have his kid. And somehow, he's not at this table.

"He did come here to hide out, which I discovered later," Jessica says. "But he'd met Mike before that."

"Where'd he meet him?"

"At a club in the city. When Ambrose was still dealing drugs."

Butch pushes his plate further out of the way, drawn in by the hidden part of the story. "Was Mike buying drugs from him?"

Jessica drops her gaze. "Mike was buying something, but not drugs. I really shouldn't be talking about this; it's all in the past." She smiles suddenly, swipes at her eyes. "I think I'm just in a mood." She stands, starts gathering the dishes. "We have lemon sorbet for dessert. I'll bring you some."

"Really wish you'd tell me what you were going to say."

"Nothing."

Butch picks up a couple plates, following her into the kitchen. "You're forcing me to guess?"

She busies herself with getting out dessert bowls, her back to him. "Please don't try to guess."

To question her any further about this would be cruel. Especially when he already knows the answer. "I don't think I really need to. Like you said, it's all in the past." As he returns to the dining room, he can feel her staring into the freezer for a couple beats before getting out the sorbet.

✳✳✳

Ambrose hasn't been to this chic coffee shop in quite a while. Used to walk by here when he first arrived in town, maybe get an espresso and a pastry if he had extra money and a little time. Sit and watch the people come and go, people with real jobs and lives. The ones on the fringe would pass by outside, glance in occasionally, recognize they'd stand out a little too much if they tried to use the restrooms here, and move on. Back then, depending on the kind of night he'd had, he occupied a liminal space between those on the inside and those on the outside.

Today, total insider, he sweeps up to the counter in his trench coat, custom-made suit and Italian shoes. Feels like a double espresso day. He gazes at the golden array of pastry in the glass case. Might be nice to get a variety of baked goods to take to work, surprise Bennie, Rajit, Terrence, and Momo, but they've probably already eaten breakfast. Tomorrow, he'll stop at that new bakery for doughnuts all around. He stopped in here on a whim anyway, maybe a shred of nostalgia, just to see what it's like coming in dressed for success, on the way to his own establishment, compared to the old days, one step away from jail or life on the streets.

Not much of a line at the counter. He gazes at the back of the head of the guy in front of him. Tall, bald, black leather coat. Looks like one of those bouncers at clubs where he used to sling molly late at night. Looks like—oh shit, it is!

Lang, his former boss.

Ambrose turns away, fight-or-flight kicking in before he remembers there's nothing to fear from that son-of-a-bitch anymore. Lang looks slightly deflated these days, a little tired. The cashier bags up a bacon-egg-&-cheese croissant as the barista fetches a large dark roast. Lang fumbles for his credit card. Ambrose takes out his own. "I got it," he says, then to the cashier, "Add a double espresso and a chocolate croissant to what he's getting."

"Yes, sir."

Lang looks over at Ambrose, stunned. "Well, I'll be goddamned. Long time, no see."

"It has been a long time. How you doing?"

"I'm good." He looks Ambrose up and down. "What the hell are you doing now?"

"Got my own business."

"Oh yeah?"

"Yeah." The barista places the pastries on the counter in separate bags and Ambrose and Lang move to the end of the counter to wait for the coffee. "You?"

"Bouncin' over at Betty's Cheetah."

The strip club. Ambrose pretty much already knew that. Wade, one of Lang's other former employees, had told Ambrose the day he scored the molly he and Bennie did that night of hers and Randy's breakup. The break-up that only lasted one night. "That must be interesting."

Lang shrugs. "Has its moments." They get their coffees and move over to a counter by the window. "So. You're working for yourself now?" He's thinking drugs.

"Uh-huh. Kind of a bed & breakfast. Sort of."

"Really? What kind of bed & breakfast?"

"A dungeon with the option of spending the night. And a cigar bar."

Lang laughs. "Now that's thinking outside the box. Whatever happened to that place you worked before?"

"Ms. Dover passed away and left it to me. Somebody else bought the building, so we moved and changed the name."

"Lucky you."

Ambrose sips coffee. "Is bouncing your main line or a side-hustle?"

"Main line. Some shit happened, things got kinda hot, so I had to step back from my own, uh, entrepreneurial interests for a while."

"I see."

Lang takes the bacon-egg-&-cheese croissant out of its small sack. "Hey, what do you hear from Butch? Still in the big house?"

"He's living with me now. In the guesthouse."

"Guesthouse?" Lang bites the croissant. "Sounds fancy."

"It's my wife's place." Watching Lang eat, Ambrose is reminded of Lev's constant eating on the road to Missoula, and back.

"You're married?" Lang repeats, mouth half-full. "I never would've figured that in a million years."

"Me neither." And Lang would never figure it was his own violent threats that helped land Ambrose on Eucalyptus Lane. Lang's the reason Bennie stashed Ambrose there when he was at the end of his rope. "I live with her and my stepson. She's pregnant, due in May." He wouldn't have mentioned that, but he said it just to tee up his next question: "Got any kids?"

"Little boy. Ivy talked me into naming him Josiah. Remember her?"

Ambrose nods, sipping coffee.

"I'm living back at her apartment in the Haight. She wants to get married." He makes a dismissive sound, eye roll like *that'll happen*.

"Married life's not so bad." Whereas Ambrose used to fear Lang, he doesn't in the least now. But Lang could still scare other people, if he wanted to. "You ought to try it."

Lang finishes the croissant, wads up the paper bag, sighs. "Maybe someday."

Ambrose hands him a business card with the new logo on it. Two crossed riding crops in a ring of barbed wire. "If you ever decide you have time for an easy side hustle, give me a call."

Lang looks at it, slightly amused. "You're serious?"

"Sure." Ambrose glances at the clock behind the counter. "I'd better get going. See you 'round."

"See ya."

Ambrose walks out, confident that Lang might just call.

✳✳✳

Randy never wants to hang out with anyone else; usually it's only the two of them, but, this morning, when he found out Bennie planned on cooking shrimp scampi for dinner, he said that they should invite Butch over. She invited Jessica and Ambrose, too, but they're spending the evening in. Ambrose has been working late a lot, though Bennie isn't quite sure why.

Randy offered to go get Butch in Palo Alto, but Butch wanted to ride the Cal-Train into the city, so Randy just went to pick him up at the station and now they're up on the roof, drinking beer and smoking cigars and taking in the sunset while she sets the table. Butch had insisted on stopping to get a hostess gift. Sunflowers. Her favorite.

She texts Randy to let him know dinner's ready and pours herself another glass of wine. Randy and Butch are in a jovial mood when they get back downstairs and, while Butch goes to wash up, Randy comes into the kitchen as she's tossing a Ceasar salad, wraps his arms around her from behind, and squeezes her in a hug. "You should've come on up."

"I had things to do down here." She glances toward the door to the bedroom. "What'd you guys talk about?"

"Mm. Just stuff." He goes over to the refrigerator, gets himself another beer and a non-alcoholic one for Butch. He pops open both bottles, sets one on the table and takes a swig from the other. "You know, now that I think about it, maybe I wasn't always the biggest fuck-up on the force."

"No one thinks you're a fuck-up."

"Hadn't learned to cover my ass when all that went down."

"But you wouldn't make the same choices again even if your ass were covered and you wouldn't get caught. . ." The wine kicks in and she puts her arms around his neck, leaning in for a kiss. "You're different now."

He gazes into her eyes, his are glassy from the beer and cigar. He's not really used to smoking cigars, but the one Butch brought him looked like a good one, from her dad's favorite cigar shop in Palo Alto. "We both are," he says, kissing her.

His cigar breath is kind of sexy. She pulls away as Butch walks back into the room. He hesitates, like he might be interrupting something, and she flashes back to the night when she and Randy were at Jessica's for dinner and Butch walked in on her and Ambrose in the kitchen, just as Ambrose was running his fingers down her back. . . Awkward. If Randy knew about that, he'd never let it go.

"Come have a seat, Butch," she tells him. "Anywhere you like."

He approaches the table as Bennie sets out the main dish: fresh shrimp atop a bed of pasta on her favorite serving platter that she bought in Italy her junior year abroad. It has a blue, hand-painted fish now hidden by all the pasta, with colorful, wavy designs around the edges. "This is sure a nice spread, Bennie," he says, surveying the table.

"That's your non-beer, Butch," Randy says.

Bennie refills her wine glass before joining them.

"Where'd you and your sister learn to cook?" Butch asks.

"We've both taken a few classes here and there. Jessica's a way better cook. I do have tiramisu for dessert, though. That's one of my specialties."

"Hell yeah," Randy jumps in. "She makes breads and cakes and cookies all the time. How you think I'm putting on these pounds?"

"You haven't put on that many pounds," Bennie informs him.

"She could open up a bakery if she wanted," Randy adds. "Fact, you really should, Bennie."

"There are plenty of bakeries around here already," she says, serving her own plate. "Anyway, I already have a job."

Randy makes a scoffing sound, before catching himself.

She looks at him. "What?"

"Nothing," he says, squeezing a lemon slice over his serving of buttery, garlicky shrimp

Butch looks at Bennie. "Ambrose told me you're one of the first people he met when he came to town. I can't imagine what that must've been like for him. Not knowing a soul, really."

"The one person he did know here was a thug named Lang that some friend from home hooked him up with. Could've gotten him killed. With friends like that, he didn't need any more enemies."

"That was me," Butch says. "I'm the one that got him in touch with Lang, and I am sorry for that." He leans slightly over his dinner, left arm on the table. Maybe some leftover habit of guarding his plate in prison. "When Ambrose called and told me he was running away, heading west as far as he could go, there wasn't much I could do about it, but I didn't want him to be destitute, you know? Living on the streets."

Bennie sips her wine, face burning from badmouthing the "friend" Ambrose had told her about. "I'm sorry, Butch. I had no idea it was you."

"I did give him damn bad advice."

"Aw, you had no way of knowing," Randy says between bites.

"Me and Lang met at state prison first time I ever got busted. I'd kept in touch with him through mutual acquaintances. I knew he lived here, so guess I was naïve enough to think he might be able to help Ambrose, somehow. It was you and your sister that did though. I'm grateful to you both."

"Ambrose has no trouble getting people to help him," Randy says. "Guess he's just got one of those faces."

Bennie shoots him a look, sharper than she'd meant to, but she's detected an undercurrent where Randy and Ambrose are concerned lately. She sips more wine, watching Randy slather butter on a bread stick.

He saw the look she gave him. "You know. Some people are just good at that," he says before taking a bite.

"So, Butch, did Randy tell you about the time he met Ambrose? He could've arrested him one night and didn't."

Butch looks at Randy. "Is that true?"

Randy shrugs. "Looked like a drug deal, but turned out the drugs were fake."

"And you let him go?" Butch shakes his head in wonder. "I'll be goddamn. That's hard to believe."

Randy picks up his beer. "Sometimes I can't believe it myself."

"So, y'all got to be friends after that?"

"No. Well, we met again later. At the coffee shop. I gave him my card and he hired me for security at Jessica's show."

"And that's where you met Bennie, right? That's crazy as hell." Butch leans on the table, grinning. "No telling where you and Ambrose would be if your paths hadn't crossed."

"No telling." Randy takes another swig of beer.

Butch twirls his fork on the pasta. "It's good to know there's still some compassion in the world."

"Have you been making any friends down in Palo Alto, Butch?" Bennie asks. "How do you like the people you work with?"

"They're an easy-going bunch. Boss is nice. I really appreciate Ms. Mary-Ann putting in a good word."

"She's big into fundraising but I've never known her to extend a charitable impulse to somebody right in front of her." After saying it, Bennie realizes how snarky that sounded. "To be fair, I haven't seen her in quite a while. She's Jessica's friend." She pours another half-glass of wine. "Actually, I shouldn't say things about Mary-Ann. She's just a bush-league snob compared to my mother."

"I take it you and your mama don't get along?" Butch asks.

"Not really." She turns her attention back to her barely touched plate as Butch turns to Randy.

"How you get along with the mother-in-law, Ran?"

"She hates my fucking guts."

"She does not hate your guts, Randy," Bennie feels compelled to say, even though he's probably right.

"She tolerates Ambrose better," Randy goes on. "Maybe because he's more presentable. Slim and trim and dressed up all the time these days. Custom suits. He's a fucking piece of work."

"Randy!" Bennie wishes he'd reign in his buzzed directness, at least throughout dinner, but Butch watches Randy like he's actually grooving on it and can't wait to see what Randy might say next. Or herself, for that matter, the way she constantly puts her foot in her mouth when Butch is around.

"At least I get along better with your dad," Randy reminds her.

"So do I. Daddy's easy."

"How you get along with your mother-in-law, Bennie?"

Randy glances up, waiting to see what she'll say.

"I haven't been able to spend much time with Mrs. Burke as of yet," she answers, looking pointedly at Randy. "I'd love to know her better."

"Ain't happening," Randy informs her.

Bennie swirls the pinot noir left in her glass. It's a luscious, magical plum color she'd like to use to paint the bathroom. She really shouldn't have any more wine tonight. "You'll change your mind someday."

"I doubt it."

Butch leans back. "Speaking of in-laws, I guess I've officially become that pain-in-the-ass brother-in-law you hear tell about."

"You are not a pain; they like having you there," Bennie says.

"They're still newlyweds. When I fell and busted my jaw that morning, I didn't see all this coming. Didn't figure I'd ever get out of that place alive."

Bennie drinks the last of her glass, before reaching for the bottle to pour one last splash.

"And here you are." Randy smiles, raising his beer bottle.

Butch gazes at the hand-painted fish peeking through the shrimp left on Bennie's Italian serving platter. "Yep," he says, finally. "Here I am."

✳✳✳

After dinner, Randy and Butch dawdle over dessert, talking, while Bennie cleans up. Butch offered to help, as did Randy, but Randy knows she'd rather do it herself for speed and efficiency. Sometimes she's in the mood for him to help and sometimes he feels like he's in her way. It's her kitchen, so he gives her space whenever she seems to need it. He can feel her tensing when the conversation turns back to Ambrose, and the new place, that it's Thursday night—cigar bar night—and that they ought to go drop in to check it out.

Randy asks Bennie if she wants to go and she says no, she just left there and has to go back for a while tomorrow. Anyway, it's getting late, but, if they're that determined, go ahead. Says she'd like to get a hot shower then to bed. She's had a little more wine than usual, maybe losing track in all the talking. She got quiet toward the end of dinner. Maybe Randy was talking too much. He did catch a buzz, but now, having eaten a good meal and drank a couple cups of coffee, he's wired and ready for anything. It strikes him Bennie might want a little down time after playing hostess. She looks tired.

Just before he and Butch go out the door, Randy remembers to ask: "Hey, Bennie," he calls into the bedroom, "will they just let us in or do we need some kind of password to get into the cigar 'club'?" Air quotes for club. It may be more like a closet.

"Say 'cigar snob' when someone answers the intercom," she calls back. "The desk clerk's name is Vance."

The place is low-key and unassuming on the outside: a quaint three-story Victorian rezoned for business that might've housed a law-office and maybe a CPA, much like Bennie said was the case with the old dungeon, ensconced in a repurposed warehouse made all modern and sleek. This new place retains a certain old-school charm, and, when they get buzzed in, Bennie's eclectic decorating is apparent in the lobby that plays up the architectural details of the staircase, carved molding, antique reception desk with a matching phone.

There are some darker, ultra-modern notes, too, including a pair of cushy black leather sofas and a black leather hassock as a coffee table, encircled with silver grommets, on a rug with a spiral barbwire design in front of the fireplace. The fire itself is fake, a video playing on a screen. Crossed riding crops above the mantel, surrounded by a circle of barbed wire illuminated in blue neon. The mirrors on the walls make the place look bigger than it is and multiplies the image and light from a modern chandelier hanging from an antique ceiling medallion in the center of the room.

The desk clerk, a chipper young all-American guy, looks up from what he was doing, smiles. Must be the Vance who Bennie spoke of. "Good evening, gentlemen." He nods toward the wooden pocket doors with stained glass insets. "Go right in."

"Hear that?" Randy asks Butch as they approach the doors. "He called us gentlemen." The bar area is dimmer than Randy expected. He has to let his eyes adjust. Just a few people here. A Japanese guy who looks to be in his 50s sitting at the bar, sipping a soda, staring straight ahead. A handful of international techies at a booth sharing a pitcher of draft, laughing it up over some stupid video on one of their phones. Possibly some acquaintances of Rajit and Terrence. One of them looks like a guy Randy might've seen getting off the elevator one day. A fat, hairy guy walks past them, going out. There's some goth-looking chick texting in a little alcove in the corner, a glass of wine before her on the table. There's a small room beyond, art deco in style, outfitted like the inner sanctum of an exclusive gentlemen's club circa 1930s. Now it sits empty, but there are cigar butts in the ashtrays and drink glasses waiting to be cleared. Mild techno from hidden speakers pulsates, making it seem like there's more going on than there is.

Butch and Randy walk to the bar. "What'll you have, Ran?"

"Beer me."

Butch orders a beer and a soda "Is it like this every Thursday night?" he asks the bartender, a young guy in jeans, a white shirt and black tie.

"Kinda slow night. The cigar crowd left a little while ago." He wipes down the counter. "I'm going in there to clean up, let me know if you guys need anything."

"Hey, where's Ambrose?"

"On the deck, out back," the bartender answers, heading off with a tray to the club room.

Butch leans on the bar, looking over at the Japanese guy two seats down. The guy seems to feel it, glances at Butch. Butch nods politely. "How's it going?" The guy gives a side-nod, faces front again. The techie crowd bursts into gales of laughter at some Hindi video on YouTube. The chick in the alcove puts her phone screen-down on the table like she's pissed, sinks into the red velvet seat, picks up her wine glass and takes a big swallow.

Randy turns to Butch. "What do you think?"

Butch picks up his cola in a slim glass. "I think, let's go out to the deck."

The deck is by far the most inviting part of this place. After the boho-bizarre tone of the lobby and oddball vibe at the bar, the deck really is the urban oasis Ambrose claims, with plants and potted palms everywhere, the soothing babble of a waterfall cascading over a wide panel of blue tiles affixed to a fence at the back. Like the bar, it has its own peanut gallery: big, bald bruiser at one table, talking to an off-duty delivery guy still wearing his work uniform. The big hairy dude who was leaving the bar now sits at a table with a slight, bespectacled young geek commiserating with Ambrose about something. Appears they're looking at a small map.

"Hey, what's going on?" Butch asks, walking right up to the table while Randy hangs back.

Even in the dim light, Randy can see all the color drain from Ambrose's face when he looks up.

He quickly folds up the map. "What the hell are y'all doing here?"

"Came to see your place," Butch informs. "It's something else. How'd you come up with all this stuff?"

Before Ambrose can answer, the bald guy speaks up: "Am I crazy, or is that Butch-fucking-Ballard's voice I hear?"

Butch's mood sours the instant he gets a look at the guy, who's left his table, now walking toward Butch in amazement. "You are crazy and yes, it's me, you son-of-a-bitch."

Ambrose rushes between them. "Butch, you don't have to—"

"What in the goddamn hell is he doing here?" Butch asks, turning to Ambrose.

"He just started working here. Part-time."

"After the way he treated you?" Butch turns back to Baldie. "Heard you fucked over my kid brother while I was on the inside. I don't know why I ever expected any better, but I hope you goddamn burn in Hell for it."

"Come on, he's no kid," Baldie protests. "And I didn't fuck him over, I gave him his start, you asshole. What are you doing out anyway?" Baldie's taller, but Butch looks angry enough to break off that guy's arm and shove it down his throat.

"Long story," Ambrose says to Baldie, trying to guide Butch back inside but Butch is having none of it.

Baldie keeps pushing. "Some guys prefer life on the inside, so maybe that explains your recidivism, Ballard. Or maybe you just miss that cute cellmate."

Randy tenses, as does Ambrose when Baldie steps closer.

"Better find yourself a new bitch, Butch."

"Hey, that's a good idea. . ."

Lang barely has time to laugh before Butch grabs a beer bottle, slams it on the edge of a table in a shower of suds, and shoves the jagged edge at Lang.

Lang backs away until he runs up against a majestic palm by the wall.

"You wanna be my new bitch, *bitch*?" Butch inquires, getting in Baldie's face.

Ambrose moves toward Butch.

"You've lost your fucking mind," Baldie tells Butch as the silent Japanese guy appears in the doorway, gripping a pistol.

"I said for you to call it a night," Ambrose reminds Baldie.

"Your nutcase brother doesn't scare me," Baldie says.

The Japanese guy is still on pause, awaiting an all-clear.

Ambrose waves him away and he returns the gun to the holster, mostly hidden under his windbreaker. Still stunned by the outburst, Ambrose grabs Butch by the arm and guides him, followed by Randy, over to a table in the corner as Vance the desk clerk steps outside.

"Everything all right back here?"

"It's fine," Ambrose answers. "Tell Jake to give everybody one more round."

Butch allows himself to be seated, still clutching the bottle neck. He finally surrenders it to Ambrose, who tosses it in a nearby trash bin. "Goddamn it, Butch. Contain yourself, you're on parole."

"I was taking up for you, little fucker."

Ambrose pulls Randy away a few feet. "What the hell were you thinking, bringing him here?"

"It's Thursday night. We came to see what's happening. It's not like you'd ever invite us, so we just decided to show up." Randy jerks his head toward the big bald guy, now talking to the big hairy guy and giving Butch the stink eye. "Who the hell's Baldie?"

Ambrose sighs. "I used to sling for him, but he works here now. Like a bouncer. You know, security?"

Randy hates the fact that, just for the moment, he feels stung. He and Ambrose have a weird, shitty relationship anyway, and now, to see Ambrose would rather have that bald jackass who did him wrong working here than his own brother and brother-in-law, it makes Randy want to tell him to fuck off. *Not that I'd ever want to work here anyway though*, he reminds himself. *Not even as a temp.* Looking around at the late-night collection of misfits and miscreants, among whom Randy might've once felt somewhat at home, he can't wait to leave.

"Help me get Butch calmed down. I'll get him an Uber and you can go home."

"Nah," Randy says. "I'll take him." Randy goes over and claps Butch on the shoulder. "C'mon, Butch. Let's get the fuck out of here." Then, looking at Ambrose: "We know when we're not wanted."

"It's not like that," Ambrose protests.

"Anyway, we're going."

When they climb back into Randy's black Jeep after that debacle of a visit, Butch is silent. After they start down the street, he finally speaks. "Sorry 'bout that outburst, Ran."

"Think nothing of it."

"I wouldn't have killed him in front of y'all. He just pisses me off."

"I gathered."

"Take me to the train station, if you don't mind."

"I'll drive you back."

"I'd rather take the train. Give me a chance to cool off."

"If you're sure. 'Cause I don't mind driving." Randy looks over at Butch.

Must be something about the light, making Butch look older. More lines, a furrowed brow. A different look in his eyes that's harder, more jaded.

"I'm sure."

✳✳✳

After Butch and Randy left, Bennie took a hot shower, smoked half a joint and fell into bed. Even though she's tired and beyond buzzed, she actually has sexy thoughts swirling in her mind. Of all times for Randy to be out. Will he mind if she starts without him? Their sex life's been tangled up, what with his bad dreams, sleeplessness, and distractions that she doesn't totally understand. His friendship with Butch figures in somehow, giving her a sense of unease. It shouldn't but it seems like she always says the wrong thing around Butch, coming off as rude, and she still cringes over him walking in that night on her and Ambrose in the kitchen. She'd almost gotten over the guilt about the night she and Ambrose did molly together and things got so heated. That was when she thought she might never see Randy again, and Ambrose was hurting because he'd found out Jessica was having a bisexual fling. No way to explain all that to Butch. Though, who knows what Randy and Butch talk about when they're alone. . .

She rolls over onto her back, reaches under her nightgown, touching herself the way Randy told her to do that first time they had phone sex. What is it about his voice that turns her on so much? What if she called him now, just to see what he's up to, let him know she's here waiting. . . But if he's having a good time, he might not feel like getting a call from her. She's teased him about his bromance with Butch, which Randy doesn't like, and he might not be in the mood for a sexy call or text right now.

She's not used to him having guy friends, so maybe she's a little jealous. Ambrose is her friend, not his, and he gets jealous of Ambrose, so Randy's new friendship with Butch evens things out, though hers with Ambrose is more complex. His with Butch is pure and simple, shiny and new. He's having fun with somebody who isn't her, and that's okay. . .

She thinks back to their wedding night, and that sweet, shining moment in time as he turned on the stereo. She's always the one planning so letting him take control was an absolute relief. She was full of joy, close to bursting as he'd walked toward her, the opening notes of Tommy Shondell's "Crimson and Clover," haunting, bittersweet, hallucinogenic, playing on the sound system throughout the lake cabin. He'd embraced her, kissed her deeply and picked her up off the floor, which she wasn't expecting. "You carried me over the threshold already. Remember?"

"I remember."

The cabin's master bedroom was awash in silvery moonlight as he laid her on the king size bed. She expected him to lie on top of her like she always asked him to do, a moment of therapeutic bliss before she started coaxing him out of his clothes, battling back any self-consciousness that seemed to grip him before an intimate situation, sometimes after. Instead, he stepped back from the bed and started unbuttoning his own shirt. She leaned up on her elbow, watching him. He took off the shirt, slowly, then started unbuckling his pants, unzipped, lowered and stepped out of them. He usually wanted to get under the covers at that point, but, that night, he took off his T-shirt, stepped out of his boxers, and stripped off his socks.

"You're always saying you want me naked," he said. "Can't get any more naked than this."

She sat up. "No, I don't suppose you can."

He watched as she slipped off her going-away dress and panties.

"Neither can I."

"My God. I love you so much."

New marriage like a shiny red penny. She tells herself they've just been experiencing the growing pains any couple might have. Their separate lives and the one they share together. She wonders if Jessica ever has a twinge of jealousy when she thinks about that morning, walking in and finding Bennie and Ambrose asleep on the floor together? She would if she knew the deep, dark fantasies Bennie once had about Ambrose, before he fell hard for Jessica and after Bennie ditched the philandering Coastie, Rob. That window of opportunity closed before it even fully opened. *Bennie, you bad girl.*

Randy likes her bad-girl side. The more outrageous fantasies they can conjure up, the better. And then there are her own mental images, yellowing around the edges like photos in an old album, snippets from porno movies glimpsed at wild parties, pictures from dirty books, artsy nudes and antique erotica she's run across over the years. Maybe it's time to add a new fantasy to her repertoire.

She's never really wanted to do a threesome, but what if instead of being caught between Ambrose and Randy in some uncomfortable way, she was lying between the two of them right now? Her two ideal men, each of whom she adores, for different reasons: Ambrose, her former love interest and current best friend, and Randy, her bad-boy partner and forever soul mate. What if any negative feelings Ambrose and Randy have for each other could be canceled out over making her most secret, most forbidden fantasy of all come true: to have both of them at the same time.

She reaches under the nightgown while cupping her left breast with the other hand, thinking about what it would be like to have both their hands on her, Ambrose leaning down to kiss her lips, then her neck, her nipples, Randy getting a "raging hard-on" as he calls it, pulling off the covers and sliding between her legs while she anticipates everything to come as Ambrose squeezes her breasts like this—

She freezes and the fantasy vanishes, leaving her all alone. She stops touching down below and feels her left breast again.

There's a lump.

Small, but it wasn't there before. At least she doesn't think so. She sits up, turns on the lamp, and takes off the nightgown as she walks into the bathroom where she flips on the light and peers in the mirror. She wasn't expecting to see her reflection looking so alarmed and that's unsettling enough, but not like feeling this—thing.

She touches her breast again with her fingertips, going in a circle, the way it says to on those infographics at the gynecologist's office. It hasn't been that long since the last exam. She's touched herself since then and, even though she can feel it now doesn't mean she would've felt it before, because it's only now big enough to notice and feel. Something's definitely there.

She puts her nightgown back on, going into the kitchen for a glass of water and a couple aspirin. Might as well turn on the TV, too, because she won't be getting any sleep tonight. No coffee, though. Maybe she's been drinking too much coffee. They say too much caffeine can cause benign cysts and she had a suitemate at Hollins who'd had surgery for that and was fine.

That could be what this is. It could be any number of things. But it's something. And she'll have to call and make an appointment with the doctor first thing Monday.

Until she knows more, she won't say a word about it.

SEVEN

Mary-Ann doesn't get out of bed until nearly noon, woozy from the sleeping pills she's been taking to block out any feelings of anger, embarrassment, hurt. Whatever it is she's been experiencing has been like a storm that she only wanted to sleep through. Long before she awakened, Bob left for a round of golf and lunch at the club with some other retired executives, old friends who've moved out of town and returned for a brief visit.

When she walks into the kitchen and sees the pristine yellow, pink, and white roses in the Waterford crystal vase she and Bob received as an anniversary present many years ago, she assumes they're from Bob, then reads the card next to the vase on the counter, surprised to discover they're from Jessica and her family—Ambrose, Beau and Butch—wishing her well and hoping she feels better soon. Lenore must've put them in the vase when she came over to do some light cleaning and straightening this morning.

Jessica hadn't been at that table at Las Dalias with the women Mary-Ann had once considered friends, but Mary-Ann wondered if Jessica would've agreed with the things they were saying. Maybe these flowers are proof that Jessica's a real friend after all. And she'd put all their names on the card. Mary-Ann doesn't know Ambrose all that well, but he and Bob seem to have some rapport since that night she introduced them at the country club. Butch's name is in a different handwriting. Would he have signed this himself? Her eyes mist at the thought.

She used to see him out cleaning the pool on mornings before she left the house to do errands, but that seems like months ago. How long has it been? She hasn't really been out anywhere nor talked to anyone but Bob and Lenore. Maybe it hasn't been as long as it seems. She takes a pink rose from the vase, breathing its sweet scent as she pours a cup of coffee and heads back to the bedroom. She hasn't been checking her phone much and dreads looking at it. There's a text from Sue Rutherford, wanting to know if she plans on going to the Woman's Club luncheon next week. Says they want to recognize her for all her years of service as president. **Please RSVP**, it says. **We'd <3 to see you there!**

Right.

Since all the committeewomen who were talking about her will be at this luncheon, her impulse is to decline, but she doesn't, yet. Might be interesting to see them honoring her with a plaque or trinket of some kind, see how they behave now that she knows the truth. She doesn't have the strength to make any kind of a scene at their staid little affair, the likes of which used to give meaning to her days, but even with all the painful soul-searching that revelation prompted, it's liberating, too. What world might lie beyond her old routine? She looks out at the backyard, at the beautiful day on the other side of the glass. Hasn't felt the sun on her skin for a while.

She was about to go take a shower, but maybe have a quick swim first. A bracing dip to get her going. She places the rose on her vanity table, changes out of her nightgown and into her swimsuit. She seems to have lost a few pounds. Maybe she'll go have a late lunch at the shopping center, look around for a new outfit. Something fabulous to wear to this luncheon, her swan song. After all, something new is about to happen, no idea what, just that events leading up to her temporary withdrawal from society were somehow fated.

If her perception was distorted like a fun house mirror, her own mirror in that huge walk-in closet reflects the real her, starting all over.

✳✳✳

Jessica asks Ambrose to see if Butch needs anything from the pharmacy, besides some prescriptions she's picking up, so he walks out to the guesthouse before heading into the city. Butch is pacing around out back, drinking coffee. Says he doesn't need anything. Ambrose doesn't mention his and Randy's impromptu visit to Arcadia, and neither does Butch. Yet. Whenever disaster struck in the past, their innate connection would kick in, and Ambrose would imagine Butch's face, like that of a jaded cherub, willing him to go on. Tough, compassionate, benevolent. But this time Butch's eyes are accusing when he sets down his coffee cup, and asks, "Just tell me this—what the hell are you up to?"

"Up to?"

"What shit you got going on at that place?"

Ambrose takes out a cigarette and places it between his lips to light it. "What do you mean, 'what shit'?"

Butch steps forward, grabbing him by the lapels so quickly, he drops the cigarette.

"Whatever crooked shit you're pulling that involves Lang, and those other freaks."

Ambrose pulls away, straightening his Burberry trench coat, rattled. Fuck Randy for bringing Butch there and nosing around. "Not that it's any of your goddamn business, but I'm not doing anything crooked, and Lang hangs out there 'cause he works for me."

"Doing what?"

"Bouncing troublemakers."

"He's a troublemaker," Butch declares.

"Last night, that was you, Butch. You can't go up and attack somebody just for trash-talking."

"What makes you even want to associate with trash like him? My fault hooking you up with him before, but if you keep that bastard around now, it's on you." Butch is so affable, sometimes Ambrose forgets that he swam with sharks and started with the same hard-luck, hard-scrabble upbringing as himself. "And who the hell's that old Japanese thug sitting at the bar like a fucking catatonic? I thought this is supposed to be a high-class establishment, but it looked like a saloon in some outlaw border town. And if Lang's involved, that means there's drugs." Butch gets closer, speaks quieter. "You can't wear those cute little outfits of yours in prison, you know."

"There are no drugs involved," Ambrose insists.

"Prostitution?"

"Fuck you." Ambrose stoops to picks up the cigarette. It didn't get dirty. Anyone could practically eat off this patio. When he straightens up, Butch is staring at him.

"I just don't understand you," Butch says. "Married to Miss America, living in that house. Boss of your own business. What fucking more do you want?"

"I may be married to her, and she's having my kid, but that house, this house—this place—is hers, not mine, so if this ever goes south, all I've got—all we've got—is what I make from my business." He lights the cigarette. "Oh, and your salary from pool-cleaning. There's that."

Butch's looks away.

"Because I don't have some golden parachute like your buddy, Randy. Jessica wanted me to sign a pre-nup, so all I get if she decides to kick me to the curb is one million bucks. That's it."

Now he has Butch's undivided attention. "Did you just hear yourself?" Butch asks. He glances around like he's been asked to believe the impossible.

Ambrose smokes the cigarette, walking over to the edge of the brick patio, exhaling into the branches of Eucalyptus. He can feel Butch behind him.

Even though Butch is no longer the hulking presence he was, there's still something intimidating about having him at one's shoulder. "Do you remember where you came from?" Butch asks.

All too well.

"And you just said, 'All I get is one million bucks'?"

Ambrose turns to face him. "You've been out of the loop, Butch, so maybe you haven't heard, but that doesn't go very far anymore. There're people around here who make that before breakfast. You can't even get a decent house for that here, and it takes money to make money. And then there'll be medical bills, and medicine, maybe caretakers, and everything else, and that shit ain't cheap. But maybe those Colombians you used to work for set you up with some health insurance policy you haven't told me about."

At a loss, Butch sits down heavily in a patio chair.

Ambrose nears. "Cushy pension plan, maybe? 401K?" Butch won't look him in the eye. "That's what I thought." Ambrose crushes out the cigarette in an ashtray on the bistro table. "Now, if you'll excuse me, I have to get to work." He walks the path from the back of the guesthouse, through the back yard, and under the trellis leading to the front on the way to get his motorcycle from inside the ivy-covered garage. A wave of guilt hits him hard when he flashes on the pain in Butch's eyes. Don't go back, he tells himself. It'll blow over.

He stands under the trellis, stuck. If Jessica got wind of the things he said during that little outburst, she'd kick him out—not Butch. When Ambrose rounds the corner, having returned to the back of the guesthouse, Butch hasn't moved from the chair.

He looks up, watery-eyed, expressionless. "Forget something?"

Ambrose approaches. "I'm sorry I was such an asshole just now. Been kind of stressed lately, that's all."

Butch stands. "You don't have to apologize to me. But if I'm the reason you're running some game that could land you in stir, I'll get out of here tomorrow, even if I have to go live under a goddamn bridge."

"I'm not doing anything illegal, Butch. And even if I were, it wouldn't be because of you, it'd be on me. I hope you can find a way to forgive me for what I said."

Butch sighs, before grabbing Ambrose in a bear hug.

Ambrose melts into that powerful embrace, letting Butch hold him for a few seconds. It's not often one gets a hug like this. Releasing all effort, he reverts to the skinny, terrified kid Butch would give his life to protect all those years ago, hiding in a closet, in a run-down house in a dusty Texas town, under the jurisdiction of a worthless father and indifferent mother. When Butch was his rock.

When the hug is over, Butch steps back, wiping his eyes. He picks his coffee mug off the table. "Be careful out there."

"I will." Ambrose starts back to the garage.

The day's just begun and he's already tired.

✳✳✳

Randy expected it to be clinical, sterile, but where this all goes down is more like a room at someone's house if that someone was New Age bordering on hippie. The couch is covered in throws with interesting designs, above it a piece of textile art in shades of sunset-pink, orange, green, and blue hangs on the wall. There are plants in macramé hangers near the window, some potted ones on the floor, and the walls are lined with book-filled shelves. A few pieces of medical equipment—blood-pressure monitor and stethoscope—are visible but not too intimidating. Nothing he can't handle, he tells himself.

Now that he's taken today's dose, he's starting to feel wired, but not jittery, noticing some colors in the textile wall art that he hadn't really seen before. Turquoise and flecks of burgundy. Maybe a hint of chartreuse along the edge between the green and blue. . . The wider swaths of color are growing more vibrant, and the different textures of yarn make the thing look more inviting to touch. He almost reaches toward it and is reminded of his first words to Bennie: "Please don't touch the art work, ma'am."

It's coming on all right.

He'd already met and grown to like the psychologist who'll guide him through all three sessions. Yvette, a young easy-going black woman in a turtleneck and blue jeans was here when he took the dose a few minutes earlier and now walks back in to check on him. "How we doing?" she asks. "Feeling okay?"

"Better than okay," he says.

"Wonderful!" She sits in a chair a couple of feet from the couch where he's sitting. "I see you have some water; is there anything else I can get for you right now?"

"No, thanks."

"If there is, just let me know. Do you mind if I take a few notes as we talk? It'll help me remember any questions I might have for you next time, but, if it bothers you, I don't have to."

"It doesn't bother me."

She reaches for the pad and pen on the end table. "Do you remember meeting Evan when you were here the other day?"

"Uh. . . Oh, yeah. The red-haired guy."

"He's my assistant. Is it okay if he sits in with us? He's already a member of our team and training to become a licensed therapist," then, as if reading his mind, she adds, "Like myself and the others here who work with patients in this capacity, he'll maintain the highest level of confidentiality. If you're averse to the idea, however, he'll only come in if we need him."

"You mean if I start screaming and throwing things?"

"Or if you want him to get you another bottled water or an apple."

He smiles, noticing his mouth feels a little funny. And dry. He picks up the water bottle and unscrews the cap. "He can come in, as long as—what you said. Confidentiality."

"Absolutely." She turns toward the door. "Evan? You may enter."

Evan, tall, thin, maybe in his mid-twenties, comes walking in, nods. "Hi, Randy."

"Evan," he responds, reaching out for a fist bump.

Evan returns the gesture, seems to relax a little and sits down in a chair over near the plants.

"How are you feeling, Randy?" Yvette asks.

"Okay," he says, listening to the sound of his own voice. "I feel okay." That seems like an understatement. He gazes up at the wall art that is now gently undulating. Inanimate things seem imbued with a gentle lifeforce, and he can see movement and feel vibrations in the walls, along the bookshelves, around the door, surrounding the plants in macramé hangers. "I don't know what I should talk about, though."

"Has anything been bothering you that you'd like to share?"

He flashes on the day in the tenth grade he hit a home run with bases loaded. His parents had been proud.

"I believe when you last saw Dr. Martell, you told him about some dreams you'd been having. Would you like to talk about those for a few minutes?"

"The well-dressed woman walking through a war zone, wearing a pink veil?"

"Sure, let's start there."

"I haven't had that dream in a couple of weeks. She kept walking away from me and I couldn't see her face. But who knows. Maybe she's safe now." Just the mention of that dream, the hope that whatever caused it might be resolved, is enough to take him back to another nightmare that he doesn't want to talk about, when he saw three of his fellow soldiers gunned down by the side of the road next to an abandoned shop. He was right there, too, saw them light up and drop like flies on a bug zapper. He remembers wondering if they'd deserved to die, then decided they did deserve it and that he wouldn't have done anything to stop it. They weren't like the good ones he knew, really good men who he would've done anything to save—if he could've. Those three guys weren't like anything. They were pure animals. And that's an insult to animals.

"Were you close to any of them?" Yvette asks.

"Only in the sense that they bunked near me. I used to hear them talking at night."

"What would they talk about?"

"All kinds of things. Sometimes they'd get high and go on this nasty kick, about things they'd done or things they wanted to do. . ."

"What'd they say that offended you?"

"It didn't so much offend me as make me sick to my stomach."

"Why did it make you sick?"

"Because they were predators. Sometimes they'd talk about seducing young girls back home. And the things they'd make 'em do. And when I say young, I mean really young, they'd talk quietly about it but I could hear 'em. Two of them did most of the talking and the other one really seemed to get off on it, giggling and making these—sounds. I think they were giving him ideas. It made me want to. . ."

"Want to what?"

The lifeforce making everything in the room vibrate in his vision still flows. That's comforting, but the silence is oppressive. "Is there any way we could play some music in here?"

"Sure; what kind?"

"Something laid-back but not sleepy. Surprise me."

Evan turns on the small stereo. Piano and marimba. Soft drums. Like walking into a cool, dim bar on a hot day.

"That'll work."

"Feel free to lie down on the sofa, if you'd like. And let us know if you start feeling too cold or hot."

He was about to say no, he was fine just sitting but now he feels himself lying back. This way he can keep an eye on the wall art, and the ceiling is a nice, neutral canvas, with gentle lifeforce. "Don't mind if I do," he says almost to himself.

"So, Randy," Yvette begins, "you were just saying that listening to those guys bunking near you made you want to do something. Is there anything you'd like to talk about related to that?"

"Like if I ever did anything—in my dream?"

"Did you? Ever confront them?"

"I should've called them out, but I never did. They acted so normal the rest of the time and some of the others liked 'em okay. But they didn't hear what these guys talked about at nights when they thought nobody else was listening."

"Do you remember the last time you saw them?"

"The day they all got killed there was some heavy fighting at the edge of town. A dust storm was coming up. I remember thinking, if I was going to die, it was a good day for it. Like the Indian chief in that old movie, about the white boy growing up Indian—*Little Big Man*. That chief would get up in the morning and say, 'It is a good day to die.' I'd already lost some close friends who. . . Am I talking too much?"

"No," Yvette says. "Feel free to talk all you want. And we can take a break, whenever you need to."

"I do tend to talk a lot," he says. "Sometimes I get sick of the sound of my own voice."

"Is there anything specific that's been on your mind? Anything related to the day you were just telling us about?"

He takes a deep breath, closing his eyes. The music flattens into white noise and the wind takes over, then dies down, and he can hear music coming through again. M4 at the ready, awash in adrenaline, toward staccato pops, explosions, roiling madness. Heading that way, he sees three soldiers gathered by the door of a vacated shop. Nearing, he's shocked to see the teenaged daughter of an Afghan couple whose home he'd recently visited. The sergeant had been talking with her father, a tribal elder, and this girl and her little sister had helped their mother serve tea. This girl had smiled kindly at him, and it was one of those rare moments, illuminated in Randy's memory, that made him truly feel part of something universal, revealing in some cosmic way that the world is a much bigger place than Gilroy or the city or even America itself and that there's something to be said for shutting up, being still and receiving kindness from strangers.

If it hadn't been for Sergeant Anderson asking him and Pvt. Frazile to walk with him that day, Randy never would've had that epiphany. Maybe one of the clearest, most revelatory moments in his life was that afternoon having tea with that Afghan family, with his sergeant, and his friend and fellow Giants fan, Private Lester Frazile. God rest his soul. God rest both their souls. God rest all their souls. . .

Evan hands him a box of tissue. "Here you go, Randy."

At first, he doesn't know what Evan wants him to do with it but then he realizes tears are rolling down his face. He can't feel the crying, and never heard himself crying but some kind of pressure's built up inside his head, like a block of ice is melting and the only way for it to come out is through his tear ducts. "Jesus Christ," he says, trying to sit up. "Have I been bawling or what?"

"You haven't been bawling. It's normal to get emotional though. Sounds like that was an important moment for you."

He can't really remember articulating it verbally. "Anyway, it was that same girl," he goes on, "Down on the ground. Her head-covering was off, and I thought she was hurt and, when I came closer, it didn't look like she was hurt, really. Just terrified. The wind was picking up and they—those guys—were trying to make her go into that empty shop but she didn't want to, and she looked so scared. And when I came closer, I could hear some of the things they were saying. One of them tried to run his fingers through her hair, and another one, Jarvis, I think it was, grabbed her and I could tell she wanted to scream but couldn't get her breath, and the dust was flying, in thick clouds. She saw me coming up behind them. Probably thought I wanted to join in, help them drag her inside and rape her and kill her. Maybe even burn up the place. . ."

". . .And did they rape this girl?"

"No, but they would have. I popped their idiot look-out and he dropped. Then I dropped Jarvis. And the one on the right, McGhee, saw those two bastards were hit and tried to take a shot at me, and I popped him, too. *Pow-pow-pow.* Nice and neat." He sighs, sits up, takes a sip of water and, as he does, sees Yvette look over at Evan.

"Do you remember what happened next?" Yvette asks, always in that calm voice.

"I think the girl was in shock. There was a dead soldier on either side of her and one had fallen across her legs, so I dragged him off. The wind was picking up something terrible. I think sometimes about what I must have looked like to her. For all she knew, I was some kind of monster with a U.S. flag on my sleeve. She couldn't see my face, so I lifted my goggles just to tell her I wasn't going to hurt her and I asked her to point the way back to her house. I'd only been there one time and. . . She was staring at me. The wind was whipping like a motherfucker. . ." Tears force their way out again. He reaches for a tissue to wipe his nose.

"And did you take her back to her house?"

"Slung my gun on my back and carried her. It was just around the corner. I set her down at the door and she ran inside, and I never saw her again. Three empty bunks that night and I finally had some peace and quiet. For a little while. Then I kept thinking, somebody's gonna come and get me. One day, they'll come and take me away. Lock me up and throw away the key." He swipes at his nose, wads up the tissue in his hand. Behind the grim words, there's hope flowing through him. *Be nice to hold onto that feeling, but it's fake, right?* "And next time I saw that house, that dwelling, it was gone."

"The house was gone?" Yvette asks.

"There was a gap where the house used to be. I don't know what happened to that girl, and that family." Again, he glimpses Yvette's and Evan's faces. With this mysterious elixir massaging his brain, lowering his inhibitions and loosening his tongue, he's vulnerable. "But you know. . . I didn't like those guys. I heard 'em talking, but. . . It couldn't have happened like I told it. It was all a dream."

"What was all a dream?"

"That I. . ." He swallows, then remembers to take a drink of water to get rid of the cotton mouth. "Could've ever pulled that off. They had it coming, but. . ."

You're her knight in shining armor, Ambrose had said to him that day behind the coffee shop.

The tears start again. He wants to give in to all the charms this MDMA stuff offers, but it's way too dangerous to feel this good. Anyway, maybe those three guys were just sent somewhere else. He heard they got killed, but maybe they didn't.

They did, but it wasn't him. He'd only wished them dead. And maybe that house where the family lived still exists. Maybe he was on the wrong road. It looked like the place he'd been before, but there's no making sense of it now. There'll never be an answer. Unless someday there's a knock at the door and they've come to get him. Now there's even more they could come get him for. He thought when he married Bennie that everything awful, including his mental and emotional issues, would recede into the background so far that he wouldn't even have to deal with them anymore.

But they haven't. Quite the contrary.

"I get so confused sometimes," he says. "It must've all been a nightmare. I used to have all kinds of bad dreams." Then, taking a page from the book of Ambrose: "That whole thing never happened."

EIGHT

Bennie read about Doug Stewart in the 40 Under 40 issue of *SFGate* and recognized his picture. He'd been a regular at Miss Dover's. One night when she and Randy had gone out for dinner at Mona Lisa's post-honeymoon, she'd seen Doug and a lady who must've been his wife. He's married, all right; she saw his wedding band. Randy didn't know who he was, but she did and spoke to him as they walked past his table. He was cordial but flustered and Bennie realized his visits to Miss Dover's must be a secret from his wife, and that she shouldn't have said anything.

Doug Stewart's from the East Coast, by way of University of Virginia, then Harvard Law. Clerked for a female judge on the Federal Circuit Court of Appeals, taught a couple of classes as an adjunct at Stanford after arriving in the Bay Area, did a bunch of pro-bono work for various charities and opened his practice in Menlo Park about a year ago. And if it did cause him any awkwardness with the wife when Bennie spoke to him that night, Bennie'll make it up to him. And then some.

The next morning, she arrives at his office at half-past nine. It's an unassuming frame house that's been rezoned for business. As she starts up the walkway to the door, she catches a glimpse of him through the window, turning and facing his desk as if he'd seen her. She walks into a pleasant little lobby: sunny, with healthy green plants.

The secretary, or maybe receptionist, looks up and smiles. The place is so small, they're likely one in the same. "Hi, may I help you?"

"My name is Bennie Burke; I have an appointment with Mr. Stewart."

"Of course. One moment, please." She picks up the phone. "Ms. Burke is here to see you." Her eyes shift back to Bennie briefly as she listens. "No, sir, the realtor's not coming until this afternoon. . . This is your 9:30 appointment. . . Yes, I'll hold all calls. . . Of course. . . I'll send her in." She hangs up. "Mr. Stewart will see you now."

"Thank you." She walks toward the door and Doug—Mr. Stewart—himself opens it for her.

He's smiling but looks ill-at-ease. "Ms. Burke, how nice to see you." Then, glancing at the secretary: "Hold all my calls, Jen."

Jen gives him a look like, *I already said I would.*

Bennie walks into his office, and he shuts the door behind them.

"Have a seat," he says, indicating the more comfortable-looking of the two chairs in front of his desk. He returns to his desk chair, folds his hands in front of him and looks like he's somehow seeking to center himself.

"Is everything all right, Mr. Stewart?" she's compelled to ask.

He straightens a paperweight and she could swear he's blushing. "I didn't recognize the name, but I recognize the face," he says.

"My face?"

"Of course. I mean, after that night we saw each other in the restaurant. You know some things about me that—I'd prefer my wife not know about. . ." He takes a deep breath and adjusts his tie, clearly uncomfortable but plowing forward anyway and it hits her that he's thinking the worst. "Whatever it'll cost to keep things quiet—"

"Mr. Stewart," she jumps in before he can finish, "I think I know where you're going and I'm afraid you're, as they say, 'laboring under a misapprehension.'"

"Oh?"

"I realize you were a valued client at—" She glances toward the door, quieter. "Dover, Inc. but my visit has nothing to do with that."

"It doesn't?" He blushes even more.

"I can see how you might've wondered about my motives, given the nature of our—acquaintance? When I thought later about speaking to you at the restaurant, I hoped I hadn't raised any unpleasant questions or put you in a difficult position. I certainly didn't mean to."

He clears his throat. "No, not at all, I just. . . It's fine, Ms. Burke. I hope you can forgive me for thinking. . ." He pauses for a couple of seconds, then: "What can I do for you today?"

"I'd like for you to draw up my will."

He looks a bit taken aback, but nods once. "I can do that."

"Wonderful." She reaches into her purse and takes out a folded-up sheet of paper on which she made some notes last night. "You see, I've just been diagnosed with breast cancer, and I'm about to undergo treatment. I want my will done soon as possible so there can be no question about my mental competency, or soundness of mind, or—well, not that someone couldn't question those on an everyday basis," she laughs a little. "But you know what I mean. I want this will to hold up in any court of law, so that there's no question about my final wishes. I don't want to give anyone room to say I didn't know what I was doing when I signed it, or that I was too sick or out of it to know." She hands him the piece of paper.

Before he unfolds it, he looks at her earnestly. "Do you have reason to believe someone might question or contest your last will and testament, Ms. Burke?"

"I hope not, but, if I'm being quite realistic, I'd have to say yes. There might be people in my family who wouldn't agree with my decisions, for whatever reason. I want someone in mine and my husband's corner who would see to it that things are carried out the way I want them to be." She watches as he starts unfolding the paper. "I know it's common to have a family member named as executor of a will and, for the reasons I've already mentioned, I'd like to consider other possibilities."

"Such as?" he asks, looking down at the paper as he slides on a pair of reading glasses.

"Could you do it? Or recommend someone that you trust and know to be reputable and independent?"

"Well, sure. . ." he says slowly, reading her notes. "I'd be happy to draw up the will, and then I'll make sure there are no inherent conflicts were I to take on the role of executor. Because if there are, I can. . ." His eyes scan the sheet again. He sets the paper on the desk, takes off the glasses and sits back, running his fingers through what's left of his hair. "This is quite an estate, Ms. Burke."

"I gained control of the money in my trust fund two years ago. I'll provide you with a comprehensive list of assets I want distributed and any additional beneficiaries. In fact, I'd like to go ahead and retain you as my legal representation, should anything happen."

"Of course."

Bennie shifts in the chair. Just thinking about how her mother would react to all this makes her uneasy. The lengths to which Pamela might go. . . "In fact, if anything at all were to ever happen to me, I want to make sure that no one, no matter who they are, can keep my husband from inheriting everything that I want him to have. He doesn't even know I'm here." She takes a check, folded in half, out of her purse and hands it to him. "I wasn't sure how much you'd want for a retainer, but this should cover things, for now."

He unfolds the check, looks at it, then at her. "For now?" He sets the check down on his desk and rubs his forehead. "Ms. Burke, this is far and away beyond any figure I would ever consider charging you for my services."

"Like I said, I need someone in mine and my husband's corner, willing to fight for our interests against any opposing force, no matter how formidable it may be. Having a will and trustworthy executor would give me some peace of mind. And if you'll handle any issues that might arise, it's worth every penny. Are you up for it, Mr. Stewart?"

He looks down at the check on the desk, then up at her. "I am. I'll get to work on this right away. In the meantime, if you have any questions or concerns, please don't hesitate to call me any hour of the day or night. I'm always at your service."

Bennie stands, content that this makes up for any discomfort he had to experience that night at the restaurant. "Thank you."

"Thank *you*, Ms. Burke."

✳✳✳

Next time Butch is over at the Bauers', Ms. Mary-Ann's car is there but no sign of her. He cleans and chlorinates the pool, then rounds the corner to the private patio by the bedroom to clean the hot tub, trying not to wonder if the curtains will be open so he can see her lying there in bed in that emerald nightgown again. None of that's any of his business. . .

He looks up, shocked to see her sitting at the table by the sliding door to the bedroom, sipping coffee and looking at a magazine. She's wearing glasses and a lounging robe with intricate, exotic patterns. Her dark, wavy hair is down around her shoulders.

She looks up, smiles. "Oh, hi!"

"Hey, Ms. Mary-Ann." He nears. "You're a sight for sore eyes."

"Why, thank you." She takes off her glasses. "I'd forgotten the time; I must look a fright." She attempts to smooth her hair, but he wishes she wouldn't. Wilder, the better.

"Nah, you look great. How're you doing?"

"Much better." She stands. "I was going to call Jessica to thank all of you for those roses. They're so beautiful."

"You're very welcome."

"Lenore told me you dropped them off. Seeing those flowers and the note helped hasten my recovery. I've been. . . Well, let's just say I'm much better now."

"I'm glad. Nice to see you out again."

"It's nice to be out. And to see you. Do you have time for a cup of coffee?"

He's caught off guard by the offer, automatically glances at his watch. "Guess I'd better take a raincheck, I got a few more stops to make, but thank you anyway."

"How about a coffee to go?"

"Well, I—"

"Just do what you need to here and I'll be right back." As she goes into the house, he catches a whiff of her perfume. Something simple and fresh: not flowery or sweet. He turns and gets to work cleaning the filter, flashing back to the other night when he couldn't get to sleep for thinking about her. Letting his mind roam free, he'd pictured things he'd like to do with her. Finally had to beat off to get any rest but, other than that, he's been a model of self-control, all things considered. He skims a couple leaves off the surface of the water, picturing a bloody car wreck to quell the hard-on making him glad he wore loose pants today. Goddamn.

She comes back outside with one of those stainless-steel tumblers with a top on it, and hands it to him. "Here you are."

"I hate to take your fancy go-cup; you might need it."

"This one's yours. When you come by, you can always get a refill." She smiles, then, like she's just remembering something: "Oh, hey—you're tall—would you mind doing me a quick favor?"

"Not at all."

"The light went out in my closet. Could you change the bulb for me?"

"Sure." He sets down the coffee and follows her into the bedroom, still imagining screeching tires and dead bodies as she guides him toward the walk-in closet that's twice as big as the cell he used to live in and filled with enough fine ladies' clothes to fill a boutique.

"I'd do it," she says. "But I get dizzy when I look up while standing on a chair. And Bob won't be home 'til tonight."

"Yes, ma'am." He reaches up, removes the old light bulb in the hanging fixture shaped like an upside-down clear bowl, and twists in the new one, hyperconscious of her standing so close. When he's done, she switches on the light.

"Oh, thank you! Here—"

He catches a glimpse of his face in the full-length mirror, flushed, as she goes out to her dressing table and slips a bill out of a green velvet jewelry box embroidered with flowers and vines.

"I really appreciate it," she says, offering him a twenty-dollar bill.

"No need for that."

"Are you sure?"

He notices the door to another walk-in closet on the other side of a wide, tall chest of drawers. Mr. Bob's closet. "My pleasure." He glances at the rumpled sheets on the bed as he goes out and thinks what it would be like to lie shipwrecked there, breathing the heady scent of sandalwood incense. Back out in the sunlight, it clings.

She follows him, still clutching the twenty. "I really wish you'd take this. You didn't have to do that, and I didn't mean to hold you up."

"No need to tip me, Ms. Mary-Ann. Glad to do it." He picks up his equipment, turns to her. "I'm just really happy you're feeling better. It hasn't been the same coming by without seeing you lately. You take care now."

"I will. You, too."

She goes back inside as he walks away, leaving the to-go coffee tumbler on the patio table.

✱✱✱

Mary-Ann seems to be doing better, Bob thinks, setting his suitcase in the foyer. Seems to be, but things were almost easier when she ordered him to be present at this or that event. He wouldn't want to admit that this new situation has thrown him off, but depressed Mary-Ann is worse than bossy Mary-Ann. He can't help but think about people he's known who went through a funk and, just when he thought they were doing better, turned around and killed themselves, the better mood brought on by the knowledge that it'll soon be all over and they'll be out of life's rat race. His first business partner, whose wife had plundered their savings before walking out on him. His cousin who'd been busted for shoplifting but had far deeper problems. His grandfather who lost it all during the Great Depression.

Depression. Seems like almost everybody's depressed these days, in one way or another. He walks into the kitchen for another sip of coffee before leaving for the weekend golf tournament down at Santa Barbara.

Mary-Ann insists she'll be fine. Says she's only going to this luncheon because it's the last. Jessica's picking her up here, so she won't be alone all day again. Supposedly they're presenting her with some token of appreciation. She says it's her "swan song," her last gathering with that club she belongs to, which also includes those women on that charity committee she's been on for so long. She's already stepped down as chair, citing personal reasons, leaving them guessing, and now stepping down as president of her women's club. Maybe they think there's trouble here at home, but, whatever trouble there is, they started it by running their mouths about her over cocktails at that damn Mexican restaurant. That changed everything.

He glances at his watch. Really should be going. He walks back to the bedroom, just to check on her one last time. She's still in the shower. He opens her nightstand drawer. There's a half-bottle left of those sleeping pills. Never would've given it a thought before, but what if seeing those women again gets her upset, and then she comes home alone in the same mood as last time.

Payton and Edie and the kids are on a trip to see Edie's parents back east, so they won't be checking in. Jessica might. Looks like she could be the only friend Mary-Ann has left after this strange debacle. Butch comes to clean the pool, but he won't come in the house. He'd asked after Mary-Ann when he didn't see her for a while, so maybe he'd notice if something were amiss.

Bob grabs the bottle of sleeping pills from the drawer and looks at the label. **No refill**, it says. **Contact your physician.** Dr Zadir will be at the golf tournament. Bob slips the pill bottle into his blazer pocket and heads back through the kitchen and out to the car. He kissed her good-bye already, doesn't want her asking what he came back for or know he'd even think she might take too many pills. Or maybe she'd be touched that he cares. Hard to know anymore. Most likely, she'd just be pissed that he swiped her mother's little helpers for her own good. It'll be too much of an inconvenience to get more over the weekend. Anyway, after this luncheon today, and one glass of pinot, she'll be out like a light, no downers necessary.

He glances again at his watch. Better get going if they're to arrive at the resort by cocktail hour. He'll call her this evening after a cigar and a couple of Pimm's cocktails.

✳✳✳

Something's happened to Mary-Ann. Whatever it was that caused her to fade from sight for a few weeks must have gotten resolved. Jessica expected her to be somewhat nostalgic heading off to her last club meeting as president, but she's jovial to the point of being giddy. Also, she's wearing her hair down, which she usually never does, and it gives her a more relaxed look, quite different from the hard-charging madam president and chairwoman who had a gavel for so long and wasn't afraid to use it. When they present her with the crystal gavel for all her years of service, she lightly approaches the podium to accept it before giving an uncharacteristically brief speech: "Thank you, ladies. It's been an honor to serve all these years, and to get to know you, each and every one. And while I'm moving on to new things, I hope all the goodwill in this room finds its way to you, just as it has to me. Good luck in the future. And again, thank you." With that, she returns to the table she shares with Jessica, the elderly Harris sisters from Sunnyvale, and Amy, the young wife of a new-in-town tech executive.

At lunch, Mary-Ann sips champagne punch, laughs more than usual, talks through the watercress sandwiches and asparagus soup, turkey salad, petit fours and lace cookies. She's usually the last one to leave a function like this, overseeing all serving and social activities and then staying to make sure cleaning is carried out properly and thoroughly but, today, after Sue presented her with a basket of wine and charcuterie from a posh new shop on California Avenue, she's ready to go, relieved to be done with the club and charity committee.

Driving her home, Jessica asks her about the new things she has planned.

"Oh, I don't know," Mary-Ann answers. "Something different, that's all. I'll keep busy." When they arrive at Mary-Ann's house, the pool-cleaning company's golf cart is parked in the driveway.

"Hey, Butch must still be here."

"Wonderful." Mary-Ann smiles. "He usually comes by a little earlier. One of the neighbor kid's toys must've gotten stuck in the intake again."

"Can I help you get that basket into the house?" Jessica asks.

"I've got it." Mary-Ann grabs the handle, along with the gift bag containing the crystal gavel, purse strap over her shoulder.

"Tell Butch I'll see him at dinner," Jessica says. "We're having tacos. You're welcome to come join us if you'd like."

"Thanks, but I'll take a raincheck." Mary-Ann steps out of the Mercedes. There's just something different about her these days. When they were all talking over lunch, she said she'd given up tennis for Pilates and yoga. She does look healthier and more toned. Wearing her hair long is definitely a positive change, and she's getting a nice tan.

There's something else too, though, that Jessica can't quite pinpoint. "It's great to have you back, Mary-Ann. I'm so glad you're feeling better."

"Thank you. For the flowers, and everything. I mean it."

"Sure. Call me."

"I will." Mary-Ann turns to take the haul from the luncheon into the house.

Jessica continues around the circular drive and back out onto the street. *Something's happened to Mary-Ann, all right. Not sure what.*

***

When Jessica gets home, she's surprised to see Ambrose's motorcycle already parked in the garage, prompting her to wonder if everything's okay. He's been gone so much lately, that his being home early prompts concern. She walks in the front door to the scent of roses, a trail of petals: red, yellow, pink, and white from the front door, through the living room, down the hallway, and into the bedroom. "Ambrose?" she calls out.

He steps out of the bathroom, wearing his Turkish cotton robe, still drying his hair with a towel, which he tosses back into the bathroom the moment he sees her. "Hey, you're home!"

"Hey, you're home," she responds. "Is everything all right? Where's Beau?"

"Everything's fine." He approaches, hugs and kisses her. "Beau's with Caitlyn at the park and then they're going for ice cream."

"Oh." She allows herself to melt into his arms, realizing just how tired she is. "What's with all the rose petals?"

"I was hoping if I pamper you this afternoon, you'd let me take you out to dinner later." He kisses her again, holding her close.

She can feel his hands caressing either side of her round belly. He hasn't been the most attentive father-to-be, and she's more than willing to let him make up for it. She doesn't have the bandwidth to play mind games or try to guilt him and doesn't want to anyway. She just wants to be close to him, like they used to be, before he got so driven, so desperate to prove himself. It's all in his head.

"I told Butch we were having tacos."

"Butch can have tacos and watch Beau while you and I go out. How does that sound?"

"Good," she murmurs as he kisses the side of her face. She closes her eyes, breathing his freshly showered scent. "Even better if I can catch a nap first."

"Sure." He guides her over to the bed, pulls back the covers, and starts undressing her.

She's conscious of how her body looks, stretch marks and all the rest, but he's so gentle and warm, she's lulled into a state of bliss. It's been a long day. "Is something going on?" she asks, almost without thinking.

"What do you mean 'going on'?"

"Just wondering what brought on all this."

He walks over to close the bedroom curtains as she finishes undressing and gets into bed. Walking back, he slips out of his bathrobe, leaving it on the floor. He looks wonderful naked.

She still can't help thinking how he might be comparing her pre-pregnancy body with now. She'd bounced back, quickly getting into shape after Beau was born, but this time, who knows? "Not like it's a special occasion or anything," she muses, watching him get under the covers.

"Every day with you is a special occasion."

She laughs. "Seriously."

He leans on his elbow to look at her. "You don't believe me?"

"I believe something must've happened that you deem special enough to scatter rose petals and take me to a nice restaurant in the middle of the week, on the spur of the moment."

He moves closer.

It feels good to be next to him like this, making her realize how hectic it's been lately, with his late nights. She often kept late hours, too, but now that she's well into this pregnancy and tires easily, it's better for her and the baby if she gets plenty of rest. Her late nights will come around again soon enough. She'll put a crib in the studio.

"I had an epiphany," he says.

"An epiphany?" She smiles. Sounds like another entry from his word-a-day calendar. "And what was this epiphany?"

"How much I love you and that I don't want you to think I'm taking you for granted. Like a certain husband once did, who shall remain nameless."

Ah. Mike.

"And that I like having you all to myself." He leans down and kisses her. "And I don't want to have to share you with anybody else again."

Mignon. "She's gone for good, isn't she?" Jessica asks.

She feels him pause slightly. "Yeah," he responds, then continues kissing her.

"You're sure."

"I'm sure."

Jessica closes her eyes, trying to shut out any memories of meetings with Mignon—or Margarite, rather—at hotels and then, for the last time, at that cheap motel. The feverish sowing of wild oats before discovering she was pregnant and then her own "epiphany" that she should marry Ambrose and then the both of them settling down to making this turbulent affair legit, solid, real. Even here in her own bed, with his warm, reassuring caresses, she chills at the chances she took with that woman who wasn't who she said she was and might've even exploited their brief but intense relationship by taking illicit videos and doing no-telling-what with them.

But that's all over now. As he slides further under the covers, still kissing her all over, she tries to get lost in pure sensation: no distracting thoughts. But what she told Butch the other night, in an insecure moment. . . He would never repeat that, or say anything to Ambrose, would he? Her face gets hot at the thought. All that about how their paths converged: hers, Mike's and Ambrose's? No need to revisit the past. And this feels so good.

Yet the lingering scent of rose petals takes her back to the morning after they first had sex, when she'd scattered rose petals all over his bed and the floor out at the guesthouse. That's when she knew, and so did he, that she was falling in love with him. And that was also the day that she found out how Mike had tried to pick him up at the night club. So much deception all around her. But that was then, she thinks, remembering the sentiment that had prompted her to scatter those rose petals. Whatever impulse made him do the same today must be real as well.

She chooses to believe it is.

Since Bennie found out she has cancer, she's been baking a lot. Cookies, mainly. Most of which she's been giving away. To Rajit and Terrence, Ambrose and Jessica, Beau and Butch. Momo and her family. She left some at her parents' house, for her dad, mainly, and their maid, the yard man, his kids, etc. Randy doesn't know just how much baking she's been doing because she boxes them up and gives them away before he can see the sheer number of cookies stacked in this kitchen. All he knows is there've been a lot of fresh cookies around lately for him to eat: Linzer hearts, snickerdoodles, mocha almond, wedding cookies, chocolate chips, madeleines, and that he's gained a couple of pounds while she hasn't, because she hasn't been eating them, just baking, processing her diagnosis the best she can and consulting with her oncologist about the best course of treatment.

When are you going to tell him? That inside voice keeps asking. She knows she should confide in him, let him support her. She'll need encouragement and someone to talk to, but since Randy's been going to therapy, and still having trouble sleeping, she doesn't want to lay this on him, too. She'd been jealous of all the time he was spending with Butch, but now. . . . He'll need a friend. She'll have to tell Jessica eventually, but Jessica has been more anxious than usual. Her pregnancy is going well, but there's something going on with her and Ambrose, and something going on with Ambrose in general. Rajit and Terrence sometimes, too. All of them seem to clam up whenever she enters their little tree house of an office in the top floor of the new location. Arcadia.

And she misses Miss Dover. She even misses Mr. Rusovich, that pervy old sweetheart. Oddly enough, she thought she saw him the other day, or someone who looked like him, right in the neighborhood near Arcadia. He was with an attractive young blonde, crossing the street down at the corner, heading for the donut shop. They were both stylishly dressed and made a dashing couple. She only saw them from behind, but it looked so much like him—that suit, that walk—Bennie checked the guest records to see if it was him. But there was no one here under that name.

Her eyes mist when she thinks about everything that's changed since the old place, for better and for worse. Everything that's going on would be hard on a good day, but, standing in the kitchen, staring at the rows of gingersnaps on a baking sheet, it's completely overwhelming. She sits down at the table, tears spilling over, and takes a deep breath. Right now, her main concern is Randy. Possessiveness has given way to worry. Her mad love for him, her need for him, still burns. He's tough, but also sweet and vulnerable. If there were ever a time when she's not around, what would happen to him? He has a good friend in Butch, but who else could ever come close to caring about Randy as much as she does? He's estranged from his family. Bennie's rocky relationship with her mom notwithstanding, she still has her dad.

She flashes back to that afternoon in Gilroy when Mrs. Burke caught Bennie and Randy at her house. Maybe "caught" isn't the right word, but Randy had picked a time when he knew she wouldn't be there, and Mrs. Burke had walked in to find Bennie, a perfect stranger in her kitchen, with Randy upstairs, after months of no contact with him. It must've been a shock. And then Randy had refused to even invite her to their courthouse wedding. Guilt creeps in when Bennie realizes maybe she should have reached out to Mrs. Burke somehow, but Randy was adamant that he didn't want her there.

Still, such a hurt look in Mrs. Burke's eyes when they left her standing in the garage that day. She'd been in tears. Bennie can't even think of a time she ever saw her mother in tears. Even though she seemed suspicious, and Randy and his mom had exchanged harsh words that day, there's a gritty frankness about Mrs. Burke that Bennie sees in Randy, a stark honesty that some people, Bennie's mother included, find downright offensive, but that Bennie finds refreshing.

Mrs. Burke's unusual New Orleans accent sounds more like she's from Brooklyn than anywhere down South, but Randy told her it's because the nuns from New York City who started the Catholic schools down in St. Bernard parish had passed it on. His grandmother had taught at a fancy girls' school in Uptown New Orleans, and his mother had received free tuition, but also had to endure the snarky remarks from some of the rich girls attending there, debutantes who looked down their noses at the little Cajun-Italian spitfire who'd just as soon tell them to fuck off as to go cry in a corner. She did tell them to fuck off, but occasionally cried as well, though she'd sooner die than let anyone know.

Randy had told Bennie these things in an unguarded moment, on a lazy afternoon at the park, lying on a blanket in the grass in a post-picnic, buzzed reverie. She listened intently, hungry for anything he was willing to share about himself, his parents, his family. Anything and anybody who contributed to making him who he is, the man that she loves beyond life itself. There's more to the story about him and his mom than he's willing to admit. He's the youngest of her children, and Bennie gets the feeling Randy and his mother used to be close. Perhaps there's a way to get them on speaking terms again. That way Randy would have somebody else to lean on, in addition to Butch. Somebody else, besides herself, who would check in, and make sure Randy's okay, and that everything's all right.

Just in case.

***

Saturday evening, Butch sits out on the guesthouse patio, trying to do some reading. He went to the library with Jessica and Beau earlier this week and checked out a book about President Lyndon Johnson and the Vietnam War. He glances at his watch. Almost six o'clock. He shifts in the chair, unable to concentrate. Already read the same page twice. Can't put yesterday out of his mind. How Mary-Ann came outside just as he was finishing up with the pool and how she was wearing a tight dress, high heels, her hair down. She said they'd given her a basket of wine and cheese and some other stuff and that he should come over tomorrow night and share in the bounty. She was in such a good mood. Might've had a few drinks at lunch. Not sloppy or anything, but. . . happy.

It wasn't until he was gathering his equipment to leave that she said, "Hey, would you do me a quick favor? Come inside for a sec?"

"Yes, ma'am." He left his things on the patio and followed her.

"Normally I'd wait 'til Bob got home but he's out of town," she explained, backing up to him and holding her hair up off her neck. "I'm just dying to change clothes. Would you unzip me?"

He didn't think he'd quite heard her right, but she was standing there, waiting. "Sure," he said, flashing on those car wrecks again. Of walking in on his mother smoking a cigarette while sitting on the toilet. Goddamn. He nearly shuddered, but then sliding that zipper down Mary-Ann's back chased away all unpleasant images and he thought about what it would be like to strip that dress and everything else off her, lay her on that king-sized bed and fuck her.

Is that what she wants? Is that why she did this?

He puts the book aside, stands, getting massively turned on at the idea she just might want that. He's alone now, no need to think about car wrecks or worse. He wouldn't want to do anything that would jeopardize his job, but she got him that job. She wouldn't then want him to lose it but, if sex is something she wants, she'd be sure he didn't, wouldn't she? And if he's misreading this, one word from her that he made unwanted advances would get him fired in a heartbeat. Who'd they believe? A rich society lady or a broke-ass ex-con?

Ambrose and Jessica are home after last evening's date night. Little fucker must've decided to take Butch's advice, taking his ass out to dinner with his wife at some nice place. No doubt got some pussy that he wouldn't have otherwise. Jessica's a million times more than that of course, but she's also a woman and might appreciate some reassurance—about everything. And that unfinished story she was telling him the other night, about how all this started. Sounds like she's been through it. Sounds like Ambrose must've been practically turning tricks.

Goddamn.

Part of Butch wants to whack Ambrose upside the head just to remind him what he's got right here. No reason for staying in the city so late, with that rag-tag bunch of outlaws and misfits he calls the staff. Why does he want those shitheads there at night? Randy's the only decent one in Ambrose's orbit and he's an asshole to Randy. There's something going on with them and Bennie that makes Butch uncomfortable, but he can't think about that now. Already burned enough daylight, sitting here in torturous indecision, thinking about showing up at Mary-Ann's door. Sure, she had a good buzz when she asked him over. Maybe it was just to be polite.

But the zipper. She had to know what that could do to him.

He glances at his watch. Time's a-wasting. It's inconvenient all right. So goddamn horny with no car, no reason to leave the house that he'd be willing to share with Ambrose and Jessica. But hell, it's just a hop and a skip downtown. He could say he wants to go for a walk, stop at the cigar shop, maybe grab a non-alcoholic beer somewhere, maybe go take in a flick at that old movie theatre on University Avenue, or that artsy one around the corner. That's what he'll tell them and, if he somehow ends up at Mary-Ann's instead, they don't need to know. But what if Ambrose wants to go with him? He won't, though, he's already committed to staying home. Jessica's cooking up a nice dinner. They're in for the night.

If Butch can slip out quietly, he'll do it. But what if Ambrose is on the patio like he usually is this time of the evening, when he's home, that is? What if Jessica's out there? Then Butch'll just handle it, he decides. Quickly and calmly. Barely been anywhere, except work and home, or to the doctor and home. They'll understand if he wants to go out on his own for a while. Just right downtown. For a beer and a movie. Then right back. That's what he'll say.

He goes in to take a fast shower, put on some jeans, a fresh shirt and hoodie. It's already getting cooler and daylight's fading. If he chickens out, at least downtown's a stone's throw from here and he'll have a good cigar to smoke when he gets back.

Fuck it. Worth a try.

***

Ambrose sits at the patio table under the big canvas umbrella, sipping a martini. Jessica's getting Beau ready for bed and then a quiet, intimate dinner. Then maybe more wild sex, or pass out on the sofa in front of the TV. No way to know anymore. Depends on her mood. And then there's what could be going on up in the city, things he can't help wondering about. Experience has taught him that these worlds often collide. They did with Jessica and Mignon, and that was just the tip of the iceberg. Funny saying, he thinks, taking another sip, lapsing into buzzed contemplation. And true. Looking at him right now, anyone would think this is all there is to it, not knowing that the massive bulk below the surface just keeps growing: his deal with Alexei, Miss Dover's deceit that still haunts him, along with Dimitri's dead body at the bottom of Lake Tahoe. Randy's knowledge of it. Those confusing, lingering feelings for Bennie. The ill-gotten money tied up in the new business. Then there's impending fatherhood. And Butch coming to live here.

This patio. Life in this house. On this street. That's the part most people see. He thinks back to the day Mike came to pick up Beau before Ambrose and Jessica went to the beach, and he told her the truth about Mignon/Margarite. He and Mike had been alone for a few minutes of awkwardness, knowing they'd have to get used to such occasions eventually. Ambrose asked if Mike wanted a drink, and Mike declined. Ambrose went behind the bar to get himself a soda, just for something to do, hoping Jessica would hurry back out with Beau. "How's it going?" Mike asked.

"Good. How're things for you?"

"Couldn't be better," Mike said, and seemed to mean it. He walked over to the bar, watching as Ambrose filled a glass with ice, leaned the way he did that night at Galaxy, when they first spoke and Ambrose thought he might be trying to pick him up, but wasn't sure. There'd been a different look in Mike's eyes that night, when he was too fucked up to care what happened beyond the next half-hour or so. But there that day to get Beau, leaning on the bar, he just looked content. No vindictiveness, either. "You and Jess getting along okay?"

"Yeah." Ambrose poured cherry ginger ale over the ice cubes, hand shaking ever so slightly. "Why?"

"Just asking," Mike said. No "trouble in paradise" question or other back-handed comment. "She's something else, isn't she?"

"That, she is."

"She seems happy," Mike said. "I'm glad for both of you. I think we're all better off now than we were—" Then, finding the right word to reference that moment when their lives all crashed into each other: "Before. Amazing what a difference a year can make, isn't it?"

"It's amazing, all right," Ambrose answered just before Jessica came into the room with Beau and his *Star Wars* overnight bag.

Was amazing and still is, Ambrose tells himself, embracing denial with another sip of the drink. Everything'll calm down. He'll keep telling himself that 'til it's so. He lights another cigarette, then sees Butch approaching from the guesthouse. "Decide to join us for dinner after all?"

"I's just thinking I might take a walk downtown. Maybe go see a movie."

"I'll drive you downtown," Ambrose says, starting to get up.

"I really need the exercise." Then, eyeing the martini: "Anyway, haven't you already had a couple of drinks?"

Now that he said that, Ambrose remains parked, realizing maybe he's not in the best shape to drive. . . "Yeah, but—"

"But what? 'Fraid I'll get into some kind of trouble?"

"Not at all. I just don't want you getting lost. Or too tired."

"I know how to get downtown. You drove me to the smoke shop that night I took the train into the city, remember?"

"Yeah, but—"

"If I walk through the campus, it's a straight shot down Palm Drive, right?"

"Yep." Ambrose notes that Butch looks more shaped-up than usual, wearing his good jeans and loafers instead of sneakers. He's also wearing that understated Stanford jacket Jessica bought him at the university bookstore, zipped up against the growing evening chill, hands buried deep in the pockets. "Call me later and I'll come pick you up after the movie."

"I'll call an Uber, or a cab or something. Don't worry 'bout me."

"I do worry 'bout you, though, Big Brother," Ambrose admits, booze kicking in just enough to stir a wave of emotion. Jessica's hormones have been all over the map, leading to highs and lows; must be catching. Maybe Butch is right. Shouldn't be driving tonight. Last thing Ambrose needs is a run-in with the law. He sniffles, rubs his eyes, then notices Butch staring at him, head slightly cocked to one side.

"Well, don't," Butch says. "I'm just going out for a little while, that's all. You and Jessica have a nice time."

"You, too. Call if you need me."

"I will. Good night." With that, he turns, walks along the stone path to the front and out of sight.

∗∗∗

Walking alone through campus and then down Palm Drive from the Stanford main quad, Butch feels slightly out of step with the easy-going mood of the evening, the wide-open expanse of time to himself and all the possibilities. If everything he told Ambrose were true, there wouldn't be this nervous sensation in the pit of his stomach. He hasn't even called or texted Mary-Ann. What if she doesn't remember that off-the-cuff invitation and is shocked that he's stupid enough to show up on her doorstep, unannounced. She might've even halfway been kidding and, if he hadn't already been fantasizing about her like a horny high schooler with a crush on his teacher, he really would go drinking at some bar, try unsuccessfully to pick up any unescorted females, then pass out in the balcony at that old movie house during the Ginger Rogers double feature. When the lights came up, he'd stumble on home 'round midnight, fall into bed and stay there until work on Monday.

He waits for the traffic light to change at the corner of Palm Drive and El Camino Real, still pissed about Ambrose's *in loco parentis* offer to drop him off and pick him up downtown. Maybe he meant well, but it felt patronizing. Like California culture shock, learning to navigate the most mundane aspects of life on the outside, and the illness inside him waiting to manifest makes him a source of concern. Just another thing to worry about. What peeves him even more is that Ambrose might be right.

Walking down Emerson Street toward the smoke shop, he feels a certain social awkwardness that makes him wish he were invisible. He pauses to look at the display window of a book shop, pretending to gaze at some first edition poetry books and catching a glimpse of his reflection, shadows of worry on his face. If only he weren't so eaten up with desire for this older married woman who reminds him of the other woman who broke his heart, abandoned him and nearly wrecked his sanity.

He buys a couple of cigars and a lighter and heads back over to University Avenue, still feeling out of step, constantly moving against the current of pedestrians. He passes the door of a small bar, thinking of going for that beer. He takes a step inside. More crowded than he thought. A couple of people glance up. He turns and walks out.

Continuing down the street, there's a line forming at the theatre box office, the aroma of fresh popcorn emanating from inside. He clenches his fists within his jacket. If he were smart, he'd just walk in there, disappear in the dark, and forget about going over to Mary-Ann's. Mr. Bob might've come home early. That'd be embarrassing as fuck, for Mr. Bob to answer the door and see Butch standing there with hungry eyes and a hard dick. Nope. Better to abort this whole crazy mission.

There's still some time before the first feature starts. Relieved at having finally made up his mind, he goes around the corner, walks down the block a to a small park with a few benches. He sits down, takes out a cigar, pausing before he lights it, that nervous sensation bubbling up in his gut. Same tension spreading down the back of his neck and across his shoulders. He places the cigar back in his shirt pocket, takes out his phone and opens the ride app, staring at it.

Maybe his mind's not so made up after all.

✳✳✳

Mary-Ann had a nice-enough time at the luncheon that day, especially with Jessica there for moral support, though Jessica had no idea she was serving that purpose, nor how much it meant. Mary-Ann had mostly avoided the members of the committee who'd fractured her sense of self that day at the Mexican restaurant, except for brief hellos, the presentation of the crystal gavel, and that wine and cheese basket she hasn't opened yet. She'd been so deliriously relieved that part of her life was over, she drank too much delicious punch. It added a sparkly glow to everything, made her feel prettier, the flower centerpieces brighter, and the contrast between that and the darkness she was leaving behind made it a stand-out day. She held it together all through lunch, feeling more like herself, only better, and it wasn't until she got home that she went off the rails.

After Jessica left, seeing Butch out by the pool, Mary-Ann felt so relaxed that she thought nothing of asking Butch to unzip her dress the way she always did with Bob when she came home from some dressy function, just the way she asked Butch to change the light bulb the other day. Jessica is a friend, and he's her brother-in-law, but he's also working in a professional capacity when he comes over and, having fallen asleep and awakened with an awful headache, she finally realized this morning that what she did could certainly be taken the wrong way. And what would Bob say if he knew? Would he even care?

She gazes down at her tablet, where she's been sitting at the counter of the isle in the kitchen, idly shopping for new patio cushions. She leaves items to be purchased in her cart, wishing she could forget the whole zipper thing, better yet, somehow make Butch forget all about it. And, as if what she'd already done wasn't inappropriate enough, she then asked him to come over and share the wine and snacks from the gift basket this evening. What the hell was she thinking? She wasn't thinking. She goes into the bedroom, looking for her sleeping pills. She'll take one now, shower, and, by the time she's dressed for bed, maybe it'll have kicked in enough to melt away some of the shame and regret for making such a fool of herself.

He wouldn't want to hurt her feelings by refusing but wouldn't want to encourage such a thing either. She is old enough to be his mother, and that's putting it kindly. Even if she doesn't feel that old, to him she must seem. . . She glances in the mirror. Oh God. She'd felt and looked much better yesterday. No telling what he must think of her being so—forward. She hadn't meant for it to be like that. So how did she mean it?

She'll just make herself scarce when he's here cleaning the pool for a while. Though she'll miss seeing him.

She walks over to the nightstand and opens the drawer, reaching for the pill bottle, only it isn't there. She rummages around in the items that are there: old reading glasses, a pink satin sleep mask, and a red-and-green plaid one, muscle pain cream, aloe hand lotion. No gentle downers to be found. Alarmed, she goes to look in the bathroom medicine cabinet, and all around the perfume bottles, the make-up and face creams—nothing.

After a few minutes more of fruitless searching through the bathroom drawers and closet, she returns to the kitchen. The pills are not in the vitamin cabinet either. She calls the pharmacy, enters the prescription number for a refill to be delivered, but a robotic voice informs her that her doctor's authorization is required, and that son-of-a-bitch is with Bob at the golf tournament in Santa Barbara. She's not in the mood to drink. That's what caused this awkward situation in the first place. There's a half bottle of expired Advil PM behind Bob's beet supplement. That'll have to do. She takes it into the bedroom and leaves it on the nightstand.

Zoned out in a steamy shower, her mind wanders to places she wouldn't normally allow. What exactly had made her ask Butch over anyway? Why is she thinking so intently about him, standing here under a steady pulse of hot water? She hasn't really thought of anyone this way in years, including Bob. She imagines for a moment what it would be like enfolded in those strong arms. Would he laugh at her if he knew what she was thinking, or would he be vaguely intrigued?

Probably the former. She turns off the water and returns to earth.

Drying off, she can't get him out her mind. It's not like he's conventionally handsome. Very appealing, though. And all those mysterious tattoos. . . At first, she'd found them strange, a bit off-putting, but now she's curious about what exactly they mean. To meet him, you'd never guess he'd done a long stint in prison. Hard to picture him consorting with the hard-core criminal element, much less being a criminal himself. She catches a glimpse of herself in the mirror. One positive side effect of this recent mental health crisis is that she's dropped a few pounds. She's quit going to the country club, in favor of the yoga and Pilates studio. She's also been eating lighter and less, so her clothes fit better. So, there's that.

She slathers herself in patchouli-scented lotion, then slips into a caftan she bought on her twentieth anniversary trip with Bob to Morocco. It always lifts her mood, making her feel exotic and adventurous. She steps into her red velvet slippers, purchased at Harrod's and threadbare at each heel, but still so incredibly comfortable. She goes back into the kitchen and, before she sits back down at the tablet, decides to open the cellophane wrapping of the gift basket from the club luncheon. She places the two bottles of wine, a cabernet and a pinot grigio, in the wine fridge and sets the Camembert cheese and prosciutto in the refrigerator, leaving packages of Carr's crackers and honeycomb on the counter. She'll put those away tomorrow, have them on hand for unexpected guests.

The doorbell rings.

She freezes.

It can't be.

Gripped with panic, she removes her glasses. Surely it isn't Butch. But it isn't Bob, nor Payton and the kids—they've gone back east to visit Edie's family for a week.

Be careful what you wish for, a voice warns her too late. You just may get it.

Oh, don't flatter yourself, she thinks, going to the front door. It could be anybody. She remembers suddenly she's not wearing make-up, and her hair's still damp but, when someone just drops by like this, unannounced, on a Saturday evening, they deserve whatever they get. She opens the door, thrilled and terrified to see Butch standing there. "Oh my God," she breathes, then, remembering herself: "Hi, Butch."

"Hey, Ms. Mary-Ann. Busy?"

"No, not at all."

"Still okay, my dropping by?" Then: "I really should've called first, so if your plans have changed. . ."

"No, they haven't. Come in." As he walks inside, she sees a small car out front pull away from the curb. "Did a friend drop you off?"

"Nah, that's the Uber guy. Said he'd be in the area when I need a ride back." He glances around. "Mr. Bob home yet?"

"He's coming back Monday." She closes the door, amazed at this turn of events. "What can I get you to drink? Wine or beer? Tea? Juice?"

"Just a glass of water'll be fine."

"Sure."

He follows her into the kitchen.

She gets him a glass of water and places it on the counter next to where he's standing. "What would you like for a snack? I haven't cooked anything, but I have all this stuff from that gift basket. How about cheese and prosciutto?" She opens the refrigerator. "I have fig preserves. Or would you like some spinach dip and crudité?"

"Please don't go to any trouble. I really just came to see you."

She pauses, about to open the package of gourmet crackers. "That's sweet. I'm so glad you did. What are Jessica and Ambrose up to tonight?"

"Quiet evening at home."

"How lovely." She places the crackers on a plate.

He leans on the counter, watching her. "How's your day been?" He eyes her damp hair. "Looks like you went for a swim."

"Actually, I never did go for a swim today. I'd just showered and was thinking of turning in early tonight, but I'd much rather visit with you for a while. Do Jessica and Ambrose know you're here?"

"Nah, I started out to see a movie, then remembered you said you'd be here." A pause. "I really missed you when you weren't feeling well. You know, missed seeing you around."

"I missed you, too. You don't know how much it meant to me when you left those flowers here that day. I know they were from all of you, but you were nice enough to bring them over, and. . . It meant so much to know someone cared." A wave of emotion swells within her chest, reminding her just how recently that was and—even though she'd managed to go to the luncheon and pretend everything was normal—she's still in recovery mode. From what exactly, she's still not sure. Nervous breakdown? Identity crisis? Midlife collapse? All of the above.

"Of course we care." He shifts to stand closer to her. "I care. A lot."

Her eyes meet his.

He holds her gaze, slowly reaches up to touch a strand of her hair. It's nearly dry now, curling up in ringlets she used to tame in a practical updo: no-nonsense. Put together. She's stopped trying to tame it, or anything or anybody, for that matter. "I notice you've been wearing your hair down lately."

"For the first time in years."

"Maybe I shouldn't say so, but it's kind of sexy this way."

"Why, thank you." There's something so easy about him. Nervous as she's been, worrying about what he might think, and now that he's actually here. . . "I'm glad you like it."

"I do."

She turns back to preparing a snack tray.

"Fact," he goes on, "I could tell you a secret, but it wouldn't be very professional of me. You know, as your regular pool man."

"You're not here in a professional capacity now. You're my guest, so talk freely."

He blushes, heightening his youthful appeal. "I wouldn't want to make you uncomfortable. It is kind of personal."

"No one here but you and me. I can keep a secret."

It feels like he's sharing a secret already. "Well, when you put it that way. . ." He pauses, like he might be having second thoughts, then takes a deep breath. "I've been having these dreams about you."

"Oh?" She looks up. "What're these dreams about?"

He shrugs, like it was risky enough bringing it up in the first place. "Let's just say they've been good dreams."

"Wish you felt comfortable enough to tell me more."

"You've been so kind to me," he says. "I just wouldn't want to say or do anything that might. . . mess things up between us."

"I don't see how anything you could say would do that." She turns to get out a couple of plates, even though she's not hungry. "We could take a tray out to the patio, if you'd like. Or do you want to go into the living room, watch TV?"

"I really can't stay long."

She opens the refrigerator, takes out a plastic container of cut-up vegetables and places them on the counter. "But you came all this way. Why don't you at least give me a hint?"

"A hint?"

"About these dreams of yours."

He laughs softly, standing so close to her, she can smell his aftershave. Whatever it is, it's intoxicating.

"Better think about that," he says. "'Cause once that genie's out of the bottle, there's no going back."

She smiles. "There are genies and bottles involved? Tell me more," she says with a sly smile, excited about what he's shared so far and craving more. . .

"I'd love to tell you everything. Better yet, I'd love to show you, but that'd be takin' my life in my hands."

"Show me," she says softly.

He leans in, holding her gaze, pausing as if to give her time to pull away if she wants to.

But she doesn't want to.

"You're sure?" he asks.

She nods.

He kisses her softly on the lips, waits, and when she doesn't object, leans in to kiss her again.

In that moment, cascading impressions of that day at the Mexican restaurant, Payton bribing the kids to spend time with her, the chasm between her perception of herself and reality, the sudden realization that Bob removed the sleeping pills from her nightstand drawer. Bob already mentioned that she was taking too many and he's worried, knowing he was going away for a couple days and that the luncheon might be some kind of trigger for her. What if he went too far, thinking she might...?

The last vestige of that old self, crippled with paranoia, makes one last play to maintain the crumbling status quo.

"Butch, did Bob——" After the first words escape, she wishes she could retract them already. She'd been going to say, *Did Bob pay you to come here tonight?* Then she realized how insulting that would be to Butch. Things were going so well before she lost all confidence.

Butch straightens up. "Um. . . No, I haven't talked to Mr. Bob much lately. Why, what were you gonna ask?"

All the toxic drama of the last few weeks sticks in her throat.

When she doesn't answer right away, he blushes intensely, in brighter splotches. "Ms. Mary-Ann, I can see you really were getting ready for bed and all. . ." He steps back, shoves his hands into the pockets of his jacket. "Probably looking forward to having a little time to yourself, and here I show up out of nowhere. I'm very sorry if I overstepped. Maybe I'd better just—get going." He flashes a tense smile.

She finds her voice before he leaves the kitchen. "Butch, don't go."

He stops. "Ma'am?"

She hurries over to him. "It was nothing, I just— You didn't show up out of nowhere, I invited you over, because I wanted to spend time with you when you're not having to work, and. . . to get to know you better." Her resistance is down, exhaustion returning. She gives in to total honesty, trying to recapture the spirit of that exquisite moment she interrupted. "Can we please pick up where we left off just now?" Without waiting for an answer, Mary-Ann leans up, kisses him.

He pulls her into a tight embrace, the most deeply romantic kiss she's experienced in years, and the fact that he *wants* her means everything.

For now, that's all that matters.

#

Would be nice to just drift off and spend the night after that epic session, but Butch has to keep an eye on the time. His first night out alone, but not spent alone, and now lying naked under the covers with this woman he's been fantasizing about for the past several weeks feels so good, he'll build on those earlier fantasies for the next several weeks—months—to come. After making out in the kitchen, he could've taken her right there on the floor, but she wanted to go to the bedroom, and he can barely remember how they made it in here. As they tore off each other's clothes, any reservations he had, wondering whether he'd read her casual invitation wrong, vanished.

She asked if he wanted the lights off, to which he'd responded: "*Hell, no,*" and proceeded to fuck her the way he'd wanted to since that first day seeing her through the window, lying here all sexy and disheveled. After things slowed down enough, he kissed her all over, trying to etch every contour of her body in his memory. During this attempt at reclaiming the man he used to be before the humiliations of prison, furtive attempts at human connection tied to his circumstances all those years, he let himself go: tasting, savoring, devouring her. The time constraint made him bolder than he might've been otherwise. He didn't want to come off as too aggressive, but she seemed to like being manhandled. Plus, she wanted him, too.

On her hands and knees on this extra-firm king-sized bed, that round, perfect ass, the curve of her waist, and that long, dark, cascading hair reminded him of one of the things he and Callie used to do when he was fucking her. When he thought she might be about to come, he'd grasp her hair with one hand, and pull back 'til she was on her knees. Holding her tightly by the waist, or cupping her breasts from behind, he'd fuck her as hard as he could, bouncing her on his dick 'til they both came 'cause that's usually how it happened. He didn't know if Mary-Ann would like that or not but turns out she does.

He loves that she does. He looks down at Mary-Ann resting her head on his arm, her face pressed against those tattoos that seem to fascinate her. "Mary-Ann?" he whispers.

She opens her eyes, looks up at him with a sleepy smile. "Yes?"

"You all right?"

She sits up straighter, grasping the sheet to keep it pulled up over her breasts. Her hair looks even better than before. Wild. "I'm great," she says, resting on the pillow. "What about you?"

"I've had a truly wonderful time."

"Really?"

"Really." He grasps her hand, intertwining his fingers with hers. "Look, I probably shouldn't bring this up, but. . ." He just doesn't want her to worry. "I was in prison a long time and all, but I just want you to know I've been to about a million doctors in the last couple months, so. . . I got a clean bill of health, if you know what I mean. 'Cept for—my chronic condition. Case you ever got to wondering about—I don't know. Hepatitis, or AIDS, or anything. I been tested for all that and it all came back negative."

"All right. Thank you for telling me." She strokes his arm with her fingertips, tracing the shape of a geometric tattoo inside his right forearm. "I think I'm okay in that department. Bob's the only man I've slept with for the past—oh, God—thirty years? Doesn't seem quite that long, but it has been. I just don't want you to think this is something I usually ever do. I've never—cheated—on him. I mean, I do love him. I think he loves me." She seems to be getting a little choked up.

Butch pulls her close, holding her, because she seems to need it. "I'm sure he does. He's a damn lucky man."

She laughs softly. "You're sweet."

"I swear to you, Mary-Ann, I will never breathe a word about this."

"Thank you." She swipes at her eyes.

"When I come here in my professional capacity, I'll continue to address you as Ms. Mary-Ann."

"And—we won't let this make things awkward. Promise?"

"I promise. Fact, I really hope we can do this again sometime. In the not-too-distant future."

"I hope so, too. Let's do."

"We will." He glimpses the alarm clock on the nightstand. "I hate like hell to go, but I'd better call a ride and get on back."

"Do you want me to drive you?"

"No, it's late. Mind if I call a car to come get me here? I mean, 'bout the neighbors, what anybody might say?"

"I'm not worried about that," she sighs, smoothing his hair. "I'm sure most of our neighbors are in bed by now. I wish you could stay longer but I understand."

"Well, I told my brother I was just going downtown. Ambrose and Jessica mean well, but they kind of keep tabs on my whereabouts. Out of concern, I suppose. Just wouldn't want Ambrose going out looking for me, if you know what I mean."

She smiles. "I know what you mean."

✳✳✳

Bennie drives to Palo Alto without calling or texting first to see if Ambrose and Jessica are home. They're not, so she uses her key to leave two boxes of cookies on the kitchen table. One for them and Beau, one for Butch.

She types an address into her GPS before leaving their house, and, as she drives to get onto the freeway, remembers that whatever her reasons are for doing this, Randy might not like it. In fact, he'll probably get downright angry when she tells him, if she were to tell him. She heads south toward Gilroy.

She parks in the driveway. The garage is open, and that silver minivan is parked inside. She steps out and reaches into the back seat to get the shopping bag containing all three remaining boxes of cookies, fighting a case of nerves as she walks to the door, this time without Randy to run interference. She rings the doorbell, heart beating faster as she waits, wondering if this was such a good idea after all and aware there's no turning back. Whatever happens, happens, whether Mrs. Burke is nice, angry, hurt, or hostile.

The door opens. "Yes?" Mrs. Burke says, a little distracted, but then a look crosses her face like, *Haven't I seen you somewhere before?*

"Hi, Mrs. Burke," Bennie says, smiling, just like she had the first time they'd met in the kitchen.

"Hi," she says, looking out toward the driveway like she expects someone else to be there as well. "You're Randy's girlfriend."

"Yes, ma'am. My name's Bennie."

Mrs. Burke glances at the driveway again. "So, where's he?"

A moment of hesitation, then: "Randy's not with me today. I hope you don't mind my just dropping by like this."

She's obviously mystified by it but curious, too. "Uh, no. . . What you got there?" she asks, noticing the big shopping bag. "Some of his stuff?"

"Cookies," Bennie answers, handing her the bag. "I've been doing lots of baking. I wanted to bring you these, and maybe just talk. If you have a few minutes."

"Sure. Where're my manners?" She steps back so Bennie can come inside, then helps her set the boxes on the kitchen table. "You made all these?"

"Yes, ma'am."

"They're so fancy," Mrs. Burke comments, gazing at the Linzer hearts and mocha almond cookies. "Jesus, they're gorgeous. Can't I pay you something for this?"

"They're a gift for you and whoever you'd like to share them with."

"This was really sweet of you. Look, I'm sorry I was such a bitch last time you were here. I was just caught off-guard, after not seeing Randy for so long. Is he still taking those pills?"

"Yes, and he's been undergoing an alternative therapy that seems to help. He hadn't been sleeping well, and he's taking his private detective licensing exam soon, so he needs his rest."

"He's really going through with that? Have a seat." She pulls out a chair for Bennie at the table and walks over to the counter. "Can I get you some coffee? I just made a pot."

"Sure, thank you."

She sets it before Bennie and, as she reaches for it, Mrs. Burke sees the rings on her finger. "My mother had a ring set just like that."

Bennie sets the cup back down on the table. "Yes, ma'am."

Mrs. Burke pulls out a chair and sits down. "That's what he was really here for last time, wasn't it?"

"I didn't know it until later."

"You're engaged already, is that it? I mean, you're not—"

"Randy and I got married in March."

Tears fill Mrs. Burke's eyes. "You got *married*? And he didn't even tell me?" The tears spill over. "It's one thing if he didn't want me there, but he didn't even tell me?"

"It was really sudden, Mrs. Burke," Bennie rushes to say. "We went before a Justice of the Peace at the courthouse. It was very low-key."

"Were your parents there?"

"My mom and dad and my sister. And my brother-in-law, Ambrose. He was Randy's best man. . ."

Mrs. Burke bursts into tears and Bennie realizes she should've answered with simple "yes," and not rattled off a whole guest list that excluded her. "My God, my baby's married!"

"Oh, Mrs. Burke, please don't cry," Bennie says, tears of her own about to spill over.

"It's all my fault." Mrs. Burke removes her glasses, wiping her eyes. "If I hadn't been so mean to him, maybe he would've at least told me. I'm surprised you'd even show up here, knowing how much he hates me."

"He doesn't hate you. I don't know everything that happened before, but I feel like whatever difficulties there are between you and him'll get worked out someday." She hopes she's not overstepping, speaking for Randy, but his mom is sitting here dissolving in tears. She hugs her and Mrs. Burke returns the hug, then has to wipe her eyes.

"Well," she says finally, "welcome to the family! Got any pictures from the wedding?"

Bennie gets her phone out of her purse, finds a shot of her and Randy that Ambrose snapped right after the ceremony. "This is my favorite," she says, handing Mrs. Burke the phone.

"Oh my God. . ." Mrs. Burke gazes at the photo. Details of the lace on the neckline of Bennie's dress are visible, and so is the color of Randy's tie and suit and his boutonniere, a white rosebud from Jessica's back yard. "He looks so handsome," Mrs. Burke says. "And you're so beautiful. You're both just beautiful." She dabs her eyes again and puts on her glasses.

"Thank you. Feel free to swipe through those," she offers, glad that she hid any more personal pictures in a different file. "I'll send these to you and put 'em on a jump drive if you'd like."

"Yes, please. Did you tell him what to wear? I got a feeling somebody did. Is this your sister?" she asks, holding up a picture of Jessica next to the window at the courthouse, holding a bouquet.

"That's my older sister, Jessica. She was my maid of honor."

"She's a knockout. And him?" she asks, holding up a picture of Ambrose and Randy.

"That's Ambrose, the best man. He helped Randy pick out that suit." Bennie watches her, looking at the phone. "Mrs. Burke?"

"Call me Linda," she says, swiping through the pictures.

"Linda. . . I just want you to know it means so much to me to share these with you. I love your son more than anything in the world."

Linda looks up at her, touched. She sets down the phone. "He must really love you, too. I can't remember the last time he was all that crazy 'bout a girl. 'Specially enough to even think about getting married. He used to say he'd never get married." Then: "Will you stay and have lunch with me? We could order Thai food from the place down at the Village strip mall."

"Sure." Bennie smiles, looking into her warm, brown eyes that are like Randy's. "I love Thai."

✳✳✳

Randy sits on the sofa, staring at the messy desk in the corner, aware he should get it organized and set things moving in the right direction, but he's unable to focus. Can't keep sitting around here, living off Bennie. It's high time he took that licensing exam. He should be out there getting cases, have a business plan for Burke Security, the firm Bennie keeps telling people about with such confidence, as if it were already real. He should be getting his post-police force/post meltdown career going strong, working for himself the way he's always dreamed, but now that there's nothing between him and those goals but air and opportunity, he finds himself yet again sitting, staring, pacing, spinning his wheels.

Finally, he gets up, walks over to the kitchen, pours himself more coffee and goes to sit at the desk, flipping through the empty pages of his planner, throat tightening. What would it take, just to get started? He remembers the days of desperation in his old apartment. He's not desperate anymore, so why does he feel that way?

Unresolved issues perhaps. His gaze drifts to the bookshelf, to the book he'd been flipping through on his and Bennie's second date, *The Subterraneans* by Jack Kerouac. That's the one that the photo of Bennie and Ambrose had fallen out. He'd stuck it between some pages near the back and, as far as he knows, it's still there. He thinks of other invisible demons from his lifetime gathering in the ether.

Not going there, though. Not now.

He walks around the living room, sipping coffee, unable to pinpoint what it would take to break through this frustrating inertia that surrounds his brain like a crinkly layer of plastic wrap he wants to tear off, to feel more like his old self. His *new* old self. But he doesn't know how. Maybe he's trying too hard. Best to just go take a shower. That might help. He gets more coffee and sits back down on the sofa to rest up for the effort showering will take.

✳✳✳

After the shower, Randy does feel a little better. He hears his phone ringing in the bedroom and goes to see who's calling, expecting it to be Bennie. It's Butch. He answers. "Hey, what's up?"

"I got the day off. You heading down this way for anything? I'd like to take you to lunch."

"Really?" Randy glimpses himself in the mirror. Still dark circles under the eyes. He runs his fingers through his damp hair. "Sure, want me to come pick you up?"

"Meet me at that old-timey diner at the corner of Emerson & Hamilton, right down from the cigar shop. Think you could be there in an hour or so?"

"Yeah, I'll be there."

"See ya shortly."

"See ya." He ends the call and gets dressed, glad to have somewhere to be. A destination. "It's a *date*," Bennie would say, laughing her ass off. "*You have a lunch date with your bromantic interest!*" Okay, fine, he thinks, putting on his watch and wedding ring. Who knows? What if somehow, this impromptu lunch with Butch could turn out to be the highlight of the whole week?

When he arrives at the diner, Butch is sitting at a table by the window, reading a paperback, cup of coffee nearby. As Randy sits down across from him, he tucks in a strip of napkin as a bookmark and places the book to one side.

"Whatcha reading?" Randy asks.

"*In Cold Blood.*"

"Indeed."

Their server, a young Hispanic guy, takes their drink orders. Butch switches to iced tea, and Randy seconds that. "Thank you, sirs," he says. "Be right back." Randy watches as he and the other waitstaff calmly go about their duties while the lunch rush intensifies. Randy could never be a waiter, he thinks. Takes focus, mindfulness, multitasking, people skills. Any of those Randy ever possessed have eroded into nothing.

"So hey, look." Butch, having noticed Randy's distraction, smacks the table to draw him back. "You're probably wondering why I asked you to come down here on the spur of the moment like this."

"I just figured you desired the scintillating pleasure of my company."

"That is a perk. And I got a job for you."

"What kind of job?"

"What do you mean, 'What kind of job?' You're a private detective, aren't you?"

Randy's stomach ripples. "I'm not *officially* a private detective."

"Yeah, but as good as. Right?"

"Haven't taken the exam yet."

"So? Think of this as a practice case and, by this time next month, you'll be bona fide." Like Bennie, Butch is so sure things will work out, that Randy decides to roll with it. Why wouldn't things work out? Of course, he'll be bona fide by then.

"Okay. What kind of case is it?" Randy asks.

"It's an investigation. I want you to find out everything about somebody. Where they go, what they do, who they hang out with, and report it all back to me. I've been saving my money, so tell me honestly what it costs. I've got it covered, up to $800, and I get paid again next week. Hell, I'll pick up odd jobs if I have to. You're the only person I'd ask to do this." He waits, then: "What do you say?"

The answer hangs in the air as the waiter brings their drinks, takes their orders: cheeseburgers and fries.

When they're alone again, Butch leans forward, arms resting on the table, his amazing collection of tattoos covered by the long-sleeved blue-and-green flannel he's wearing over a white T-shirt. "I believe you were about to say, yes."

"Okay. Yes." Then: "Maybe first I should ask who I'm investigating."

Butch takes a pen out of his shirt pocket and jots something inside the back cover of the book he's been reading, before sliding it toward Randy. "I'm sure it goes without saying, this is top secret. Just between you and me."

Randy peers inside the back cover and reads: **Ambrose Ballard.** "Are you fucking kidding me?"

"You know as well as I do, there're things going on with him that don't smell right. Maybe it's none of my goddamn business, but—" Butch glances around. The lunchtime din is rising, a Gene Krupa/Anita O'Day song on the jukebox blending with all the chatter. Butch speaks so only Randy can hear. "He's been putting Jess through Hell, and a woman in her condition shouldn't have to wait and wonder and cry herself to sleep thinking he doesn't want to come home to her. Agree?"

"Agree."

"You've been around him more than I have. Can you tell a difference in him lately?"

Randy squeezes a lemon wedge into his iced tea. "Not really. I mean—" Randy's about to suggest that Ambrose is always squirrelly on some level but decides to rein that in for now.

"Figure out what it'll take to get you started. I'll pay you that today before we part ways and settle up for expenses and whatever else next time we meet. Is that acceptable?"

"It is."

"Good." Butch exhales, sits back.

Randy sits back as well, avoiding Butch's steady, penetrating gaze. Now that they've taken care of the Ambrose business, Randy feels all Butch's attention shifting his way with a laser focus.

"So. What's new with you?"

"Not much." Randy sips iced tea, just to have something to do so he doesn't have to look at Butch. It's like he knows something's up. "Haven't been sleeping worth a shit, as you can probably tell."

"Something preying on your mind, too?"

Randy's throat tightens, as he realizes that yet again the firewalls around certain parts of his life have to be fortified. What would happen if he confirms Butch's worst fears and tells what he already knows? But he doesn't know everything, like why Ambrose killed the guy they dumped in the lake that night. As for any killing Randy's done. . . That was different.

You're her knight in shining armor, Ambrose said that day by the dumpster behind the coffee shop, voice dripping with sarcasm at Randy's claim that he'd been looking out for Jessica the night he recorded them having sex through their bedroom window, figuring Ambrose was a con-artist. *Touché.* That move was pretty fucked up, but Randy was in a very fucked up place. Then, through all that, he met Bennie and, on that amazing second date, she said he reminded her of Philip Marlowe, the detective in Raymond Chandler's novels, which he took as a huge compliment. The fact that she knew that Frank Miller quote about noir heroes like Marlowe, that they're knights in "blood-caked armor," sealed the deal that he and Bennie were meant for each other. He realized the next day that he'd fallen madly in love with her.

He glimpses out the window, a crumpled flier rushing down the sidewalk in a gentle gust of wind, lifting off the pavement in a whirling dervish, then dropping into the gutter out of sight. It's not like there's a dust storm brewing or anything. Blue sky all around.

"Randy? You okay?"

Randy rouses himself. "Better than okay. Just landed my first client, right?"

"I hope this turns out to be the most boring case you ever have, 'cause there's nothing to even find. Know what I mean?"

"I totally do."

Butch looks down at the table. "You must think I'm just some meddling poor relation."

"I think nothing of the kind," Randy says, focus shifting from his own anxiety-induced navel-gazing to Butch's concern for Jessica and Ambrose.

"Guess I looked like the only troublemaker that night you and me went to his place, but something ain't right. Does Bennie talk about work much?"

"Not really. But hers is more like office stuff. She's only there during the daytime."

"I'm thinking those IT guys only work daytime, right?"

"Usually." Randy thinks back to last week, taking out the trash after he and Bennie had steamed crab for dinner. Rajit and Terrence were just getting off the elevator. They'd looked pretty exhausted but, when he asked them what was happening out on the town, their smiles looked forced and, before Terrence could speak, Rajit quickly said that they were just having a beer with some of their old housemates. Terrence smiled and nodded. Randy was buzzed up, full of crab and beer himself, but something seemed off. Randy just chalked it up to their eccentric nerdiness, but it was weird—even for them. "But not always," he says in answer to Butch's last question.

"Bet he'd shit a brick if me and you just decided to drop by there again one night."

"I bet he would." Randy can't help but smile at the prospect. Why does the thought of pissing off Ambrose make him smile? Oh, wait—several reasons why.

"Only if it wouldn't hinder your investigation, of course," Butch says. "I wouldn't want to get in the way of anything you have to do. You're the pro."

Randy flashes on that Hunter S. Thompson quote he used to have on a poster in his old bedroom, with the Gonzo-peyote fist on it: **When the going gets weird, the weird turn pro**. It was through watching Ambrose that first time that led to a transformation of Randy's whole life. Those days when watching the gutterpunk, as he'd called him then, before he knew his name, was his *bete noir*, his very own white whale and reason for getting up in the morning, just to see what the squirrelly motherfucker was up to.

One night Ambrose was pulling a botched drug deal and, not long after, he's on the arm of a beautiful heiress, living in her guesthouse, then sleeping in her bed. How that all somehow led to the same outcome for himself, Randy is still processing. But even after all that, Ambrose is still pulling some shit involving murder and cover-ups—and possibly other things that would devastate Bennie and Jessica. So, Randy has a stake in this. It's personal. Spying on Ambrose will be different this time. Plus, it's his job to find out these things. Butch just gave him the push he needed. It's a start. "Thanks, Butch," he says just as the waiter serves their food. Perfect cheeseburger and fries. Hot off the grill. The smell of victory.

"For what?"

"For making me a pro."

ELEVEN

A couple of days later, Randy takes his feet off the coffee table as Bennie looks under the throw pillow on the other end of the sofa. "I have to run back to my office," she announces. She was about to start cooking dinner when she became distracted, looking all over for something that didn't seem to be here.

"What the hell for?"

"I think I left my tablet there and I won't be able to rest until I find it."

"Can't it wait 'til tomorrow?"

"But all my stuff's on it, and I wanted to take it with me to—" She sighs, exasperated. "I need it for some things."

"What things?" he asks, stretching lazily before a thought hits him like a bolt. He sits up straight.

"Just—lots of things."

"You're right. You'll rest easier once you get it." He goes over by the door to put on his shoes. "I'll drive you."

"No, it's okay. I'll just go there and back." She turns to grab her purse. "You can take a shower while I'm gone."

He pauses, hands on his hips. "Are you saying I stink?"

"No," she laughs. "You just look like you're in for the night."

"We'll both be after we get your damn tablet." He grabs the keys out of the leaf-shaped bowl behind the sofa. "Ready?"

The place is nearly dark when they get there, except for the security lights and a couple of inside lights on a timer to give the impression someone's here. It's quiet. No guests, nor workers. Just a rare and miraculous opportunity. Once inside, Bennie goes to her office. "Hey, what else is upstairs?" Randy asks from the center of the lobby, eyeing the staircase. "I didn't get to see it all last time."

"Two suites on the second floor," she calls back. "Then at the top, just the computer room and Ambrose's office. Oh, and Momo's dressing room's on the second floor."

"Is there a bathroom up there?" he asks, already moving toward the stairs. He doesn't want her to show him around, not now.

"Yeah, but there's one down here, too, if you have to go."

"I'd better use the one furthest away," he says, easing up the first couple of steps. "Trust me, you don't want me using the one closest."

"Oh. Okay."

He takes off up the steps, pausing when he hears her add: "Be sure and jiggle the handle when you flush. This is an old house, you know."

"I will," he assures, and rushes the rest of the way up the long staircase and up to Ambrose's little sanctuary at the end of the third-floor hallway. When he walks in, he stops to look at the view from the window. The sunset's turning from shell-pink to deep purple and the lights are coming on all over the valley and beyond. Beautiful sight but no time for that. Using a handkerchief that he wadded up in his pants pocket, Randy takes the mini-cam out of his shirt pocket. He'd left it in the middle console of the Jeep with no idea how he'd ever get in here until Bennie dropped this golden ticket right in his lap. He looks around for the best place to put it, aware that, if he already had his license, he'd be stretching—no, *breaking*—the limits of legality by leaving it in someone's private office, but this is personal, and somewhat unofficial, except that Butch insists on paying him for it, which makes it quasi-official, but fuck labels. It has to be done.

He looks up at the bare rafters that give the room a rustic look even with the sleek desk, computer, sofa and mod-looking chairs. There are photos of Jessica and Beau, Ambrose and Jessica, Bennie and Momo, one of Rajit and Ambrose at their backyard wedding. . . The only wall decor is an abstract painting hanging behind the desk. Green and blue squares and a few slashes of bright yellow and red. It has the initials *JEB* scribbled at the bottom. Maybe it's one of Jessica's rejects. Not her usual stuff, though.

Aware of the clock ticking, Randy looks around for a place where this cam can get maximum coverage but not be seen. Those tech nerds are smart but maybe not the most observant bastards. Maybe they don't even come in here that often and, even if they do. . .

He turns, searching for the perfect location, and keeps coming back to that painting. The top of the canvas. There's a board angled above it but not too much in the way. Randy takes off his shoes, pulls a chair over to the wall, steps up, and places the tiny contraption on top of the painting. He steps back down, pulls out his phone, and opens the corresponding app to check the view.

It's disorienting seeing himself on there. He'd already considered there could be cameras in here, maybe in the hallway.

Ambrose and the tech guys have cameras placed downstairs for security, but they don't want to be watched. "Testing," he says, checking the sound. It fucking works. He walks around the office, checking visibility from every part of the room, including from behind the desk, and looking to make sure the tiny cam is practically invisible, and it is. The only way they'd find it is if they're really looking for it, and they won't be, he tells himself.

Randy stuffs the handkerchief back into his pocket, looking around to make sure everything is just so. Heart pounding, he's reminded of the afternoon he got Sandy away from her desk computer at the art museum at Stanford to find Jessica's address on that mailing list. He did find it and went to that house and the rest is history. That whole thing led to Ambrose and Rajit breaking into Randy's apartment to delete the video he took of Ambrose and Jessica through their bedroom window. The night of the red jumpsuit fuck-fest. Been a while since he's had this rush. Feels kind of good, but he doesn't want Bennie to find him in here when he's supposed to be taking a shit.

He leaves the office, goes into the bathroom and flushes the toilet, lets it stop running, then flushes again, waits and jiggles the handle, just like Bennie said.

Bennie meets him at the bottom of the stairs.

"Find your tablet?" he asks.

"Right where I left it."

He watches her set the burglar alarm before they walk out.

There's a burglar alarm. Good to know.

✳✳✳

The following week, Bennie had just finished straightening her desk when Ambrose walks in, still wearing his coat, carrying a small red shopping bag. "Hey," he says, "I didn't know you'd still be here."

"I didn't expect to still be here."

He looks around, taking in the extreme orderliness. "You really cleaned out some stuff."

"Just getting organized."

He smiles. "Wish my mind were this organized. Heading home?"

"In a few minutes."

"Come upstairs. I want to show you something."

She was about to arrange the office supplies in the cabinet, though no one would care, and Randy's home waiting for her. Maybe it is time to call it a day. "Sure."

When they get up to his office, he sets the bag on his desk, removes a small red velvet box, opens it. It's a diamond ring shaped like a flower, with a pink diamond in the center, surrounded by smaller yellow diamonds. "For Jessica's birthday," he says, beaming. He hands her the box, and she gazes at fiery stones glinting in the waning light.

"It's absolutely beautiful."

"Think she'll like it?"

"She'll love it."

"I hope so. I've never been able to get her anything this nice."

She hands him back the box and goes over to the window, looking out.

He sets the velvet box on the desk and walks over to her. "What's the matter?"

"I have to go away for a few days. It may turn into a few weeks. I've been wanting to tell you, but it never seemed to be the right time."

"A few weeks? You and Randy going on a big trip or something?"

"No. . ."

"What then?" He can see the tears. "Wish you'd just tell me, you're kind of scaring me."

She turns to him. "If I tell you, you can't breathe a word. I mean it, not a word to anybody. Understand? Not even Jessica."

"I understand."

"I've been diagnosed with breast cancer and I'm going in for a lumpectomy and then radiation treatment."

He's stunned. "Cancer?"

"The prognosis is pretty good. I mean, if all goes well. Which it should. It's not like it runs in my family, that I know of. Leave it to me to be different, right?" She attempts a laugh to lighten things, but it just sounds weak and nervous.

"Oh, God, Bennie. . ." At a loss, he finally just embraces her. He smells good. A citrus-y scent so rich, it makes her mouth water. He pulls back to look at her and she sees tears in his eyes. "How've you been keeping this to yourself? Randy knows, doesn't he?"

"No." She feels guilty even saying it. "But he's had so much going on. I didn't want to tell him until I was sure about what direction things might take. You know, sure as one can be."

"What's he got going on that's more important than you?" Then: "Remind me; does he even have a job?"

"Ambrose—"

"Oh, I know he's says he's taking that detective test or whatever. Someday. Doesn't he keep putting it off?"

"It's next month."

"And your parents— Nobody else knows?"

"Randy's mom's the only one. And my lawyer. And now you."

"Lawyer?"

"I had a will made when I found out. Needed to have that done anyway. What if I got killed in a car wreck and didn't have my affairs in order?"

"And Randy's mom? I thought he hardly even speaks to her?"

"He doesn't, but I do. He doesn't know we've gotten close, but— Oh, it's complicated."

He hands her a couple tissues from the box on the mini-fridge.

"Thanks." She wipes her eyes. "I don't know why I haven't— It's hard enough talking about it. I just haven't been able to talk about it with anybody but her. The only reason I'm telling you is because I might have to take off for a short while. I've got a temp agency looking to find some help. You've started fresh since losing Miss Dover. Maybe you'll like seeing a fresh face around here for a change."

"Nobody's face is fresher than yours," he insists. "Besides just the work thing, I hope the biggest reason you told me this is because we're best friends. We are still, aren't we?"

"Of course we are."

He embraces her tightly.

Without meaning to, she flashes on the night she discovered this—lump. Maybe all this is some karmic retribution for even daring to dredge up old, forbidden fantasies, for even going there in her imagination when she adores Randy and would follow him to the ends of the earth. But there's also the kink factor, the memory of the night things got heated while she and Ambrose were doing molly, and her latent jealousy over Randy hanging out with Butch so much, even though Randy needs a real friend . . . and here she is hanging out with Ambrose, telling him her biggest secrets. Randy would be so jealous if he knew she were here, if he saw Ambrose holding her like this.

"You'll beat this cancer, Bennie," Ambrose whispers into her ear. "I love you, you know."

"I know. I love you, too." Secure in her devotion to Randy and despite any free-floating fantasies that linger regarding Ambrose, she hugs him back, unafraid of letting him feel how much he means to her.

"Can I kiss you?" he whispers. "Just this once?"

"You said that once before. Remember?"

"I know, but this could really be the last time."

"You mean 'cause I might die?"

"There's a way better chance I'll die before you will."

She sniffles, trying to make sense of why he'd say that. "Ambrose. . ."

"It's true," he whispers, just before pressing his lips to hers. Quite an innocent kiss, really, though no one, especially Jessica nor Randy, would see it that way.

It strikes her that she's been unfair to Randy and Jessica and her parents—everyone she hasn't been honest with. Not telling them something like this. She gently pulls away. "I'd really better go."

"See you tomorrow?"

She pauses at the door, barely glancing back. "See you tomorrow." She goes out, closing the door behind her.

***

Randy knew spying on Ambrose would be different this time, but nothing had prepared him for the tangle of intrigue captured on the little clearance-priced piece of equipment he'd planted in that office. By piecing together live conversations between Ambrose, Rajit, and Terrence, one-sided phone conversations between Ambrose and some guy with a half-ass Russian-sounding name, the very least that's been going on is cyber-theft, possible money laundering and smuggling of some kind, likely drugs. Hell, of course it's drugs, but the nitty-gritty details of all that are murky. Then there's still the matter of the body at the bottom of Lake Tahoe, but that won't go into the report for Butch. It was before he even met Butch. Anyway, it'd be too much for Randy to explain and for Butch to handle, and it makes Randy an accessory after-the-fact.

Even with Randy's penchant for blurting out inconvenient truths, and clumsy lies, that would just be too much. He's stripped naked for Bennie, physically and emotionally, the latter easier than the former, but she's the only one he'll do it for, despite her teasing him about his "bromance" with Butch, which sounds too gay for comfort and the perverse high he gets telling her secrets he'd never tell anyone else. Wait, do his therapists Yvette and Evan count?

No, that's a secret corner of the universe. Still seems like a scene from a movie, seen in bits and pieces from a long time ago, one he's never really sat down and watched beginning to end. Maybe it was a movie after all.

Tahoe won't go into the report.

Neither should the nefarious way he acquired this information, breaking rules left and right, and he hasn't even gotten his license yet. When he's a bona fide private detective, he will follow the rules. This is a favor for a friend.

Oh, bullshit. It's a clusterfuck all around.

He's been making notes about what goes on: dates and times and any other observations in his pigeon shorthand, kept in a strong box with his pistols in it under the bed, the key stuffed into the toe of one of his crummiest sneakers in the very back of the closet. There was a time when collecting all this dirt on Ambrose would have brought him joy, but now it just makes him numb.

He takes a bottle of beer out of the refrigerator and pops it open. Bennie'll be home soon. She texted she's going to the store and asked if there's anything special that he wants for dinner. **Nah**, he'd texted back. Whatever she wants is fine. He flops onto the sofa and opens the spy cam app on his phone. Zipping past the dead-zone footage, he finally sees Ambrose walk in, followed by his adorable girl. Bennie hasn't been present during any of the illicit discussions going on behind the scenes, so it looks like she's blissfully ignorant of what's really been happening, which is a tremendous relief.

Randy turns up the volume, takes another swig of beer and puts his feet up on the coffee table to watch another installment of *What The Hell's Ambrose Up To Now*, guest-starring Ms. Bennie Burke.

TWELVE

When Bennie arrives back at the apartment, Randy's waiting for her like she expected, only something's off. He's unusually quiet. She asks what he wants for dinner, and again, he says it doesn't matter, whatever she wants. As she's unloading the few groceries she bought and placing some bananas and apples in the fruit bowl on the counter, he walks over and embraces her from behind, turns her around to face him. She smiles, hoping this means his mood's lightening. "To what do I owe this pleasure?" she asks, putting her arms around his neck.

"What do I have to do to show you how much I love you?"

"Nothing. You're doing it now."

"Not enough, though." His eyes are bloodshot, dark circles more prominent. "C'mon, there must be something you need that I'm not giving you."

"There isn't. You do plenty."

He releases her, goes over and opens the refrigerator.

"Randy, what's wrong?"

He laughs softly, like, *Where to begin?*

She watches as he pops open a beer, her mind racing. It's almost like. . . But he can't know about the cancer. He's just been so fragile, so on edge. She doesn't want to upset him further until she knows more about what might be ahead. Until then, there's no point in telling him. But who is she kidding? There's nothing routine about the way she's handling this, which is all wrong.

"I'm going up on the roof to smoke a cigar," he announces, grabbing one Butch gave him from the box on the table by the door. "Call or text me when dinner's ready."

"I'm thinking chick-pea tagine for tonight. Sound good?"

"Sounds great."

She watches as he shuts the door.

✳✳✳

Mary-Ann tells herself that she's just helping at the orchid show, only because they asked her so nicely and because none of the ladies at the garden club were among those at the Mexican restaurant that fateful day her old world began to crumble. Plus, coming back out to the Crescent House, a Queen Anne-style Victorian with ample gingerbread woodwork around the edges, is always a pleasure. Named for the brass weather wane featuring a crescent moon encircled by stars atop one of the fanciful round towers above the front porch, the property was willed to the garden club by a wealthy former member.

Bob didn't even seem to mind coming with her, talking to a couple of his golfing buddies near the bar set up in the back yard. Most everything takes place outdoors and it's a beautiful afternoon. A croquet game is already in progress beyond the glass greenhouse. Jessica said she'd try to make it, and there she is, lovely as ever, so very pregnant. Ambrose is with her, too, looking handsome in a linen suit. Haven't seen him in a while. And Butch. . .

She's never seen him this dressed up. Khakis, navy blazer. He looks wonderful, but somewhat ill-at-ease, fiddling with his striped tie. Jessica told her last time that she wished he would get out more, seemed almost too content to sit out on the guesthouse patio, reading books, staying home to watch Beau when she and Ambrose go out. Jessica said she wished they could find him a date. A date! Why yes, of course, why shouldn't he have a date? And why had it made Mary-Ann cringe inside when Jessica said it? Anyway, seeing Butch, Mary-Ann feels like she did in high school when a crush walked past her in the hallway, that nervous rush when he would look her way. . .

She greets Jessica and Ambrose, air-kisses all around and, as they proceed toward the garden and green house to see the displays of prize-winning orchids, Butch lingers behind. "You look great," he says.

"Thank you. So do you." Then just to show she wouldn't be jealous if he hadn't come stag: "I'm surprised a young man as handsome as you didn't bring a date."

"I thought about it, but it just didn't work out."

"Oh?"

He speaks quietly. "There's this woman I really like. Would've invited her but she had plans this afternoon."

"Oh." Her heart falls. "That's a shame."

"Isn't it?"

"Well, tell me about her. I mean, who is she?"

"Society lady with gorgeous gams. Long, dark hair. Brown eyes. A lot like you."

"Is that so? Does this woman have a name?"

"Oh, she has a name." He leans closer, whispers in her ear. "And I'm fucking crazy about her." He gives her hand a gentle squeeze, and a smoldering look that sends her heart reeling before he ambles off to join Ambrose and Jessica.

She turns to watch him walk away. He glances back, sees her looking, winks. She turns away, and there's that sweet tingle that goes back to the high school hallway. Pure, unbridled joy.

As the afternoon drifts into evening, Mary-Ann goes into the kitchen just to see how things are going with the caterers. Nothing to worry about, everything under control. Mrs. Margaret Denechaud, who willed this place to the garden club, would be pleased with today's event. Mary-Ann remembers her holding court in the solarium, surrounded by rare plant specimens from all over the world. A few guests venture in from time to time to view the photographs lining the hallway of the late Mrs. Denechaud's travels, from the Amazon jungle to the gardens of Versailles, Kew, Sissinghurst. Mostly family portraits in the parlor, including a sedate portrait of herself above the fireplace, the last she ever commissioned.

After making the rounds to make sure no dessert plates have been left in the solarium, no abandoned drinks on the Steinway in the parlor, Mary-Ann returns to the kitchen. Servers come in with empty trays and go back out to the party replenished There's a stack of plastic boxes at one end of the counter under the cupboards, dainty antique cups and saucers from the last event held here. The plastic boxes of glassware are taking up valuable real estate, having been pushed aside to make room for cardboard boxes of finger sandwiches, and now sit precariously near the edge of the counter.

Even though Mary-Ann could easily claim "not my job" to put it away, her innate sense of responsibility kicks in, plus the fact that she's tired of the social swirl out on the grounds. All talked out, though buoyed from that encounter with Butch. He, Ambrose, and Jessica may have left by now, and Bob is out there somewhere, drinking, smoking, and comparing golf scores, or maybe starting to look at his watch. She hasn't had anything to drink. She'll put these priceless relics away for old time's sake. Almost time to call it a day.

"What're you doing in here?" a familiar voice enquires.

She turns to see Butch standing in the kitchen doorway. "Well, well. Speak of the devil and in he walks."

"Were you speaking of the devil?"

"No, but—I was just thinking about you. Figured you all might be heading back to Palo Alto."

"Eh, they're still out there. Some lady asked Jessica to paint a portrait of her orchid, and Ambrose is jaw-jacking with Mr. Bob and them. How come you're hanging out in the kitchen?"

"Just checking on things. Old habits die hard. I used to be vice-president of this garden club."

"Did you now?"

"I was going to put these boxes upstairs and go back outside."

"I'll do that for you. Where do they go?"

"Up in the attic. There's a dumbwaiter around the corner."

He places the boxes on the little elevator contraption and she presses the button that sends them to the attic.

"There. Thanks for your help. "

"What else you need?"

"Nothing. I'll get them off the dumbwaiter and send it back."

"All the way up there? Aren't you afraid you might see a ghost?"

"I haven't heard of any hauntings here but one never knows. After all, the Winchester House is less than a half-hour away, and it's simply riddled with ghosts."

"I'd better go with you, just in case."

"I don't want to keep you from the party."

"It's no party without you. Let's get it done so you can go back outside and enjoy yourself."

No party without you. . . Tears prick her eyes and she realizes she's still healing from everything that happened. Subconsciously, maybe that's why she retreated into the kitchen, even though no one asked her to, and she's not needed in here. Thrilled as she was by what he said earlier, she didn't want to talk too much, say the wrong thing, make him feel awkward, or give herself anything new to worry about. "That's sweet of you," she says.

"What?"

"That you care whether I enjoy myself."

"Of course I care." He gently hands her a handkerchief from his pocket. "Got something in your eye?"

"I'm all right."

"Show me where to go unload that stuff."

✳✳✳

Butch follows her up three flights of stairs, pausing on each floor for her to show him around, give him a whirlwind tour of this mansion full of antiques, travel souvenirs, and exotic ephemera collected by the rich old woman who lived here. "She traveled the world," Mary-Ann says, "but always came back. No children, no relatives left by the time she died while on an excursion in the

Galapagos. Good for her. She went out doing what she loved. Can't ask for more than that."

By the time they make it up to the attic, Butch is slightly winded, but turned on from looking at Mary-Ann's ass in that turquoise sheath dress. He takes the boxes out of the dumbwaiter and places them on a shelf next to some other see-through plastic boxes that appear to contain silver and flatware. The attic is full of plastic boxes and a few cardboard, most overflowing with decorations for every season, holiday, and occasion: artificial Christmas trees of all sizes, bunny rabbit figures, baskets, bells, and bows and red, white, and blue bunting.

"Thank you again for doing this," she says.

"My pleasure."

She glances at him and starts back toward the short flight of steps to the door.

He grasps her hand. "Do we have to rush back so fast? It's a long trip downstairs, maybe we ought to rest a minute."

"Oh, dear, I hope this hasn't worn you out too much."

"No, but. . ." He pulls her closer. "I've missed you."

"But you see me every week. Sometimes almost every other day."

"Not like that night."

She smiles. "That was quite a night, wasn't it?"

"I'll never forget it."

"Me neither."

He'd like to keep this up for a little while longer: flirting, building anticipation, art of seduction and all that, but he's hungry for her, starving, gazing at that ass all the way up those creaky wooden stairs, walking through this Victorian oh-so-proper house with its doilies and settees interrupted with the occasional fertility statuette or nude goddess. He's feeling like a bull in a China shop, wanting to grab her, toss her onto one of those slender four-poster canopy beds, tear off her clothes, go down on her and fuck her all over again.

He wraps his arms around her, rubbing her ass through that dress. He never thought, when Jessica insisted on his coming to this thing, that he'd ever get a chance like this. "I'd kiss you, but I don't want to mess up your lipstick," he murmurs into her ear before kissing her neck. She's wearing a diamond pendant on a chain, and he tries to picture her wearing that and nothing else, even though Jessica, Ambrose, or both might be looking for him, and Mr. Bob might rouse himself off that cushy chair, buzzed on bourbon and cigars, and start looking for Mary-Ann. But Butch can't go back downstairs, not without some release. . .

"I think I could fix it." She kisses him full on the mouth, before some innate sense of guilt or paranoia kicks in and she pulls back. "How long have we been up here?" she asks.

"In here? Just a couple minutes." He turns her around, reaches down for the hem of her dress, raising it, sliding it over her thighs.

"What're you doing?"

"This won't take long." He slides her panties down her shapely legs to the floor. Lace panties and those high heels. "Step out."

"Butch!"

"You don't want to?"

"Yes, but we don't have time."

He embraces her from behind, kissing her neck.

She melts into him. "Do we?"

"If we hurry."

She steps out of the panties.

He places them in his coat pocket, unbuckles and unzips, sliding his hand between her thighs. "Spread your legs," he whispers. That encounter at her house was high risk enough, but this is tight-rope-without-a-net risky with people downstairs, Mr. Bob around, Jessica and Ambrose always conscious of his whereabouts. No margin for error, but goddamn, she looks good.

"What're you doing?" she asks as he fumbles in his wallet for a condom.

"Grab that handrail," he softly commands, remembering how she reacted before when he gave her directions. She's a woman of the world, knows her mind, but maybe gets tired of having to figure out everything, and he has so little control over anything in his life, but knows what he wants in this moment and, as long as she wants it too. This drop in a sea of time'll shine in his memory like that big diamond solitaire around her neck on a silver chain, dangling just above her smooth, tanned, ample cleavage.

She gasps as he enters her and the attic is silent except for his heavy breathing and the gentle, insistent slapping of the front of his thighs against the back of hers, that firm, lovely ass, doing her best not to cry out, maybe biting her lip 'til it bleeds to keep from giving them away, drawing the attention of some buzzed sight-seeing guests who might come nosing around to see whether there are ghosts in this house.

The old floor slightly creaks as his weight shifts. "Bend down further," he whispers.

She does what he says, allowing him to penetrate deeper. "Oh my God."

Momentarily, any guilt or paranoia is blotted out by streams of molten gold overcoming them. That's how it feels. Even if every party guest were watching, it wouldn't matter. He wouldn't be able to stop and she wouldn't want him to until they finish and he tightly embraces her, still inside, pulsing like aftershocks of some rock-candy mountain earthquake.

He hears her gasp when he pulls out, strips off the condom, and, unsure what to do with it, wraps it in his formerly neatly folded handkerchief, and sets it on a shelf as she lowers the hem of her dress, straightening up. He tucks in his shirt, zips and buckles back up.

She turns, kisses him, straightens his tie, smooths his hair. "Um. . ." She pauses, smiling, flushed. "Thank you for helping me bring those boxes upstairs," she whispers.

He grasps her hand, kisses it, but it's not nearly enough, so he pulls her close, kisses her deeply. "'Til next time?"

Her eye makeup is still intact, eyeliner having only slipped slightly from the intense few moments they shared. She has a dewy, dreamy look that's most attractive. Her lipstick's paler, but not smeared, at least not so's he can tell in the waning light. "'Til next time. Do I look okay?" she asks.

"You look beautiful." He runs his hands over her shoulders. "Do I look put back together?"

She turns him around, looking him up and down. "Perfect. You look extraordinarily handsome." Then, peering around at the floor: "What happened to my underwear?"

"It's in my pocket."

"Can I have it back?"

"I was hoping I could keep it. Can I? At least 'til—if I ever get to come see you at your house again?"

"If? Please say '*when*.'"

"When."

"Okay, I guess." She seems amused that he'd want to keep them. "What'll you do with them in the meantime?"

"Put 'em under my pillow."

She laughs softly, then remembers: "How long have we been up here?"

"Not long. You want to go back downstairs first? I'll wait about five minutes and, if anybody asks me where I've been, I'll just tell 'em I was walking around, looking at pictures."

"Maybe it's best if I do go back down first. Let's walk down to the next floor and then I'll go back out to the garden. If anyone's looking for you, I'll tell them I saw you in the parlor earlier."

"'Kay. Maybe I'll go out front and have a smoke."

She leans closer, with that look of concern he often sees on Jessica's face. "Are you really supposed to be smoking?"

"No, but don't tell anybody."

"Such a bad boy," she sighs, steps back. "You're sure I look presentable?"

"Perfect."

"We'd better go."

He follows her back down the short flight to the door that leads into the hallway between a couple long-vacated servants' bedrooms. Before she opens it, he whispers, "Mary-Ann?"

She turns back to him.

He kisses her once more. "Thanks for letting me steal a few moments of your time."

She looks touched, eyes lighting up in a way that gives him hope it won't be too long before he can be alone with her again. "Thank you, too, Butch." A kiss on the cheek and she goes out.

He stands by the door until he hears her high heels pause, turn the corner at the landing, and start down the next flight of steps. As he's about to start his descent, he remembers the handkerchief with the used condom in it that he left sitting next to a plastic box full of that red, white, and blue bunting. Better just get rid of it. He goes back, grabs the handkerchief and stuffs it in the opposite jacket pocket from the one her panties are in.

As he goes back down the short flight of creaky stairs, he's hit with a wave of fatigue so complete and debilitating that he has to sit down on the bottom step. He loosens his collar, takes a few breaths, trying to steady himself. The doctor did say things like this would happen, just a matter of time. But it can be managed, they said. It's a fact of life now. No time to think about it. There's all the time in the world to contemplate everything sitting out there on the patio behind the guesthouse. Suddenly, he fervently wishes he were there. But then he wouldn't have gotten with Mary-Ann, and memories of this afternoon will get him through many lonely nights.

When he feels able, he makes his way back down to the second floor, pauses, pretending to look at a picture of a Balinese temple on a wall in the wide hallway as a couple walks past, admiring a Hindu statue sitting on an antique teakwood cabinet. He finds a bathroom, shoves the handkerchief with the condom into the bottom of the trashcan, washes his hands, pats his face with a little cold water, and continues downstairs and onto the wide porch.

He sits down on a wicker swing, starts to light a cigarette, but doesn't because it's enough just to sit still and take in the view as the sun begins to set. His phone rings. He takes it out of his interior pocket, expecting it to be Ambrose or Jessica looking for him, but it's Randy. "Hey, Ran," he answers. "What's going on?"

"I wish I fucking knew," Randy replies.

"What's the matter?"

"Everything."

"That covers a lot of ground." Then, quieter: "Is it about Ambrose?"

A scoff at the other end of the line. "Isn't everything about Ambrose?"

Butch sits back in the swing, a queasy sensation starting in the pit of his stomach. He glances down at the shoes Jessica helped him pick out on the way home from his last doctor's appointment. Light brown, richly detailed, fairly expensive even on sale, and with a glob of cum on the tip that he hadn't noticed before. He starts to reach for his handkerchief but it's in the trash upstairs, and he doesn't want to use Mary-Ann's delicate panties for this purpose, so he reaches down and wipes it off with the palm of his hand, then reaches inside his jacket and wipes it off on his shirt. Damnit, Butch, you filthy bastard. "Pretty much," he answers. "What'd he do now?" He's shocked to hear what amounts to the sound of a dry sob. "Randy? What the hell?"

"I'm all right."

"Where you at?"

"Home. Up on the roof."

"Where's Bennie?"

"Downstairs, cooking dinner. Are you at the guesthouse?"

"No, a garden party somewhere out in the country."

"Garden party? Let me guess. Ambrose is there, wearing a white suit with a pastel shirt and tie, looking like the goddamn Great Gatsby. Am I right?"

"Uh, come to think of it—yeah."

That sound again. Pure derision. "Go back to your party and don't tell him I called. Don't tell anybody you talked to me."

"Randy, I gotta say, you've got me worried."

"I'm fine. Sorry I bothered you." Then, as if to try and lighten the mood: "I'm having a beer and one of those cigars you left here. Great smoke. Thanks."

"You're welcome." Butch sees a couple of cars leaving. This shin-dig's winding down. "I'll call you when I'm back at the house, a'ight?"

"I'm starting to get a buzz."

"If you're buzzin', stay away from the edge of that roof," Butch says with a smile, but means with a vengeance. Whatever's upset Randy and has to do with Ambrose sounds like more than buzzed talk.

"Don't worry, I won't do handstands on the ledge or anything."

"See that you don't," Butch says, flashing on that Sunday afternoon when he and Randy were walking back to their apartment from a nearby bar and some teenager was out stopping traffic so his friend could come flying down a hill on a skateboard while another guy got it on video. The skateboarder made it, and their whole group cheered. It was a cool sight to behold: kid flying at top speed down that crazy-steep incline just below Coit Tower, across a wide street and into the next block before they all high-fived and hauled ass.

Same daredevil impulse that had himself and Mary-Ann in its grip just a few minutes ago, and maybe the same one that used to have Randy when he pulled all that shit that got him fired. That grips Ambrose with whatever shit he's pulling now, and that possessed Butch like a demon when he was engaged in the activities that got him locked up all those years. Wherever that impulse comes from and whatever it is, it's powerful and persistent.

Call over, Butch goes back through the house and down the steps to mingle among the last of the orchid-lovers.

THIRTEEN

Ambrose knocks on Bennie's and Randy's apartment door. Heavy rain this morning and Jessica's at home finishing some paintings for that upcoming Santa Fe exhibition, so he drove the car today. Rajit's Mini-Cooper is in the shop, and Ambrose is picking up him and Terrence and might as well give Bennie a ride, too—just texted her a few minutes ago.

Randy answers the door.

"Happy Monday." Ambrose smiles.

"What the hell are you doing here?"

"I'm playing chauffer today." He holds up the car keys. "Got the Mercedes."

Randy's scowl reminds him of that morning he came here homeless and desperate, and Bennie's then-Coast Guard boyfriend had given him that same look. "Does she know that?"

"I texted her."

Randy steps away, leaving the door open, calls out. "Bennie, your ride's here."

"Coming!" Bennie walks out of the bedroom, looking all fresh and perfect, in a retro yellow dress with blue flowers. "Good morning." She tosses her purse and red rainslicker on the sofa and heads back into the bedroom. "I'm almost ready. Be right back!" She disappears into the bedroom, and they hear the bathroom door close.

Randy leans against the sofa, arms folded.

Ambrose shoves his hands into the pockets of his trench coat.

Randy stares at him.

The silence is too much. Even the TV is on mute.

"So," Ambrose begins. "Who pissed in your cereal?"

"Ha."

"Ha." Still nothing.

"I should beat the shit out of you for asking."

"Fuck's the matter with you?"

Randy nears, pokes his finger into Ambrose's chest. "You're what's the matter with me. What are you, a fucking sociopath?"

"No more than you are."

Randy takes a deep breath, exhales. "If Bennie wasn't in the next room, you and I'd have a frank discussion right now about rules and boundaries and how you wouldn't know the truth if it came up and bit you in the balls."

"Which truth is that?"

"*Which*? See, that's what's wrong. You're used to picking whichever one suits you at the moment."

"And you're not?"

Randy fixes him with a bloodshot stare.

Awaiting a smart-ass retort, Ambrose detects a deep sadness sopping at the edges of all this anger.

Without breaking the stare, Randy calls out, "Hey, Bennie. Your best friend's waiting."

"Just a second!" she calls.

Ambrose speaks quietly. "This isn't about Tahoe, is it?"

Randy's bluster's preferable to this dead-eyed resignation. "Why would it be? That never happened."

"Ready!" Bennie walks out, wearing her red rain boots, puts on her slicker and grabs her purse. She approaches Randy, kisses him on the cheek, and, noticing he looks tense, caresses the side of his face.

He grasps her hand and kisses it. Sweet.

Ambrose looks away just as there's a quick knock on the door.

He opens it to Rajit and Terrence. "Good morning," Rajit greets. "We are here to claim our ride to work and possibly a free breakfast, please."

"Right this way," Ambrose starts out.

"I'm coming." She hugs Randy, then heads for the door. "I'll call you later," she says before going out.

As Ambrose closes the door, Randy is still standing there, staring like before, only darker. What if he somehow knows about Bennie's diagnosis? Or what if something new's come up that's causing all this weirdness? If he knew about what happened in the office the other day. . . That could cause a look like that. But he doesn't know. Ambrose walks down the hallway, unable to get that image out of his mind's eye. Randy standing there, accusing him of something, but he's not sure what.

As Ambrose steps onto the elevator with Bennie, Rajit, and Terrence, who are chatting, laughing, he can't shake an eerie feeling. Whatever it is that's eating Randy is bound to come to light. Maybe Butch can get it out of him. Randy likes Butch. Butch likes Randy.

In fact, sometimes it's like Randy's the brother Butch never had.

***

After Bennie leaves for work with Ambrose and the nerds down the hall, Randy paces around, pausing every so often to look out at the rain. The grayness of the day matches his mood. By late morning, though, the sky begins to lighten, and the rain goes down to a drizzle before stopping altogether, leaving the streets slick. He'd been in a surly funk but now, as the coffee kicks in harder and the clouds in his head clear, he realizes he may have fucked up big-time, tipping his hand by being such an asshole to Ambrose this morning.

The more Randy tries to get his mind off it, the more he thinks about Bennie and her reasons for not telling him about her cancer. That she's worried about him, that maybe he's too weak to handle it and she's telling this to *Ambrose* of all people, goddamn it. And Ambrose using it to hug and kiss her and let her cry on his shoulder.

Randy got the feeling he'd do more if she'd let him. Way more, even with his pregnant wife at home.

But what if Ambrose starts wondering why Randy was so pissed today. May be overthinking this, though. Ambrose may have forgotten it the minute he left. Even so, there's no way to concentrate on anything constructive when Randy's got so much on his mind and heart. Everything bad in life that he thought was in the past comes rushing back, along with his worst fear: He could lose Bennie. She's even been in touch with his mom, for God's sake.

The impulse strikes that he must get back into Ambrose's office and retrieve that mini cam. What if it's discovered and connected to him somehow? But that little device is the only way Randy knows any of the vital information that's driving him up the fucking walls. Should've held it together better.

He opens the spy-cam app. Nothing happening. Ambrose isn't even there. But just as Randy's about to log out, Ambrose walks in, sits at the desk and turns on his computer. Flopping onto the sofa, Randy stares at the tow-headed cock-sucking son-of-a-bitch who somehow has the power to destroy his whole world. If Ambrose weren't married to Jessica. If she weren't pregnant. If Bennie weren't married and even though she did let him kiss her because they're "best friends" and they "love" each other, she did tell Ambrose that she loves Randy most of all. Randy closes his eyes, chaos engulfing him like the wicked undertows at Ocean Beach.

"Jesus Christ. . ." he breathes. *My life is a clusterfuck.*

When Randy's able to focus on his phone again, Ambrose is sitting back in his chair, like waiting for something to load on the computer, then he stands and starts walking around, looking at objects on the shelves, behind framed photos on the cabinet behind his desk. Ambrose's cell phone rings. He picks it up. "Hello? Yeah, it's a go. . . Haven't really figured out how to work that yet." Ambrose sits down on the sofa and props his feet up on the coffee table. Expensive shoes. He probably likes to stare at them, whatever they are.

Randy glances at his own sock feet propped on his coffee table.

"I haven't forgotten," Ambrose says. He puts his feet on the floor, leans forward. "Sure, it's most generous. . ." He sighs. "I think I can pull it off, but this has to be the last time. . . It just does." He stands, goes over and looks out the window. "Thanks, but I had a late breakfast. . . Just soup and salad, maybe. . . Okay, if you insist. 1:30ish? . . .All right. See you then." He ends the call, looking around the room once more, then goes out.

Randy starts to log off, then Ambrose walks back into the office, glancing around at eye-level again, then up around the ceiling. His eyes almost come to rest where the device is hidden.

Randy cringes, feeling exposed.

Ambrose takes out his phone and makes a call, pacing around. "Hey, where are you?" Still on the phone, he goes over to turn off his computer. "I was just thinking. . . Let's do a bug-sweep this afternoon. Tell Terrence to make sure that zapper's charged. . . Nah, I just think it's a good idea, that's all. . . 'Kay. I have to go out, I'll be back between 2:30 and 3:00. . . See you then." He ends the call and leaves.

Randy logs out, heart racing, brain scrambled. He gets up, pours some more coffee.

Only one thing to do now.

✳✳✳

Randy approaches the front door of Arcadia with take-out from Chossi's, Bennie's favorite sandwich shop. He smooths his hair, conscious of cameras that might be watching.

Bennie's plenty surprised to see him, as he knew she would be, and claims she's not all that hungry—they ate a late breakfast—as he knew she'd say. "It's sweet, but you didn't have to do this."

"I was kind of a pill this morning, so figured I'd try and make up for it."

"You weren't a pill to me," she says, taking paper-wrapped sandwiches, bags of chips, and gourmet chocolate chip cookies out of the to-go sack and placing them on her desk.

"Nevertheless, I wasn't in the best of moods, either. You can eat what you want and have the rest later." Difficult standing still when he's dying to go upstairs and get his hands on that damn mini camera while no one's around, not even that Momo-chick. "Hey, I'll be right back; I just have to go to the bathroom."

"I'll go get two sodas from the bar. What do you want to drink?"

"Dr. Pepper if you got it." He heads for the stairs, hurrying so she won't remind him there's a bathroom downstairs. Up in Ambrose's office, he slips out of his shoes, shifts a chair over by the painting, steps up, grabs the mini cam off the painting, and shoves it into his jeans pocket. He steps down and back into his shoes, moves the chair back, heart still racing, neck burning that way it does at times like this. As he starts back out, Bennie meets him at the door.

"What're you doing up here?"

"I was on my way to the bathroom and thought I'd stop in and say hi to Ambrose. He's not here though."

"No, he went out." She goes over to the mini fridge. "There wasn't any Dr. Pepper at the bar, but Ambrose likes those too, so— Hey, jackpot!" She takes two cans out of the fridge. "You already talked to Ambrose today when he came by our place, I'm surprised you want to come up and say hi again. Unless. . ." She nears. "By any chance, were you a pill to *him* this morning?"

Hard to know how any attempt at nonchalance might translate with all this stress cortisol coursing through him. By tomorrow he might look ten pounds heavier, but now that his mission's accomplished and the mini cam's in his pocket, he feels positively buoyant. "Why you say that?"

"It's no secret to me he's not your favorite person. Or is there something else you want to talk to him about?"

"Nope, just came up here to take a shit."

"Randy," she laughs. "You and your shits."

"Executive washroom, right?"

"Actually, the one on the first floor's way nicer. And we do have air freshener, you know." She starts out. "Anyway, let's go eat."

He gently pulls her back, takes her face in his hands, tilts it so she'll have to look at him. "Sorry, I forgot to ask. . . How's your day been going?"

"It's been going fine. Especially now that the rain stopped and the sun is out."

"Good. Because if something were wrong, you'd tell me before anybody else. Wouldn't you?"

She glances aside. A definite tell.

"'Cause I'm your husband and I love you. More than life."

"I love you, too," she says. "More than life itself."

"Do you really?" He's close enough to kiss her but holds back.

"Of course," she whispers, leaning slightly forward, wanting the kiss.

He's still no good at that tantric, sexual withholding crap some yogis are into. Apparently, his old neighbor Brianna wasn't either because, even though she was a yoga fanatic and talked that mumbo-jumbo, she'd still fuck anything that moved, including the old Randy.

Bennie likes this teasing. He wants to get her turned on, wants to seduce her in this same room where not so very long ago Bennie hugged and kissed Ambrose, and Randy never should've seen that, shouldn't even know it but, since he does, he wants to purge that energy from this room, his mind, his memory, and hers.

He grazes her lips with his, then gives her a real kiss, one of those long, dizzying kind that takes their breath away. "Prove it. Take me in one of these rooms and fuck my brains out."

"Randy!"

"That's what they're for, isn't it?"

"Well—not exclusively. Anyway, we've got guests coming in, and the rooms are set up for them."

"Okay, how 'bout right here, on the sofa?"

"Now you're being ridiculous," she laughs.

"Why not? It's not like there are any cameras or anything in here. Right?"

"No, but Ambrose will be back soon."

"Let's give him a cheap thrill."

She steps back, puzzled and amused. "What's gotten into you?"

"I don't know," he answers. Getting crazy with *her* beats going crazy *alone*. The chaos still swirls slowly, like a lazy whirlpool, but he feels a little better now. "Hey, I got an idea."

"What's that? Or should I be scared to ask?"

He places his hands on either side of her waist, pulling her closer. "Let's go downstairs, get our lunch and take it home. We'll eat and fool around and take a nap."

"But it's not even two o'clock. I have things to do."

He pulls her closer, hoping she can feel the hard-on happening just from talking about sex with her, whether it's in this room, one of those freaky suites or this afternoon at home. If he can get her to come home, Ambrose doesn't get to drive her back and, if that bastard values his life, he'll refrain from calling, texting, or daring to knock on the door. "Please, Bennie," he whispers into her ear. "I need you."

"Well. . . Okay. When you put it like that." She starts to replace the sodas in the fridge, but he stops her.

"Bring those with us."

"I should text Ambrose that I'm leaving early."

"Just leave a note on that Post-it. We'll role-play. I'm the boss. You're the secretary. You've got to write what I tell you."

"Hm. Okay." She sits at the desk, picks up a pen, and looks up with a slightly naughty smile. "Ready for dictation, Mr. Burke."

"Put, **'I left early today.'**"

She writes, looks up. "Any explanation?"

"To go fuck Randy's brains out."

"Randy! I can't—"

"'Okay, okay. Put, **'Because Randy said so.'**"

She writes. "Anything else?"

"Sign it, **'Sincerely, Mrs. Randall J. Burke.'**"

She smiles again, biting her lip as she complies, and when she's finished, she leaves the Post-it next to Ambrose's laptop. "Let's go." She goes out first.

Thanks for the free sodas, asshole—should write that on a Post-it. Signed, **Your mortal enemy, Randall-fucking-Burke.**

FOURTEEN

Butch is on the guesthouse patio, reading a book, smoking a cigar when Randy arrives. "Oh, hey, Ran." Butch puts the book aside, rests the cigar in a ceramic ashtray "Thanks for coming. Want a drink?"

"No, thanks." Randy pulls up a chair and sits down. Butch trusted him to collect this information, and he trusts Butch. Has to, or there's no way he could ever go through with this.

Butch sits back down, eyeing the manila envelope Randy has in his hand. "Got something for me?"

Randy hands him the envelope. "It may not be what you wanted, but it's the truth." Difficult looking Butch in the eyes, so Randy fumbles for a cigarette.

Butch lights it for him. "That's what I asked for." Butch opens the envelope, takes out the exam blue book into which Randy transcribed all his notes. It's as neat as Randy could make it, handwriting instead of typing it because he doesn't want a copy of this sitting on a hard drive, some cloud, vulnerable to any motherfuckers who might ever hack his computer. Ambrose and Rajit did it once, and maybe he deserved it, but Randy essentially hacked Ambrose's office to get this, so they're even. Butch sits back and starts to read. Randy's heart beats faster. Butch turns a page, shifts in his chair, the expression on his face going from neutral to *Goddamn.*

Randy's impulse is to get up and walk around the patio. Should've taken Butch up on that drink. He thinks about that dungeon: how people go there to be tied up, titillated and getting off having the shit beaten out of them, and how that makes no sense whatsoever. Yet here he is, hand-cuffed to his decision to tell all, watching Butch's face even though he doesn't want to, dreading the inevitable questions.

Butch gets to the last couple of pages. "This thing that happened up at Tahoe. . ." he says, then, reading from the notes: "'**Subject was seen**. . .' Was there a witness? Or you saw this?"

Randy clears his throat, shrugs. "Just what it says."

"I know what it says. . ."

Taking another drag from the cigarette, Randy feels nauseous. Whatever imp of the perverse led him to include the Tahoe incident in that "quasi-official" report has abandoned him completely, left him defenseless, his mother's accusing voice echoing in his head, *You brought this on yourself.*

"It is what it is, right?" Butch stands, reaches down and grabs Randy up by the collar, forcing him to look him in the face. "You tell me," Butch quietly demands.

"I'm just the messenger," Randy says, still unable to look Butch in the eye.

"I get the impression you were a participant."

Randy tries to swallow, but his mouth's parched, that drink he refused calling his name.

He drops the half-smoked cigarette as Butch clutches him in a hard bear hug, speaking directly into his ear: "Was it you, Randy?"

The only thing keeping Randy from collapsing onto the pristine brick patio is Butch's embrace. Again, caught in a trap of his own making.

Butch pulls back, takes Randy's face firmly in his big hands, staring him down. "Answer me."

The last thing Randy expects is compassion but, since Butch seems to be the only one these days who can see into his soul, that's what he feels. Kind of like that first day with his therapists Yvette and Evan, only he'd had to tell them; they couldn't read his mind like Butch can, like Bennie used to. He'd thought he was finally getting his life straightened out, but it remains a goddamned mess. Could still end up in jail, or on the streets, broke and alone. May never pass that licensing test. Never know if Bennie truly loves him the way he loves her or if she really wanted Ambrose all along. The fair-haired gutterpunk that's never satisfied, not even with the best of everything. Randy feels silent tears forcing their way out, but he pretends not to notice and so does Butch.

Jesus Christ, that's so gay, old bad-cop Randy would say if he were watching this, but here-and-now Randy miraculously feels a weight lifting as Butch lowers him back into the chair, goes and fetches him that drink while Randy pulls himself together, somewhat.

Then Butch gets himself a soda, flicks his lighter and lets the exam blue book burn before dropping what's left into the metal firepit. Once that's done, Butch sits across from him, taps Randy on the knee to get his attention. "You all right?" Butch asks.

Randy wipes his damp eyes with his shirt sleeve. "I'm all right."

"Do you know who it was? The guy in the bag?"

"I have no idea."

"Whoever he is, I bet he had friends. Or family. Somebody knows he went missing." Butch leans back, relights the cigar, gazing at Randy through the smoke. "Whatever gadget you used to get this information. . . Is it still there?"

"I had to get it out."

"What do you mean you 'had' to?"

"That guy that works there, Terrence, has a bug-sweeper and— I just didn't want to take a chance."

"And this trip to Miami?"

"Said it'd be the last for some time."

Butch leans forward, elbows on his knees, staring down at the patio bricks. "Wonder what kind of situation he's walking into if he does this thing."

"That, I don't know."

"Got some kind of tracking device to see where he goes?"

"I'll get one."

Butch looks up at the sky, then back at Randy. "When do we think this might be happening?"

"Soon."

"Wonder where he'll tell Jess he's going?"

"I don't know. He's a damn good liar." Then: "No offense. Him being your brother and all."

"None taken."

Better liar than I am, Randy thinks. But not better than Bennie. If she was telling Ambrose the truth that day, this window of time they're talking about could coincide with her scan and God-knows what else. If Randy came up with some reason he couldn't be around, would that force her to tell him? "You want me to follow him?"

"To Miami? Are you fucking kidding me?"

"I could do it."

"Not by yourself, you couldn't. I wish I could, but I'd have to come up with something to tell my boss, my parole officer. Jessica'd be all over it with a million questions. It'd open a whole can of worms."

"I'll think of some way. Maybe I could fly to Jacksonville and rent a car. See what route they're taking and follow 'em to Miami."

"You really think you could find him like that?"

"I could try."

Butch still looks skeptical. "I don't know. What would you do when you even got to Miami?"

"Hide and watch. Call an ambulance if there's a shootout."

Butch sighs, flicks the ash off his cigar.

"Sorry, Butch. I didn't mean to imply there'll be a shoot-out."

"If he's hauling drugs, anything could happen. I know that firsthand. Whoever it is he thinks he can trust, he can't."

"He referred to it as a caviar shipment when he talked with the Russian guy on the phone. Mentioned something about the last of a 'gold-labeled' product. That everything would need to go smooth, and this is the last time."

"Uh-huh." Butch looks jaded beyond words. "One last job." He takes a puff from the cigar and exhales slowly. "Famous last words."

✻✻✻

Bennie invited Linda up to the city to accompany her to her last scan before the lumpectomy, then they drove over to Sausalito. Over lunch at The Spinnaker, one of Bennie's favorite restaurants with its big windows and spectacular views of the Bay, she learns more about Randy's rift with Linda and the rest of the family and why Linda still blames so much of it on herself. She said there was something different about Randy when he came home from Afghanistan. He seemed more reckless, confident, and had high hopes for his new career in the police department. She and Randy's dad had been really proud of him.

Even though Mr. Burke had some health problems, he was still working, fixing heaters and air-conditioners, and she was still working at the board of education and very involved in the church and community. People she knew were encouraging her to run for city council, and she toyed with the idea but then found out Randy was under investigation, and it got in the local paper. There was gossip and the people who'd been encouraging her to run didn't mention it anymore, and she decided it just wasn't the time.

Not long after, she got a call at work that Mr. Burke had suffered a massive heart attack while sitting in his truck in someone's driveway as he was preparing to go to the next job. Linda was devastated and lashed out at Randy for causing it. Randy barely made it to the funeral and his brother and sister distanced themselves because they blamed him, too. Linda said she thought he'd been drinking before the funeral. He wore sunglasses through the whole thing and, when he took them off to rub his eyes a couple of times, she could see that he was feeling real pain and that he did blame himself. But at the time, she wasn't interested in alleviating it, considering the misery he'd caused his father and, to a lesser extent, her.

He disappeared for a couple days right after the funeral, then came back to find the appeal had been denied: He was officially off the force. Then there was that scene at the station, and that flashback out in the street. Then he was in the hospital for the better part of a month, mostly alone, because she only went to see him that once, to bring him some clothes. And then he wouldn't take her calls, wouldn't see her. And he wouldn't when he got home, either. No texts. Nothing. Until she saw him that day at her house with Bennie.

Linda gazes out the picture window as a sailboat glides past. For a moment, Bennie can see it reflected in her glasses. ". . .And I've been thinking about it a lot since I saw you and him at the house that day. How alone he must've felt when his dad died. How I never really talked to him like I should've. Nor listened to him, either. And I still don't know his reasons for doing some of the things he did."

The server, a young woman near the end of her shift, offers to take their plates. Bennie orders coffee and Linda tells the server, "I'm still working on it." Linda sighs as the server walks away. "I wish I'd done things different. I don't know what I would've done exactly but turns out everything I did was wrong. Part of it's 'cause I listened to other people, but I won't make that mistake again." She picks up her wine glass, shrugs. "So, he's not the perfect son. I'm far from being the perfect mother."

✳✳✳

Mary-Ann wondered if it was her imagination that Bob's been kinder and more attentive, or whether he *really* changed in subtle ways. Driven and busy as he was when they first got married, he still made time to pamper her or make sure she got pampered, paying for her to go on yoga or spa retreats when she used to do that sort of thing, before she got so involved with social clubs, charity work, and party-planning, admittedly much of it motivated by a desire to make a name for herself, to carve out a parallel track for her own influence apart from Bob's sphere. Since then, she and Bob adhered to their own interests, showing up for each other when they had to, but resigned to routine, punctuated by occasional trips for milestone anniversaries.

But she found out it wasn't just her imagination when Bob took her out to dinner Friday night, commented on her new dress, and told her he likes that she's wearing her hair down, like when they first met back at UC-Santa Cruz. His compliments were all very nice, but she never would've guessed the surprise he had in store between the main course and dessert. A trip to Majorca in two weeks, and it's nowhere near a milestone anniversary. She pretended to be happy that night and must've pulled it off, but when she tells Butch the next time Bob's out of town, she cries, distraught at the idea of going to another part of the world right now, curling up under the covers, allowing Butch to put his arms around her, enjoying the feel of his skin, his warmth as he holds her close.

"Well, that's a good thing, isn't it?" he says after hearing about the trip to Spain. "How long will you be gone?"

"Almost a month," she sniffles. "He rented a beachfront villa with a private pool."

"Damn. Sounds like he's doing it up right." Butch watches as she wipes her eyes. "What's the matter? You really don't want to go?"

"It's not that so much as. . ." She pauses. Maybe it sounds trite, but it's the absolute truth. "I'll miss you."

"I'll miss you, too, but— Hell, I ain't going anywhere. I'll still be here when you get back."

Tonight, Mary-Ann is especially mindful of how it feels to be held by him, to absorb every second of wild adventure that's been this whole wonderful affair. Because what if while she's gone, it cools and ends? What if he meets someone his own age? Less said, the better. She doesn't want to sound whiny, or needy. Older woman making a fool of herself over the younger man. It's a given she wouldn't leave Bob, and Butch wouldn't want that. He likes and respects Bob. He's said so and she believes him. "It just came out of nowhere, that's all," she tries to explain. "The last thing I expected was to be going on a big trip right now."

"Maybe he figures the break'll do you good." He fondles her hand, her fingers. She just had her nails done. "It might, you know."

"I suppose. . . He'll be doing some business while we're over there, but the rest of the time. . ."

"He wants to spend with you."

She takes a deep breath, pulls herself together. "You are a true gentleman, you know that?"

He laughs softly. "No but thank you very much."

She kisses him on the cheek.

"I'd better get going. Mr. Bob coming back tomorrow?"

"Tomorrow afternoon."

Butch checks his phone as she slips into her robe and goes over to the dresser.

"Actually, if he'd been here tonight, he might've gone into the city to your brother's place."

"Really?"

"Well, the cigar club there, I should say. It's mostly a bar, isn't it? Or a boutique hotel?'" She runs a brush through her hair. "I was never really sure."

". . .Something like that."

"Whatever it is, he seems to enjoy it. Bob doesn't always connect with young people, but he and Ambrose kind of hit it off. He thinks Ambrose has real potential."

Butch looks up, puts the phone down. "That's nice to hear."

"Quite true. Otherwise, he wouldn't have invested in that humidor, cigar bar thing."

Butch, about to get out of bed, pauses. "Mr. Bob's got money invested in Arcadia?"

"Mmhm." In the mirror, she notices Butch is still sitting on the edge of the bed. "Something wrong?"

He rouses himself. "No. . . I just didn't know that. That's all."

They freeze when they hear something in the driveway.

"Oh my God," she says, stress levels soaring. "That cannot be Bob back already!"

"Shit." Butch jumps up, grabs his clothes. "What do you want me to do?"

"Wait one second."

They listen.

They sound of a car door slam. The back door opening, closing.

"Go—this way." She opens the glass door leading to the bedroom patio.

He kisses her fast as he goes out.

She glances around. "Wait!" She grabs his phone off the nightstand, hands it to him, clothes clutched against his chest. After another quick inspection of the bedroom, she takes a deep breath, attempting to pull herself together before walking into the kitchen, forgetting to step into her slippers. The tile is cold on her bare feet.

Bob's back is to her as he peers into the refrigerator. He takes out a plastic container of empanadas that Lenore made yesterday, turns and sets it on the counter. "Hey, you're up."

"Thought I heard you come in." She smiles, going to get a glass from the cabinet. "How was Sacramento? I didn't expect you back until after lunch tomorrow."

"Eh, we had brunch with the state rep, played a nine-hole round with the new lobbyist. Long day. I just felt like getting on back.

Glad you woke up." He grabs the end of the ribbon belt of her robe, and she struggles to keep it closed. "Sleeping in the nude, are we?" He kisses her on the cheek. "Sexy." He grabs a dish from the drainer, turns back to the empanadas.

"I was just about to take a shower," she tells him. "I went for a swim and then fell right into bed. Chlorine is so drying. You know."

He puts his plate of three empanadas in the microwave and turns it on. "Go get a hot shower and slather yourself in that pachouli lotion I like," he says, taking off his jacket and tossing it over a chair. "I'm going to watch the end of the ball game." He pauses to get a beer out of the refrigerator. "Keep the bed warm for me." He smiles in a way he rarely does anymore and disappears into the living room.

The microwave *ping*s, causing her to jump.

She hopes Butch makes it home all right.

✳✳✳

Ambrose dreaded this and now that he must leave in two days on this last trip for Alexei, there's no putting it off any longer. "It's an entrepreneur conference in Rapid City, South Dakota," he tells Jessica over breakfast Saturday morning, using the most boring location he can think of. "You're welcome to go, but I don't think there'd be much for you to do. You might want to stay here and finish some work and we'll all go to Santa Fe for the show next month."

"I don't know," she says, reaching for the bottle of maple syrup to drizzle over her organic yogurt-strawberry-granola bowl. "Mt. Rushmore's nearby. I could take Beau to see the sights while you're at the conference."

"Yeah. . ." Damnit. This place isn't quite as middle-of-nowhere as he thought. "If I go to that one. There's actually another thing going on in Kansas City that week."

"Hm." Having drizzled syrup over the bowl, she catches the last drop on her index finger, licks it. "So, we'll go see the fountains instead. That place is famous for those."

"Right." He watches her digging into her calcium- and fiber-rich breakfast. He's having black coffee. Alexei says it's all set up, a cakewalk, though these things can always blow up a million different ways, that's why he's paying handsomely to make sure the last of the gold-labeled opium arrives without a hitch. None that can't be dealt with, anyway, another reason for the pay. Ambrose had heard Jessica talk about Mr. Bob's wife's swan song luncheon, marking the end of her time as chair of that fundraising committee, and as president of some club. This is his own "swan song" opium delivery. Some high roller in Miami bought the whole batch, cloaked in a shipment of domestic caviar.

Alexei even agreed for Ambrose to fly home and for Lev to take his time driving back, see more of the country, stay in motels at night. He can eat junk food and listen to obnoxiously loud music the whole way back, but Ambrose won't have to see or hear it. It's all planned out. Plus, Ambrose gets the feeling this may be Alexei's "swan song" in a way. He said it was the last of his Afghan opium stash. He's indicated he may be looking to get out of the drug trade, skin trade, even the agri-scam hustles, maybe looking to get into something more legit, but still lucrative. He even mentioned something about the music business, which sounded kind of interesting. How it came up in conversation, Ambrose can't recall exactly, but first things first.

He watches Jessica, eating her healthy breakfast. So pretty, so content, so unaware that she's cock-blocking him from the biggest payday of his life. Some smart-asses like his dad would say, "Biggest payday of your life was the day you married her!" But Ambrose doesn't see her that way. She's his wife and the mother of his child. Besides, he can't afford to see her as some golden ticket because, unlike Randy, he signed a pre-nup and, unlike Bennie, Jessica asked him to. "If you and Beau come along, I won't want to do any conference stuff, I'll just want to hang out with y'all," he says, getting up for more coffee.

"So, what are you saying? You don't want us to go?"

"That's not what I'm saying."

"This is the kind of thing Mike used to do."

"Now you're comparing me to Mike?"

"Well. . . If the shoe fits."

"What the hell's that supposed to mean?"

She props her elbows on the table, looking at him. "It means, you don't want us to go with you, and I really don't think you're being forthcoming about the reason."

He walks back over to the table. "You think I'm lying?"

"I didn't say that. I just don't think you're telling me the whole truth, that's all." Then she shrugs like, *There it is*, and shuffles over in her cushy bedroom slippers to get the orange juice out of the refrigerator. "Honestly, Ambrose, please give me a reason to believe you, because I could use one about now." Up until this moment, she'd been unruffled by his wishy-washy travel plans, but she's fed up.

This is bad. He never thought he might have to resort to anything like a nuclear option. "I didn't want to tell you this, but it looks like I have to because I really think at least one of us should be around. Just in case."

"Just in case what?"

"You've got to swear you won't breathe a word, because I've been sworn to secrecy. But if I don't tell you. . ." There's no coming back from this. A part of him wants to believe he'd never do it if he really thought it was the wrong thing to do. . .

"Sworn to secrecy about what?"

"Bennie's been diagnosed with breast cancer, and she's scheduled to have surgery sometime later this week."

Jessica's look goes from smug skepticism to shock. "Bennie has breast cancer? And you didn't tell me?" Then, realizing: "*She* didn't tell me? Why?"

"She has her reasons. I don't really understand it either, but she says she's worried about how Randy'll take it, because he's been going through some mental or emotional. . . stuff lately. He doesn't even know. She doesn't want anyone to know, at least until after this surgery—or lumpectomy—and she finds out what happen next."

"Oh my God." Still stunned, Jessica walks over to the glass patio door, looks out at the yard, then walks back. "She hasn't even told her own husband?"

"No. She only told me because she's taking off work a while."

Jessica, rattled to the core, eyes watering, still eyes him in a way that's disconcerting. "And because you two are so close."

"What's that supposed to mean?"

"She considers you her best friend, right? So, she would tell you."

". . .And Randy's mom."

"Randy's mom?" Another shock. "She doesn't tell him, but she tells his mother instead of me? Instead of our mother and dad? My God." Jessica paces for a moment, still trying to wrap her head around not just the news, but the silence about it. "I've got to call her," Jessica announces, about to grab her phone.

He moves to stop her. "No, no, no—don't call her! I said you had to promise not to say anything."

"But I didn't promise, did I?"

"I thought it was understood you wouldn't, not now. Just be here for her, in case she needs you. She'd do the same for either of us."

Jessica touches her fingertips to her forehead like trying to get a grip. "Okay," she says finally. "I'll take today to process this. If you want to go to your conference, go. I'll be here in case she needs me, but eventually I'll have to talk to her about it."

"But not 'til she's ready, right?"

Jessica looks at him and he can tell she's getting exasperated again.

Time to table this discussion. Spilling Bennie's secret had the desired effect of distracting Jessica from his own. But he'd blown up a bridge in the process.

Whenever Jessica does confront Bennie, Bennie will never trust him again.

✳✳✳

Mary-Ann sits on a lounger next to the pool, the Mediterranean sun tanning her skin and lightening her hair. Bob went out fishing this morning with a couple old friends here for the season. She's been trying to stay off her phone as much as possible, and not think too much about what Butch may be doing. Her mind keeps wandering back to the times they've been together: that outrageous afternoon at the garden party, last time when they almost got caught and he disappeared naked through the patio hedges and into the night. All those things would've been unthinkable but, after her break with the old way of doing things, any and everything seems possible. Even the idea that she can balance her marriage and a torrid affair with a man half her age, and all involved will live happily ever after.

It could happen.

Payton's been texting her photos of the kids' trip to Disneyland, and she responds as a loving mother and grandmother, but, really she couldn't care less. Of course she loves them all, but they're no longer the center of her life, not like they were. Maybe partly because she's no longer under the impression she's anywhere near the center of theirs. She barely even takes up space on the sidelines, now that they're getting older. She's accepted—no, embraced—the new normal: that to them she's a pinch-hitter babysitter and human ATM. Next time one of the kids ask her for clothes, toys, or a little extra cash to take to computer camp, she'll lovingly suggest they *get a job*.

She takes a sip of mosto, adjusts her bathing suit to try and minimize tan lines, and returns to dutifully replying to photos of Kylie and Tyler wearing mouse ear hats and Stanford T-shirts, posing with Mickey and Minnie until the AI takes over and the words "how cute," and "adorable" automatically pop up and she can get back to her daydreaming.

Someone grabs her shoulders from behind and she nearly yelps. Bob flops down in the lounge chair next to her, having changed into his cargo shorts, Hibiscus-print Hawaiian shirt, and topsiders.

"My God," she gasps, heart pounding. "You scared the hell out of me."

"Yeah?" He smiles. "Who're you texting? Your boyfriend?"

"No! Why on earth would you say that?"

"Just kidding." He settles back comfortably. "You've been looking hot these days. Wouldn't surprise me a bit."

She sets her phone aside, nerves jangled. "I can assure you, that's not the case at all." She sips her drink. It's cold, perfect for early afternoon. Like red wine without the alcohol. "I could say the same about you. Were you really out fishing all morning or having brunch with some young, sweet *senorita*?"

"No need to go looking when I got a fine piece of ass sitting right out here by the pool."

"Bob!"

"Just saying. I already got more than I can handle."

She turns on her side, staring at him. "With me?"

"Yes, you. Who else?"

She doesn't have an answer.

✱✱✱

Now that Butch has come around to the idea, Randy must pull the trigger. He's flying blind since he took the mini spy-cam out of Ambrose's office, but he had Butch put a tracker on Ambrose's motorcycle while it was parked in the garage. Randy's put in some time watching Arcadia from down the street at night, telling Bennie he's studying at the library. It's hard to focus at home, he told her; there are too many other things he'd rather do there. The date for his exam is looming, but so is this trip, and he has to figure out where this goddamn delivery truck is parked.

If he still had the spy-cam in place, there could be Miami as well as Bennie's cancer updates, but she's not spilling to him. Whenever she leaves the house, she could be going to meet up with his mother, or for a doctor's appointment, or both. Or taking a treatment, and that's why she's been coming home and taking so many naps, for all he knows. They've been ordering out more, and she's been eating less. She doesn't look sick, but she's lost weight while he's put on a good five pounds. He's in the dark because she's keeping him there, and she has her reasons.

He's agonized over this long enough and must accept her decision, respect her wishes and roll with the punches. That's not how he feels in his heart, which is a cauldron of turmoil. Nothing left to do to hold on to what sanity he has left—but to let go.

"Butch wants me to drive him to Big Sur," he announces at Sunday breakfast.

"Oh?" She's still lingering over a single toaster waffle.

"Yeah, he has a few days off. Wants to go on a short road trip, spend a couple nights, see some sights. He's paying for gas."

"When's this trip happening?"

"End of the week."

She looks taken aback. "Really?"

"Yep." He takes his plate to the sink. "You don't mind, do you? Might be glad to get me out of your hair for a while."

"I don't mind," she says. "That actually works out fine."

"Great. I'll be at the library. I'm going to ace this exam, you know."

"You totally are."

"And when I do, I'm hoping you'll quit that job at Arcadia and come work with me," he tells her, watching to get her reaction.

There's something frightened in her eyes that makes him feel guilty.

"Does that sound like a plan?"

"We'll talk about it when you come back."

"All right. I'm going to take a shower." Far as she knows, he's living in blissful ignorance. Just the way she wants it.

FIFTEEN

This road trip is turning out to be everything Ambrose dreaded. It's hard enough riding all day and into the night but driving for so long gives him too much time to think. After listening to Lev's blaring pop tunes, when Lev starts to drift off in the sleeper, Ambrose adjusts the radio to something more soothing. At least in this older truck, the sound of the engine is enough to blunt the sharp edges of his conscience. Lulled by the subtle roar of the motor and the endless miles of interstate, it's easy to forget his own reality back in the Bay Area, mesmerized by this magical nowhere-land of the open road.

Back when he had no place to call home, the road was all he had, so it felt like home. Now, weighed down by far more responsibilities, he's living from mile to mile, pushing everything else to the edges. When he left Texas to come to California, he had only one responsibility: himself. To stay alive, and there's still that, but also impending fatherhood, Jessica's growing distrust, his betrayal of Bennie, Butch's disapproval of the people he's hanging around, his discomfort over Butch and Randy being so tight. Add in Alexei, with his silky, seductive tales of untold riches and future backing for things Ambrose would very much like to look into, even though he should absolutely know better by now.

Know what? Not to trust Alexei? What about Miss Dover, Maxim, Jessica when she was with Mignon/Margarite? Alexei can be an asshole, yes, but how can you trust anybody? Bennie'll wonder the same thing pretty soon, and it pains him that she'll have to. It makes him sick to think about, so he focuses on billboards to distract himself. Somewhere in the middle of the night, he jerks the wheel, realizing he was about to fall asleep and had better stop somewhere.

Lev's still snoring, and Ambrose pulls into a motel and pays cash to lie flat on a bed for a couple of hours. Lev crawls in the back of the cab, and the snoring continues. The back of the truck is locked. Ambrose realizes he's not thinking too clearly. Not a good way to be, pulling into Miami with a shit-ton of opium and intent to distribute. He was almost this tired the night he and Randy dumped that body in Lake Tahoe. There's been something else disconcerting about Randy, but can't think what right now. That weird conversation. *Who pissed in his cereal?* It's like he knew things. Clean bug-sweep, though.

Fuck him. He's crazy.

Ambrose pulls the spread off the bed and falls onto the sheets, down for the count.

✳✳✳

Having picked up their trail in Gainesville, Randy sits in a rental car in the back corner of a cheap motel somewhere outside Leesburg, staring at the parked truck. Ambrose went into the motel room alone, so where's that big, hairy ape? Randy sinks into the seat, considers getting out the binoculars, but peering through binoculars wouldn't reveal anything. The tracking device is doing its thing, so nothing left but wait and see. Déjà vu. It was through watching the hairy guy's comings and goings to and from Arcadia that Randy found the delivery truck. Wearing a hoodie over a black baseball cap and scarf to obscure his face, heart in his throat, he placed it under the fender by the right front tire and hauled ass.

While this is all valuable experience, he realizes that, if he already had a license, much of the shit he's been pulling lately could get that taken away in an instant and he'd still be nothing more than a snoop. But it's for Butch, who's worried about his brother, and for Bennie's sake. She trusts Ambrose and has no idea what all he's into. And Jessica. . . Jesus, poor Jessica.

Randy quietly walks around to the back, pretending to look for something in the trunk while he takes a piss. There's a small sign on a light pole near the back fence that says, **Property under surveillance**, but this is a rather sketchy motel. He hasn't seen any cameras, not even earlier with binoculars. He strolls closer to the truck. No one visible in the cab. Ambrose's traveling companion must be in the sleeper, behind the seats. Randy takes a step nearer, then hears the door unlock, and hightails it to the car.

Momentarily, he sees the big, hairy guy get out. He appears to be taking a piss next to the truck, leaning against it with one hand before he zips up and climbs back into the cab, jarring Randy out of his pre-dawn reveries about the old him and shit he used to pull—*used to*. How far he's come and how stuck he still is at the same time. Same regarding Ambrose, for that matter. He's come so far. No longer a nickel-and-dime dealer hanging from the edge of a pier, but still slinging for somebody, even though he's got everything. Risking it all to get a little more. Why? And why does Randy feel like he and Ambrose are still in the same boat, different pond?

Need coffee and cigarettes. A toothbrush and a shower. Bet Ambrose would shit a hot brick if Randy showed up at the door of that motel room to avail himself of the facilities. But revealing himself is not an option. Not yet anyway. *My God, Bennie. I love you. Why do you trust him and not me with the truth, when I'd die for you?* His mom knows about Bennie's cancer. Can he afford to take comfort in the fact that, in addition to Ambrose, she confided in his mom and not her own. He thinks back to a time when he trusted his mother, when she was his fiercest and most vocal protector.

He rubs his eyes, looks at his watch. **2:15 AM**. There's a convenience store right around the block. All quiet here for now. He drives out of the parking lot, gets the coffee and smokes. When he returns, all's still quiet and another 45 minutes before the door to the motel room opens and Ambrose walks out, heading for the truck, carrying a knapsack. He climbs into the driver's seat, cranks up.

And this caravan of lost souls lumbers south.

***

Still early morning when Ambrose and Lev roll into Miami and find the address in Coral Gables. Ambrose drives the truck through a back gate designated for deliveries and even the backstage view of this Mediterranean mansion with stucco walls and a red tile roof is impressive itself, with lush grounds landscaped to within an inch of their life, surrounded by palm trees. He drives the truck into an empty garage, waved in by an elderly yard man who approaches when he gets out. "*Hola*," he greets. "You are Ambrose, no?"

"I am. And you are?"

"Abraham," the man says, shaking his hand. "Go upstairs and rest a bit. Shower if you wish. There's food in the refrigerator. I'll be back soon."

"Thank you."

Lev rolls out of the cab, stumbles up the stairs. By the time Ambrose makes it up to the sunny little apartment, Lev is already passed out in one of the twin beds, snoring. Ambrose showers, standing under the hot water, letting it massage his head, the back of his neck and shoulders, loosening the tension. He eats one of the Cuban sandwiches and a few bites of cut-up fruit from the kitchenette. He's been running on coffee and cigarettes for so long that coming in for this cushy landing is a pleasant surprise, though he doesn't want to get lulled into a false sense of security. He changes clothes, wishing he'd brought something more appropriate for this tony setting.

Still jeans, a plain white T-shirt and old boots, but at least he's wearing clean underwear. Same stale flannel. Should've brought the black blazer. The day keeps getting hotter but at least that would've given him a sense of authority.

Abraham returns in about an hour. He leaves Lev lying in bed. As Abraham guides him over to the main house, Ambrose glances back at the garage. No armed guards this time, no unloading of equipment, but, now that they're here, Ambrose's job is done anyway. After this meeting with the customer, he'll book a flight back to San Francisco and Lev's on his own. Meantime, however, Ambrose feels like he's watching himself walk into this Florida dreamhouse, determined to walk out. The polished-nickel .38 pistol is tucked into the back waistband of his jeans. Abraham makes no move to search for or confiscate anything. It's like he really is just the gardener.

Ambrose walks across the Spanish tile floor in the wide hallway, through double doors into a large, wood-paneled room with a brick-and-tile fireplace, expensive artwork on the walls, floor-to ceiling windows with a view of a formal garden beyond. Above is a metal chandelier that looks like it was pilfered from some Moorish palace. Bright sun illuminates the gleaming floor. At one end of the room is a baroque desk with a high-backed leather desk chair facing the wall.

He flashes on Alexei's office back in the old ballroom. This is different, but. . . He hears the doors *click* shut with a faint echo, turns and Abraham is gone, but Ambrose has the feeling he's not alone. Someone's sitting in the desk chair, but he can't see who. He slowly walks up to the desk, conscious of his own footsteps. Whoever this is knows he's here. Cinnabar foo dogs on either end of the mantel stare at him. Ambrose clears his throat.

The person in the chair doesn't move.

Any tension washed away in the shower creeps back into his neck and shoulders and he grows hyperconscious of the gun wedged into the back of his jeans. Can't afford to be slow on the draw if this is a set-up, but, if that's the case, he's doomed anyway. The money coming to him from all this seems like a remote illusion, as does everything that makes up his life back on the west coast. In his near-exhausted state, he's not sure where he is nor how he got here, feeling suspended like a fly in amber. Whatever's happening here, he wants it over with. Sleep or death will follow. "Excuse me," he says. "I take it Abraham informed you the delivery's arrived from San Francisco. We'd like to get unloaded and be on our way as soon as possible, so, if you'll tell us where to leave the caviar shipment, we'll get on that straightaway."

Nothing.

"I have word from Mr. Rusovich the transaction is pending, so if you or anyone here would like to inspect the shipment before that goes through, please feel free. Mr. Rusovich guarantees satisfaction."

The leather desk chair slowly turns and he finds himself staring into the face of the woman he last saw outside the macaron shop in Paris: Phoebe Grace, aka Miss Dover.

Her new look is all soft neutrals with a few hard edges. The beige cashmere sweater with a cowl neck collar, white and beige boucle skirt. Sky-high heels. The straight-edge cut of the radically straight, long, blonde hair, the claw-sharp fingernails encrusted with diamonds or at least high-end crystals.

He laughs from the shock, but it comes out more like an exasperated sigh. That exalted, other-worldly feeling he had after dumping the body at Tahoe engulfs him. "I'll be damned. We meet again."

"I've been racked with guilt ever since the last time we met," she says, tears starting behind her stylish glasses. "And after all my warnings about that man, you come in here like his robot errand boy, talking about unloading contraband for that motherfucker?"

"I said we have your caviar shipment. I'm the delivery man, not anybody's errand boy."

She stands, walking around to the front of the desk. "I took this dive to get him off all our backs. I left you a business so you wouldn't ever have to be out on the street again, and this is what you do with that opportunity? I thought you'd learned your lesson."

"I've learned some things, all right."

She walks closer to him, eyes narrowing.

He gets the feeling Phoebe Grace won't slap him like Miss Dover would. Anyway, he's in no mood to be slapped.

"You feel betrayed, is that it?"

"It's not just a feeling. Guess I was stupid enough to believe everything you told me. I might've even damned my soul for you, whoever you are."

She looks at him closely and for the first time he realizes what else is different about her. She's wearing lighter contacts. *"Damned your soul?* You did no such thing."

He wishes he hadn't said that. It wasn't murder, it was self-defense. *It was him or me. Had to be. At least I think so. I don't know anymore.* This is no time for that unraveling feeling to hit, but then again, maybe this is the perfect time. End of the road.

Phoebe Grace steps closer. "You killed for me, is that what you're saying?"

"I didn't say that." He'd forgotten what it's like being near her, how much he'd missed her before he knew what she'd done. "But you don't know what it did to me when I thought they'd killed you." Like up at Tahoe, he's held it together enough to complete a Herculean task and, once again, seeing tracers, starting to crumble right at the end, but not before completion.

She picks up the phone off the desk and opens an app, showing him the screen. It's Alexei's glass house. Still morning on the west coast, rays of sun glancing across the waves. "At least if I'm damned, it's for killing the right one." And just like that, the house explodes into smithereens, a fiery conflagration of glass and metal flares, glinting in the golden light before collapsing into the rocky cliff.

He grabs the phone from her, a lump rising in his throat big enough to be a choking hazard, the bubble of denial he's inhabited for the last several months starting to spin. "That's a fake," he says into the void. "Who'd you pay to make this video?"

"Video?"

"What program did you use?" The pain in his throat makes it hard to speak. "Not that I give a damn."

"We had to destroy him before he destroyed you."

"Who is 'we'?"

A door opens at the other end of the room.

Ambrose turns to the dim silhouette of a man in a suit. Double-breasted, he can see the glint of brass buttons. Reluctant to turn his back on Phoebe Grace or the phantom in the doorway, Ambrose turns sideways, backing up so he can see keep an eye on them. "Are you the guy who placed the order?" Ambrose asks the phantom. "Or did she? 'Cause I just made one hell of a trip to get it here and I want some guarantee of payment."

"If I wasn't sure if this was the right thing to do before, I'm sure now," Phoebe Grace says. "It had to be done."

The phantom in the doorway steps back into the adjoining room. Before the door closes, Ambrose catches a glimpse. White hair and thick-framed glasses as he turns to shut the door.

Ambrose flashes on the photos Miss Dover used to have in her office, the ones with her fairy-godfather and friends of the international set. Another one of Alexei's old enemies and vice versa.

Ambrose realizes he's caught between warring factions whose feud has far outlived its usefulness.

Sick to his stomach, dizzy and confused, he hasn't really had this sensation since that day he got beaten up by two of Lang's flunkies, then limped over to Golden Gate Park on his old motorcycle, sat on a bench, cried, and called Bennie to see if the offer still stood to stay at her sister's guesthouse. Even the night he'd had to dispose of Dimitri's body, he'd had a focus, a mission to accomplish before passing out from exhaustion. Now the mission is in limbo. Aborted. Water muddied.

"At least you won't get blamed for this awful explosion out on the west coast," Phoebe says, walking back to the desk and sitting down in the chair. She tries to appear calm, but he gets the feeling she's play-acting, that something about this hasn't exactly gone the way she wants. "You're nowhere near the scene."

As he takes the pistol out of his waistband and starts toward the desk, he hears the door at the other end of the room open again, and the racking of a weapon, from somewhere. The phantom's not holding a gun, but someone hiding in here is. In case Ambrose felt like killing her? But even if he didn't know that killing her would mean bleeding out on this beautiful floor, he was never going to do it.

"Pretty fucked you're so worried about me being under Alexei's thumb when it looks like you've got a Svengali of your own pulling the strings. I believe this is yours." He lays the gun in front of her on the desk. "I never want to see or hear from you again." He turns and walks out of the room, denying himself the satisfaction of registering her reaction in favor of showing her the freezing-cold indifference he wants her to feel. He closes the door behind him, then he's back into the bright sunlight, fighting the urge to stop and throw up the Cuban sandwich churning in his gut.

Lev is probably still sleeping in that room over the garage. No sign of Abraham anywhere. Maybe that was him Ambrose heard racking a gun. That makes perfect sense.

How best to find out if Alexei's house is really gone, or if that was some hoax just to rattle him, get him back in line. He takes out his phone, thinking to have Maxim take a drive out for a look, then he remembers to tap on the SF local news app and, sure enough, **Breaking: An Explosion. Details to follow as they become available**. So, what now? He looks up. Palm trees everywhere, but not his palms. Sunshine everywhere, but not his California sun. Still clutching his phone, he walks to the closed gate at the end of the driveway, overcome with a desire to go home.

But the money. . .

Fuck the money.

He tries the gate, but it's locked. He stares through the bars, then looks up, trying to gauge whether he's up for a hard climb, before remembering to look for a box with a sensor that'll open it. Sure enough, there it is on a thin pole a few feet from the driveway. He walks up to it and presses a yellow button. The gate slowly swings open. He walks out to the curb and sinks down onto the concrete.

✳✳✳

After all the soul-crushing, ass-deadening hours of riding, waiting, and watching, Randy finally sees Ambrose walk out of the delivery entrance to that piece of real estate priced to rival any parcel in Silicon Valley. Having melted onto the curb, Ambrose looks sick, sitting there slumped over, clutching his phone. There doesn't seem to be anyone else around. This is what counts for a back alley in these parts more manicured than the main drags of most neighborhoods. Trash carts lined up with metric precision, no junk, no litter, not even a candy wrapper.

Whatever mission Ambrose and his traveling companion were on, whatever fallout must've occurred, it appears to be over. Randy hasn't been in touch with Butch since yesterday, and whatever Butch might've thought Randy could do to prevent whatever might happen, Randy's been nothing but an observer.

'Til now.

He slowly gets out of the car and starts walking toward Ambrose. For the first time in a long time, Ambrose looks like the gutterpunk he used to be and nothing like the dandy he's become. He actually looks kind of. . . pitiful. "Hey."

Ambrose looks up, with a faint smile. "Randall," he says softly. "What're you doing here?"

"I could ask you the same thing." Randy glances around, wondering if they're being watched. If some homicidal kingpin or cranky property owner might walk out and take aim at them with a .357 Magnum or chase them away with a tennis racket and call the cops. Everything is so quiet. Randy figures he himself must be delirious by now or he wouldn't be out here, talking to his subject of scrutiny. His rival, brother-in-law, and best man.

His fellow fuck-up.

✳✳✳

Phoebe Grace watches through the window as Abraham places the **For Sale** sign back on the front lawn.

Sergei approaches. "The meeting didn't go exactly as you'd hoped," he says.

"No, it didn't."

"What was your hope for this—reunion?"

"To make up with him. Didn't happen. What are you going to do with their shipment?"

"It's being taken care of. The caviar will find a home and the opium will be sold to the highest bidder. There'll be enough for us to spend some time in Fiji, perhaps. After your fashion show." He nears. "I had Abraham give Alexei's stooge enough money to return to California." He smiles. "Perhaps Alexei remembered him in his will."

She'd held it together in the presence of Ambrose, but now that he's gone, likely forever, she's still reeling from seeing that explosion. Ambrose thought it was fake, and she'd tried to convince herself that it was for the best. An era that needed to end for better things to emerge. There was a time when she was Ambrose's mentor, and to be replaced by Alexei, of all people, and seeing Ambrose do Alexei's bidding, had nearly choked her. She hadn't saved Ambrose nor herself by faking her death to escape the past. All it had done was relegate them both to the dark side. She'd become Ambrose's worst enemy and made her enemy his friend.

She can feel Sergei looking at her, what he's about to ask. "Tell me, my dear, have you considered my proposal any further?"

"Yes."

"And?"

"It'll be in name only. I'm not feeling very warm and fuzzy these days." She turns to him.

He's smiling, unruffled by her pronouncement. "I understand. It's for companionship."

She doesn't need him for protection anymore. He told her he'd lost his taste for murder, but he's mean as ever, the vindictive old bastard. Come out of retirement just for her. Whacking Alexei and leaving his corpse at her doorstep like a cat leaving a dead bird as present. He'd mentioned Alexei's will. Wonder if Sergei will be changing his own will to provide for his new wife. His companion, eventual caretaker, and only living relative. Of course he will. She'll make sure of it. She can manage enough warmth and fuzziness for that. "You're sure they can't trace that explosion back to you?"

"What's to trace? A propane tank malfunction. These things have been known to happen. It's most unfortunate."

She gazes out at the green expanse, at the shadows cast by the palm fronds swaying in the breeze. Then, thinking more about what happened with Ambrose than any sabotage performed by Sergei's small cadre of loyalists: how Ambrose had looked at her, told her he never wanted to see her again. How he'd left the gun on the desk, walked out and shut the door forever on their friendship.

"Most unfortunate." Sergei reaches into his coat pocket, takes out a light blue box and opens it for her. It's a platinum engagement ring, at least four carats. Such a big diamond. Small consolation for the loss of a friend.

"But," she has to acknowledge, gazing into its fire, "life does go on."

✳✳✳

Sequestered at a motel in the city while Randy's tracking Ambrose, Butch alternatively paces the floor, goes outside to smoke cigarettes or stares at the TV, feeling useless. Last he heard from Randy, there were closing in on South Florida, and since then, Randy might've had his hands full staying off Ambrose's and that Russian guy's radar. This was bat-shit crazy, dispatching Randy after them, but then Randy was crazy enough to be down for it. The only thing crazier is that Ambrose is even doing this God-awful thing in the first place.

He thinks back to that night he had dinner with Randy and Bennie and how Bennie was the one who told him how Randy could've arrested Ambrose that fateful night they met but let him go. Let him go. Ambrose had done well with that second chance, but somewhere, somehow, things went awry. And Butch feels solely responsible. He falls asleep watching a movie in bed and is awakened by his phone ringing on the nightstand. He fumbles around to answer it, expecting it to be Randy but it's Mary-Ann. "Well, hello there."

"Good morning, you." It's so good to hear her voice.

He sits up straighter, propping himself on the pillows. "How're things on the sunny coast of Spain?"

"Not too shabby. How are things there?"

"Okay, I guess. You and Mr. Bob still loving life there?"

"This is a beautiful place," she says. "And Bob's—well, he's been different lately."

"Different how?"

"Not terribly different but. . . something. Maybe he's just learning how to let loose."

Butch smiles. "Let loose?"

"I think he's actually been enjoying himself."

"I imagine what he really enjoys is being with you." A pause. "Don't you think so?"

"I guess. He said something funny when he saw me texting the grandkids the other day."

"Funny *ha-ha*, or funny *weird*?"

"Funny weird. Sort of."

"What'd he say?"

"Something like, 'Are you texting your boyfriend?'"

Butch settles further into the pillows. "Mmhm. And what did you say?"

"I said no, of course."

"Well, there ya go."

"But. . . You don't really think he knows. About everything. Do you?"

Butch sighs. When it rains, it pours. "Did he sound mad, or—"

"No, quite the opposite."

"Then I don't think I'd worry about it."

"Really?"

Butch rolls over, hugging the pillow into a ball, still clutching the phone to his ear. She's seeking reassurance and there's no reason not to let her have it. Sounds like something Mr. Bob would say, just kidding her. And even if he does know, there's nothing Butch nor Mary-Ann can do about it. "Am I your boyfriend, Mary-Ann?"

Silence, but such lush silence that he can feel her lying in the Mallorca sun, gleaming with expensive tanning oil, smelling of coconut and patchouli, her hair maybe swept up off her neck, damp with sweat.

"Yes." He can almost feel her blushing through the tan. "Does it bother you that I feel that way?"

"Hell, no. I'm glad you do."

He hears an awkward laugh on her end. "But back to your question, I don't know what Mr. Bob knows or doesn't. You and him are having a good time over there, that's all that matters."

"Oh, Butch." He can hear emotion creeping into her voice. "How are you really doing? I hope you haven't been working too hard."

"Nah." He rolls over on his back again. "What kind of bathing suit are you wearing, if you don't mind my asking?"

"How did you know I'm wearing a bathing suit?"

"What else would you be wearing?"

"It's a one-piece. Dark brown. Kind of plain."

"I'm sure there's nothing plain about it." He thinks of that diamond solitaire necklace she was wearing the evening of the garden party. That diamond, resting between her breasts while she's all oiled and scented. He unzips his pants. "Where y'all going tonight?"

"Early dinner. Maybe a walk on the beach."

"That sounds romantic. What else?"

"What else?"

"What do you plan on wearing?" he asks. So hard right now. "Tell me everything, so I can imagine you taking it all off."

SIXTEEN

Ambrose wakes with a start, still wearing a seatbelt. For a moment he wonders if he fell asleep driving and somehow rolled to a stop, but he wasn't driving, this isn't the truck, and there's no Lev, only the Atlantic, straight ahead. He sits still, starting to remember the surreal scene that took place in the room of that Coral Gables mansion. The shock of seeing Miss Dover/Phoebe Grace, and that white-haired guy who stayed in the shadows like a stage manager.

The haul to Miami had been a hoax, with Phoebe Grace and the man in the double-breasted suit trying to kill two birds with one stone: her trying to make up with Ambrose and him dealing Alexei a death blow all at the same time. That old guy doesn't know Ambrose from Adam, but if he could convince Phoebe that snuffing Alexei once and for all was in her best interest *and* that of the mixed-up young man who he's sick of hearing her obsess about. . . She said she'd been racked with guilt, but so what?

So, this was all for nothing. Ambrose left the truck, the drugs, and Lev behind. If Alexei really is dead, Lev's out of a job. Maybe the white-haired man will hire him. Ambrose rubs his face, remembering that somehow *Randy* showed up in all this. Ambrose takes a deep breath, smelling the salty air. The Randy part must've been a dream. No way that could've happened. He unsnaps the seat belt.

Then whose car is this? He looks around at the disposable coffee cups and junk food wrappers on the floorboard. Randy's brand of cigarettes in the console. His watch. A weathered Giants baseball cap laying on the driver's seat. Ambrose gazes out at the beach. It's not too crowded, just a few swimmers and sunbaskers. Randy's out there, bathing in the surf.

Ambrose gets out of the car, walks the beach. He sinks onto the sand and draws his knees up to his chest. Forgot to look at his phone. It's in the car. There's no way he could talk to Jessica right now, no way he could dodge questions or make up stuff that's happened at the fake conference he's supposed to be attending in Rapid City. No way he'd want to talk to Butch either.

Ambrose looks up as Randy approaches, dripping wet. Now that he's up close, Ambrose can see he's wearing boxers that could pass for swim trunks, but the brand is emblazoned around the waistband in capital letters.

He grabs his shorts and T-shirt, tosses them on the ground and plops down. "Fuck it," he says, "Had to take a dip. I was filthy."

Ambrose's mind races, spiraling, while Randy sits still for a moment, staring at the waves.

"How did you know I was here?" Ambrose asks, finally.

"I'm psychic," Randy answers.

"Did Butch put you up to this?"

Randy focuses on the waves. "Nobody put me up to it. I was just curious. You know what a nosy bastard I can be."

"Nosy enough to follow me across the entire continental United States? You're that nosy?"

"Yep." Randy wipes droplets off his face with his T-shirt.

"It was Butch, wasn't it?"

Randy slips on the shirt. "Let's just say it was somebody who. . ." Looks like he's searching for the word, then throws up his hands. "Who *loves* you, okay?"

Without thinking, on so little sleep, Ambrose takes a blind stab at the answer. "Bennie?"

Thoroughly disgusted, Randy shoves Ambrose's shoulder hard, knocking him back on the sand. "*No*, it was not Bennie, you stupid son-of-a-bitch."

"I just meant—"

"Shut up!" Randy's bloodshot eyes remind Ambrose he's on no sleep too, haggard, nerves frayed. "Look, we're dropping off that piece-of-shit car at the airport, flying back and then you're on your own. And I put those tickets on my card, so you owe me for yours, motherfucker. It's bad enough I'm not there with Bennie now."

"What do you mean, 'It's bad enough' you're not there?"

"I've just got to get back to her, that's all." Randy's voice sounds like he really is at the end of rope before going into meltdown.

"You know, don't you?"

Randy busies himself shaking the sand out of his shorts. "Know about what?"

"Never mind."

Randy gets up, steps into the shorts and looks out at the Atlantic. "Yeah, I know about Bennie's cancer."

"She told you?"

"I told you, I'm fucking psychic."

Ambrose lies back on the sand, a headache coming on. He covers his face with his hands against the sun. Left his sunglasses in the delivery truck. Nice ones, too. Damn.

Randy nudges with his foot. "Hey."

Ambrose keeps his eyes closed.

"You got a gun or anything we need to get rid of?"

"No. You can tell Butch I didn't kill anybody."

"Told me that once and you lied, remember?"

"I'm telling the truth." She was already dead anyway. "Dead to me," Ambrose mumbles.

"What?"

Ambrose opens his eyes, not meaning to look up the leg of Randy's shorts. Strange, feeling so stoned while sober. "I see your junk."

Randy reaches down, grabs Ambrose by his shirt and pulls him back up to a sitting position. "You know, if I could go back in time, I'd arrest you that first night I ever laid eyes on you, for your own good." He releases the shirt. "I was pretty fucked up back then but, if I'd been on my game, bet I could've come up with a million reasons to keep you in jail."

"So, you'd be a better dirty cop?"

"Not dirty, just smarter."

"Well, it's all over now, so it doesn't matter."

"It is not over," Randy informs him. "You came all this way to commit God-knows how many felonies so, if I would've run you in that night, maybe you would've learned something."

Ambrose stands, brushing sand off the seat of his pants. "You're not the one to teach me. Stop talking like I'm a goddamn three-year-old."

"Your three-year-old stepson's smarter than you, and, speaking of that, have you forgotten you have a pregnant wife at home? Maybe you'd better take care of her and leave my wife the fuck alone."

"You watched me take care of my wife that night you stood outside and recorded us having sex, so maybe you learned something about taking care of your wife. You're welcome."

Flushed with anger, Randy throws a punch.

But Ambrose jumps back and Randy drops, grabbing him around the ankles.

Ambrose falls to the ground.

Randy's next punch lands.

Ambrose manages to get in a punch before they roll, getting covered in sand, wrestling like two scrappy kids before Randy somehow pins him, breathing hard.

Someone yells and, when Randy looks up, squinting in the sun, Ambrose grabs him by the neck, rolling over on him.

"Get *off* me, you cock-sucking bastard," Randy chokes out.

"Hey, everything all right over there?" some buffed-out guy in a Speedo inquires.

"Everything's okay," Ambrose calls back.

"I said, get off me," Randy commands, shoving Ambrose.

Ambrose goes limp, spent. Not much of a fight but it took everything out of him. They both sit still, catching their breath.

Finally, Randy stands up. "Shit, I've got a plane to catch." He heads for the steps to the parking area, Ambrose trailing. Randy gets to the top of the steps, still brushing off sand. "Goddamnit, I gotta go rinse off again 'cause of you." Randy heads back down the steps and starts for the water. "Nothing like sitting on a plane for five hours with sand in the crack of your ass."

Ambrose's nose is mostly numb from the punch but beginning to ache. He wipes it with his fingertips. No blood.

They get odd looks walking through the airport and from the flight attendants, too. Can't wash away the bush-league injuries from that ridiculous beach skirmish: Ambrose's swelling nose and Randy's blackening eye. Grim, bruised and bedraggled, they look like wanted criminals. No first-class seats this time, just crammed into coach. Ambrose tries to sleep but can't, and Randy constantly fidgets before finally drifting off, his head drooping over onto Ambrose's shoulder.

Ambrose requests a pillow from the flight attendant and passes it to Randy. Like on the flight to Paris, not knowing what was facing him there, he thinks of this time high in the air, unreachable, as a respite from the shit-show awaiting upon landing. All the loose ends and lies he'll have to secure and maintain. And if Alexei is dead. . . Another strange kind of grief to wade through. He settles back, closes his eyes. Randy's light snoring would normally drive him up a wall but, in the moment, it's oddly reassuring, given everything that's happened in the last 24 hours.

He recalls the response his grandpa back in Riviera used to give when asked how things were going. "Just another day in paradise."

Another day in paradise, indeed.

✳✳✳

Linda was with Bennie when she got the results of her scan, and she'll be there tomorrow for the lumpectomy. Apparently, so will Jessica. Bennie found out when Jessica called and confronted her that Ambrose had spilled the beans before going on his trip. Bennie doesn't really have the energy to be angry. She asked a lot of him. The jig is almost up anyway. When Randy gets back, she'll have to sit down and tell him. She'll make up for that news with the news that she's quitting Arcadia to stay home for a while, be with him to help him start his business. After these last couple days, she realizes that, in keeping this from him, she'd missed the fact that they could be stronger together. If he'll forgive her for keeping this secret so long, whether anyone else does or not.

She hopes the phone confrontation with Jessica is no indication of how Randy will react. After finding out the procedure is tomorrow, Jessica sounds pissed that Bennie hadn't asked her to go. "I figured you were busy."

"Too busy for something like this?" Then: "Look, I'm glad you have a good relationship with Randy's mom but it's not like you don't have our mother and me to turn to. We're family, you know. *Your* family?"

A sigh at the other end of the line.

"But you do what feels best for you."

And so, she does. Linda goes with her to the hospital to get checked in, waits through all the pre-tests and fluffs Bennie's pillow, while Bennie waits to go into the operating room.

"I really wish you'd go get something to eat," Bennie tells her. "I'll be fine. It's not like I'm going anywhere."

"I'll go get something from the cafeteria in a little while." Linda picks up a newspaper, then sits down in the recliner near the bed.

"I know this has been a lot on you. I'm really grateful for everything you're doing for me."

Linda looks up with a puzzled expression. "What do you mean 'been a lot on' me? What else would I do? You're family."

"I know, but—"

"But what?" Linda still gazes at the paper through those retro, white-framed glasses perched on the bridge of her nose, using the close-reading part of the bifocals. "There ain't no 'but,' dawlin'."

Bennie, smiles, sinking further into her pillows, finally starting to relax when there's a tap at the door and Jessica walks in, all smiles and sunshine, followed by Pamela, who isn't.

She does look concerned, though. "Bennie, darling!" Pamela comes over to the bed and hugs her. "Why didn't you tell us what was going on with you? How are you doing?"

"I'm fine. Better when this is over."

"I told Mom you wouldn't be here long, but she insisted on bringing an overnight bag," Jessica says by way of warning her that Pamela wants to stay with her. Or says she does, or feels she ought to.

"You don't have to do that, Mother, I'm going home this afternoon."

"Honey, it's no trouble at all. Why, I'll just take you home with me!" She stops, just noticing Linda.

"Hello," Linda says and, before she has to introduce herself, Bennie jumps in.

"Mother and Jessica, this is Randy's mom, Linda. She came up from Gilroy. Linda, this is my mother, Pamela, and my sister, Jessica."

"Oh, yeah," Linda says with a bright smile. "I saw your pictures on her phone, from the wedding. You all looked beautiful; it's pleasure to meet you both."

"Randy's mom!" Jessica exclaims, going over to hug her. "Your son's a great guy. I'm very proud to be his sister-in-law. Thank you for everything you're doing for Bennie."

"You don't have to thank me. Gives me a chance to get to know my new daughter-in-law better. I can see why Randy fell head-over-heels in love with her, she's the best thing that ever happened to him." She looks at Pamela. "You have such charming daughters," she says. "I hope you and I can get together for lunch sometime, I mean, what with our kids being married and all."

"Yes," Pamela says. "We'll have to get together one of these days." To Jessica: "I'm going downstairs to get some coffee. Want to come along?"

"Sure. We'll be back in just a few minutes, okay?" Jessica turns back to Linda as Pamela heads for the door. "It was wonderful meeting you, Mrs.—Linda."

"Same here, sweetheart," Linda says, watching as they go out.

Once they're gone Bennie turns to Linda. "I'm sorry," she says.

"Sorry for what?"

"That my mother's so rude."

"Aw, your mom doesn't even know me yet. Think she's upset I'm here? Sounds like she came to stay with you."

Bennie sinks back into her pillows.

"Was she against you and Randy getting married?"

"She doesn't agree with most of the choices I make. I've never done anything like she wanted me to." She looks over at Linda. "Randy's so lucky to have you."

"He wouldn't agree."

"He's just working through some things." She misses Randy terribly but, for now, Linda's here. Randy's closest blood relation. "Can I call you 'Mom,' sometimes?" she asks.

Linda's eyes well with tears. She takes Bennie's hand in hers. "Anytime, sweetheart."

***

Bennie wakes up. Must've been dreaming but already can't remember about what. It's absorbed by the cool hospital room glow. She turns toward the window and sees daylight through a thin break in the curtains, then an image of Randy by the bed, gazing at her. He looks different somehow, anxious beyond words and, while the vision is welcome, it's also jarring: the manifestation of her guilt for hiding this from him. The image moves closer and it's not blaming or sorrowful or accusatory. She reaches a hand toward it, expecting the image to disappear, but it doesn't.

"Hey," it says, grasping her hand and kissing it.

"Hey. . ." A flood of emotion coursing through her body forces tears from her eyes. "Is this you?"

"It's me all right." He gently embraces her.

His arms feel strong and being held like this again must have healing properties because the joy in her heart radiates like a supernova, dispelling all fear because Randy's home!

"I missed you," he whispers.

"I missed you, too. Guess I have some explaining to do," she says, because even though the happiness glows, the faulty physical her is still in the material world surrounded by hospital.

"You don't have to explain anything."

She can see the truth. "Someone's already done it, haven't they?"

He smiles. "Maybe I'm just psychic."

"Maybe." She touches his face, her mind and vision getting clearer. "What happened to your eye? You got hurt?"

"It's minor."

"You didn't have an accident on the way home from Big Sur?"

"Nothing like that."

"Did you get in a fight?"

"Nah, don't worry about it."

"You look so tired."

"I'm all right." He lays her back on the pillows.

She reaches up to touch his face and he kisses her hand again. She waits to see if he'll kiss her. If he means it, if he's not deep down furious with her.

And then he does kiss her.

Sweetest homecoming kiss *ever.*

✳✳✳

Ambrose watches them through the window. It's a sweet scene all right. They're beautiful in there together but something about it makes him sad. It hurts to look but he can't turn away.

After a few moments, they stop kissing and then they're talking to each other, close. A nurse walks into the room. She smiles at them, saying something as she pulls the curtain around the bed and Ambrose turns away at last. He walks toward some chairs near the end of the hallway and sits down, head in his hands. Anyone would think he's on the brink of despair, but it's not that—just confusion. He hears someone walking this way, looks up and sees a woman approaching Bennie's room. She sees the curtain closed and pauses, like she's unsure whether to proceed.

Ambrose stands. "Are you here to see Bennie?"

She walks closer, points at him, smiles. "You look familiar."

"I do?"

"I've seen your picture. You were Randy's best man at his wedding, right? You're Ambrose. Married to Bennie's sister."

"Are you Randy's mom?"

"Please, call me Linda. You were my son's best man and we've never even met. But give me a hug."

The thought of someone hugging him doesn't appeal, more for Mrs. Burke's sake than his because he feels covered in miles, sand, and coach cabin air. Nevertheless, he allows her to hug him.

"I met Jessica earlier," she tells him. "What a pretty lady. Nice, too. You and Randy both lucked out!" Her smile fades as she looks at him closer. "What happened to your nose? You get hurt?"

"Tripped on some stairs. It was the craziest thing. I'm all right though."

She gives him a knowing look. "Sure you weren't in some brawl?"

He laughs. "No brawl."

She turns to look through the window again. "You know who's in there with Bennie? Is it a nurse?"

"And Randy's in there with her."

"You're kidding me. I thought he was—" She glances at the door again, fighting an impulse to go in. "How is he? Never mind; I'll see for myself soon enough, right?" She paces back to look through the window, but the curtain is still closed. "'Course, I'm probably the last person in the world he wants to see. Maybe it's good I went down to the vending machines." She sets her large purse on a nearby chair, looks inside and takes out two bags of chips. "Want a snack?"

"No, thanks. You go right ahead."

She's about to open a bag but drops it back in her purse, returning to look in the window as the nurse pulls back the curtain partway, giving Bennie and Randy some privacy. The nurse walks out of the room, and heads back up the hallway.

Ambrose sits, feeling compelled to make polite conversation but he has nothing to say, so he casts his gaze to the floor.

Linda walks back over to him.

He tries to arrange a more pleasant expression.

"Are you sure you're okay?" she asks.

"I'm fine."

She looks through the window again. "Want to get something to eat?" she asks. "Let's you and me get a fast bite—my treat."

✳✳✳

Ambrose hadn't wanted to go anywhere but, like her son, Linda Burke has an intensity that's hard to resist. She doesn't really look old enough to be Randy's mother, nor have kids even older than Randy. And she's hyper-alert like not much gets past her, unlike his mother, who didn't know and didn't want to know what was happening with him and Butch.

"What do you do for a living, Ambrose?" she asks, after the first bite of her California burrito. They're sitting in a booth at a taqueria a few minutes from the hospital.

"I'm in the hospitality industry," he tells her. "I run a bed & breakfast."

"You don't strike me as an innkeeper." She studies him as he dips some green salsa onto his quesadilla. "Where's this bed & breakfast?"

"Used to be in the Sunset District but the property got sold so we moved to Noe Valley."

She slices into the burrito again. "Who is 'we'?"

"My partners," he says, thinking of Rajit and Terrence.

"So, how'd you meet Bennie's sister?"

"Bennie introduced us. She and I worked together. I was between apartments, so Jessica let me come stay at her guesthouse and we hit it off." No need to mention Jessica was already married then.

"Lucky you. She's a beautiful girl."

"She is." He can feel something else coming.

"Did you and Bennie ever date before you got with her?"

"No, we never dated," he answers between sips of prickly pear iced tea. "Why do you ask?"

She shrugs. "You just seem close. You look out for her, don't you?"

"I care about her a lot."

"Am I'm being nosy? I don't mean to be."

". . .No." He glances up at her, but she's not looking at him, not looking at anything.

"Used to get on Randy's nerves when I asked so many questions. He'd call me 'the quizmaster' and go to his room or leave the house. Hang up the phone. Then when I realized he was lying to me most of the time anyway, I stopped askin'. Shoulda never stopped though. Even if it did piss him off. That's a mother's job sometimes. Being a pain in the ass. You talk to your mom a lot?'

"No, ma'am. She's back in Texas. Into her own stuff."

She sets down her fork, pushes her plate away. "I'll get a take-out box for this. I'm going to the ladies' room, then I'll come back and order Randy something to go. You'll give it to him, won't you? In case he won't talk to me?"

"I would but I think he'll talk to you, Mrs. Burke."

"From your lips to God's ears." She places her hand on his for a moment and he notices her blue nail polish. "Call me Linda."

"Okay. Linda."

She stands and starts toward the restrooms. He watches her go. She takes off her glasses and rubs her eyes on the way before she disappears into the hallway.

✳✳✳

When they get back with Randy's take-out, he's just walking out of Bennie's room as a different nurse walks in pushing another cart with electronic equipment on it. Randy still looks exhausted, even more so now but happy. He notices Ambrose first, walking down the hallway, carrying the take-out bag. When he sees Linda, his eyes get bigger, instinct kicks in and he seems a second away from bolting.

"Randy," Linda calls to him, steps quickening. "Come here!"

He doesn't so much walk toward her as stop where he is.

She rushes up to him and throws her arms around his neck. "It's so good to see you!"

He slowly puts his arms around her, having to bend slightly because she's about a foot shorter than him. He looks at Ambrose and mouths the words, *What the fuck?*

Ambrose shrugs. Let him deal with being hugged. Ambrose barely got a half-assed hug from his own mother after being gone for so long. Then again, maybe she did the best she could. Maybe Jackie just doesn't have it in her.

Randy and Linda sit down in some nearby chairs and Ambrose gives Randy the paper bag. "Here you go," he says. "Steak burrito."

"Thanks."

Linda can't seem to look at Randy long enough. "I saw the pictures from your wedding and—I never got to tell you, *Congratulations.*" She leans closer, speaks quieter. "You know, I'm sorry 'bout the way we left things. I've thought about it *so* many times. I was just worried for you, you know? And when I walked in that day and you were there, after so long. . . I won't lie; it was a shock."

He leans back in the chair, looks back up the hallway.

Sensing resistance, she straightens up, "I love spending time with Bennie. I really hope now that—I'll get to see both of you more."

"Maybe. . ."

Ambrose looks up and sees a tall, slim man—balding on top, in a dapper gray suit and navy tie—step off the elevator, carrying a briefcase. He starts toward them. There's something familiar about him. A more hangdog version of this guy used to come to Miss Dover's. He walks right up to Bennie's door and, noticing there are medical staff in the room with the curtain drawn, pauses before knocking. He turns to see Randy, Linda, and Ambrose staring at him.

Randy steps forward. "Can I help you?"

"Hello," the man says. "Are you related to Mrs. Burke?"

Randy inadvertently glances at Linda, then: "Bennie Burke? I'm her husband."

The well-dressed, balding guy smiles. "You must be Randall?"

"Correct," Randy answers. "I didn't catch your name."

"Douglas Stewart," the guy says, handing Randy a business card. "I'm her attorney. I have a couple of papers for her to sign, just thought I'd bring them by. Save her a trip to Menlo Park." He leans closer, lightly placing a hand on Randy's shoulder. "And if there's ever *any*thing I can do for you, Mr. Burke, please don't hesitate to call."

✳✳✳

Later, while Bennie rests for a few minutes prior to being released, Randy allows himself to be talked into joining Linda for a cup of coffee. Ambrose slips into the recovery room. Bennie's eyes are closed but she opens them when she hears him approaching even though he was trying to be quiet. "Hey," he says. "How're you feeling?"

"Not too bad." Her eyes narrow. "What happened to you?"

"Happened?"

"Your nose is all swollen."

"I know. I—" What to tell her? "It's nothing."

"I don't believe you." She reaches out to take his hand. "Did you and Randy get in a fight or something?"

"What would make you say that?"

"He has a black eye."

"It's a coincidence, that's all."

"You told Jessica everything about me, didn't you?"

He leans closer. "I'm sorry. I'd never have done it, but I had to go out of town, and I was worried about you."

"And Randy?"

"Randy? No, I didn't. . ." Wait. How *did* Randy know, if his mom didn't tell him? Did Jessica?

"It's okay," she says.

"It's not okay. I let you down."

She sleepily smiles. "It'll be all right."

He's so relieved, he kisses her hand. "It is. I mean, it will be. God, it's so good to see you smile." He feels tears coming, but there's no need for that.

"Jessica said you were gone to some conference. Where'd you really go?"

"It's a long story, but it's over."

"You'll tell me someday. Promise?"

"I promise. You just get better." He swipes his nose, having forgotten how tender it is from Randy's punch. "What comes next?"

"A few weeks of radiation treatment. Then I hope to be good as new."

"You'll be good as new."

"Of course she will."

He turns to see Jessica standing in the doorway.

She walks over, gazing kindly at Bennie, less kindly at him. "What happened to you?"

"Nothing. Why?"

"You look like you got punched in the nose. Did you get into a fight?" Jessica asks.

"It's a bee sting, I think."

Jessica looks insulted at his explanation.

Bennie, still groggy, closes her eyes. She'd normally jump in to help, but he's on his own.

"A bee sting," Jessica repeats. Then: "Can I see you outside?"

He goes with her to a waiting room across the hall, to the farthest corner near some windows, away from a small group. He sits down in a chair, fading fast, second wind spent.

"You look terrible."

"You make up for it by looking gorgeous," he says. "Where's Beau?"

"At home with Caitlyn. Where have you been? I want the truth."

"You know where I've been."

"I called the Rapid City Chamber of Commerce and every big hotel in town and there hasn't been an entrepreneurship conference, so I know you've been lying again. It's bad enough you kept the news about Bennie to yourself for so long, but how can I *ever* trust you when you won't trust me?"

"I trust you."

"How can I believe you really love me?" The emotional hitch in her voice strikes a chord in the room and the group in the other corner—a middle-aged couple, young guy in a Cal-Berkeley T-shirt, and a preppy-looking guy in his thirties—glance their way before turning back to their conversation.

"I do love you." After seeing the house explosion on Phoebe Grace's phone and still not having been able to make sense of that, Ambrose feels like he's losing his last grip on sanity, watching his life not just fall apart, but explode, all for something that never happened. It wasn't even a real delivery; just a trick played on an idiot.

"I thought things were better this time, but they're worse; *this* is worse." She reaches into her purse, looking for a tissue. "It's like a repeating nightmare."

"Don't say that, Jess."

"What would you call it?"

"I'm sorry I didn't tell you, but I didn't know if you'd understand."

"Understand what?"

"I took a part-time job driving a delivery truck to make extra money."

She looks puzzled. "What were you delivering?"

"Caviar."

"Caviar? If you needed money, why didn't you just tell me?"

"I don't want to have to ask you for money. And I don't want you to feel like you have to pay for everything, because you don't."

"But you have a job and so does Butch. And I—" A beat. "I work."

"I know. You're an artist. Say it."

She brightens slightly but still seems to be holding back tears. "I'm an artist." A tear escapes and she wipes it away. "Anyway. We're a family, and we're all contributing." The light from the windows surrounds her, giving her hair a halo effect while emphasizing the shadows on her face. "You and I are having a baby together. Doesn't that mean something to you?"

"Means I got you pregnant."

She looks stricken, but he can't think what else to say.

"Can we do this later?" he asks, just before he collapses onto the floor.

SEVENTEEN

Butch took the train back to Palo Alto when he got word from Randy that he and Ambrose made it home and he'd tell Butch all about it later. Whatever mission Ambrose was on seems to have been aborted right at the end and Randy wasn't making much sense. Meanwhile Bennie's in the hospital for a procedure—Randy didn't say what—Randy's mom is there and so is Jessica, and Ambrose had a fainting spell but he's okay now. Bennie and Jessica think Randy and Butch have been in Big Sur, so Randy said to stick with the story.

Butch showers, naps for an hour, and ventures over to the main house later in the afternoon. This time it's Jessica sitting at the patio table, glass of water with a slice of lemon in front of her. "Hey, Jess." As he approaches, he notices how upset she looks, even just staring into space. He hopes he's not the source of any of her anguish. "How's Bennie doing?"

"She okay. Back home now."

"Where's Beau and Ambrose?"

"Beau's spending the night at my parents' house and Ambrose is asleep. How was your trip?"

This poor woman's been lied to so much. Does she really believe he's been to Big Sur, or is this a question she knows the answer to? Randy said to stick with the story, so. . . "Beautiful place; that's for damn sure." He braces for any follow-ups, having read a Big Sur guidebook while holed up at that motel in the city. He almost asks her how she's holding up, but that might be jumping ahead. For all he knows, what does she have to hold up under? All the deception surrounding her? Young husband turned problem child? Two brothers-in-law snooping around, discovering things that could up-end her life yet again?

"Oh, Butch," she says just before the floodgates open. She stands and throws her arms around his neck, crying.

Nothing to do but hold her, then sit quietly while she tells him all about it.

✳✳✳

Back at the hospital, Maxim pauses before pushing open the door to Alexei's room. He hadn't believed footage of the explosion, had checked and double-checked, and yes, it was the house, the purchase of which he'd arranged. Alexei is lucky to be alive. The question arises, whether Maxim will be much longer after walking through this door. But it's bound to happen sometime. Maxim has decided he wants to return, wants Lilly here with him if she'll stay, if she'll accept his proposal. He hasn't asked her yet, but he will. This week.

He'd received a brief voicemail from Ambrose, although no voice was on it, just garbled background sounds, leading him to wonder if it was a pocket dial or if Ambrose had seen the same footage and didn't know what to say. Ambrose wouldn't be in on any of this, would he? But the Dutchess. . . Such a wild card these days. And Sergei. Nothing is as it seems, and no one. Except Lilly. She's gone shopping, then will meet him back at the hotel. She doesn't know he's been getting his condo back into shape, cleaned up from the months of neglect so that he can offer her a space to redecorate, a canvas for her to go wild with imagination—if she'll stay within his budget, which is rather tight these days, until he gets his business affairs back up and running.

He takes a couple deep breaths, centering himself, then opens the door.

Alexei lies in bed, apparently sleeping. He looks beaten and banged, his head wrapped in bandages, gloves on his hands, no doubt covering severe burns. Maxim approaches the bed. Alexei's eyes open slowly. "Maxim? Where have you been?"

"I went on a trip."

Alexei winces, attempting to maneuver himself to better fix Maxim with a stony glare. "How wonderful."

"I just returned and heard what happened. I'm glad to see you're alive."

"Are you?"

"Of course," Maxim responds. "I know that we've had our differences, but you are still my brother. I wish no disaster on you."

The glare weakens, painkillers perhaps making it difficult to maintain. "You are among the few."

"How did you survive? Were you inside the house when this happened?"

"I was a having a small wine cellar put in just below the kitchen. The workers were off for the day, and I went down to see the excavation. It was shaping up beautifully. I remember being quite pleased with what they'd done and then—*ka-boom*."

"What do they say caused the explosion?"

"A leak in the propane tank. I think it was an attempt to kill me." Alexei's gaze shifts toward the ceiling, eyes flinty and intense, a departure from just moments ago. "Have you heard from Ambrose?"

Maxim tenses. "Eh. . . No. You don't think—"

"That it was him? I seriously doubt that. Not this time." Alexei focuses on Maxim. "What have you heard from our old pal Sergei?"

"I've not spoken to him in some time."

"Nor have I. But I believe this is him speaking to me. I suppose I have no choice but to answer."

Maxim glances toward the door, leans closer. "But you do have a choice. Please don't perpetuate this—battle. It isn't worth it. Take the insurance money, go someplace else and be happy."

"I'm not going anywhere. I want to rebuild. In spite of the loss of that last shipment. The only way I can stomach this whole debacle is to see it as a sacrifice to the gods of fortune."

"What shipment is that?" Maxim asks.

Alexei eyes him wearily. "If you happen to speak with Ambrose, tell him I want to see him." The flinty glare leaves Alexei's eyes. He sighs, starting to look sleepy again.

"Yes, of course." Maxim straightens up, realizing there's much he doesn't know. Strange things taking place and, for the moment, everyone's asleep at the wheel. He glances at the clock on the wall. Lilly will want to know where they're going for lunch. She needs to decide what to wear. "I'll check in on you later. And relay your request to Ambrose. Goodbye for now."

"*Ciao.*" Alexei waves, before sinking back into a drugged slumber.

✳✳✳

The new normal continued when Mary-Ann and Bob returned from Spain, but with another dimension. Payton and the kids surprised them with a welcome home party. When that was over, there was a week of resting and getting reacclimated following that month of getting reacquainted in Majorca, where the Bob she used to know re-emerged. He was ribald and flirty and made her feel that way, too. They'd previously settled into such a middle-aged rut that she didn't know they'd ever climb out. With her reawakening she had to grapple with the fact that the old her had been repressing herself and suppressing Bob. She pushed so hard with her fundraising and committee work all those years, thinking it was making her a more likeable, more popular person, someone others could depend on to take care of the details no one ever thinks about, that it took 'til now to realize it didn't make her more loveable, no matter how detail-oriented she may be. Quite the opposite.

While she and Bob were in Majorca, he didn't seem so put-upon and bored as she's come to regard him. He enjoys not being forced to go to fundraising galas and other events. He can do things for fun, not because of an ultimatum or obligation. If she hadn't had her near-breakdown, she never would've learned all these things about Bob nor herself. And Butch would still be only the pool man instead of her lover—her *boyfriend*, as Bob teased.

She hadn't felt much guilt before because she was so caught up in her own emotional storm, and she doesn't feel much now because, if it weren't for her relationship with Butch, she might not have rediscovered this side of Bob. Who knows if he would've rediscovered it in himself? She once wondered if any of Jessica's drama would touch her because of putting in a good word for Butch to get the pool-cleaning job. Now she has her answer. Things can't go on forever like this (can they?), but instead of any let-down feelings at returning from a glorious trip, she's excited to be back, deepening her relationship with herself, with these two men in her life.

And thank God all the recent drama hasn't erupted into any sort of scandal.

Mary-Ann goes out to speak to Butch when she sees him arrive to clean the pool on Wednesday. "Welcome back, Ms. Mary-Ann," he tells her as she approaches, then quieter: "I'd pick you up and swing you around but one never knows who's watching."

"That's so true," she says, aware of someone next door speaking with the foreman of the yard crew and pointing at a sickly palm near the foot of the driveway. "How've you been?"

"I've been all right."

"Just all right?"

He smiles. "That's good as it gets when you're not around."

She asks after Jessica and Ambrose, and Beau.

He says all are fine but doesn't make eye-contact.

"Jessica's due pretty soon, isn't she?"

"'Bout another month and a half."

"Do they know if it's a boy or girl?"

"Little girl."

"That's wonderful! Jessica must be thrilled."

"She can't wait." Somehow, though, something doesn't seem right. His smile fades, a shade of melancholy coming over him, even though he's trying to look pleasant. "I've missed you."

"I've missed you, too." She nears. "Is everything really all right?"

He tries to laugh but it comes out a sigh. "As it can be."

"Jessica's not having any—difficulties, is she? I mean, she and the baby are all healthy."

"It's nothing like that. How's Mr. Bob?"

"Just fine. He went to a board meeting this morning, then over to the club to work on his swing. He signed up for a tournament in Fallbrook this weekend."

"You going with him?"

"No, but he wants me to meet him in Palm Springs on Monday, spend a couple of nights and fly back with him. His doubles partner has a private jet he's just dying to christen." A step closer. "I suppose I could've gone to the tournament, but I still need a little beauty rest."

"You look tanned, rested, and ready to me," Butch remarks, prepping a water test kit.

"Why, thank you."

He briefly looks up from what he's doing. That spark. Those eyes. "What'll you do here by yourself all weekend? In between naps."

"I was thinking maybe you could come over Saturday. I can show you the pictures from our trip." Then, just to give him an out: "Unless of course, you already have plans. In which case, we'll make it another time."

"I don't have any plans." He seems sincere in wanting to come over, but there's something. . . He glances toward the driveway. "I'm pretty sure Jessica and Ambrose'll be hanging out at the house. If something comes up, I'll text you, but otherwise. . . Shall we say seven-ish?"

"Seven-ish is perfect." Another thought occurs. "Unless you'd like for me to pick you up a little earlier. Maybe somewhere on campus? We could ride out to the beach and see the sunset, then back here for a while. Would you like that?"

He sets down the test kit. "I would." Then: "How 'bout you pick me up at the Oval. I'll be out there 'round 5:30."

"5:30 it is. I'll see you then."

He nods, eyes sweeping over her once more before he heads off toward the pool.

***

The trip to Miami was like a "lost weekend," a surreal journey that led to the past and back again with Miss Dover's/Phoebe Grace's failed attempt at making amends, and the opium delivery left there hanging. It brought back memories of the bogus drug deal that unleashed the wrath of Lang, sending him to stay hidden in Palo Alto.

Thinking Alexei was dead and then finding out that he wasn't was another whiplash, although Alexei's death and resurrection wasn't carefully choreographed like Miss Dover's; it was real, a matter of fact and record. The news initially reported no survivors in the propane tank explosion that had reduced the beautiful mid-century modern lightbox of a beach house to smithereens, but when Maxim called and said Alexei wanted to see him, it took another day for Ambrose to pull himself together to visit him at the hospital.

Alexei's sitting up in bed, bandaged, wearing a hospital gown instead of one of his many custom suits. Even though he wasn't in Miami that day, and lightyears from the fisticuffs on the beach, it seems that everyone connected with that trip had been roughed up in various ways—except for Phoebe Grace and her elder Svengali who no doubt took a private jet back to Paris, leaving Ambrose empty-handed and Alexei semi-homeless.

He'll be in the hospital a couple more days, then take up residence at a Richmond District apartment while the house is rebuilt. So sayeth Maxim, who's gone to Napa for the weekend with Lilly.

Alexei had been dozing but opens his eyes as Ambrose approaches the bed. He looks so human and vulnerable without his custom-made armor. "Ah, Ambrose. How are you?"

"Well, and you?"

"They tell me I'm lucky to be alive. So, I'm feeling very lucky."

Ambrose flashes on that day at the nursing home back in Texas, visiting his dad. Carl looked sickly but was still a smart-mouth son-of-bitch, with no remorse for what he'd put Ambrose and Butch through all those years ago. Looking at Alexei right now, Ambrose feels more affection for this man he used to hate and fear, more than his own father, whom he no longer fears but still hates. "Maxim told me what happened."

"And Miami. I did some checking on the canceled transaction. Lev informed me how the shipment was intercepted."

"Lev's back?"

"He was forced to unload the shipment at gunpoint but, before he was allowed to depart, saw Sergei and a tall, slim woman with blonde hair leaving the address in Coral Gables in a black SUV."

"I'm sorry for the way things worked out. She— They showed me a video of the explosion. I thought you were dead. *They* thought you were dead."

Alexei's face hardens and for an instant he looks like his old self.

"I feel so stupid for not realizing it was all a set-up."

"You are not stupid. This woman. Who is she?"

Ambrose can't meet Alexei's stony gaze. "Her name's Phoebe Grace."

"Ah, yes. Alexei's protégée. Your former boss, yes? Risen from the dead."

Ambrose looks up. "You know?"

"The bane of my existence for too long. She and Sergei deserve each other. May they both rot in Hell." He faces straight ahead, smiles wistfully. "Or should I be more philosophical now that I have my own second chance? Shall we say, 'Leave them to Heaven'?"

"So, the shipment. . . How do you write off a loss like that?"

"Cost of doing business—of that particular type. In other words, I eat it."

Ambrose shoves his hands into the pockets of his coat. Alexei's willingness to cut his losses by moving on reminds Ambrose of his own losses incurred that trip. Things with Jessica are hanging by a thread. It made him betray Bennie, again gave Randy enough rope to hang him out to dry, and he's noticed Butch eying him with looks alternately suspicious and pitying. It's sickening. And his mind still goes back to things Randy said that rainy day when Ambrose came to pick up Bennie. Randy's not psychic, but he has some strange connection with Butch.

He's the one who brought Butch to Arcadia that night. Clued him in to things going on there, which made him aware of Ambrose's side interests, his renewed association with Lang and other members of the night staff Ambrose had seen fit to surround himself with for a greater sense of security while he procured the best security of all: sizable chunks of money enabling him to play bigger in all aspects of life.

"Oh, well," Alexei sighs. "We lick our wounds and heal, then come out swinging, yes?" He makes a weak fist and holds it out for Ambrose to bump.

Ambrose makes his own fist, touches it to Alexei's. "Absolutely."

✳✳✳

The winding drive down the La Honda Road through the redwoods to San Gregorio Beach couldn't have been more beautiful. Mary-Ann and Butch have never gone anywhere—didn't dare, but this evening is different from other times they've been together. Butch is sweet as ever, but a little quiet. He again told Jessica and Ambrose he was going to see a movie downtown, maybe grab a bite of dinner or do some reading at a coffee shop, so time is limited, but neither of them seems rushed, holding hands, wading in the surf.

The water is cold, and the wind is up. There're only a few other people on the beach and at a distance, so Mary-Ann's not too worried about anyone reporting back to Bob. She's wearing her Jackie O-style sunglasses. Feels incognito, even a bit glamorous.

Sitting on a blanket, watching the spectacular sunset, she shivers in the wind and Butch wraps his arms around her to keep her warm.

"Thank you for bringing me here," he says.

"You're more than welcome. This is one of my favorite places on earth."

"Now it's one of mine, too."

She melts into his embrace, looking out at the ocean.

"I want to tell you something, Mary-Ann, and I hope you don't take it the wrong way."

She looks up, dreading anything that might cloud this moment. "What is it you want to tell me?"

"I love you."

She's unsure how to respond since that's the last thing she expected him to say. It thrills and terrifies her. "Are you serious?"

He seems to sense her confusion as she turns to him, takes off her sunglasses. "And I know you and Mr. Bob are tight and got a good thing going. Like I've said before, I'd never want to hurt him, or cause any trouble between y'all." His gaze shifts back to the tide, waves licking the sand and rushing back out. "But you've been so damn good to me. There's only one other woman I ever loved, and she broke my heart. At first, you kind of reminded me of her, but the more I got to know you, the more I forgot about her and all that pain. . ." He pauses.

She remembers to breathe. "I'm sorry you got hurt like that, Butch."

"Is what it is," he sighs. "I don't know what things are going to be like for me, in the future. You know, health wise, how much I'll be able to get around. I'll manage it best I can, but whatever happens, I just want you to know how special you are to me." He looks at her, tears in his eyes.

Her heart breaks for him.

"And that I love you. I always will."

"Oh, Butch. . ." She gets up on her knees, wraps her arms around his neck. "Why did you think I might take that the wrong way?"

"I don't want you to feel like I'm putting any pressure on you, I just had to tell you." He knows a side of her no one else does, barely even Bob, though now she feels like Bob wants to know her better. But something in her relationship with Butch has shifted, even before this confession, when they were driving here, not talking much. At ease just being together. This relationship's evolving into something deeper. It's like he wants her to know that, even if the sex goes away, what they have won't. Ever.

"I love you, Butch," she says, holding him tighter. "I'll always love you, too."

EIGHTEEN

Tonight, the sex with Mary-Ann was slower, sweeter, than their typical feverish rush. Afterwards, they lay in bed, holding each other, and then he remembers the photo he'd found in some of his stuff, from around ten years ago, when he was spending time in South America. It's of him and three of his old colleagues in the smuggling biz, on the expansive patio at the campo, near the pool, looking out over the mountains. Callie's there, sitting in her husband's lap, in the wheelchair. They're all drinking, smoking cigars, dressed for a night out clubbing in Medellin, though, whether they actually made it to the clubs, he can't remember. No doubt there was a luxury car and a driver at the ready in front of the hacienda, just in case anyone took the notion. Hard to believe how dumb he was then, thinking he'd already reached the pinnacle of success in his early twenties. Before things nosedived.

"I can't believe this is you. Such a young kid." Mary-Ann gazes at the photo in amazement. "You were handsome then, but even more now. Who are these men?"

"Alfredo, Julio and Bobby. I used to work with them."

"In your—former profession?"

"Mmhm."

She studies the photo carefully before handing it back.

He rubs her tanned shoulder, smooths her silky hair, then, realizing he's getting lulled into a state of comfort that could lead to sleep, glimpses the clock on the nightstand. "Hell, I better get going. Look at the time."

"I'll drive you and drop you off just down the block from Jessica's if you want."

"No need for that, I'll call the ride service." He gets dressed and kisses her goodnight at the sliding door to the patio. He turns to watch as she draws the curtains.

She's wearing that caftan with the exotic Moroccan print, her hair down. Seeing her briefly through that panoramic window looks like a scene from a movie.

He walks past the hot tub, following the curving flagstone path out toward the pool, aiming to hang a left at the driveway and keep to the shadows near the ivy-covered wall between their yard and the neighbor's. His ride should be here soon. As he nears the patio table nearest the driveway, out the corner of his eye, he sees a tiny light move. An orange dot.

"How's it going, Butch?" comes a voice from the darkness.

His eyes have barely adjusted to the dimness but, even so, he detects the redolent scent of a fine cigar.

Busted. Bigger than shit.

Butch walks over to the table.

Mr. Bob is sitting there, laid back as ever. The end of the cigar glows as he takes another puff, exhaling into the sky.

"It's going all right, Mr. Bob. How you doing?"

"Just fine." He pushes the other chair out from the table with his foot. "Have a seat."

Butch glances toward the driveway, wishing he'd left earlier, but who knows how long Mr. Bob's been out here?

Poor Mary-Ann. Wish there were some way to warn her, but it's too late now. *Goddamn.* Butch sinks into the chair.

"Care for a smoke?"

"No, thanks. I really gotta be getting on home."

"What's your hurry?"

Butch shoves his hands into his jacket, clenching his fists. "Getting kind of late, that's all."

"Yeah." Another puff of the cigar.

"Thought you were off on a golf tournament this weekend. Ms. Mary-Ann said she was going to meet you in Palm Springs on Monday."

"My partner's daughter went into labor up in Spokane. He and his wife took off to be with her. So, I just came on back."

Butch nods, unsure what to say next. He can feel Bob watching him. When he finally dares to look Bob in the eye, he gets the feeling Bob's enjoying this on some level, but maybe that's just a feeling. "Guess you're wondering what I'm doing here."

Bob leans forward, flicks the long cigar ash into the large Cohiba ashtray on the table. "I think I know what you're doing here. You've been spending time with Mary-Ann. You two have become close."

"I guess you could say that." *Shoot me now.* If there were any way to spare Mary-Ann one second of pain or anxiety that comes from this, Butch would gladly take a bullet and die happy. "She's a nice lady. You're a lucky man."

"I think so."

Silence.

Butch chews his lower lip. It's been an emotional day, and this is a minefield he wasn't prepared to negotiate. It's hard playing poker against such an ace poker face as Mr. Bob's.

"I've just started realizing it lately," Bob says finally. "How lucky I am."

Butch nods again, at a loss for words.

"I think a lot of that's because of you."

"Because of me?"

"Maybe I just needed to look at her through the eyes of the pool man." Another puff from the cigar. "Course you're much more than that. When she went through that rough patch, you knew what she needed more than I did. And I've been married to her for over thirty years."

Finally able to exhale, Butch runs his fingers through his hair. Sweating. "I don't know 'bout that, Mr. Bob. She's her own woman, knows what's best for herself. She's done a lot for me, too. An awful lot."

Bob sighs, leans back in the chair. "Well, anyway. Whatever's been happening, she's back to being the woman I fell in love with in college." He laughs, rolling the cigar between his thumb and forefinger. "Hell, since she started hanging out with you, our marriage is better than it's been in years. I don't know what that says about me. Probably not much."

"She showed me some pictures from your trip. Both of you look real happy, so I guess that says something. Something good."

"Turned out to be like a second honeymoon. Somehow, I think I've got you to thank for that."

This conversation's certainly taking the opposite turn from what Butch expected. "I think it just speaks to how you really love each other."

Bob laughs softly, gazing at him through that expensive cigar smoke. "You know, you and your brother are really something. Can't imagine what you must've been like as kids."

"We're both lucky to still be alive."

"Tough, huh?"

Butch shrugs. "There's plenty that got it worse. But, yeah, growing up with our folks was no walk in the park."

"How's Ambrose these days?"

There's a billion-dollar question. "Well, he's 'bout to be a daddy, so. . . there's that." It's so quiet, he hears a car coming, then sees the headlights as it slows, stops down at the end of the driveway. "Looks like my ride's here."

"I'll let you go then. Nice talking to you, Butch."

"Same here, sir." He stands, still weak in the knees. "You have a good rest of your evening."

"Thanks."

Butch starts away.

"And, Butch?"

"Yessir?"

"I won't tell Mary-Ann that I saw you here."

"You're a mensch, Mr. Bob."

Bob laughs, flicks his lighter, re-lighting what's left of his cigar.

✳✳✳

Bennie told Jessica she and Randy had plans for her upcoming birthday, and not to do anything special, but Jessica said she'd be out of town next week, going to Santa Fe for the opening of her exhibition. She's taking Beau with her but didn't mention whether Ambrose was going. Butch is staying home. Bennie still can't shake the feeling there was something off about his and Randy's trip to Big Sur, but she can't exactly point to what, so she tries to focus on herself and not think about it. Jessica insisted they drive down for Sunday lunch, then cake and ice cream. Now that Bennie's taking radiation treatment, her appetite comes and goes, but she accepts the invitation. It's a beautiful day for it. She smoked a joint before they left and Randy's doing the driving.

"If you're still tired from that last treatment, you could've just told her you didn't feel like it, you know," Randy reminds her, referring to Jessica. "She'd understand."

Bennie leans into the seatbelt like a sling, just enjoying the view. Randy looks handsome wearing jeans and that gray linen blazer she bought for him, Aviator sunglasses: so smart and cool. Her sex drive's plummeted, but she'll think about how he looks today as she gets stronger post-treatment. It'll help her get back to normal. "I know, but she seemed to really want us to come over."

Randy appears to be getting back to normal, too. Been sleeping better: stopped tossing and turning so much. She gets the feeling their sex life would already be back, hotter, even—if he weren't having to wait for her to catch up. But he's been so patient. He knows she wants him. She's not even jealous of Butch anymore. If Randy has to have a friend, it might as well be Butch. *Keep it in the family.* And Randy's learning to accept that Bennie' close with his mother, no longer shutting her down every time she mentions Linda, or that maybe the three of them should go out to dinner. Linda wants to have a big crawfish boil this spring and invite everybody over, including hers and Jessica's whole family (of course Pamela will find a reason not to go), and Linda's other kids and grandkids. Randy still says he's not going to some quasi-family reunion held in his mom's back yard, even if Linda is calling it a belated wedding celebration since she didn't get to see the wedding itself. Randy draws the line at reconnecting with his siblings, still saying that'll be a cold day in Hell.

Bennie presses the button that opens the sunroof, marveling at the perfect square of glorious azure. She hasn't felt this happy in a while. Only midway through treatment, she believes that in the not-too-distant future she will be good as new, and everything will be all right. Especially if she can hold onto this wonderful feeling, even when she's not so stoned that she's practically flying. She turns to gaze at Randy again. "You look great," she declares.

"Thanks. So do you."

"Know what you look like today?"

He flashes her a smile. "No, what do I look like?"

She blissfully leans back in the seat. "A real detective."

He looks pleasantly surprised. "Do I?" He adjusts the rearview mirror. "From your lips to God's ears, angel."

✳✳✳

Another patio cookout and Ambrose is tending the grill. Randy's feeling too good to go over and skirt any issues that would make Ambrose squirm. Randy's attention is on Bennie and making her happy. He's already debriefed Butch about the things he saw on the trip to Miami, the gaps in his knowledge and blanks in what Ambrose was willing to tell him. Today looks like any Sunday afternoon family get-together but, behind the scenes, there's scaffolding, hanging wires, and loose boards in the form of secrets, lies, and unfinished business to tip-toe around. *Mostly because one of us has been up to some shit that would destroy this altogether. One of us doesn't deserve all this because he doesn't appreciate it.*

Jessica looks lovely as always but tired. She walks over to Ambrose, touches him on the back as she speaks. He goes inside. She gazes into the embers, her hand resting on her belly. A little over one more month to go and she looks like she's ready to pop. Bennie, followed by Beau, walks out by the roses beyond the swing set. He hops on his tricycle, pedaling along the flower beds, pointing to her certain roses, giving them imaginary names. Still stoned from earlier, Bennie seems delighted by Beau's impromptu garden tour, pausing to take in the scent of each rose that has its very own name: a loopy but most sincere flower child.

Later, sitting on the garden bench beside Butch, Randy looks up and sees Beau walking over, a dandelion in each hand. Beau presents a dandelion to each of them, pleased with himself. "Well, looka there." Butch holds his up, gazing at its tiny complexities. "What'd I do to deserve this pretty thing?"

"You're my two uncles."

"Hey, that's right," Randy recalls. He has several nieces and nephews on his side that he never sees—because seeing them would mean seeing their parents. There's only Beau on Bennie's side, at least until the new niece comes along, that is. Holding up his dandelion to look at it, he sees Bennie in the background, lingering next to some yellow daylilies. He can see her through the delicate blossom. It's superimposed on her, like a shot in some early experimental flick he saw in film appreciation class, a random elective he took that contributed to his store of useless knowledge. Only it isn't useless, he's thinking now, contemplating fleeting beauty, the fragility of life, and his love for Bennie that'll outlast all the earthly bullshit the Devil can possibly throw at him. He doesn't want to start crying, not now. He thinks of Yvette's calming voice: *Don't forget to breathe.* After a couple of deep breaths, the moment passes. "You know what people do with dandelions sometimes?" he asks Beau.

Beau is more than ready. "Make a wish!" Beau exclaims.

Randy wishes for Bennie to be cancer-free at her next follow-up, then blows on the dandelion blossom, like blowing out a candle on a birthday cake, and watches the feathery petals travel into the breeze.

Bennie remains over by the daylilies, having been joined by Jessica who walks arm-in-arm with her over to a new patch of rose bushes. These haven't bloomed yet but are about to.

"Think I'll get my wish?" he asks Beau.

"Sure," Beau answers with utmost confidence before turning to Butch. "Now you."

"Make it a good one, Butch," Randy urges. "If you could have any wish come true, what would it be?"

Butch pauses, glances around the yard for a moment, contemplating. Finally, he sighs. "A'ight. Here goes." He blows on the dandelion and Beau passes his hand through the bits of puff billowing before them. "Think it'll come true?"

"It will," Beau chirps before jumping back on his tricycle and going over to join Jessica and Bennie.

Randy and Butch remain seated on the garden bench, still holding their dandelion stems.

"What'd you wish for?" Randy asks.

"Can't tell you that." Butch smiles. Randy watches as Butch twirls the empty stem between his fingertips, follows Butch's gaze back over to Bennie and Jessica, then to the patio, where Ambrose is sitting near the grill, texting. He has his feet up on a patio chair.

The soles of his shoes are red.

✳✳✳

Jessica arrives early at the restaurant, seated at a table on the patio and whiles away a few minutes answering e-mails on her phone before she sees Mary-Ann walking outside from the main dining room, guided by a waiter showing her to their table. Jessica waves and, when Mary-Ann approaches, she rises for a quick hug hello. Mary-Ann is tanned, toned, and looks fabulous. The waiter takes their drink orders and leaves them with lunch menus.

"Thank you for meeting me," Mary-Ann says, getting out her reading glasses. "I guess we could've had lunch somewhere quieter, but is this okay with you? You're positively glowing, by the way. All well with you and the baby?"

"Everything's going fine. We found out it's a girl."

"Oh, congratulations!"

"You look great, Mary-Ann. How was Majorca?"

"Beautiful. How are Ambrose and Beau?"

"They're fine," Jessica tells her, not prepared to get into it. "Ambrose has been working a lot and Beau's excited about starting preschool."

"And Butch?"

"Butch is doing all right, too, but. . . a little tired lately."

"Tired—how?"

"Sometimes he has to be reminded to get enough rest, that's all. Honestly, between you and me, I don't know how much longer he'll be able to work full-time."

Mary-Ann sets the menu aside. "What about that experimental treatment he's taking, isn't that supposed to be helping by now?"

The waiter brings their drinks. "Are you ladies ready to order?"

"We need a couple more minutes," Mary-Ann informs him.

"Yes, ma'am."

As he walks away, Jessica peruses the menu even though she knows what she wants. "I guess it's more of a marathon than a sprint with these things. They said it could take time to see results."

"How much time?"

"I don't know exactly. He has an appointment with the specialist next month, so we'll find out more then. I know there's only so much they can do, but I'm researching some other doctors, too. Exploring every lead I can regarding alternative treatments, just in case." She sips her hibiscus iced tea as the chatty lunchtime buzz surrounds them. With so much going on, it's good to be out and sweet of Mary-Ann to care so much.

Maybe she's remembering how Butch brought her those flowers when she was going through that rough time. She seems completely over that now, only she looks distracted, almost upset.

"Mary-Ann, is everything all right?"

Mary-Ann makes a failed attempt at a smile. "Of course. I'm just worried. About Butch, that's all."

"I know."

Mary-Ann's eyes cloud.

"Has something happened that we should know about?"

Mary-Ann pauses, gathering her thoughts. "The other day, at the house. I brought him something to drink, and he dropped it, then he had to sit down because his balance was off. It just—frightened me. . . I shouldn't even be telling you this."

"Of course you should. He's wouldn't tell Ambrose and me something like that for fear of worrying us, but it's better if we're aware."

"Don't tell him I said anything. Please."

"I won't, if you don't want me to."

"I don't want you to."

"Okay." This would be a good time to change the subject, given that Mary-Ann seems so ill-at-ease, but the fact that there's all this tension there makes Jessica curious. "May I ask why not?"

"Why not what?"

"You've been so kind to Butch since he first came here. I'm sure he appreciates it. Appreciates you. When you weren't feeling well all that time, he really missed you."

Mary-Ann slips her reading glasses back into their case. "He told you that?"

"Sure, he did."

Mary-Ann looks like she's about to cry. "That's so sweet," she says. "I'm—Bob and I—are both very fond of Butch."

Jessica is hyper-aware of the chatter swirling around them in an ebb and flow of restaurant noise, maybe partly because Mary-Ann, normally one of the chattiest people she knows, is sitting here so preoccupied, like a rock around which the bustle swirls. Again, good time to change the subject. Ask about Majorca, about her son's and daughter-in-law's trip back east, with those three kids of theirs. Ask if she and Bob are going to the Master's this year. But Jessica's intuition says none of that's as important as what's going on with Butch.

"He's a wonderful young man," Mary-Ann sighs, gazing off into space with watery eyes. "I can't tell you how much he—his friendship means to me. I just want him to be okay. You understand. I want him to be happy."

Jessica nods, still trying to figure this out. "Speaking of friendship," she begins, "you and I are friends, right?"

"Of course."

"Then why do I feel like there's something you're not telling me?"

"Why on earth would you think that?"

"Because you seem upset."

"I'm not upset."

Quick glance around. "Did something else happen?"

"What do you mean?"

Here goes. She speaks quieter but not so quiet that she'll have to repeat herself. No one's listening, there's a crescendo of ambient sound as a large group enters the patio. "Is something going on between you and Butch?"

"What would be going on?"

"You tell me."

Mary-Ann makes an attempt at looking insulted, but it falls apart when she can barely contain her emotions. "I don't know what you're thinking but you'd be wrong if you're implying that there's anything untoward going on between myself and your brother-in-law."

"You can tell me, Mary-Ann." Jessica leans closer. "Are you and Butch having an affair?"

Mary-Ann would be a terrible poker player. "How can you possibly ask me that?"

The waiter serves their salads. Neither of them lifts a fork.

"I can see you're upset," Jessica begins. "But if there's something you need to tell me, I hope you feel like you can."

Mary-Ann reaches into her purse for a pack of tissues, and Jessica flashes on the other day at the hospital doing just that when she and Ambrose were talking, before he fell in the waiting room, insisted he was fine and slept in the car all the way home.

Jessica feels guilty for pressing the issue with Mary-Ann. Jessica's intuition certainly isn't fool-proof, especially not where Ambrose is concerned. Now, she wonders if she's erred on the side of meddlesome and should've changed the subject after all. "Look, I'm sorry. Let's—"

"Okay, I'll say this," Mary-Ann blurts. "Butch and I've become very close." A pause, quick glance around.

Everyone's wrapped up in their own conversations, texting, eating and drinking.

"In many ways, everything that's changed for the better in my life lately is because of him and I just. . ." Quieter. "Adore him with all my heart. I love Bob, of course, and this trip to Spain helped us reconnect in ways I never dreamed, but—and—Butch is very special to me, too. Always will be."

"So, you Butch have been lovers. Is that what you're saying?"

"I've said all I have to say on the subject."

Jessica finally stirs around in her salad, in shock but excited somehow, too. Maybe it's seeing Mary-Ann, and Butch, in a whole new light. Now that she knows the secret of Mary-Ann's transformation, it feels like their friendship has been elevated to a new level of intimacy. After all her own unease of the last few weeks, this revelation makes her see herself differently, too. "Can I ask you just one more thing?"

Mary-Ann looks up from her salad. "Shoot."

"What's it like?"

Unlike before, Mary-Ann looks Jessica squarely in the eye, smiles. "Amazing."

NINETEEN

Back at Arcadia, Ambrose sits behind his desk, staring at a blank computer screen, contemplating the immediate future. Bennie's radiation treatments are over, and things are looking good. It's a cause for celebration, but she's also given him notice that she's quitting, which is unsettling at best, alarming at worst. He'll still get to see her, of course; they're family, but not seeing her practically every day is a bleak prospect. She'll be with Randy almost all the time, helping him get his grimy dreams off the ground.

"What about you?" Ambrose had asked her. "What about what you want for yourself?"

"This is what I want," she said, and "I promised I'd help him ages ago. Anyway, I'm kind of still deciding what I want to be when I grow up. The cancer threw me, but I'm getting focused again." Then she'd taken him by the hand and looked him in the eyes. "You need to take some time to do that, too," she said. "Before the baby gets here. Don't you think?"

The baby's due in a month and fatherhood is enough to worry about without the palpable tension between himself and Jessica. Butch has been making himself scarce. Or maybe it just seems that way. At times he just seems tired as anyone might be after cleaning pools all day, and others, the MS appears to be leveling up its efforts against him, though he'd be loath to admit it. He's seen a specialist who's more or less content to see how things unfold but Jessica's learned about another specialist in London, who's working on a cutting-edge experimental treatment. She's willing to fly there to have a consultation with Butch, or, if Butch being on parole is a factor, having the doctor flown here.

Once again, she'll move Heaven and Earth to save Butch. Ambrose has to wonder if she'd do the same for him. He doubts it, leaning back in his chair, clasping his hands behind his head as he looks up at the ceiling. Why does he doubt it? Because he finally went too far? Somehow it doesn't seem far enough.

A knock. "Ambrose? It's me." Bennie.

He straightens up, rubs his eyes. "Come in."

She opens the door, a swirl of pink in a new retro dress with full skirt, tiny waist, and that sweet-sexy neckline he's seen on women in old movies. Bennie and her vintage style. Vintage Bennie. The days of anticipating which candy-colored outfit she'll wear next are numbered. She looks anxious.

"Good morning. What's up?"

"You need to come downstairs right away."

He starts toward the door. "What's the matter?"

"Some men are here to see you."

"What men?"

"I don't know." Her anxiety escalates his as he starts feeling clammy beneath his clothes. "They have badges like cops, but they're not wearing uniforms." She leans against the doorframe, catching her breath. "I think they're with the F.B.I.."

He stops. "The F.B.I.? What'd you tell them?"

"That I just got here, and I'd see if you're in."

He doesn't know if it's because all the blood's rushed to his head or fled from it, but he can't think straight. That stuff Alexei said about Ambrose's ability to land on his feet might've been true once but, now, the only way he'll land on his feet is when he drops from the bottom of the fire escape after slipping out the window. "I'm not in," he says, about to walk past her when two dark suits block his way.

"Mr. Ballard?" one of the suits begins, flashing a badge. "I'm Agent Jameson, and this is Agent Riley of the Federal Bureau of Investigation. We have some questions we'd like to ask you."

"Am I under arrest?" Ambrose panics, instantly forgetting their names.

The one talking, with the face of a clean-cut, blue-eyed solid citizen, smiles that way some doctors do when they're trying not to upset a potentially unruly patient. "We just want to talk to you."

"I don't want to talk without a lawyer present."

Blue-eyes glances at the other dark suit, this one decidedly not so friendly-looking.

"All right, Mr. Ballard. We'll wait while you phone your attorney."

Ambrose calls Miss Dover's former attorney, Teddy Simmons. Teddy's secretary puts him through to the man himself. Teddy remembers Ambrose from the reading of Miss Dover's will, still thinks she's dead, has fond memories of her and is willing to help the friend of such a good friend (*Oh, if you only knew*, Ambrose thinks).

The two agents and Ambrose wait in the office until Teddy drives over from Oakland, which takes about a half-hour. The whole time, Ambrose sits behind the desk with his arms folded, or his hands resting on the desk blotter. Anything so that he looks steady and they can't see his hands shaking, can't see the earthquake happening inside him. He doesn't want to give them the satisfaction. Already fucked up enough asking if they were there to arrest him, as if there's something to arrest him for. They heard him tell Bennie he wasn't here, so must already figure he's deceptive, a possible flight risk about to sky out before they reached the top of the stairs.

Blue Eyes sits on the sofa, the other one looks out the window between slow paces across the room. "Nice view," he comments.

"Thanks."

Bennie appears in the doorway. "Um. . . Would anyone care for coffee?" Ever the hostess. She can't help herself.

Ambrose shakes his head, *Don't bother.*

Blue Eyes politely declines, so does his partner.

Bennie's eyes briefly meet Ambrose's before she starts back down the stairs. If there were one thing he would tell her, it'd be to let Rajit and Terrence know to stay the fuck away from here until further notice. They may yet get a knock on the door to their apartment, but this would be a perfect time for Rajit to go visit his folks in India, or for Terrence to go see his uncle in Jamaica. It may be too late for that, though. Ambrose realizes with a jolt that it may not even be cybercrime they're here about. It could be Dimitri. But that wouldn't be F.B.I. business, would it? The fact that there's more than one reason they could be here speaks volumes. Didn't even realize he was in so far over his head until he stepped off a ledge into the deep.

Ambrose flashes on Dimitri's pale blue face with that neat hole in the forehead, eyes open, gazing peacefully at him from the freezing depths of Lake Tahoe. *Come and join me, comrade,* he seems to say. *The water is fine.*

***

Bennie drives home in a panic after Ambrose leaves Arcadia with the two agents and Teddy Simmons, Miss Dover's former attorney and apparently Ambrose's current one. Randy isn't home, thank God. No way to explain her agitation and headlong rush down the hall to Rajit's and Terrence's apartment.

Rajit answers the door in a T-shirt and running shorts. Terrence is on the sofa, shirtless, wearing boxers, his feet on the coffee table, eating a large bowl of cereal, and his laptop open on a cushion beside him. "Bennie, what's wrong?" Rajit asks as she walks in without an invitation.

She pauses momentarily, again catching her breath. "Ambrose is in trouble."

Rajit and Terrence exchange looks, Terrence pausing his bite of cereal midair. "What kind of trouble?"

"Two F.B.I. agents just escorted him out of his office. You don't know anything about this, do you?" she asks, looking at Rajit. "What's been going on that I don't know about?"

Terrence sets the cereal bowl on the coffee table, shifting to the edge of the sofa like he's ready to spring into action but doesn't know which direction to go.

"What would be going on?" Rajit asks.

"Don't act like you don't know. You and Terrence are upstairs with him all the time. What's been going on that would make the F.B.I. want to talk to him?"

"I really don't know, Bennie. What did they say?"

"They didn't say it in front of me, but it's got to be bad, right?"

"It doesn't have to be. We'll just wait and see. Perhaps it's something to do with one of our clients, or—"

"Don't tell me that! When I went up and told him they were there, he said, 'I'm not here,' and was ready to take off. It was like he maybe knew what they were there for." Near tears, she collapses onto a puffy pod-like beanbag chair near the window. "We used to be a team, but now I have no idea what's going on."

Rajit starts pacing, running his fingers through that thick, luxuriant hair, only now it's a mess. Even though he looks shell-shocked, he stops pacing long enough to walk over, kneel, and look her in the eyes. "I'm sure we'll find out soon enough. All this stress isn't good for you. Go try and relax and pull yourself together. We'll let you know if we hear anything, and you do the same, okay? I'm sure we'll get to the bottom of this and all will be fine." His big, brown eyes look so sincere, she calms down a degree.

"You think so?"

He smiles reassuringly.

"You don't think this has anything to do with drugs, or—"

"Nooo," Rajit and Terrence both say at the same time. "Not a chance," Terrence adds as a coda.

"I guess I should call Jessica."

"Wait until we know more," Rajit urges. "There's no need to upset a lady in her condition."

"Maybe. . ." Bennie muses. "You think I should at least call Butch?" Then, remembering his condition, too: "Guess I shouldn't upset him, either. . ." Back to panic mode: "But they're all going to be upset if Ambrose somehow gets arrested!"

That seems to send a shudder through Rajit and Terrence, too, even saying it out loud.

"But they wouldn't do that, would they?"

"Nooo," Rajit and Terrence intone again.

She can see that they're humoring her, but she wants passionately to believe them. She scrambles up off the beanbag chair, looking out the window at the blue sky and sunshine, Coit Tower rising like an alabaster temple of hope above its surrounding trees. Her innate sense of optimism kicks in weakly, a willing suspension of disbelief. No news is good news, they say. And there's no reason to totally assume the worst. . .

Then why did Ambrose say, "I'm not here"? Whatever this is all about, they'll know soon. In the meantime, she'll go back to her apartment and busy herself making lunch, maybe bake some cookies. She thinks of calling Momo, but no. Not yet. This window of time and blissful ignorance, the gap between the knowing and not knowing, may be her last refuge from the coming storm.

Better enjoy the sun while she can, because, once again, dark clouds are gathering.

✳✳✳

The moment Bennie walks out and Rajit closes the door behind her, he sinks to his knees, in the throes of a delayed panic attack. Terrence is already on his feet, grabbing his duffel bag from the closet and tossing it on the sofa. "We've gotta get out of here," Terrence announces. Rajit curls into a ball, rolling over on the rug.

"Where could we have fucked up?" Terrence stops.

"Wait, we really don't know what this is about. Maybe we didn't fuck up. It could be something different altogether, right? Maybe this has to do with something he did on one of those trips." Rajit now lies silently on the floor, staring up at the ceiling.

Terrence throws on some jeans and a *Mad Magazine* **What, me worry?** T-shirt that was laying in front of the TV. "Whatever happens, I have to get to an ATM," he says, shoving his wallet into his pocket and stepping into a pair of ragged denim Vans parked near the door.

Rajit sits up slowly. "You're pulling out all your money?"

"Damn right."

"Won't that look odd, if they're watching us?"

"If they question me, I'll tell 'em I've been saving for a car. I was looking at Kias online so, if law enforcement's tracking us, it's plausible, right? Not like it's out of left field. We're legit. We pay our taxes. They can't touch us."

"You're delusional."

Terrence pulls on a black zipper hoodie, grabs one more bite of cereal and places the bowl in the sink. "They got nothing on us," he mutters, walking back to the door. "There's nothing they could have on us. . ."

"What if Ambrose spills his guts about that transfer? Would we be accessories? Co-conspirators? *Perpetrators*?"

Terrence pauses, considering the possibility. "He doesn't strike me as the gut-spilling type."

Rajit slumps, staring at the floor. "Anyone might become a gut-spiller if they're staring down a 20-year prison term."

Terrence kneels, grabs Rajit by the shoulders and gives him a good shake. "Would you stop this? We can't afford to lose our shit and assume the worst!"

Rajit starts to tip over again and Terrence lightly slaps both sides of his face. Rajit swats him away.

"Buck up, buckaroo!" Terrence says, straightening up. "Get a shower. Get some clothes on." Before he closes the door: "Is your car gassed up?"

"Half-tank."

"Good enough. I'll be right back." He goes out.

Too drained to move, Rajit lies back, closes his eyes. Five more minutes of floor-rest as the last of the old normal drains away, and a new normal, fraught with paranoia and adrenaline spikes, begins. This never would've happened if he'd married Meera and moved back to India when he had the chance. But it's far too late for that now. He opens his eyes.

Or is it?

 TWENTY

Ambrose sits in a swivel chair next to the bedroom window, gazing out at the guesthouse. Sunlight slants through the trees, creating pools of light on the walkway and closely cropped grass. The roses are starting to bloom, but he won't be here to see them come into their fullness, because he'll be spending the next year at Folsom State Prison, a minimum-security facility in Represa, two-and-a-half hours away. It could be way worse, but still. . . No more sitting on the patio, plotting his next move, thinking of ways to get ahead. Now he'll be doing that in a prison cell, common room, and prison yard, surrounded by other nonviolent offenders who dropped the ball when it came to cooking the books, embezzling, and evading the tax man.

There'll be other stuff, too. He'll hear all about the transgressions of inept individuals whose schemes went awry The sob stories and misadventures, miscalculations that led to their unfortunate incarcerations. Now Ambrose has his own to share. At least parts of it.

Jessica comes out of the bathroom, hair and what little make-up she's wearing looking perfect. But she's exhausted, her sunny glow dimmed, dark circles under her eyes. He sat up with the baby last night to give her a break and try and bond however briefly with the daughter who may or may not remember him from the intermittent visits he'll be allowed. He couldn't sleep anyway. Neither could she. All she could do was lie in bed, dreading today.

Not only does she have to endure the shame of her husband being a jailbird and all the gossip, but her mother couldn't wait to remind Jessica of her warnings about getting mixed up with such trash, a nobody from nowhere who'd been taking advantage of her all this time. He'd heard them in the kitchen one day while he was lying on the sofa, nursing a headache, the monitor around his ankle tightening with each passing day. "You may never be completely rid of him because of this baby," Pamela told Jessica, "but you have to cut him loose, honey. Erase him from your life and your daughter's. He was no good from the beginning and why you couldn't see that is still beyond me." No comment from Jessica. "But then," Pamela continued, unable to resist, "look what happened with Mike."

Then Ambrose heard Jessica sigh, tears in her voice, "Mother, please. . ." before taking the conversation out to the patio.

He's the one who deserved that lashing but Jessica was getting the brunt. He did this to her and, for that, he's truly sorry. He deserves all of it and more for not having enough faith in her and in their marriage.

She sits down at her dressing table, putting on her earrings. He stands behind her, watching her reflection. This reminds him of that long-ago night when she came home from a party, wearing that silky red jumpsuit she used to have. That night, she'd sat here, taking off her earrings just before he started untying the ribbons down the back of that outfit. It slid off when she stood up, and he took her in his arms, and after that: the best sex of his life. Little did either of them know someone was watching them through the window in the darkness. Someone who turned out to be Randy, of all people. But she doesn't know about that. And she never will.

Still sitting at the dressing table, she goes about straightening some things in her purse.

"Jess?"

She looks up. "Hm?"

"Do you want a divorce?"

"I don't know yet. Do you?"

"No, but if you ever decide you do, I'll respect your decision."

She turns to him. "Do you love me? At all?"

"I do. I'm sorry for all the embarrassment I've caused you. If you don't want to wait around for me, I understand." He sits down on the end of the bed. "You might even meet somebody else."

"I doubt that. Even if we did get a divorce, I don't think I'd ever want to marry again."

"You might change your mind. Beau and Ariel need a dad at home. I love both of those kids." He's been so numb and detached, he didn't expect to feel all these emotions erupting. He can't go walking in to surrender himself feeling like this. Maybe he should've waited to have this talk with her, or done it sooner, but it never seemed to be the right time. Today, time is up. "I know Beau has Mike, of course, and Ariel. . . She has you as a mother. Probably better off without me in her life full-time anyway."

Jessica comes to sit next to him. "That's not true."

"Butch is staying on, right? Maybe he can be her surrogate dad while I'm gone."

"He's her uncle; you're her dad. She'll know you're her dad."

Can't let all this hit him now. "Thanks." He takes her hand. "What if Butch takes a turn for the worse?"

"I'll take care of him. He'll always have everything he needs."

"Really?"

"Of course."

Ambrose gets up and goes over to the window.

Butch walks out of the guesthouse. He's wearing a coat and tie with khakis. Semi-formal. It feels like they're waiting to leave for a funeral, only no one's dead, so no need to go all-out, just dress up enough to show some respect for the semi-solemn occasion of Ambrose surrendering himself to the authorities.

Ambrose is aware he's been using Butch to justify what he's doing, but the thing that busted him: avenging Miss Dover's death when she wasn't dead. Getting tossed out of paradise for being greedy and too stupid to live. The Devil must be laughing his ass off.

"You do what you need to," he says, "about getting a divorce, or not." Through the window, he watches Butch pace the edge of the patio like he's hesitating to come inside, letting Ambrose and Jessica have a few more minutes together.

Butch glances at his watch, runs his fingers through his hair, and finally sits down in a chair. He takes his phone out of his pocket and places it screen-down on the table.

"It's not what I want," Ambrose says, still watching Butch out the window. "It's not what I want, but what I want doesn't matter. Just follow your own heart."

✳✳✳

It's official. The wish Randy made on the dandelion has come true, just like Beau assured him it would the day of Bennie's birthday cookout. Bennie is cancer-free. Randy made reservations at her favorite Italian restaurant, a little place that's quaint verging on kitsch, with checkered tablecloths adorned with basket-wrapped Chianti bottles used as candleholders. Pictures of the Mona Lisa adorn nearly every surface, in every form imaginable, from a copy of the real deal hanging over a jukebox, to myriad renditions of the same enigmatic image rendered in watercolor, crayon, mosaic, colored pencil, computer code print-out, dried pasta, and every iteration in between.

They both ordered lasagna; Bennie got the spinach version. Both had plenty left over to take home. Randy told her to leave room for dessert and, after ordering, slipped away from the table and asked the waiter to put the pink candle Randy brought on Bennie's slice of tiramisu, extra sparkle to match the sparkling heart pendant he's giving her, thanking her for all her patience and encouragement that led to his passing the licensing exam on the first try. He's already approached Doug Stewart about working for him as an investigator and, miracle of miracles, Doug is down for it. The diamonds in the pendant are small, but the sentiment behind it. . . The things he wants to tell her stick in his throat sometimes.

Bennie's radiant, wearing a black-and-white gingham dress and red lipstick. He can't look at her long enough as she toys with the heart pendant on its gold chain around her neck, gazing back at him. No words, because each knows what the other's thinking.

Finally, Randy feels compelled to speak: "I don't mean to get all maudlin," he says in case she can tell he's getting overcome with emotion, "but this has pretty much been the best night of my life. And tonight's not even over yet." He picks up his wine glass. "To many more years together." Then: "Many, many more years."

She raises her glass of sparkling white grape juice, having been laying off the wine during her convalescence. "To many, many more years. Together."

After the *clink* of glasses, he sets his down on the table. "Hold that thought," he says. "I'll be right back."

✳✳✳

When Randy says he'll be right back, Bennie figures he's gone to the men's room and settles back to await his return, soaking up the over-the-top romantic Italian restaurant atmosphere, with the scent of garlic and oregano in the air, a new layer of candle wax dripping onto the basket of their wine bottle candleholder. She's thrilled by the new pendant on the chain around her neck that he was so proud to present to her as a surprise. She clutches it again, grateful for this chance at those many, many more years with him.

Even with all this, she's mindful of what Ambrose must be going through, and Jessica and Butch, too. Ambrose seems to be holding up pretty well, going through some kind of transformation, but she isn't really sure what kind. Time will tell. Meanwhile, she and Randy are on a journey to a new phase of life together, having survived this cancer scare, his mental health crisis and whatever's happened regarding that that he refuses to share. There are still things she doesn't know—she can feel it—but someday, she will. He's a detective who contains mysteries.

For now, she's grateful for every moment they have together. Everyone everywhere nowadays says to "practice" gratitude. She thought she had been, but hopes she's been doing it right. Maybe it's a little more complicated than she thought. Maybe she should lean into it harder.

She sighs, takes a sip of her grape juice, gazing up at the constellations of tiny red, white, and green LED lights draped all around the top of the bar, the tops of the windows, above the hanging plants, around the doorway. The sun is setting, and its waning light makes everything look pink and magical, and she's not even drinking real wine tonight. She hears the opening notes and vocals of "That's Amore" wafting from the jukebox and turns to see who selected one of her all-time favorite Dean Martin songs.

It was Randy, and now he's walking back toward the table. He knows that song always makes her smile. He holds his hand out to her. "May I have this dance?"

She laughs, thinking that having made the gesture just for fun, he'll just go ahead and sit down, finish his tiramisu and order another espresso. People don't really get up and dance here. There's no room.

But he's waiting. He's serious.

She can feel herself blushing. Everyone else is just sitting at their tables or cozy booths, eating, chatting and sipping at the bar. "Um. . . Randy. . ."

"Come on," he coaxes. "Don't leave me hanging here." Leaning closer: "I'll make it worth your while later." After what's seemed like a somber season for them, that sparkle's back in his eyes. Or maybe it's the lights.

If she were drinking real wine, she'd have a buzz, but the buzz must be originating from something else. "Oh, really?" she says.

"Yes, really. What've we got to be afraid of." He grasps her hand. "Live dangerously."

When he puts it like that. . . Despite the self-consciousness and mild embarrassment at being conspicuous, she rises from her chair, lets him take her in his arms. She holds onto him, glad he's such a good lead, making her feel safer and more loved than she's ever felt.

The other customers and waitstaff recede to the point of disappearing. Lights glow brighter still as darkness falls like a velvet curtain outside and she's lost in Dean Martin's voice, the Italian melody, the over-the-top lyrics that match these surroundings. Other vocals join Dean's in the chorus, and it sounds like they're in this room. What a killer jukebox to be such an antique; the sound is crystal clear and so real. . .

When she looks around, she's shocked to realize the other customers are grooving on their little impromptu floorshow and singing along with the jukebox. She looks at Randy. "Oh my God," she breathes. "Is this real?"

He grins, blushing a little himself.

"Did you tell them to do this?" she asks.

"No—how could I?"

The chorus grows louder, stronger, like the whole song's alive. Observers, well-wishers, waitstaff, busboys—the voices of all present join with Dean Martin's quintessential croon for the final notes and then they all cheer and applaud, laughing with Bennie and Randy as they take a brief bow and return to their seats: breathless, teary-eyed but for all the best reasons.

Another night of many in the magical city. Bennie's heart overflows, cup runneth over. Tonight, she's the happiest woman on earth, and the most grateful.

Turns out she must've been doing it right after all.

✳✳✳

Sunday morning in the dayroom and Ambrose and some of his fellow inmates from the Bible Group are gathered around the TV, watching the preacher from Houston. After waiting all week, it's sustenance for the week ahead. He can get through this if there's something he can learn that'll guide him through the rest of his life. When he gets out, he'll still have time to try and get it right, and be better for having course-corrected, even if it is happening behind bars. A GPS recalibration. Compass reset.

He tries to be on his best behavior while not looking like a soft target, walking a fine line between Jesus-freak and marginally insane ex-gutterpunk. Which direction the scales will eventually tip remains to be seen. He's whoever he has to be, depending on the circumstances, while he figures out who he really is—something he's never taken enough time to do before. Now, he has time.

Jessica and Butch visit bi-weekly. For now, anyway. Sometimes she brings Beau and the baby, but usually just her and Butch. Butch is still walking with a cane, but the new treatment seems to be slowing the progression of his MS, and he's been in good spirits. He's dropped a few pounds, but still looks healthy. He and Jessica look like a married couple, just going by appearances. If they stop to eat lunch on the way home, anyone seeing them would think they're a couple, and if the kids are with them, the parents of two beautiful children. If Butch and Jessica really are hooking up on the down-low, behind closed doors,

Ambrose has no way of knowing. It's better if he doesn't know. He meant what he said when he told her to follow her heart.

At least he meant it at the time, but, if he knew it were really happening, how would he feel?

Time will tell.

Bennie comes to visit regularly. Every once in a while, with Jessica and Butch, a couple of times with Momo, sometimes Linda, but usually alone. Randy came with her once and didn't have much to say. He's been really busy, Bennie says, working as an investigator for that lawyer who stopped by the hospital that day, Doug Stewart, and putting together his security consulting business. He's been taking online classes and getting additional certifications to beef up his credentials.

Ambrose tries not to roll his eyes when Bennie talks about Randy. Who knows if what Randy tells her is true? But then, like Randy said to Ambrose that rainy day, "You wouldn't know the truth if it came up and bit you in the balls."

Touché, and neither would you. Ambrose is no more swayed by Randy's bullshit than Randy is his. Maybe they have more in common than either will ever admit, only Randy's on the outside and now Ambrose is on the inside. It's not fucking fair, but neither is life. It's a rigged game, no matter how you look at it. And somebody ought to cut Randy's dick off and sew it to his chin.

That's not a very Christian attitude, Ambrose reminds himself. He recalls the preacher talking last week about not judging others and staying in one's own lane. "After all, their race is not yours and your race is not theirs. Be a blessing unto others."

But I don't trust that son-of-a-bitch.

Love your enemy. Pray for him. Ambrose did pray for Randy once, feeling sorry for the stupid bastard for about a half-second back when Randy was on the skids. But that small voice inside sometimes whispers the thing he knows deep down but can't yet face in bright daylight: *Randy's a rat.* Ambrose doesn't have proof, but the F.B.I. must've had a tip; that's all they needed to go on their little egg hunt, and the prize egg was the money transfer.

But Ambrose gave the prosecution plenty of rope, even falling on his sword for Rajit and Terrence, because he was the instigator. He claimed he had no help with the actual theft. He didn't want them to go to jail for doing just what he told them to do. Teddy was pissed, figuring Ambrose was covering for somebody, but Ambrose stuck with his story. This was a crime of opportunity and, once it was done, he didn't know how to reverse it, he claimed. Ambrose said he researched how to do it, tried it, and lo-and-behold, it worked. He couldn't do it again if he had to, having forgotten the intricacies involved. He'd certainly never want to do such a thing again, and he's truly sorry for all the trouble he's caused.

On a visit one day, Maxim had conveyed to Ambrose, in a round-about coded way, that Alexei held no ill-will towards him and, if someone blew the whistle, it wasn't Alexei, who does not like scrutiny from the media nor authorities and whose had a more than enough media attention following the glass house explosion to last a lifetime.

In fact, Alexei went to Teddy and swore an affidavit claiming he and Ambrose had become friends since this happened, that he had no idea who'd taken that money but had confidence that, if it was a disgruntled former employee or something similar, it could be settled internally and amicably. He asked that the court show leniency and hoped that this impetuous act by a young man, whose impulsive nature may have once gotten the better of him, would not permanently dim an otherwise bright future, and his ability to be a productive member of society, with many positive contributions to make.

So, a year. If they'd gotten him for killing Dimitri, it could've been life—or death. He'll take the year.

A year for doing things he wouldn't have done if he hadn't thought Miss Dover were dead. If he hadn't been lied to, duped. He really had thought the two of them had a special relationship. Maybe he hadn't realized it but, for a while, she was his fairy godmother in a way. Gave him a job, talked straight, wasn't afraid to slap sense into him. Miss Dover seemed to care about him more than his parents, who hadn't reached out once since Butch told them Ambrose had gotten into trouble and was going away to prison for a while.

So, what happened? Maybe that phantom Sergei was the devil who'd tempted her. The devil wears Armani suits and Prada sunglasses. She had her Russian devils mixed up when she warned him about Alexei. Sergei turned out to be more of a threat, killing off the Miss Dover who Ambrose loved with worldly temptations, to resurrect her as a pastel-clad ice diva with fake blue eyes. Sergei had sucked the soul right out of her. And when everything else falls away, a soul is all a person has, Ambrose realizes. He'll use this time in prison to learn to care for his soul. He feels lucky he hasn't totally lost it already.

If Ambrose felt like the TV preacher from Houston was exclusively talking to him when he'd watched in the living room back in Palo Alto while Beau scribbled outside the lines in his coloring book on the coffee table, now he feels that way even more, especially during today's sermon about accepting God's grace, and growing through tough times.

A scuffle breaks out near the foosball table, where an inmate made a disparaging remark about another's girlfriend. It sparked a confrontation loud enough to drown out the TV just at the crux of this week's message, the takeaway that Ambrose and other members of the Bible Group like to reflect upon to apply God's word in their lives. Only now they can't hear the TV because somebody called somebody else's woman a butt-ugly cunt.

It's hard enough holding it together without some brain-dead loud-mouth stepping on Ambrose's last nerve. Time to call on the gutterpunk, the one who's been loudly spreading the word about his AIDS diagnosis to deter would-be rapists from day one, and whose utter fearlessness makes others afraid.

Ambrose stands, faces the disruptors, and yells at the top of his voice: "WOULD Y'ALL KINDLY SHUT THE FUCK UP? CAN'T YOU SEE WE'RE TRYING TO HEAR THE GODDAMN PREACHER!"

He gets both angry and bewildered looks from the games area, and one or more of those geeks or goons may yet try to beat his ass or sink a shiv into his neck when he least expects it, though there's a fairly low likelihood of that here. The other Bible Group members are momentarily unsettled, some possibly offended by his choice of words, but the outcome of his outburst is that now they can hear the TV, so they'll keep their mouths shut, too.

Ambrose sits back down in the chair, draws his knees up to his chest, and wraps his arms around them, having said his piece.

He'll walk through this fire one day at a time. Faith will get him through, and God will smite his enemies. Or at least make it so they get what's coming to them. *This too shall pass.* One day, he'll leave here and go back to that collection of custom suits waiting in the closet at the house on Eucalyptus Lane, go forth and share his testimony, maybe even spread the gospel.

He tries not to think about Ariel too much. Pamela told Jessica to erase Ambrose from her life and Ariel's. Jessica might one day decide to do that, though it doesn't look like she has yet. Still, maybe it would be for the best if he and Ariel pretended each other doesn't exist. At least not until he's worthy of any love that she might have for him as her dad. Only if he's ever really worthy.

One day, he'll learn whatever lesson he's supposed to learn.

And things will get better from there.

Thanks for reading! Find more transgressive fiction (poems, novels, anthologies) at: Outcast-Press.com

Twitter & Instagram: @OutcastPress

Facebook.com/OutcastPress1

Amazon, Kindle, Target, Barnes & Nobel

Email proof of your review to OutcastPress@gmail.com & we'll mail you a free bookmark!

From the greasy spoon to gourmet sit-in, these 20 stories curated by Craig Clevenger (author of *The Contortionist's Handbook, Mother Howl,* and *In Filth It Shall Be Found*) show diners are where heists are plotted, bodies get dumped, and police are tipped off. They host drug deals to premeditated murder and mob mutiny. It's all fluorescent-lit, fly-riddled entertainment to the drunk, recovering, or wish-they-were.

MORE FROM
OUTCAST PRESS

Citrus Springs isn't just a bunny-dotted, zinnia-speckled city nestled in Florida's rare dewy hills. It's a state of mind, albeit an altered one. With "In Bloom" on blare, Paige Johnson gives life to the Wonderland tarts and bitter Xanax fiends who reside in tangerine dreams.

Whether these 40+ illustrated poems tell the tale of South Beach sugar babies or Bay Area scrapers-by, the characters are always in search of ecstasy, novelty, meaning. An infatuation so intense, it's psychedelic.

ABOUT THE AUTHOR

Twitter: @NevadaMcPherso3

Instagram: @NevadaWrites

Nevada McPherson hails from the haunted Milledgeville, Georgia, but is a graduate of L.S.U.'s MFA Creative Writing Program and has gone on to pen several award-winning screenplays, four graphic novels, short fiction and nonfiction. She is best known for her brand of neo-noir that blends steamy romance and crime fiction. Her work can be found in *Deep South Magazine, Noir City*, and *Twisted Pulp Magazine*. Her most recent piece, "Scattershot," about two female bounty hunters traveling the American southwest in the 1970s, is in *Starlite Pulp Review #2*.

When not writing, McPherson enjoys reading, cooking, yoga, and spending evenings porch-sitting with her husband and chihuahua. She also loves gardening and may be only one or two houseplants away from becoming a crazy plant lady. More about Nevada's writing and artwork can be found at:

www.nevada-mcpherson.com

www.ingramcontent.com/pod-product-compliance
Lightning Source LLC
Chambersburg PA
CBHW022136240626
47153CB00007B/2382